Jennifer Armintrout was born in 1980. She has been obsessed with vampires ever since the age of four and her first crush was on Vincent Price. Raised in an enormous Roman Catholic family, Jennifer attributes her interest in the macabre to viewing too many funerals at a formative age. Jennifer lives in Michigan with her husband and children.

BLOOD TIES

ASHES TO ASHES

Jennifer Armintrout

All the characters in this book have no existence outside the imagination
of the author, and have no relation whatsoever to anyone bearing the
same name or names. They are not even distantly inspired by any
individual known or unknown to the author, and all the incidents are
pure invention.

First published in Great Britain 2010.
MIRA Books, Eton House, 18-24 Paradise Road,
Richmond, Surrey, TW9 1SR

© Jennifer Armintrout 2007

ISBN 978 0 7783 0401 2

55-0510

MIRA's policy is to use papers that are natural, renewable and
recyclable products and made from wood grown in sustainable forests.
The logging and manufacturing processes conform to the legal
environmental regulations of the country of origin.

Printed in Great Britain
by Clays Ltd, St Ives plc

This book is dedicated to Jill, Warnament,
The Wallses, Katy and Scott.
Because without you all, my head might
no longer fit through standard-sized doors.

ACKNOWLEDGEMENTS

These people had something to do with
this book getting finished:

My critique group, Chel, Chris, Cheryl, Marti,
Mary and Martha by proxy.

My husband and son, who whine, complain, beg for
attention and generally harass me. Until a cheque comes.

My agent, Kelly, and my editor, Linda.

Everyone who bought books one and two.

And, oddly enough, Dr Carrie Ames. She might not be
real, but she does the hard part of this job.

Prologue

"Hey, Baker! You give her the seven o'clock meds yet?"

Don swung his legs from where they'd been propped on his desk, knocking the tower of empty soda cans from the corner. "Yes. I did. At seven o'clock. Check the sheet."

Leave it to Sanjay to ask a stupid question. Don shook his head and watched the new guy retrieve the clipboard from the hook beside the door and frown at the words. How he'd managed to live a hundred years was a mystery. Hell, Don had had close scrapes in his own twenty years as a vampire, more in his thirty years previous. How someone with double the lifespan could wander around in a state of constant confusion—

"Then this doesn't make any sense." Sanjay flipped the pages on the clipboard, but it was clear from the rapidity of his movements that he couldn't possibly be reading the charts. "It doesn't make any sense!"

"What doesn't make sense?" Always with the drama, these Movement scientists. "I gave her the meds."

Sanjay's worried brown eyes flicked up to meet Don's

gaze. "I know you did. I see it on the chart. But her brain activity is…too active. It's like she hasn't been sedated at all."

"Chill out, chill out. There's a reasonable explanation for this." The newly assigned guys tended to flip out over every little thing, but he'd seen what had happened the last time the Oracle had shrugged her meds. "I'll feed her another tranquilizer, keep her as down as I can until morning report. Dr. Jacobson will take it from there."

The meds for the Oracle were fed to her hourly, through a tube that first dissolved the sedative in warm blood, then injected the whole solution through intravenous lines. It was so simple. And Don hated it.

It wasn't as if he wanted glory, like the big guys got. Or danger, like the assassins. He just wanted a job that a trained ape couldn't pull off.

Hell, at least he could watch TV between doses. And the faster he got things under control, the faster he could get back to *Will and Grace* reruns.

Slipping the key to the tank room from his pocket, he slid it through the card reader. The door popped open with a hiss, and he stepped inside. It was ten degrees colder than the rest of the facility—the monitoring equipment and various pumps and containment machinery would overheat if it wasn't—and the rest of the facility was damn cold. Don rubbed his hands together and blew into them. It smelled like blood in this room, but it always did.

"Honey, I'm home," he called to the slumped figure of the lab assistant asleep at his workstation. Couldn't handle the day shift.

The blinding white of the room was interrupted on one

side by the huge, dark wall of glass. Inside, floating suspended in gallons and gallons of blood, was the Oracle. Sleeping, if the tranquillizer had worked. He popped two tablets out of the meds cabinet and strolled to the access tube, whistling while he did so, hoping to annoy the lab tech enough that he'd wake up. "I hope they check the security tape in the morning. Because you will be so busted."

The meds pump was attached to the wall just below where the glass ended. He knelt down and pulled the drawer open. The tablets would be inserted into a clear, glass chamber inside and dissolved. The whole process was a pain in the ass, but she'd built up a resistance to nearly all the sedatives that came in liquid form. Don didn't know why it worked, but he was glad it did. The bitch could get downright nasty when she woke up.

He blinked in disbelief at what he saw in the drawer. The glass chamber, which should have been empty to receive the next dose, was still filled with blood. Hands trembling, he followed the intravenous line to where it disappeared into the wall. A chunk of a pill that hadn't dissolved was stuck in the thin plastic tube, forcing the flow of the blood to a trickle.

The Oracle had never gotten her sedative.

The rest happened too fast. He looked up, saw the face of the Oracle, pale and inquisitive, touching the glass. Her eyes were open. He staggered back, screaming, tripped over his own feet and landed at those of the sleeping lab assistant. Blood pooled around the guy's sneakers. He wasn't just sleeping.

Don opened his mouth to scream, but the sound never made it out.

One: Inevitability

*"C*arrie, I think it's time you call Nathan."

I knew that statement would come, sooner or later. I'd just been hoping it would be much, much later.

We were lounging in Max's bedroom, the only room in his spacious, opulently furnished condo that had a television. For the past three weeks, all we'd done was lie around during the days and prowl various blues clubs at night. It wasn't as though I hadn't had time to talk to Nathan. I just hadn't wanted to.

When I didn't answer, Max sighed heavily. He folded his arms and leaned against the carved headboard of his antique bed, the only piece of furniture in the room that wasn't modern. He seemed strange and anachronistic on it. Having been turned in the late seventies, Max was the youngest vampire I knew. Besides myself, of course. He'd adapted to the changing times much more easily than some vampires did. Max kept his sandy-blond hair cut short and spiky, and his uniform of T-shirts and jeans helped him blend so perfectly with the twenty-something population of Chicago, I forgot at times that he was really old enough to be my biological father.

Clearly, he was about to pull chronological rank. "It's been almost a month now. I don't mind you crashing here. Hell, most nights you've been one mojito away from a rebound fling, and being the only male here, I'm digging the odds. But Nathan is my friend. If you're splitting up permanently, he deserves to know."

I refused to argue that the only thing my sire and I had between us was the blood tie, our weird psychological link that made us privy to each other's thoughts and emotions. Even that didn't connect us so much, lately. Nathan seemed to be blocking me from his mind. The few times I'd tried to communicate with him, I'd gotten only terse, vague answers. I supposed it was better than begging me to come back, but it stung nonetheless.

Still, Max wouldn't take simple logic for an answer. The many, many times I'd tried to explain my nonrelationship with Nathan, Max had refused to see reason. "He wouldn't have asked you to stay if he didn't love you," he'd insisted. "Just because he doesn't admit it doesn't mean it's not true."

"Oh, kind of like you and Bella?" I'd quipped, effectively ending the conversation. I should have cut Max a little more slack. After all, he had just gone through a nasty breakup himself, no matter how he denied it. Obviously, he had transferred the situation with Bella onto Nathan and me to avoid dealing with his feelings.

"I don't think I can handle talking to him right now," I said, knowing full well how lame that sounded.

"It'll only get worse the longer you wait." Max knew he

had a perfectly valid point. I could tell from the gleam of triumph in his blue eyes. "And if it's horrible, so what? We're going down to Navy Pier tonight. You can drown your sorrows in cotton candy. No one can be sad with cotton candy."

I raised one eyebrow. "Not even a vampire with a profoundly screwed up love life?"

"Cotton candy is to vampire suffering as kryptonite is to Superman." He reached for the cordless phone on the nightstand and handed it to me. "Call him."

Helpless, I looked from the alarm clock to the phone. The days had gotten longer. Though the sun wasn't down yet in Chicago, it was almost nine Michigan time. Nathan would be getting ready to open the store. If I called now we wouldn't have long to talk. That was a good thing, considering I had no clue what I would say to him.

I took the phone and punched in the number, a pang of homesickness assailing me as I imagined Nathan navigating the cluttered living room to get to the phone in the kitchen. An overwhelming desire to be home again gripped me, and my heart pounded in my chest in anticipation of speaking to him. The line clicked and I wet my lips, preparing to answer his "Hello?"

"Nathan Grant's residence," a sleepy, female voice purred over the line.

As quickly as my heart had warmed to the prospect of speaking to Nathan, it froze again with the realization of who this was.

"Hello?" she asked, the word marked with a distinct Italian accent. "Is anyone there?"

Bella.

With shaking hands, I hung up the phone. I couldn't look at Max. How would I break it to him that Bella, the only woman he'd ever had feelings for, no matter how he tried to deny them, had apparently extended her stay at Nathan's apartment by a good three weeks?

I was having a hard enough time explaining it myself. My mind jumped from one possibility—Bella's employers, the Voluntary Vampire Extinction Movement, had discovered she'd helped us find a cure for Nathan, leaving her with no job or residence—to the next—she'd missed her plane and had to wait for a much, much later flight—but none of them dislodged the sick feeling in my stomach.

"Carrie, what's wrong?" Max frowned at me as though he'd be able to discern my thoughts if he stared hard enough.

I opened my mouth cautiously. I wasn't sure I wouldn't throw up. "He wasn't home. I guess I dodged that bullet."

"Yeah, well…you're still calling him when we get back." He eyed the window, where rosy sunlight sneaked in around the edges of the curtains. "I'm gonna go take a shower. By the time we're ready, the sun will be off the streets and we can head out."

I nodded and watched him start for his bathroom before I left for my own room.

Max's penthouse condo took up three stories in a corner of an old building near the museum campus, the lakeshore park where the city's big attractions clustered. It wasn't the hip, happening part of Chicago I'd imagined

Max inhabiting, but he hadn't had much choice in the location, as he had inherited it.

Marcus, the former owner of the place and Max's late sire, stared accusingly from an oil painting on the landing. Max had always described his sire with glowing words, but it was hard to imagine the grim-faced man in the powdered wig as being "loving" and "fatherly."

Though it had happened twenty years prior, Marcus's death still haunted Max. I saw no need to heap another broken heart on him by revealing his werewolf almost-girlfriend was boning Nathan, the man he considered a close, loyal friend.

How could he? I fumed silently as I took the stairs to the guest rooms on the lower level. I flopped onto the ornately carved bed in my neoclassical guestroom and pulled the duvet over my head.

Cold tears escaped the corners of my eyes. Nathan had made it clear from the beginning that there would never be anything between us except the blood tie, but each new reminder stung more than the last, because I'd never really believed him.

I thought it had been settled the night Bella's spell let Nathan relive losing his wife. He'd as much as said there would never be anything between us. I thought it was because he hadn't yet gotten over killing his wife. Now, less than a month later, he appeared to have moved on. So either he'd needed seventy years and a month to get over his guilt, or it hadn't been the memory of Marianne at all. He just wasn't interested in *me*.

My parents had raised me to be a logical thinker. Logic

insisted that the most plausible assumption was the correct one. Nathan was probably still screwed up, he just wasn't going to be screwing me.

Because I didn't want to break the news to Max yet—he was still in deep denial over Bella—I acted as if nothing was wrong as we gorged ourselves on cotton candy and elephant ears on the pier.

Unfortunately, Max picked up on my vibes. "Carrie, what's going on? You're not acting right."

"I'm acting fine," I snapped, then instantly regretted it. It wasn't his fault I had nonstop images of Bella and Nathan engaged in myriad sexual positions. "I'm sorry, I'm just—"

"Homesick?"

Worried the man I love is at this very moment fucking the woman you refuse to admit you love.

"Yeah, I guess." I tried to sound more cheerful when I said, "You know what's a good cure for homesickness? Alcohol."

Max grinned. "Now you're speaking my language. Let's take a turn on the Ferris wheel, then we'll find some."

I've never been a fan of heights, so I should have been grateful to be preoccupied on the halting trip to the top. Somehow, I couldn't be grateful for the torrid images of Nathan and Bella that swamped my mind.

It occurred to me that he'd never be able to hang on to Bella, who had Call of the Wild stamped all over her. Knowing they were probably doomed to failure cheered me up a little.

Still, I couldn't shake the torturous scenes, or the self-deprecating commentary that went with them. *Of course he's attracted to her. She probably doesn't wear pajama pants in public or go a day without washing her hair. She's also a size four around her hips and the size of a small solar system around her chest.*

Feeling fat, ugly and petrified of falling to my doom, I closed my eyes and sighed.

Max apparently took it for an expression of contentment, because he looped an arm companionably around my shoulders and sighed in turn. "I know, this is awesome, isn't it?"

"I'm not really into being off the ground. But the view is nice."

"The view is gorgeous." He looked at me as though I was insane for not appreciating the experience. "But that's not what I was talking about."

It was my turn to give him the are-you-insane? look.

"This." He gestured broadly, as though he could encompass the entire city with his arms. "Hanging out, screwing around, just being normal people."

"Normal people who drink blood and burst into flame in sunlight?" I snorted. "But far be it from me to interrupt your little delusion."

He settled against the seat and replaced his arm around my shoulder. "You know what I mean. For the past three weeks there hasn't been any occult shit going on. Not a peep from the Soul Eater. No faxes from the Movement. No drama."

Except for in our love lives. But you don't know that part yet.

"Well, there was that whole thing where I broke up with my sire and you got dumped by Bella." I'd sworn to myself I wouldn't bring her up again, but I was desperate to get him off his life-is-great kick. The way he talked with his hands when he was happy seemed bound to tip us out of our car.

Not that I begrudged him his I'm-on-top-of-the-world attitude—okay, maybe a little—but when he found out about Bella and Nathan he would come crashing down from his high as quickly as if he'd fallen from the Ferris wheel.

Instead of arguing with me, he chuckled. "You're trying to pick a fight."

"Guilty as charged."

He inhaled deeply. The air smelled of the city—hot cement and traffic exhaust—and carnival food, the scents of humanity only a vampire could truly appreciate. "Try all you want, I ain't gonna bite. Nothing can ruin tonight for me. Nothing."

With a parody of his contented sigh, I leaned my head on his shoulder. "If I don't get a drink soon, I'm going to stake you."

As promised, when we escaped the Ferris wheel of doom, we headed for our nightly circuit of bars and blues clubs. At a few we were becoming regulars. At the rest, Max had already established himself as one.

We'd thrown back enough alcohol to kill a small rhino by the time our final stop on the booze tour announced last call.

Squinting at his watch through heavy-lidded, red-rimmed eyes, Max frowned in drunken confusion. "What? It can't be last call yet."

"It is," I insisted with the knowing, superior tone of a complete inebriate. "And it sucks."

"It does." He looked around the bar, his mouth set in a grim line. "The band is going to leave."

"Yeah." I rested my forearms on the table and dropped my head onto them. I heard the scrape of his chair, and when I looked up he was swerving across the empty dance floor toward the musicians on the tiny stage. He spoke to them a minute, pointed at me, then returned with a confident, drunken swagger. The band started a slow blues ballad and he gestured for me to join him.

If I'd learned anything since coming to Chicago with Max, it was that he enjoyed any activity that required putting his hands on a woman. I stumbled toward him. It wouldn't be the first time we'd danced drunkenly in a bar at closing time. And that struck me as just a tad pathetic.

Not so pathetic I wouldn't do it again. I liked being close to Max, in a totally platonic way. He was the guy friend I'd never had. Actually, until I'd become a vampire, I'd never had any friends. It was nice being with someone who didn't expect anything from me short of just hanging around.

Unlike Nathan. I was supposed to stay at his side, waiting for him like a faithful dog, should he ever need me. The unfortunate comparison put me in mind of Werewolves, and I had to blink back cold tears.

Max's arms tightened around my waist and he leaned his head against mine as we shuffled clumsily to the music. "Can we just keep doing this forever?"

"Dancing?" I mumbled, toying with a lock of hair at the back of his neck.

I felt his chuckle deep in his chest. "No, stupid. Just doing this. Going out and having fun and not worrying about falling in love or being alone. Nothing ever has to change, we'd never have to worry about getting hurt. Wouldn't that be great?"

If I hadn't been drunk, it would have sounded as messed up as it really was. Instead, I looked up at Max as though he'd cured cancer and world hunger simultaneously. "That's so smart."

"I know." He frowned. "I always get my best ideas when I'm drunk."

The bartender called us a cab—rather ungraciously—and I'm sure Max overpaid the driver when we got out at his building.

"This place—" I interrupted myself with a dainty belch. "This place looks like Dracula's castle."

"I know. It's depressing." A fleeting look of sadness crossed his face. "That was Marcus for you."

When we got into the elevator, Max stood a little closer than usual. When we got out, he took my hand for the short walk to the door. Instead of opening it, he pulled me flush against his body and kissed me, the scent of Bell's Two-Hearted ale lingering on his mouth.

I had consumed a lot of alcohol myself, but not so much to silence the alarm bells going off in my head. I jerked back so fast our teeth clinked.

"Max, what the hell are you doing?"

Dazed, he squinted at me for a few seconds before he focused his eyes, then grinned. "Oh, come on, Carrie. You know you're curious, too."

I was. Max was like the star quarterback every girl wants to date. Still, he was an emotional wreck and not thinking clearly. "I know you're upset about Bella—"

"This isn't about Bella." He laughed a little too loudly. "Jeez, you're always talking about her. Are you sure *you* don't want to fuck her?"

"No, but if we went to bed now, you wouldn't be fucking *me*." I jabbed my finger into his chest, not merely to make a point but because touching him just seemed good.

He grinned again. "Believe me, this isn't about Bella."

"It is." I slid my hands across the front of his T-shirt—Max has great pecs—and gave him a shove.

Rolling his eyes, he held up his hands. "Okay, it's about Bella. Peri...peri—you know, when you see out the corner of your eye?"

"Peripherally." I nodded. "How so?"

He linked his arms around my waist and pulled me forward so I stepped on his toes and our feet tangled dangerously. "I like women. Everyone knows it. I don't fall in love with women, though. So, how come I haven't had casual sex since Bella?"

"Because that wasn't casual sex. You really liked her." I leaned against him, purely to regain my balance, I'm sure.

"You're insane. You women all are. You think men have to be in love to stick their cock in somebody." He inclined his head for another kiss, but halted. "You know that's not true, right?"

I quirked an eyebrow. "Gee, we're drunk, we both just got dumped—"

"You got dumped."

"Whatever." I rolled my eyes. "Do I think you love me? No. I think you're trying to get laid to prove to yourself you don't care about Bella."

"Is that so evil and wrong?" His lips were a millimeter from mine.

I shrugged. "I guess not."

He kissed me again. Max is an insanely good kisser. But there was desperation in it, and sadness. I didn't need a blood tie between us to feel it.

"Let's do this, Carrie," he whispered, sinking his fingers into my hair. "Let's just have fun."

It made an insane sort of sense. As we tumbled through the door to land on the Persian rug in the foyer, I convinced myself that this wasn't terrible. People did this every day.

Max's mouth never left mine as he rolled us both over so that I straddled him, still fully clothed. With a chuckle, Max sat up. I felt him, hard and eager, through his jeans, but he didn't appear uncomfortable. In fact, he seemed more at ease and himself in this intimate situation than he ever did while doing mundane things. I wondered if I was with the real Max now, or just another character. Maybe that was part of his practiced magic. I pitied the women who didn't see it for what it was, because they could fall in love with a man like Max, who made them feel they were the most important woman he'd ever touched.

Luckily for me, I couldn't fall in love with him. I was already in love with a man who didn't find me very important at all.

As if on cue, the phone rang.

Max glanced at me, half imploring. Then guilt crept into his expression, and I couldn't look at him anymore.

I groaned and climbed to my feet, more wobbly than I had been when I'd been plastered. The realization that I had been about to have sex with Max forced the rest of the alcoholic haze from my system, leaving awkwardness it its wake.

"Hey, while you're up, can you get that?" Max asked sheepishly.

"Fine. But if it's one of your girlfriends, I'm not going to be very good cover."

I was surprised anyone would hang on the line for as long as it took me to reach the telephone in the kitchen. Every ring seemed sure to be the last, until I picked up the phone and said tiredly, "Hello?"

"Carrie?"

Nathan.

Two: Reconnected

"Carrie?" Nathan repeated over the crackling of the line, his soft Scottish accent curling around my heart like a possessive hand.

I swallowed the lump in my throat and tried not to focus on the fact I was standing in Max's kitchen wiping his kisses off my neck. "Yeah, it's me."

There was a long, heavy pause. "It's good to hear your voice."

My throat went dry. *I will not cry, I will not cry.*

But my emotions were too raw. The alcohol left me with nothing to buffer them. I wiped at my eyes and prayed my voice wouldn't fail me when I spoke. "It's good to hear from you, too."

"I tried to get ahold of you earlier. You must have been out." He probed gently at the edge of the blood tie, and I shut him out firmly. He laughed softly. "Got something you don't want me to know?"

"I'm a little tipsy, is all. We just got in."

"Ah." Nathan didn't sound as though he believed me.

He hadn't yet offered any information about Bella. The suspense had me twisting the phone cord around my arm. It would be better to do it like a Band-Aid, I decided—as quickly as possible so the pain wouldn't last. "I tried to call you earlier."

He cleared his throat. "Yeah, that's what Bella said."

I rolled my lips over my teeth, pressing them until they were numb.

"She said you hung up."

I managed a tight laugh. "Yeah, I thought I had the wrong number. I didn't expect her to be there. Do I still have a room?"

My chuckle sounded so lame, if it had been a horse, some farmer would have shot it.

"Of course you do," Nathan said, his voice so soft I had to strain to hear it over the static. "Listen, has Max heard anything from the Movement?"

I tried to stay out of Max's personal business, but I did remember the comment he'd made on the Ferris wheel. "No, he said he hasn't heard anything lately."

"Bella has." His casual use of her name sent spears of agony through my heart. "There's too much to explain on the phone. We're headed down there right now."

I imagined her in the seat next to his, looking gorgeous and out of place in the rusty old van. "I'll tell Max. I don't think he'll be happy about her coming here."

"Why not?" Apparently, Nathan had gone brain dead.

Then I remembered he'd been possessed by the Soul Eater's evil spell the whole time, and probably missed the weird dynamic going on between Bella and Max. Still, she should have had the common decency to clue Nathan in. "No reason. Forget I said anything."

"Okay…" He cleared his throat again. "Listen, we're about an hour out of the city. We're hoping to get to Max's before sunrise, but if we can't, is there a parking garage or something nearby I can shelter in?"

"Yeah, there's parking under the building. If you buzz up from there you can get straight in." I winced as I said those words. I should have told him he'd be better to stop in Gary, Indiana for the day. Better yet, he should have turned around and headed back to Grand Rapids.

The kitchen door swung open behind me, nearly flattening me to the wall. Max strolled in and stretched his arms over his head. His shoulders popped and he groaned loudly. "You know what's just as good as sex? Ice cream. Nah, that's a lie. I'd rather have had sex."

I covered the mouthpiece, but it was too late.

"Is Max having trouble getting reacquainted with the city?" Nathan asked, amused.

"I think I'm cramping his style."

On the other end of the line I heard muffled talking. *You're on the phone to me, your fledgling, your blood, and you can't wait a few seconds before you talk to her?*

Without being able to stop it, my annoyance filtered over the blood tie. Nathan got it, and I felt his relief at our renewed connection. "You're right, that's rude of me. Listen, I'm going to let you go. I can explain everything when we get there."

We. It was like he used the word as a weapon against me. "Fine. *We* will be here."

He hesitated. "Okay…well, goodbye, sweetheart."

Sweetheart. It was all I could take. I hung up the phone and crumpled to the floor.

Max knelt at my side before I could draw two sobbing breaths. "Carrie? Are you okay?"

I couldn't speak. I could only cry against his shoulder.

"What's the matter? Is something wrong?" He sounded as alarmed as any man faced with a woman's tears. It must have been doubly distressing, considering what we'd almost done in his foyer. "Is it me? Was it something I did?"

Shaking my head, I wiped my nose on the back of my hand, but I couldn't control my sobbing enough to make an intelligent sound.

Max pulled me tighter to his side, as if trying to absorb my suffering through his skin. "You're really freaking me out. What's the matter? Is it Nathan?"

It most definitely was Nathan. Anger roared to life in me, drying my tears. Nathan and Bella were coming here. I'd come here to get away from Nathan and clear my head, and he was bringing more pain my way? He was like the opposite of an ambulance; he brought portable disaster.

"That was him," I muttered. "He's coming down here with Bella."

"Bella?" Max frowned. "I thought she was going back to Spain, like, a month ago."

I gave him a minute. Max was a smart guy. I was confident he would figure it out.

He wasn't as quick to believe as I had been, but the comprehension slowly crept over his face. "No. No way."

I nodded vehemently. "When I called the apartment this evening she answered the phone."

"Well, that doesn't mean anything." He was assuring himself as much as me. "Maybe something came up, she got reassigned. It happens all the time."

"She hasn't been using my room." I was half-glad. I couldn't imagine going back there if she'd usurped my boyfriend—no, my sire; I'd have to get used to the difference—and my bed.

Max nodded. "Well, I'm sorry he hurt you."

Fresh tears filled my eyes at the ragged pain in his voice. "I'm sorry *she* hurt *you*."

"For the last time, she didn't hurt me! I don't give a shit about her!" He stood and stormed angrily through the door.

Numb and cold on the kitchen floor, I stared at the container of ice cream Max had left on the counter.

I don't know how long I stayed there, watching condensation form on the cardboard. It was leaving trails and pooling around the softening bottom when I finally moved.

I had to pull myself together. It was bad enough I would have to face Nathan knowing he'd chosen Bella over me. I didn't have to let him know how destroyed I was.

I headed downstairs to my bedroom. In the bathroom, I flipped the shower on, as scalding as I could make it, and stood under it until the water turned frigid and the steam dissipated. Outside, the sun would no doubt be coming up. They would be here any minute.

No sooner had I thought it than there was a soft knock at the door. "Carrie?"

Max peeked around it, eyes modestly shielded, and threw me a towel. "They're here."

"Thanks, I'll be right up."

"Okay." He stepped out, then came back. "He looks like hell, Carrie."

"Good."

I meant it. Nathan had played me the entire time I'd known him, refusing to get into any kind of relationship with me, but oh, he could have sex with me. That was okay. I could live in the same house with him. He could beg me not to leave him, and tell me constantly how destroyed he would be if I did. But he wouldn't give up the memory of his dead wife for me.

But he would for Bella. She possessed some magic key, some ingredient I didn't have, that changed his mind and made him want to be in a relationship with someone.

In a relationship with her.

I dressed, not bothering to try and look good. It would be transparent if I spent another half hour blow drying my hair and putting on makeup.

At the top of the stairs I found Nathan and Bella sitting at opposite ends of the couch. Though I registered their distance, it wasn't enough to stop my knees from going all watery.

Once we're turned, vampires never age. Nathan had remained frozen in time at thirty-two years old. A very fit, very attractive thirty-two. Once, I'd jokingly mentioned he must have had a pretty tough exercise regimen in life to get such great arms. He'd chuckled and said, "No, it was from carrying Marianne. She couldn't walk, toward the end." His gray eyes had shone with sadness for a moment, then just as quickly changed back.

Now, his gaze snapped to me and he lifted his dark head as I ascended the last few steps.

Max turned as I came fully into the room, and he winked at me encouragingly.

Nathan rose as if expecting, I don't know—a hug? For me to leap into his arms?

Whatever it was, it wasn't something I wanted to give him. I waved him aside and flopped into the armchair near the kitchen door. "No need to get up on my account."

His fingers clenched and worried against each other before he sat down again.

Bella looked from him to me, her eyes slightly narrowed and her mouth quirked in an amused smile, but she said nothing.

"Now that you're both here, I guess I can break the bad news." Nathan leaned forward and rubbed his hands on the knees of his jeans. It was a nervous habit, and the denim on his thighs was nearly white with wear. "I'm just going to say it."

"Get it over with," Bella practically snarled.

Trouble in paradise? I shot Max a look, but his gaze was fixed on Bella.

"I was trying to." Nathan slid her a sideways glare. "Something happened at Movement headquarters. That's why you haven't had word from them. The Oracle got loose."

"No." Max's exclamation came as a whisper. Not much scared Max, but I knew the Oracle did. An ancient vampire with powerful telekinesis, she had been held under strict supervision by the Movement. Max had actually been on a team assigned with moving her to the high-tech facilities she'd been kept in of late. Not all the team members had survived.

Nathan didn't respond, but I'd seen that expression on his face many times. He was just as scared as Max. "She killed her handlers, most of the staff. Miguel is gone. So is Breton. She was located in the hospital wing, so most of the destruction is centered there."

"Anne is dead," Bella said dispassionately, never looking at Max. "The Oracle set fire to everyone in the hospital wing."

"Like, with mind powers?" I asked quietly.

Bella frowned at me as though trying to comprehend my stupidity. "No. With the rubbing alcohol from the supply room and someone's lighter."

Max moved to the window, his jaw clenching as Nathan droned on about procedures during cessation of communication, and whether or not it was safe for me or himself to be involved.

I went to Max and laid my hand on his shoulder. "Are you okay?"

He nodded. "Yeah. I'm just… You know, I knew it. All those years ago, when we moved her to the new facility, it's like I could feel that she was planning something."

Bella snorted. "How could you know the mind of the Oracle?"

"I don't believe the mind of the Oracle concerns you," Max growled at her. "How many werewolves died at her hand?"

Her exotic face went pale, but Bella's golden eyes narrowed. "I am sorry she could not be of better service to you in your campaign of hatred against my people."

"Everyone just calm down." Nathan stood, entirely too reasonable for the emotional climate of the room.

When I'd first seen him, I'd just been relieved to be in

the same room with my sire. I hadn't noticed how tired he appeared, hadn't taken in the dark circles beneath his eyes or the grim set of his mouth.

His gaze flickered over me a moment, and his exhaustion seemed to intensify. "The Oracle didn't break out on a whim. Like Max said, she must have been planning it. Let's all turn it in for the day and discuss this like reasonable adults after sundown."

"Great, I'll show you guys to your rooms." Max emphasized the plurality. It comforted me to know that though they would probably end up together Max was letting them know he disapproved of it.

Nathan seemed surprised. He looked at me, then back to Max with a shrug. "Sounds good."

"Okay. Night, all." I gave a noncommittal wave and turned to the stairs.

Look back.

The suggestion over the blood tie was so strong, I had to give in. When I glanced over my shoulder, Nathan's gaze locked with mine. I couldn't discern the emotion there, whether it was guilt or apology or a silent plea for me to come to him.

I shook my head, refusing them all.

Though I was tired, sleep did not come immediately. My brain swam with imagined horrors. I'd experienced firsthand just a taste of the Oracle's power. I'd seen what she'd done to Anne, the cheerful, eternally teenaged receptionist of the Movement. The Oracle had tormented her with a vision of her spine being shattered, then, years later, she'd made it come true. What had she made those poor vampires in the hospital wing see? It must have been agony for them.

Despite the fact their agenda and my continued existence were mutually exclusive, the vampires I'd met at Movement headquarters had been nice to me, especially Anne, who'd taken me to see the Oracle despite the restrictions against it. That had ended with a skirmish in which the Oracle had tossed Anne around like a rag doll, and tried to rip my head off my shoulders. We'd been relieved, afterward, to learn that Anne had survived her injuries. But in hindsight it seemed she'd been doomed from the start. Because of the Movement's strict policy against medical treatment for life-threatening injuries, Anne would have been slowly recuperating, with no help but her body's own healing ability. She would have been completely defenseless when the Oracle torched the place. I think Nathan was right. The Oracle didn't seem to do things willy-nilly.

I rolled onto my side. The bed seemed bigger and oddly empty, now that my sire had arrived. I ached to lie at his side, listening to his gentle snores and occasional nonsensical sleep babble. Now, that was for someone else.

It made me feel a bit better to review their icy behavior toward each other in the foyer. Maybe Max's idea of deliberately putting them in separate rooms wasn't so crazy, as neither seemed inclined to crawl into bed together today.

How could Nathan have kept this from me? Despite the distance that always remained between us, I'd been honest with him, hadn't I? And I'd put my soul on the line in order to save him from the Soul Eater's torturous spell. In my mind, he owed it to me to be honest, even if it inconvenienced him a little.

I wish he had used that same, compassionate line of reasoning.

Nathan had Bella. She was exotic and passionate and dangerous. She was so different from plain, white-bread me. With all the sex and romance, Nathan probably just didn't have time to think about me and how much I might be hurt.

Not for the first time, cold tears streamed down my cheeks over my sire.

I'd nearly cried myself to sleep when there was a soft knock at my door. Probably Max coming to commiserate. I wiped my eyes hastily. If he could pretend not to be bothered, I certainly could do the same. I might even start to believe it.

"Come in," I said, hoping my voice sounded thick with sleep and not tears.

The door eased open a crack and Nathan, not Max, slipped inside.

I sat up, clutching the covers defensively to my chest as though he would be able to see through my T-shirt to my broken heart—had it been there. My actual heart was in my suitcase, removed from my chest by Cyrus, my first sire. "What are you doing here?"

He held up his hands like someone anticipating an attack. "Please, just hear me out."

"Do you really think we have anything to say? After the way things went when I left?" I scoffed. "Or especially now?"

"I know. And I'm sorry. I should have been honest with you." His words further confirmed my fear.

I drew in a shaking breath, forcing myself not to break down in sobs. "That would have been nice."

"I can't apologize enough. I know that. And I know I've put you through hell." He looked down at his hands. "But I've missed you so much."

"It would appear otherwise." I would not let his wounded-little-boy demeanor soften my righteous anger.

For a second, he appeared taken aback. "I don't want to be separated from you like this again. You belong with me."

A sick feeling wound through my stomach, something like hope with reservation.

Though I didn't speak, he came to the bed and sat down. "I've been selfish. I wanted to hang on to a past that I can't change. But I had no right to string you along the way I did. I swear, Carrie, if you come home, that will all change."

I blinked back tears. Here were the words I'd longed to hear from him, and yet…

"What about Bella?"

Nathan frowned. "What about her?"

"I don't know if she'd be too keen on having me around. Maybe, if she were another vampire, she could understand, but she's a werewolf. They don't have any concept of the relationship between a sire and a fledgling." *Or how frustrating they can be.*

A horrible scene played through my mind where Nathan replied, "You know, that makes sense. Good night," and returned to her.

Instead, he stared at me as though I'd lost my mind. "Carrie, Bella and I… I think there's been some miscommunication. We're not involved with each other."

"She was staying at the house," I stated stubbornly. "Why has she been there for a month then? Why didn't she go back to Spain?"

"She did," Nathan insisted. "She followed the Soul Eater to San Francisco, did recon, then went to Spain. She had to take commercial airlines because she couldn't contact the Movement. When she got to headquarters, she found it destroyed, and came back to Grand Rapids, because it was the only way she knew how to contact Max."

"But you said she wasn't using my room…and you were shielding your thoughts the whole time." I was beginning to feel like a total ass, and I didn't like it. It would almost have been worth it to hear he *had* been sleeping with Bella, just to keep from realizing how crazy I'd been acting.

A slow smile spread across Nathan's gorgeous mouth. "You really thought I was cheating on you?"

"It wouldn't have been cheating, since we don't have a relationship." I looked down at my hands and found them twisting the bedspread. "Nathan, I don't want to be your fledgling. I want to be the woman you love. It's never going to happen as long as you can't let go of Marianne."

I thought he would flinch or turn away at her name, the way he used to, but he held my gaze, drawing me into his steel-gray eyes. "Marianne is gone. It makes me sick to say it, but in a way, everything turned out better for us the way it did. She wasn't the woman I married. She'd given up. I know I painted her as a saint, and I don't mean to. But something about the illness twisted her. She was often depressed, sometimes openly hateful. She blamed me, once, near the end."

"Oh, Nathan." I couldn't help interrupting.

It was as if he hadn't heard me. "Even if she had lived— that is, if I hadn't done what I did to her—she would have died later. If I'd made her a vampire…well, she was too scarred. She still wouldn't have wanted to live.

"I could have given Marianne new life, could have protected her and cherished her for the rest of our time on earth, but I couldn't have given her her soul back. She'd lost that long before I killed her. The spell Bella did…that you did…it made me realize that. It sounds melodramatic, but really, you saved me."

Tentatively, I reached for his hand. I seriously expected to wake up when I touched him, but his fingers closed over mine, almost crushing, until he realized what he was doing and relaxed his grip.

"You're my fledgling. No matter what else happens between us, it's my blood in your veins. You're the only family I have. It's you I want to be with." He lifted my hand to his lips and pressed a soft kiss there.

My pulse pounded. "But not the way I want it to be. That's the part you keep glossing over."

A sad look came over his face, and his gaze dropped to our clasped hands. "If I told you now that I'm ready to…to love you, I would just be setting us up for disaster. The spell showed me the truth, but there are still parts I can't accept, even though I know them to be true. When the time comes that I can completely let it go—and it *will* come—it's not going to be some werewolf I choose. It's going to be you."

Instantly, guilt crashed over me. Nathan had been soul-searching, and I'd been…whoring it up. "I have to tell you something."

A wary look crossed over his face, followed by an obviously forced smile. Trepidation vibrated down the blood tie. He thought I was going to reject him. He let go of my hand. "Okay."

"Well, I thought you were…involved…with Bella." I closed my eyes and resisted the urge to slap my forehead with my palm. "Obviously, I jumped to a conclusion. A stupid, stupid conclusion."

He nodded, the oppressive fear of rejection letting up a bit. "And?"

"And?" I bit my lip, deciding the best way to do this was quickly. "I almost slept with Max."

I mentally counted to three, waiting for Nathan to explode. He did, but not as I expected. With a howl of laughter, he fell sideways off the bed.

"Nathan! It's not funny!" I pounded the mattress. "I almost slept with Max!"

Peering over the edge of the bed, I saw Nathan wipe tears of laughter from his eyes. "Oh, I heard you. I bet it was dead romantic, too."

"Oh, shut up," I admonished with an involuntary laugh. "I can't believe I thought you slept with Bella."

"I can't believe you did, either. I can barely stand her. Do you know she chews her toenails? I mean, she doesn't clip them off like normal people, she puts her foot in her mouth and chews them!" He shuddered in disgust. "I thought you'd give me a little more credit."

Our laughter subsided into charged silence. Nathan sat

up, resting his forearm on the bed as he studied me. "Carrie, I don't want you to do anything you don't want to. If you don't want to come home, tell me."

Home. Our home. My chest squeezed as though it would suddenly collapse. My mind raced for some proof that this was an elaborate trick to break my heart again. "I do want to come home. But I can't promise I'll wait for you. It's too unfair to ask that of me. So…"

"So?" he asked, a reluctant smile quirking the corner of his mouth.

I hated to kill the happy expression that might grow there. "So, I'll think about it."

His smile held the promise of happiness. Realistic happiness, but still, more happiness than we'd had. "Carrie?"

The way he said my name, the way it sounded heavy and meaningful on his lips, gave me chills up my spine. "What?"

"I've been dying to kiss you."

At those words, the chills ran straight from my spine to my stomach, raced down my arms and pulled a soft, "Oh," from my throat. I swallowed thickly and nodded, wetting my lips, which had become suddenly parched in anticipation.

Wordlessly, he climbed into bed beside me and we kissed as though we'd never done it before. Not because it was clumsy and awkward, but because there was more to it on both ends than there ever had been. There was a fierceness in him I'd never experienced before, not born of desperation, or fear of losing me, as when I'd first become his fledgling. It was something between determination—determination to let go and make this right—and confidence I would be there when all was said and done.

I wished I could be as sure as he was.

But my body was certain of what it wanted. No matter what had transpired between us, I needed him on a primal, visceral level. His blood was in me, making me a part of him. I couldn't seem to touch him enough, even as his mouth covered mine again and again, even as his hands found their way to my back, pulling me tight against him.

I rose on my knees before him, and he mimicked my action, pulling his shirt off in the process. I actually moaned at just the sight of him, his pale skin pulled taut over hard muscle. The scars from the Soul Eater's spell still marred his chest and arms, and I wondered briefly at the power of a magic that could leave permanent marks on a vampire. But rational thought fled when he reached for me. Like always, Nathan could make the complications of the world disappear for me when I was in his arms. Not because I was an affected flower prone to swooning, but because everything about him—his body, his mind, his scent, his touch, his problems—everything was larger than life.

And you always get caught up in it, and you always fall, and he's never there to catch you.

I ignored that warning voice, ignored every thought in my self-righteous brain, because Nathan was touching me, so everything was all right.

He slipped my T-shirt over my head and bent his face to my neck. It was nearly impossible to stay upright with his skin rubbing on mine, his mouth burning a trail across my collarbones. It was too much sensation after being apart too long, and when I moaned, felt an echoing shudder in his body.

"I've missed this," he rasped, lifting my breasts in his hands to kiss the tops of them. "God, I've missed this. I've missed you."

I clutched his hair in my fingers and held his face close. He smelled wonderful, like the sandalwood of his soap and the heavy opiate smell of the incense he burned in the shop. I almost screamed in need when his hands slid to my back and curved over my buttocks, pulling my vulnerable, naked flesh forward to make contact with the rough denim of his jeans. I reached between us and fumbled with the button at his waistband, and he pushed my hands away. "Wait, wait. Slow down. We've got all day."

"I don't want to take all day," I panted, punctuating my statement with a firm tug at his jeans.

His eyes darkened and he stared down at me for a long, silent moment. "I'm so glad you said that."

In a few frantic seconds, he'd shucked his pants and pulled me to straddle him as he lay back on the bed. I gripped the base of his cock and squeezed, gliding my fingers up, over all the hard, straining length of him. He hissed and clutched at my thighs, and the desire I felt through the blood tie magnified my own. I rose above him and positioned him at my entrance. My flesh throbbed at the first touch of him; my body shuddered when he flexed his hips and slid inside.

"God, Carrie," he managed through clenched teeth. "You feel so good."

I wanted to answer him, to say something witty and self-assured, but he pressed his thumb to the hot, tingling bit of flesh at my center and all I could do was let out a hoarse cry.

It had been far, far too long since I'd been with him like this. It was more than a physical connection. With the blood tie between us, I could read his thoughts, feel his desire and experience the pleasure he felt as if it were my own. My skin burned where his hands touched me, my body tensed and spasmed around his cock as I rode him. I lost track of the times I cried out in release, lost to the feeling of his thickness stretching and spreading me, the hard, ridged length of him pounding into me. When he grabbed my hips and jerked me down, so hard against him it was almost painful, I felt him throb inside me and fell forward onto his chest, my arms too weak to support myself.

The tears that came to my eyes were unexpected. I swiped them away and carefully moved off of him, blocking him from the blood tie with what little mental strength I had left. He'd felt my sudden overload of emotion, though. The relief at being reunited with him. The uncertainty whether I could trust him to heal the wounds inflicted on him by his sire. But most of all the fear that I would be hurt again.

His hands shook as they smoothed my tangled hair from my face. "You can trust me now, Carrie. You can trust me, because I can trust myself not to hurt you."

I leaned against his cold skin, buried my face in his neck. The scent of my sire's blood, primal and familiar, filled my senses.

I'd missed him so much—the feel of him under my hands, the weight of him, solid and sure, at my side. As much as I hated the codependent notion of needing another person to

make you "whole," the blood tie did make us two halves that
were only completed by each other.

It would be so much easier if I didn't love him.

Three: Possessed

Max couldn't believe her nerve.

There Bella sat at the kitchen island, her head bent over a book, occasionally turning to take a bite from the sandwich she held in her left hand. She perched on a stool, her right foot on a higher rung than her left, so she could rest her elbow on her knee and still turn pages.

How could she look so relaxed after all that had happened? When people he'd known for years—he assumed she'd known them, too—were dead. Tortured to death by the Oracle, who now roamed around unchecked. Oh yeah. Perfect time for a sandwich.

If I kick that stool right now, there's no way she'd be able to get her balance before her ass hit the floor. The thought brought a bitter smile to his face.

"Making yourself at home, huh?" He strolled to the refrigerator and opened it, noting with annoyance she'd used all but the dregs of the mayonnaise and replaced the jar, anyway.

He pulled out a bag of blood and popped it in the microwave. "So, get a good day's sleep?"

She didn't look up. "You know I do not sleep more than a few hours at a time."

"Oh, right." He snapped his fingers. "It's a dog thing. So, do you have to circle around three times before you can lie down?"

This time, she gave him a warning glance before wordlessly returning her attention to her book.

"Sorry, didn't mean to interrupt story time." He set the timer and then turned, leaning back against the counter. "Here's a funny story. Tell me if you've heard it. A building full of vampires gets roasted from the inside out and everyone dies."

She didn't look up. "You think I do not care about what has happened to the Movement?"

"You're right. That *is* what I think. See, you haven't shown much love for vampires. None of your kind have. And maybe what I thought was you being brave and stoic was just you…not giving a shit."

The microwave dinged and he pulled out the pleasantly warm bag. Eschewing a cup, he bit through the plastic and purposely let some blood dribble down his chin, for good measure.

Her nose twitched at the coppery smell. With a noise of disgust, she tossed her sandwich down and slammed her book shut. "You are a pig."

"And you're a bitch. Yet here we are." He drained the bag, though he really hadn't been hungry to begin with, and tossed it aside. It landed with a wet smack on the floor beside the trash can.

Bella looked as though she might throw up. Nothing would have pleased Max more.

But it wasn't in the cards. Instead, she stood, tucked her book beneath her arm and headed toward the door. Her hand was on the smooth, painted wood when she whirled to face him. Her stony, cool facade had cracked, her high cheekbones coloring deep red.

"I am sorry you cannot accept my rejection of you for what it is. That is, that you cannot see beyond your pride, to the many reasons we could not be together." Her voice quivered slightly on the last word. "And I am sorry it taints your view of the situation we are in."

He chose to ignore that final part. "Oh, please. If you think I'm nursing a broken heart, don't waste your time feeling sorry for me. It's Carrie I'm smarting for."

Bella snorted derisively, than sobered. "What are you talking about?"

"I think you know." He folded his arms across his chest. "I knew you were going to make a move on him. I had a sick feeling about it when I left you at his place. How could you do it? When you saw how torn up Carrie was, how could you do that?"

"How could I do what?" Bella raised her hands in the classic pose of innocence. "I think you have finally lost your mind, vampire."

"Stop trying to play dumb! You know exactly what you did. You've been fucking Nathan!" Max rounded the island and stepped so near to her he had to ball his hands into fists to keep from touching her. This kind of closeness was dangerous. He could lose his temper and grab her, or lose his willpower and—

No. You went down that road before and it sucked.

"You think I am sleeping with your vampire friend?" She had the nerve to laugh at him, as though the idea was ridiculous. Placing her palms flat on Max's chest, she gave him a shove. "You dare to accuse me of this when last night I could smell *her* all over you?"

Ouch. But what he had been doing didn't matter, Max reminded himself. It was Bella's immorality they were talking about. "Listen, what Carrie and I do is our business. But you knew how messed up she was when she left Nathan, and you still moved in for the kill. For your information, she was really hurt when she found out about the two of you. She could have slept with me to get her mind off it. But she didn't."

"When she found out about us?" Bella snorted again. Max wanted to hit her. "How, exactly, did she find out?"

The uneasy feeling that maybe something was amiss, maybe some critical piece of information had slipped through their keen investigative fingers, crept into the back of his mind. "I don't know. When she called, I guess."

Bella only nodded.

In the eerie quiet of the kitchen, even the buzzing of the fluorescent lights could be heard, layered with the drumming of water dribbling into the sink and the ticking of the sleek steel clock on the wall. From the rest of the house, not a sound.

So, where are Nathan and Carrie, genius?

Almost the exact moment he thought it, a smug smile

began to grow on Bella's face. "I am sorry the only outlet for her troubled mind was in clumsy foreplay with an inadequate partner."

He threw the rest of her sandwich at the swinging door as she passed through it.

When I opened my eyes to find myself in an empty bed, my fuzzy brain snapped to alert. Okay, it snapped to panic.

You made it all up. It was a dream.

There was no way the day before hadn't been real. No way I hadn't spent the last few hours sleeping comfortably in Nathan's arms.

I'd tossed back the blankets and was about to swing my legs over the side of the bed to begin a frantic search for him when he stepped out of the bathroom, a toothbrush in his mouth and a towel wrapped around his waist. He paused in his brushing long enough to give me a look implying I had lost my mind, then retreated to the bathroom again.

Flopping back on the pillows, I smiled. The curtains were open, the sky had faded to twilight and Nathan had turned on the bedside lamp. The soft, golden light shone through my eyelids when I closed them, and it felt almost like turning my face to the sun. I wondered if I'd ever woken up so happy.

The faucet turned on, as briefly as possible because, as I'd heard many, many times, water conservation is everyone's responsibility. I slipped out of bed and padded across the thick carpet to the bathroom. Nathan leaned over the sink, spitting toothpaste into the basin.

It's demented that you find that sexy, I told myself. I

yawned and leaned against the door frame. "You know why vampires have to brush their teeth?"

He raised an eyebrow as he wiped his mouth with a hand towel.

"So they don't get bat breath."

Drying his hands, he considered me silently for moment. "I'm rescinding my offer of letting you come home."

I slapped his shoulder. "Listen, don't be too hard on Max today, okay?"

Nathan looked as crestfallen as a child who's had his favorite toy taken away. "Why not?"

"Because I have a feeling he's going to feel pretty foolish about all this. You know, when he finds out." I shuffled my feet on the carpet.

"Why, because you feel foolish?" He shook his head. "Don't you have any faith in me? Any trust?"

I raised an eyebrow in answer.

He rolled his eyes. "Fine. I won't give him a hard time. You women are so picky about these things. And by you women, I mean you and Max."

"Get out," I ordered. "I'm going to take a nice, long, water-wasting shower."

With a grin, he asked, "Will you require assistance with that?"

"You've already taken a shower," I pointed out, gesturing to the towel.

"I'm dirty enough to take two." He winked.

We'd found that although the blood tie didn't come with built-in sexual attraction, it did ramp up whatever attraction already existed. Now that we were on familiar footing again, it didn't surprise me that he was suddenly in a randy mood.

"I don't doubt that. But we've got bigger things to worry about than your libido." I pushed him toward the door.

He went, grudgingly. "Fine. But you are in such trouble in the morning."

I don't doubt that, I thought, grim reality intruding unpleasantly. *I'm sure by morning, we'll all have jumped feetfirst into trouble.*

We found Bella upstairs, stretched out on the leather sofa in the foyer with a book in her hands. Though I now knew the truth of what had transpired between her and Nathan, her treatment of Max still kept me from warming to her.

She sat up, her eyes moving from me to Nathan and back again. "Max is in the kitchen."

Nathan seemed to sense the reason for her trepidation, and, because it's the kind of person he is, he snarled, "I'm going to kill him," before tearing toward the kitchen.

Bella didn't look nearly as alarmed as Nathan had probably expected. She lifted one elegant eyebrow and glanced back to her book. "Is he really going to kill him?"

"No. I banned him from teasing Max. I never thought to forbid him from teasing you." I slid my hands into the pockets of my jeans. "Listen, I'm sorry."

She looked up, mild surprise registering on her face. "For what?"

I thought for sure she knew, the way she'd been hesitant to tell Nathan where to find Max. I jerked my thumb toward the kitchen door. "Be-because I almost slept with Max."

"Ah, I understand. You would be more sorry if you had completed the act." Her attention once again drifted to her book.

"That's not what I meant. He's kind of your…territory." I winced at the dog terminology. "That didn't come out quite right."

"Max does not belong to me, and I do not wish him to." Bella closed the volume with a frustrated sigh. "I do not wish to continue this conversation, either. There is much we need to do. Tell the men we will all meet in the dining room in fifteen minutes."

She left without another word.

I knew Max was in full-blown denial about his feelings for Bella, but I hadn't realized the reverse was true. According to Max, she'd ended their fling, but in typical Max fashion, he was sure she still wanted a relationship with him, while he, on the other hand, couldn't care less about her.

Maybe he was right. A definite angry vibe had radiated from Bella, the same type I'd projected to her when I thought she was competition for Nathan.

In the kitchen, Nathan leaned against the counter, sipping blood from a mug, while Max wielded a mop angrily across a vicious blood spill on the floor beside the trash can.

"Did we kill someone this morning?" I crossed my arms and eyed the mop, which was soaked pink and seemed to be doing nothing but spreading watery blood over the bright white tile.

Nathan made a snort of disagreement into his cup. He swallowed with a grimace and licked a bit of blood from his upper lip. "Max threw a tantrum."

"You're a guest in this house," Max snapped, jabbing the mop at Nathan's feet. "Remember that."

"And I appreciate your hospitality. Speaking of which, when do I get to nearly have sex with you?" Nathan took another sip from his cup, ignoring Max's murderous scowl.

I smiled, covering it with my hand when Max's glare fixed on me. "Well, Bella wants us to meet her in the dining room."

"I guess it was too much of an inconvenience to stop in and tell us herself?" Max tossed the mop aside in disgust. "Maybe I had plans or an agenda or something. She can't just move in and start ordering us around!"

"I didn't think you'd mind so much if she moved in." Nathan barely dodged the saltshaker, the object nearest Max when the comment enraged him.

"Methinks you hit a nerve." I went to the refrigerator and pulled out a bag of blood.

Nathan took it and handed me his nearly full mug. "I've already had two cups. You finish this off."

I stood, sipping my blood in silence, while Nathan studied me covertly, pretending to be interested in his bare feet, the floor tiles and the pots and pans suspended over the island. He knew I hated being watched while I fed, but his surreptitious looks made my stomach fill with butterflies.

Max cursed fluently as he scrubbed the stained tiles with a roll of paper towels and an absurd quantity of glass cleaner. As the minutes ticked by, it became painfully apparent none of us wanted to be the first to appear at Bella's meeting.

"What do you think we're going to talk about?" I ventured finally.

My voice ruptured the quiet so suddenly, Max hit his head on the counter as he straightened in surprise.

Blind to his distress, Nathan shrugged calmly. "A battle plan, I assume. With the Movement gone, we have no centralized form of communication. We won't be able to get information from other operatives, and we don't have the means to track the Oracle without Movement connections."

"Not to mention the Soul Eater," I added softly. A flicker of pain crossed Nathan's face at the mention of his sire. "He's still out there."

"I hate to say it, but that might have something to do with the Oracle's disappearance," Max commented, still holding a hand to the top of his head.

As though the air had been sucked from the room, I gasped, and Nathan took a great, hissing breath at the realization the two vampires were likely connected.

"What could the Oracle want with the Soul Eater?" I asked quietly.

"What wouldn't she want with him?" Nathan replied grimly. "She has power, but she's been isolated for centuries. Think of what that would do to you."

Max nodded in agreement. "You'd definitely lose touch with a lot of your connections."

"And it would be easier picking up an evil coup in progress than starting your own from the ground up." My throat clenched. "My God… You don't think…"

Max looked from me to Nathan and back again, his jaw tight. "It would be handy to have a god in your pocket, and totally possible if you got in on the ground floor."

The door from the dining room swung open and Bella

stuck her head in with a disgusted look. "I did say fifteen minutes, did I not?"

Max shot us a withering glance and mimed choking the life out of what I assumed was an imaginary werewolf.

Like the rest of the condo, the dining room was oversize and ostentatious. I had seen it only a few times—once on the tour, another when I'd become disoriented and taken the wrong door from the foyer. Max rarely used the room at all. He preferred to drink his meals in the stark, antiseptic kitchen, rather than mahogany-paneled, windowless grandeur.

Bella had set up at one end of the massive table, in the clean, golden light of one of the dual chandeliers. She seated herself at the head of the table, behind a miscellany of archaic-looking objects, some of which I recognized as items Nathan sold in the bookstore. The others—a piece of black, concave glass resting atop a wire stand, and a large collection of what appeared to be desiccated chicken bones—were totally foreign.

Max took the chair to her left and scoffed at the heap of bones. "Dinner?"

Nathan pulled out a chair for me on her right and sat between Bella and me.

Though she'd clearly heard his comment, Bella didn't give Max the pleasure of a response. "I tried diligently all day to make some kind of contact with my fellow assassins. Unfortunately, the werewolf contingency has all but fled Spain to return to our ancestral forests, and I know very few vampires."

"Surprise, surprise," Max muttered under his breath.

"I do not want to alarm you." Bella turned in her chair

so she faced Nathan and me. "But I feel we are at a marked disadvantage against the Oracle. And I fear…"

"That she might be looking for the Soul Eater?" The question slipped automatically from my mouth.

She nodded, her expression hard, and continued. "I have pored over the meager library Max keeps—"

I glanced his way, sure his head would blow off his neck at that. The "meager" library had belonged to Marcus, and Max took all slights against him, intentional or not, very seriously. His face remained impassive, and he leaned back in his chair, arms folded over his chest.

Bella, ignorant of her affront, continued speaking. "It appears there was a breakdown in Movement communication in France during the Nazi occupation. A handful of assassins found themselves unable to contact headquarters or track their quarry. They turned to divination to re-establish communication and monitor the whereabouts of their mark.

"Though in this case it would be unrealistic to try and open a line of communication with the Movement, we could certainly use those same means to glean information about the Oracle and what she intends to do now that she is free."

"Or Nathan could do it." Max's voice seemed overloud, and we all turned to stare at him in varying degrees of horror as he continued. "He has a blood tie with the Soul Eater. If he's working with the Oracle, Nathan would know it."

At the thought of Nathan making contact with his terrifying sire, the one who'd possessed and tormented him, the blood in my veins turned to ice. "No!"

My denial was echoed by Bella. "He was possessed

once by the power of his sire. My spell freed him, but I cannot guarantee I could do so again."

"She's right," I agreed vehemently. "Nathan, you can't even consider doing something like that. He would find you in a minute."

Beside me, Nathan drummed his fingertips on the table. "I think you're right. We try Bella's way, first."

Max snorted. "Listen, I'm not trying to shoot down the one solution anyone has come up with, but I'm not sure this is exactly the most efficient way to go about finding the Oracle and figuring out what her plans are."

"What would be more efficient?" Bella demanded. "Traveling the world door-to-door, knocking and asking if the Oracle is inside?"

Rolling his eyes, Max turned to Nathan and me. "Listen, you guys can't really believe this is our best bet? Random patterns of cards and gazing into a crystal ball?"

Though I felt as though I was betraying him, we didn't have much else to go on. I spread my hands helplessly. "Well, it couldn't hurt to try. If the Movement has fallen apart, it's just a matter of time until every non-Movement vampire figures it out and we end up with a crisis on our hands."

"So, we're going to prevent this from happening with our super New Age mind rays?" He shook his head. "I'm sorry, I just think we're barking up the wrong tree."

Nathan grimaced as though he hated being cast in the peacekeeper role. "Listen, Bella hasn't been able to contact anyone. I've been out of the Movement for two years, so I don't know anyone's number or location anymore. You might be able to track somebody down, but even if you do, how are we going to find the Oracle? We've got documented evidence that this approach works. Why not try it before we declare ourselves royally screwed?"

"Max, you were still in the Movement. You have to have the company directory or something, right?" I hoped he did. I didn't like the looks of those chicken bones any more than he did.

Max shook his head. "It was Movement policy never to reveal the identities of their assassins, even to other assassins."

"Any assassins who knew each other, like Max and me, chose to contact one another outside of the Movement." Nathan glanced briefly at Max. "Sometimes I wonder why I chose to contact him."

"It was a policy that applied only to vampires," Bella added. "The werewolves involved in the Movement were all from the same pack. You would consider that family, or extended family. We have a code of honor, and our own consequences if we should break it. But the vampires…imagine if one vampire knew how to find all of the assassins? And then they found themselves in the company of a creature like the Soul Eater?"

"So, they kept your locations, and to some extent, your identities, secret so the information couldn't be tortured out of you?" I looked to Nathan for confirmation.

"Or sold to the highest bidder." He gestured to Max. "Max and I became acquainted when we were given an assignment together. But if we hadn't both agreed that it would be handy to know another assassin nearby—or relatively nearby—we might not have exchanged contact information and stayed in touch."

"But what about the meeting? You had a dozen Movement assassins in your bookshop." I shuddered at the thought of some of them coming after us as we'd been living peacefully in the apartment upstairs.

"That was a strike team Rachel personally assembled. They already knew who I was and where I could be found. And I trusted them all for a reason." Nathan put a reassuring hand on my knee.

"Nathan was never quite as secretive as some of us." The way Max spoke the words implied he thought Nathan was an idiot for trusting anyone. "I do have a blood donor who's pretty active in the city. I might be able to get some contacts out of him."

"We may still be, in Nathan's words, royally screwed," Bella pointed out. "Of the four of us, I have the most experience with the occult, but divination has always escaped me. I may be able to pick up a few clues, but I will not know if they apply to our situation or not. Have any of you ever done anything like this?"

"I own an occult book and supply store," Nathan reminded her, not a little sarcastically. "I've used tarot cards before."

"Ah, good." Bella's face lit up. She reached for a box of cards and slid them across the table to him. "That can be your job. Since he has expressed disinterest in helping us, Max can try to reach other assassins through his donor."

"What about me?" I eyed the pile of bones. I wanted to be included, but maybe not *that* included. "I'm a quick study. Give me something to do."

She considered the array of objects before her and

pushed a jewelry box toward me. I opened it to find a slender crystal dangling from a delicate chain.

"A pendulum," Bella informed me. "Nathan, can you instruct her? I thought perhaps it could be used to try and pinpoint the Oracle's location on an atlas."

"I'm sure she'll get the hang of it." He winked at me.

"Good. We should all keep track of our results." She sounded like one of my old professors explaining the etiquette of laboratory experiments. "Until we know specifics about our situation, everything is important."

She reached for a bottle of what looked like ink and poured it into the glass bowl, which she lifted from its stand to swirl it a few times. Then, taking a lighter from her pocket, she lit the charcoal in the small, tabletop cauldron at her left.

"So, are we dismissed then?" Max asked, his tone dripping with sarcasm.

Caught up in sprinkling foul-smelling powder onto the burning block, Bella didn't look at him. "Yes, of course. We need to get to work immediately."

Max waited until we were in the foyer, at least, before he exploded. "You've got to be kidding me! She comes into my house, assigns us jobs, declares herself Dwight fucking Eisenhower of the occult, and stinks up my dining room with…whatever that was?"

"Honeysuckle and camphor," Nathan supplied. "They're powerful divination aids, but they smell better fresh than burning."

"No shit." Max's face had turned a queer shade of red. "Listen, she's got to go. I don't care where, she's just got to get out of my house."

A terminally stupid person could see his problem wasn't with incense and tarot cards. Still, I had to proceed cautiously. Any mention of his feelings for Bella caused a total shutdown, in which Max would storm off and nothing would be resolved. "I know you're having a hard time with her here, but look at us. Three of us against the Oracle? Possibly against the Soul Eater, as well?"

He didn't respond, but the muscle at the corner of his jaw ticked. He didn't like what I was saying, but he knew I was right.

"Bella has an advantage over us," Nathan added. "She can go out in the daytime. We need her for that, at the very least."

It was clear from the way Max shifted his gaze silently between Nathan and me that he didn't want to admit we were right. He groaned and tossed his hands up. "Fine. But you guys are paying for the air fresheners when she's done in there."

Nathan laughed. "It's a deal. Now, where can we go to work?"

"In the library. Or the parlor. Or one of the fine guest accommodations, either upstairs or down." Max shrugged. "Do it in the hot tub, I don't care."

A warm flush crept up my neck as I caught sight of Nathan's lascivious grin. "That's not a good idea. But thanks," I said. "We'll be in the library."

"Do me a favor and keep *her* out of it. If it's so 'meager,' she'll have read everything already," Max said petulantly. "I'll be upstairs, trying to get answers out of Bill."

"We could have done it in the hot tub," Nathan groused

as I led the way to Marcus's library. "It would have been more fun than this divination business."

The look I gave him made it clear "this divination business" was all we were going to be up to.

The library, situated at the front of the building, was by far the most impressive room in the condo. The ceiling reached to the second floor of the apartment. Books lined the walls. Iron spiral staircases led to the balcony that wrapped three sides of the room, holding the second tier of literature. I wondered how many personal libraries Bella had seen, and what they must have been like to make this collection seem unimpressive.

Nathan whistled in awe. He set the cards down on one of the leather armchairs near the enormous fireplace and scratched his head as he glanced around. "Not too shabby."

"I'd offer to leave you two alone for a minute, but I fear what you would do." I motioned him to the far wall. The huge windows overlooked Grant Park and the shore of Lake Michigan beyond. I pointed out the aquarium at the edge of the view. "Max has connections. He got us in after hours."

"Weren't all the fish sleeping?" Nathan chided. He stood silently, taking in the lights of the city for a minute, then turned to me. "You don't…like him, do you?"

"No, of course not." I suppressed the urge to tack on *You idiot.* "Not the way you're thinking."

He smiled, probably mentally adding the "you idiot" part himself. "I'm sorry. I know it's stupid to think that. But you know, here he is, nice house in a big city, young guy—"

"You're a young guy," I reminded him. "Young looking, anyway."

A faint flush colored his usually pale face. "I know that. But I've been alive a hundred years, and I'm starting to act my age."

Starting to? "In all fairness, Max is technically in his fifties."

"Max is a teenager, no matter how old he gets." Nathan's cool gray eyes scanned the street below us. "I understand why you came here. You wanted to be around someone you can identify with."

"What I want is someone who can love me." I studied him carefully to gauge his reaction. "Someone who can love me as much as I love him. But I wasn't looking for that in Max."

Nathan lifted a hand as though he would touch me. I brushed it aside and pointed toward the fireplace. "We have things to do."

He taught me how to use the pendulum. First, he showed me how to hold the cord so the crystal hung perfectly still over a book. I asked two questions. The first, "Is this a book?" caused the pendulum to swing in tight, clockwise circles. The second question, "Is this a dead fish?" resulted in wide, counterclockwise swoops.

"That's all there is to it," Nathan explained. "Clockwise for yes, counter for no. At least, for you. It varies from person to person."

It was much easier than Bella made it sound. She either had a gift for overcomplicating things, or she had greatly underestimated my intelligence. Probably the latter, as werewolves didn't put much stock in the intellectual equality of other species.

I dangled the crystal point over a map of the world, moving it from area to area and asking, "Is the Oracle here?" while Nathan laid out one complicated spread of cards after another. As soon as I made inroads to the continent North America, I flipped to a new page in the atlas and started working on the states and provinces. Occasionally, the pendulum would swing erratically, and I'd have to go through the process of recalibrating it. Then I'd start over from my last reasonable answer, sometimes to find it had changed. Every yes I got, I wrote down. Though the Oracle couldn't really be in all those places at once, Bella had said to write everything down. I would let her sort out the details.

We'd sat in silence for an hour before Nathan looked up and frowned. "Do you hear that?"

Now that he mentioned it, I did. Every few minutes, a rhythmic bang came from the upper level of the library.

I rose slowly, staring at the walls. The sound grew louder and more violent, actually shaking the crystal chandelier suspended high above us. "It sounds like it's coming from—"

"The dining room," Nathan said, breaking into a run toward the doors.

We were coming up the stairs to the foyer just as Max ran down from the third floor. "What the hell is that?"

Nathan didn't answer, but rushed to the doors leading to the dining room.

Before he could touch them, they flew open, as if with a gust of wind, but as there were no windows in the dining room, the force must have come from an unnatural source. Nathan toppled back and I rushed to help him up.

"Holy shit," Max whispered, his eyes wide.

I followed his gaze through the open doors. Bella hung lifeless, suspended in the air as though nailed to an invisible crucifix. A supernatural wind howled in a cyclone around her, the various objects she'd carefully spread on the table caught up in the maelstrom. They whirled around her like ornaments on a mobile, almost merry as they weaved and bobbed, the occasional chicken bone or rune stone flying free to smash into a wall.

Bella's head, limp and heavy on her neck, snapped up. Her eyes, usually preternatural gold, were opaque with blood, her olive skin pale and her lips the blue of a corpse.

As the three of us stared, horrified or dumbstruck or maybe both, Bella's lips began to move.

But the voice that issued forth wasn't Bella's.

It was the Oracle's.

Four: Oracle

"You have sought me, and now you have found me, children."

The voice, which I'd heard outside of my head only once before, sent chills down my spine. Even under Movement control—and heavy sedation—the Oracle had been able to maim Anne, one of Max's few friends at headquarters, and she'd nearly broken my neck. If she'd been able to hurt Bella from wherever she was, she could still damage us.

Nathan reached for me, snagging my arm and pulling me behind him, as if he could shield me from her wrath.

Bella's head turned, her blood-occluded eyes fixing on him with startling intensity. "Do not move again."

"Listen to her, Nathan," Max warned. "She'll kill you."

Her eyes moved to Max. "I know you."

"Yes, you do. And that's a friend of mine you're possessing." Max took a step toward her. "And you're going to have to leave."

"You fear me, vampire?" Bella's head sagged for a moment, then snapped up again. "I have no power over you now. Any harm you visit upon me in this form will only hurt her."

"If you don't have any power, how are you here?" I asked, trying to keep my tone reasonable. She might have tried to kill me before, but she'd also given me key information in finding Cyrus. It seemed unlikely she'd contacted us so dramatically only to slaughter us where we stood.

"Listen well, vampires. The age of your reign is drawing to a close. Those who resist will be killed. Those who do not may be spared. Chaos shall rule, order shall be abolished. Do not stand in my way and you may live." Bella's arm twitched. The Oracle's control seemed to be slipping.

"What if we help you?" Nathan edged forward. "If we don't oppose you, we may live. If we help you, will you offer us asylum?"

A laugh filled the air, but it didn't come from Bella. Her head drooped forward, her body slouching in midair. "You wish to help me?"

"It's better than dying." Nathan shrugged, as if he didn't care either way. "Better than trying to fight you."

"That path will surely lead to death," the Oracle warned, her now bodiless voice shaking the walls. "If you wish to gain my favor, abandon your pursuit of the pawn I need to ensure my rule."

"The Soul Eater?" Max whispered, as if she wouldn't hear us.

"He goes by many names. Abandon your pursuit of him and you may know my mercy." Another wall-rattling boom split the air. "Upset my plans and you will know my wrath!"

The wind came again, this time sucking into the dining room as the Oracle's presence left us. The doors slammed closed, shutting us out, just as Bella's body dropped to the floor. We heard the noise of her impact, and Max darted forward.

When he grabbed the door handles, he cursed. "It won't open!"

"She must have meant the Soul Eater." Nathan rushed forward to help him, but in true Nathan fashion his mind was on the bigger picture. "When you said his name, she didn't deny it."

Max didn't respond, pulling so hard at the door the wood splintered around the handle. "Come on!"

"Let's try through the kitchen," I urged, but no sooner did I say it than the doors let go easily. Nathan stumbled backward and landed on the marble floor with a curse. Max, who'd obviously braced himself in the certainty they'd get the door open, managed to stay on his feet. He ran into the dining room, shouting Bella's name.

I helped Nathan to his feet and hurried after Max. "Don't move her! She could have broken her neck in the fall."

It was too late. Max had already pulled Bella into his lap, and was slapping her ashen cheek lightly with his palm. "Bella, come on!" He looked up at me. "Carrie, she's not breathing!"

"Lay her down!" I caught her wrist as Max moved her to the floor. "No pulse!"

"Do something!" He pounded his fists on his thighs. "There has to be something you can do!"

"Do you know CPR?" I asked, tilting her head back.

Max shook his head. "Only from movies. Tell me what to do."

"Pinch her nose shut and breathe into her mouth when I tell you to. I'll do chest compressions." I turned to Nathan. "Call an ambulance."

"No!" Max shook his head. "The full moon is tomorrow night. If she's in the hospital all doped up, she'll change."

"Nathan, get the phone." I met Max's worried gaze. "If we don't get her back in two tries, we're calling an ambulance."

Grim-faced, Max nodded.

I've always hated doing CPR. Most of my experience with it came from the E.R., on seventy-and-over patients who'd gone into cardiac arrest. Their ribs were usually so brittle from bone loss they cracked like wishbones under my hands.

Bella was built stronger than that, whether by virtue of being younger, or because of her species, I have no idea. I got through the first set of compressions without breaking her bones. "Breathe now!"

Max didn't hesitate. Bella's chest inflated with the force of the incoming oxygen, but it fell again when Max pulled away.

I gripped her wrist—still nothing—then began another set of compressions.

At the cessation of compressions, blood traveling through the heart slows. Resuming the process doesn't bring the circulation back up to speed. It's like accelerating to seventy, dropping to fifty, speeding up to sixty, then dropping to forty. Bella's fingernails showed signs of cyanosis. Blue is never a promising color.

But we didn't have to call for help. This time when Max breathed for her, her body shuddered and she choked to life, taking great, panicked breaths.

"Bella, you're fine, you're fine," I assured her, checking again for a pulse. Though a little slow, it was strong. I nearly sobbed with relief.

"Calm down, baby," Max urged, brushing her hair back. "Just calm down. You're fine."

She opened and closed her mouth, vomited spectacularly, then visibly relaxed, shutting her eyes as her head dropped back to the floor.

"Let's get her to a bed," Max said, scooping her up.

Bella's eyes opened to slits and she laughed weakly. "Always trying to get me into your bed, vampire."

"You know it." If Bella's eyes hadn't closed again, she would surely have seen the mix of relief and sadness, and the determination not to show them, that crossed Max's face.

"You take care of her. I'll tell Nathan not to call the paramedics," I offered. Max and Bella needed time alone. If near death wouldn't inspire them to talk without sniping at each other, nothing would.

I found Nathan in the kitchen, slumped over the island with the phone in his hands. When he looked up, his eyes were rimmed with red. "Is she—"

"She's fine." I pulled out the stool next to his and climbed onto it. "Banged up, but she'll pull through. I'm not so sure about you, though."

Nathan sniffed and tried to cover it with a laugh. "Oh, I'll be fine. Just rattled my nerves, is all."

Because she was possessed.

My gaze dropped to his arm, where he'd rolled up the sleeve of his sweater. Though vampires heal quickly, for some reason the self-inflicted marks he'd carved under the Soul Eater's influence had never completely faded.

I went to his side and put my arms around him. "It still bothers you."

"You're damn right it bothers me!" he snapped, pushing away from the island and stalking to the other end of the kitchen. "Jesus, Carrie! She found us. She nearly killed Bella!" He looked instantly repentant for his outburst. "She could have chosen you. She could have done that to you."

"Nathan," I whispered, my heart twisting in my chest. "She didn't pick me. She attacked Bella. There hasn't been a time since I've know you that we haven't been in danger. Why is it so different now?"

"Because now…" His hands fisted at his sides, and he looked away. "It's just different."

Because now you love me, I finished for him across the blood tie. He shook his head. The denial didn't skewer my heart the way it would have before. "You love me, and you're afraid to lose me."

"We've got to take care of this," he said, changing the subject smoothly. "We have no idea if anyone else even knows what happened. If we're the only ones, and we wait… I don't even want to think of the consequences."

He was right. I hated it, but he was right. "What do you suggest we do?"

"Tonight? Nothing. There's no time. But tomorrow

night we meet up again and we make an actual plan. Something concrete. Something—"

"Bloody and violent?" The rage emanating over the blood tie was almost frightening. "You know, we might have a better chance of success if we didn't make this personal."

Nathan jerked his head toward the door. "Tell that to Max."

"Good point." I went to Nathan and leaned my head against his chest, waited for him to put his arms around me. He hesitated, until I said, "We've been through worse, haven't we?"

I felt the low rumble in his chest, but the laughter wasn't enough to produce sound. "No. But there is a first time for everything."

Though I wanted to stay there, held by him forever, my thoughts strayed to the pair upstairs. "I'm going to go check on Bella."

There was a smile in Nathan's voice when he spoke. "Always on call?"

"Old habits die hard." I tilted my face up, expecting a gentle peck and receiving instead a long, thorough kiss that left my limbs trembling. "What was that for?" I nearly gasped when we parted.

"If anything like that ever happened to you—" He broke off, his fingers bunching my T-shirt where his hands rested against my back. "I swear, Carrie. I don't like what I am, but I would kill anyone who hurt you. I'd kill them, and I'd enjoy it."

I didn't know what to say. I don't think I'd ever seen Nathan so angry before. At least, not an anger that wasn't fueled by grief. I pulled away from him, tried to smile. But he'd frightened me a little, and the expression felt fake. "I know, Nathan. I know."

And I didn't doubt him for a second.

I had no idea where Max had put Bella, but she wasn't in any of the guest rooms on the upper floor. A quick check of Max's room revealed it empty. I suppose, given the carnage of empty ice cream boxes and drained beer bottles we'd left there, it was no kind of environment for a patient.

I was about to try the rooms downstairs when I noticed the imposing double doors to Marcus's room were open a crack. The brass key with its heavy tassel, which Max usually hung from his bedpost, dangled from the keyhole.

"Now, what are the chances that got there by itself?" I mumbled, easing the door open a bit farther.

I'd never been in this room, and though I'd never met Max's sire, the moment I peered in the place screamed Marcus. Stern, heavy furniture; ugly, masculine colors; scratchy-looking, expensive fabrics. No wonder Max kept it locked up at all times.

The room was dim. A bedside lamp with a gold shade and beaded fringe provided muted, warm light. Bella lay in the center of the bed, dwarfed by the antique monstrosity. The huge canopy nearly touched the ceiling, and I estimated there would be room for four people on either side of her. Max sat with her, holding her limp hand in his.

For a minute it looked as though he would lean forward and kiss her forehead. I cleared my throat, so he wouldn't go all "emotional shut-down Max" on me when he noticed I was there. "Knock knock."

"Who's there?" he asked with a note of black humor in his voice. "If you say banana, I'm going to hit you."

I walked slowly into the room, feeling somehow criminal for invading this private sanctuary. On the nightstand, in dark wood frames, sat an assortment of snapshots of Max. It was an uncomfortably intimate thing to see. "She's out again?"

He nodded. "But she's still breathing, if you couldn't tell from the snores."

I dutifully took her pulse and monitored her respiration, timing it by the ticking of the ornate gold clock standing in the corner. "She's going to be fine. Whatever the Oracle did—"

"Don't. Not around her." He positioned her hand on her chest in a way that made her eerily resemble a corpse.

"If there's anything else you need—"

Max waved a hand dismissively. "Go. If she wants to do this again, it's not like the two of you will be able to stop her. And I think if she makes a return appearance, Bella's gonna need a lot more than CPR to help her."

"Don't talk like that," I begged quietly. "Listen, we can talk about this tomorrow night. Right now, we all just need some time to think. But this isn't a lost cause."

Max shook his head. "I hate to tell you, but life isn't always like this for us. You came into our world at a really bizarre time. I wish I could tell you this kind of high-concept shit goes down every couple of months, but it doesn't. So pardon me if the Pollyanna shtick doesn't make me feel all warm and fuzzy inside."

Our world? That stung more than the aspersions he cast

on my optimism. I might not be as old as he or Nathan, and I'd never been a part of the Movement. Sure, there were things I didn't know, but I was learning. I'd killed Cyrus— even if it hadn't stuck—and I'd kept the Soul Eater from devouring Nathan. I'd willingly been possessed by the soul of his dead wife to break an evil spell. I might not have a vampire extermination record as impressive as Max's, but I thought I'd earned some pretty impressive street cred.

The thought that I might be wrong, that I may not have seen anything yet, froze the marrow in my bones.

Five: Defenses

Max woke at the sound of Bella's scream.

He'd been curled up at the end of her bed like a dog—he'd hoped in her post-possession panic she wouldn't notice—where he'd fallen asleep watching over her.

There was no time to berate himself for napping on the job. Bella clawed at the blankets, then her clothing, shrieking in utter panic.

Grasping her shoulders, he called her name, shaking her lightly. "You're okay, baby. I'm here. I'm here."

Her pupils changed size as she tried to focus. Frowning, she pushed back the hair that had escaped from her long braid. "I know. That is why I was screaming."

The fact she could make a wisecrack bolstered his faith that she would be all right. At least, for now. "You scared the bejesus out of me."

"That is what I was going for." Her voice broke a little, as though she might cry. Of course, she didn't. Max was reasonably sure werewolves were born without tear ducts. Or hearts.

"Can I have a glass of water?" Her voice was hoarse,

probably from screaming. She'd always sounded like that, after they'd—

He didn't just force the thought aside. He clubbed it unconscious, threw it into a crawl space and walled it up alive.

He grabbed a bottle of water from the bedside table—he'd come prepared—and twisted the top off before handing it to her. Partly to see the look of annoyance on her face when she realized he thought her weak and incapable of caring for herself, partly because he took bizarre satisfaction in caring for her. He waited until she'd gulped down half the water before asking, "Are you okay?"

She nodded. "I am fine. I am sore all over for some reason, but I am fine."

"Well, after you blacked out, we all took turns kicking the shit out of you." He smiled weakly. "Do you remember what happened?"

She shook her head vehemently, then winced and rubbed her neck. "The last thing I remember, I was looking into my scrying bowl, and I was starting to get a picture. Then I woke up here. I had the most terrible dream."

"Do you remember what it was about?" He briefly considered grabbing a pen and paper, but decided that might seem insensitive. Not that he would normally treat her with perfect sensitivity, but she'd had a rough ordeal. She deserved at least a day to rest before the interrogating began.

When her gaze met his, her eyes held a hint of hopelessness. "I saw a man. He had white hair…. And the Oracle. She was there, feeding off of his blood. And she was becoming strong from it. I do not know why it was so disturbing, it just was."

"The Soul Eater." He shook his head. "When you blacked out, the Oracle…she took over your body."

"What?" Bella shrieked, her face pale.

He laid a hand on her knee to calm her. Even through the blankets and her clothing, he imagined her skin searing his. "Don't be freaked. She didn't make you go crazy or kill anyone, like the Soul Eater did to Nathan. She used you to speak to us. Basically, she just popped in to announce her presence."

Bella's brow furrowed. "I knew that."

"Well, then you weren't as bad off as we thought," he stated, for lack of anything better to say. He could have murmured, "Tomorrow is another day," or "Every cloud has a silver lining." That would have been just as brilliant.

"Somehow, I knew that." She started to shake, her eyes wide. "How did I know that?"

"It probably leaked into your subconscious. I mean, she could have left, like, psychic residue…."

Bella quirked her eyebrow. "Residue?"

"I'm sorry, I'm not hip to the whole mental communication scene." He tossed his hands up.

"You are a vampire. What about the blood tie? That does still happen, does it not?"

You have no idea. Everywhere Max looked—at Marcus's bed, Marcus's chairs, Marcus's obscenely expensive rugs— all he saw was a hole where his sire should have been.

Of course, he couldn't expect a werewolf to be sympathetic with that. "I'm just trying to help."

"I know." Her voice was uncharacteristically soft. "She is on her way to meet the Soul Eater."

Max frowned. "We assumed that—"

"She is on a boat. It is a cargo ship of some kind, headed for…Boston." Bella shook her head. "Why would she give you that kind of information?"

He decided to ignore the chills racing up his spine for a moment. "She didn't."

They stared at each other for a long minute. Vaguely, he noted the ticking of the clock in the corner, and the click that registered it was about to chime. When it sounded, they both jumped.

"How did I—"

He cut her off. "I don't know. Do you know anything else?"

"Many things." She trembled openly now, and a tear slid down her cheek. "She killed a sailor sent to check on something in the hold. *Hold.* That is not a word I would use."

"It doesn't come up in a lot of my conversations, either." He brought his clasped hands to his mouth. "Maybe it's a fluke."

"Fluke? I have her memories in my head. You think that is a fluke?" Bella moved as if to get out of bed, and Max put his arm out to stop her.

"You've had a bad night. Just take it easy." He tucked the blankets in around her legs.

"Take it easy?" she screamed, kicking the covers back. "Do not tell me this! I have been used as a puppet!"

"Look, there's no reason to panic. At least, not yet. She didn't have enough power to continue inhabiting you."

Bella covered her face with her hands. "Why me? I am not one of you. Why did she not seek one of her kind?"

"I don't know." He'd wondered the same thing. More

specifically, he'd wondered why it had to be Bella instead of himself. He would have gladly changed places.

She tried again to get out of bed, but her arms shook, not up to the task. She fell back on the bed with a startled cry, as if pain and muscle fatigue were things she'd never experienced.

He moved to help her, repeating, "Take it easy. You really took a beating tonight."

"A beating?" She snorted. "I am strong. Nothing the Oracle could do to me would matter."

"You were suspended five feet off the ground and she dropped you. And I'm sure your ribs hurt after the CPR."

Smooth, Max.

"CPR?" She frowned.

Max rolled his eyes. "Cardiopulmonary resuscitation. You kind of…died."

"Died?" She bolted upright.

"Just for a second!" He held out his hands, prepared to stop her if she tried get up again. "Minutes at most. Carrie brought you right back."

Bella raised her fist as though to strike him. He braced himself, so he wouldn't flinch when she hit him.

But she didn't. She broke into sobs.

Max, having long ago dismissed the idea that werewolves, Bella in particular, had feelings, had no clue how to deal with the situation. In his mind, female tears were like acid, and he had never willingly wetted himself with *that*.

Still, Bella was usually so unshakable, so collected, so stone cold…. It killed him to know something could bother her so much.

"Hey, don't cry." He reached to put his arms around her, painfully aware of how awkward he felt. When she didn't lash out at him or drive a stake through his heart for trying to help, he gave her a hug and a brotherly pat.

It didn't surprise him at all that his gesture didn't help.

"I hurt so much," she sobbed, her words almost incomprehensible, given her tears and her accent. "It hurts to cry and I cannot stop."

"Just…you know, get it out." He rubbed her back gently. Physical contact had always distracted him from his troubles. She couldn't be much different.

"That feels good," she sniffed. "My back is like a fishing net, it has so many knots."

He let the opportunity to ridicule her primitive, old-world folkism pass, and slid behind her on the bed.

"What are you—"

"Nothing sleazy. A back rub will help." Before she could argue, he pulled her between his legs and went to work on her shoulders.

She groaned and her muscles seemed to melt under his hands. "Wait."

Here we go. This is where she goes off on her "You're getting it all wrong, I don't feel that way about you" kick.

To his surprise, she leaned forward and pulled off her shirt. "The fabric was chaffing."

Faced with the smooth expanse of her warm back, he suddenly couldn't trust himself. He fixed his gaze on the dark lines of the curse tattooed on her arms, silently vowing not to notice the black straps of her lacy bra or the two tiny moles just above the small of her back, the ones he'd bent to kiss as he'd taken her from behind….

Just a friendly back rub for an injured person. Keep your dick out of her. It! Keep your dick out of it!

She moaned a little as his hands worked the base of her neck, and he shifted to keep her as far from his growing erection as possible.

"How long was I unconscious?" she asked, pulling her braid forward over her shoulder.

The silky rope of hair brushed his knuckles, sending shivers up his arm. "Well, we weren't with you when it started, and you were…gone when we got there. But after Carrie got you back, I brought you up here and that was about…six hours ago?"

Bella turned her head slightly. They couldn't make eye contact, but in profile he saw her mouth curve into a smile. "You carried me here?"

He shrugged. "You couldn't exactly walk."

"And you stayed with me?"

"Every second." He cleared his throat. "Except for when I went to get the water and the extra towels and the first aid kit. Those seemed kind of important to have, just in case."

"Ah." She faced forward again and wiggled her shoulder, signaling he should continue what he hadn't even realized he'd stopped.

Trying hard to infuse every brush of his fingers against her skin with platonic feeling, he kneaded her back, then her shoulders and finally her upper arms, trying the entire time to block out her satisfied groans and whimpers.

When his hands started to ache, he tentatively pulled away. "That better?"

"Yes. Thank you." She didn't withdraw.

In fact, to his great and keen dismay, she leaned against him and reached back to loop an arm around his neck. "I missed you."

"Did you?" He'd missed her. At least, part of him had.

She gave a little sigh. "Do you know you are still the only man I have ever slept with?"

"Congratulations. You went a whole month without boning someone else." He felt her laugh, and smiled, though it hadn't been meant as a joke. Somehow, the thought of her with another man horrified him more than the dangers posed by the Oracle and the Soul Eater combined. "Listen, I should go."

"No." Her arm tightened around his neck. "Stay with me."

What would it hurt? He didn't particularly want to travel down the road his thoughts were leading him on, but he couldn't help it. Every moment of every day, he thought of her. Not because he wanted to, but because there was some broken pipe in his brain that kept sputtering out toxic drops of her until his head was completely polluted. Now the leak had become a flood, and his fear—a very real, paralyzing fear—was that his brain would never dry out. He'd just stagger through the rest of his life drowning in *her.*

But it infuriated him that he couldn't just turn off the way he had with all those other women. She was dangerously close to becoming an obsession, and if he didn't control himself now, he might never be able to.

He shoved her off him under the guise of clumsy gentleness, and tucked the blanket around her, pointedly ignoring the hint of dark color that peeked over the lacy edge of her bra. "You had a bad night. We both did. You're not physically up to anything...physical."

"Werewolves heal quickly." She cocked her head.

"Yeah, well." He scratched his neck, a nervous tic that seemed to emerge only around her. "*I'm* not up to it."

Frowning, she crawled forward, rising to her knees to loop her arms around him again. "Did you get hurt?"

He didn't return her embrace. "Yes."

She finally got it. It took her long enough.

With a wounded look, she eased away from him. "You are not still angry about what happened between us?"

"Of course I am!" he cried. "Jesus Christ, it's only been a month! What kind of inhuman bitch are you, to ask me that?"

Her eyes flew open in shock, then narrowed again. "Not a human. I did not think that was news to you."

"Don't change the subject!" He stood and paced angrily at the side of the bed. "You can't do this. You can't just decide we're chums when you're lonely or horny or—"

"I am scared!" she shouted over his tirade, her voice hoarse. "I do not want sex, I wanted you to stay with me. You have an annoying habit of cuddling. I thought if we had sex, you would stay, and I would not be alone here. I am sorry if I opened your wounds regarding me, but what was I supposed to do?"

She was more human than she gave herself credit for. He felt like an asshole, and he hated that she could make him feel that way. "First of all, I don't have any wounds because of you."

She glared at him, hurt shining in her eyes even as she prepared for another round of fighting.

He let her stew for a minute, then sat beside her on the bed. "And second, all you had to do was ask."

The way his voice went rough, the way he had to clip his words short to get them out made him crazy. He was going to say something stupid. He knew it, and wouldn't be able to stop it.

"All you have to do is ask for anything, and I'm not going to be able to tell you no." He swallowed. *There it was.* "And that's probably why I hate you so much."

She smiled and kissed him, a friendly peck, thank God, and pulled him with her onto the bed.

As she arranged the covers around them, he glanced at the clock in the corner. "You know, it's not exactly my bedtime."

"Stay," she implored, twining her fingers with his.

His lips quirked in a reluctant smile. "And I'm not exactly dressed for bed, either."

"Stay," she repeated, yawning.

He did.

During the day, while we slept, the atmosphere in the house seemed to change. If the Oracle had intended to shake our confidence by nearly killing Bella, her plan had backfired. By the time we gathered for another—hopefully uneventful—war council, we'd all found some sort of peace with each other.

Max, however, hadn't found peace with his dining room, so we met in the library. Bella lay curled before the fireplace in a pose that betrayed her canine blood. Max sat at her side, occasionally giving her head an affectionate scratch. Each time he did this, Nathan, seated in the stiff-backed wing chair next to mine, rolled his eyes.

I gave him a warning glance and cleared my throat. "So, she can see into the Oracle's head? Like with a blood tie?"

Bella shook her head. "No. I am not familiar with your vampire tie, but I know I cannot control what I see."

"So, the Oracle is controlling it," Nathan murmured pensively. He stared straight ahead, the way he always did when working out a difficult problem.

"Not necessarily." Max tried, and failed, to make eye contact with Nathan, so he turned to me. "It sounds more like the Oracle gave Bella accidental access. Mind residue or something."

"There are still things that are hidden to me. I know where she is going. I know someone is with her. But I cannot see who." Bella's smooth forehead creased in concentration. "Another vampire."

"That narrows it down," Max quipped. At Bella's hurt look, he added a hasty, "Sorry."

There was a pause. Nathan still stared into the flames of the fireplace, his steepled fingers pressed to his lips as he leaned forward, elbows on his knees. Max looked uncomfortably from him to me.

I shrugged. "So, where's the Oracle going, then? I mean, we don't have much, but that's something."

"Boston," Bella answered quickly. "She is on a ship."

"Do you know when she'll arrive?" If she'd already come ashore, she could be anywhere.

Bella nodded. "Soon. She is still at sea, but she becomes restless. They will land in a few days."

"That doesn't give us much time." Max seemed in danger of slipping into the same concentration coma Nathan was already in. Luckily, he snapped out of it quickly. "We'd better get moving."

"All of us?" I'd just taken a long, perilous road trip, and I didn't feel inclined to go on another one. Where I really wanted to be was back in Grand Rapids, living in skewed domesticity and half-assed reconciliation with Nathan. "I mean, shouldn't someone stay behind and try to find the Soul Eater?"

"Yeah, you're right. Maybe you and Nathan should?" Max smiled. "Seriously, though, it's a good idea. Bella has to go to Boston, because she's the one who'll be able to get clues and necessary info from the Oracle's brain. I've got experience with the Oracle, albeit a drugged up, restrained Oracle, but it is experience. And the Soul Eater is really your and Nathan's area of expertise."

"So, I guess it's settled then," I said slowly, looking for any reaction from Nathan. "You'll go to Boston and we'll…"

"Nobody is going anywhere," Nathan said finally. His meaningful gaze locked on each of us before moving back to the flames.

"So, we're just going to sit around until the Oracle hooks up with your daddy and they turn the world into a nightmare of chaos on earth?" Max shook his head and lifted one arm over his head. "Raise your hand if you think that's a bad idea."

"It is a bad idea," Nathan agreed. "But it's also a bad

idea to rely on information from the Oracle, especially considering how we got it."

"Information from the Oracle is rarely wrong." Max turned to me. "Remember Anne, the receptionist? She told you the Oracle had given her a vision of her back breaking, and it happened."

It had happened, in gruesome detail, before our very eyes. "But she didn't know when. She told me the Oracle doesn't give specifics, and that's why she didn't believe it would happen."

"If the Oracle is telling Bella she'll definitely be in Boston in a few days, doesn't that seem a little suspicious?" Nathan turned to the werewolf. "I don't doubt you're getting visions, and that they're genuine. But you said yourself there were things you couldn't see."

"You think she's setting a trap?" While I didn't question Nathan's intelligence, I did question the Oracle's sanity. "She doesn't seem to have it together enough to do something like that."

"While I'm going to Boston regardless of what any of you chuckleheads say, you do have a point." Max stood and leaned against one of the massive marble columns framing the fireplace. "On the other hand, I've seen her tear a man's head clean off his body, so I'm disinclined to think she's not evil enough to set us up."

"Well, at least we agree on something," I grumbled. "She's capable of killing us all."

"That kind of thinking is not constructive," Bella snapped, glaring at me.

"If you go to fight the Oracle, you will lose." Nathan

gripped the arms of the chair and rose to his feet. "Don't be so stubborn about this that you get yourself killed!"

"Hey, hey!" I shouted, standing quickly to step between Nathan and Max. The testosterone level was growing to an unmanageable level. "We're not going to get anywhere fighting."

"That I can agree with," Bella sulked, still lying calmly on the floor.

I shot her an angry glance and turned to Nathan. "At the very least, Max and Bella should try to find out more about this Oracle situation. Now, if that means going to Boston—"

"Which I'm going to do, anyway," Max snarled.

I raised a palm to silence him. "If that means going, then maybe they have to go. But they don't have to engage in full-on combat. They can do some recon, find out what she's up to, and get back to us."

I turned to Max. "You have to admit, it's pretty stupid to rush in to kill her when we don't even know what she's got planned. What's to say that if we kill her, the Soul Eater can't finish whatever it is she's started, if she's started anything at all?"

"You have a point," Max conceded.

Nathan wasn't so easily swayed. "And if the Oracle has an ambush waiting?"

"Max and Bella are Movement trained assassins." I refrained from pointing out Bella had been seriously injured and that Nathan and Max had been rendered powerless by the Oracle. "They're more than capable of taking care of themselves. Remember your training?"

"I remember," he said with gritted teeth. "But let's suppose they go and follow the Oracle, and learn all her secrets. What are we going to be doing?"

"Well, we'll check out what's going on with the Soul Eater," I replied lamely.

"Without any Movement contacts and no idea where to start looking?" Nathan laughed derisively. "What are you going to do? Wave a magic wand? Or are we going to go back to the tarot cards?"

His contempt steeled my resolve to be the victor in this argument. "Nope. Not tarot cards. Think about it. You've got a blood tie to the Soul Eater. I realize it's a risk to contact him, but it's even riskier to let him roam around unchecked."

I slipped my hand into Nathan's back pocket, jerking him forward so our pelvises bumped. Almost before the thought fully formed, before I had any time to register shock at what I suggested, the words slipped past my lips: "And I've got Cyrus."

Six:
Conversations with Live People

"Hello?"

I don't know what I was expecting when I dialed the number Information had given me. I guess I was still reeling from the discovery that Cyrus even had a listed number. When his voice came across the line, I was stunned. Whatever it was I thought would happen, Cyrus answering the phone wasn't it.

"Hello?" he repeated. "Look, I can hear you breathing, and it is neither sexy nor interesting. If you'd like to call back when you have something sexy or interesting to say, I will be happy to chat. Until then—"

"Cyrus, it's me." I swallowed thickly. "It's Carrie."

There was a long pause. I wondered if he'd hung up, anyway.

"Carrie." His voice seemed faint and far away. "How are you?"

"I'm fine." I glanced across the room, where Nathan sat

on the overstuffed sofa, pretending to be absorbed in one of my dog-eared Terry Prachett novels.

I stood beside the bed. I'd been sitting on it when I'd first made the call, but the sound of Cyrus's voice had pulled me to my feet. It seemed way too intimate, perverted even, to be lounging on a bed, talking to Cyrus, with Nathan in the room.

"I'm fine," I repeated, turning my back on Nathan. "And you?"

"As well as can be expected." His heavy sigh made a harsh, static sound on the line. "I have a job now."

"A job?" I heard Nathan's grunt of stifled laughter and pointedly ignored it. "That's great. What do you do?"

"Do you promise not to laugh?" Cyrus didn't seem too concerned, considering he was already chuckling himself. "I stock shelves in a grocery store."

"No!" The very idea rocked the foundations of reality for me. Cyrus, my power-hungry, Euro-trash former sire, working in a grocery store?

He gave another heavy sigh. "You wouldn't believe the number of times a day I would trade my soul for a pair of fangs. Really, the customers…my God, it's as if they're brain dead."

I laughed the sympathetic laugh required for such a comment, and we lapsed into uncomfortable silence.

"So," I began uneasily. "You're back in Grand Rapids for good then?"

He made an affirmative noise. "I found Mouse's sister. I can't say I made any real progress there. But she knows what happened. At least, she knows the sanitized version."

"How did she take it?" Cyrus had told me very little about the girl he'd named Mouse. When he'd left Grand Rapids to seek out her next of kin, I'd been under the impression he'd had little hope of finding anyone.

"She asked me for a hundred bucks and offered to, ah, compensate me for it." He sounded as though the subject made him tired. "She didn't even care."

"At least *you* cared." It was a stupid thing to say, but I'd never been good at condolences. "Where are you staying?"

"In a horrible apartment downtown, near the college. The absolute worst part of the city. Hippies as far as the eye can see." I heard the smile in his voice as he added, "Near your sire's place, actually."

"Uh-huh." Great. All notions of domestic bliss, or however close Nathan and I could come to it, shattered by geographical coincidence.

"It wasn't my idea, really," Cyrus rushed to add. "Dahlia set it up for me."

"Oh, so you've been talking to Dahlia." I turned and met Nathan's suddenly alert glance with a worried one of my own. "That's comforting. What did you have to do to earn her help?"

"Still jealous, are we?" Cyrus laughed. "Don't worry. It was a trade—the mansion for one room with a kitchenette and a tiny bathroom with a stall shower and a door that doesn't close all the way. Doesn't seem like a fair trade, but life has been consistently unfair to me for a while now."

"Oh, how nice. I didn't realize I'd been invited to the pity party," I mused.

He laughed again. "Carrie, I stock bricks of pasteurized,

processed cheese for seven dollars an hour. Indulge me if I miss the comforts of my former life a bit."

"Have you been keeping an eye on your health?" I asked, changing the subject. "You're not immortal anymore, you know."

"I'm painfully aware of that. I'm also painfully aware of the fact I have no insurance, and the world seems to turn on the revenue generated by insurance companies." He waited a moment before asking, but I could feel the question coming. "Perhaps you wouldn't mind being my caregiver. Just until things are settled. I have the most insufferable allergies—"

"I don't think that's such a good idea." Historically, me and any expanse of unclothed Cyrus flesh were a potentially unstable combination. "But maybe we can go to the drugstore when I get back, take a look at some of the over-the-counter allergy meds. Some of them are just worthless, but—"

"Ask him about the Soul Eater," Nathan interrupted. I'd pushed his patience too far. He sighed heavily and tossed the book aside, clearly weary of his role as phone chaperone.

I narrowed my eyes at him and clamped my hand over the receiver.

Too late. "Is that Nolen I hear in the background?"

Clearing my throat, I made an affirmative sound. "And it's Nathan now."

"I know, I know." I could practically hear Cyrus's eye roll. "So, how is *Nathan?*"

Agitated. He was still looking at me expectantly, his big

arms folded across his chest. "He's fine. He wants to know if you've heard from your father."

"Oh, yes. Of course I have."

Wow, that was easy. "Oh?" I asked cautiously.

"Yes. We went fishing and then to a baseball game, and after that he took me to the toy store and bought me everything I wanted. And a pony." If sarcasm were liquid, it would have dripped from Cyrus's words.

"You know I have to ask," I snapped. "Something is going on, and so help me, if you have anything to do with it—"

"How, Carrie?" He sounded tired, in the way only a human could. Physically tired beyond anything a vampire could feel, a mass of dying tissues and an inability to stand another second of bullshit. "How could I, in this failing, mortal body, be a part of anything my father has planned? Do you think I've been spending any amount of time in the company of vampires? Do you know any humans who do?"

"Dahlia," I answered, for both counts. "She hung around you."

"Like an anchor," he agreed.

"And you've been talking to her lately, if she got you the apartment." I waited a moment, unsure if I would push him too far with the question. Then I decided to hell with it, I had to ask. "You're not trying to become a vampire again, are you?"

The silence was so long I wondered if he'd hung up. When he spoke again, his voice was thick. "Do you think I would want to be one of *you* again? After what happened to…her?"

It stung that he wouldn't say her name to me, as if I were unworthy of hearing it, or guilty by association for being part of the species that killed her.

Not that I could blame him. When his father had raised him from the dead, Cyrus had come back human. Mouse had been his human caretaker and, as often happens in cases of desperation and captivity, they'd fallen into a warped kind of love.

Then I'd completely misread the situation, kidnapped Cyrus—Mouse's only protector against the vampires holding them—and left her to die. Not a day went by that I didn't dream of her ruined body, lying in the bed where we'd found her. That I didn't wake up sick with guilt at the thought I could have saved her if I'd just listened to Cyrus instead of rushing to chloroform him.

But then, anyone who'd been alone with Cyrus for more than five minutes would have rushed to the chloroform.

"I'm sorry." I lowered my voice, but not for Nathan's benefit. "But I'm not sorry for asking."

"Of course you're not." He snorted derisively. "You're never responsible for anything where I'm concerned."

"Cyrus," I began, while Nathan stood and crossed the room, as if he'd be able to defend me over the phone.

I waved him away as Cyrus's angry voice cut me off. "I have to go. I have a finite amount of life left and I don't want to spend it arguing with you."

"Fine, I'll let you go," I said coolly. "But first, tell me what you know about the Soul Eater."

"I don't know anything about him!" Cyrus snapped. There was a pregnant pause, and I could nearly hear him throwing up his hands. "Dahlia stops by every now and again with groceries or money. Next time I see her, I'll find out what I can and I'll contact you."

"I would appreciate that, thank you." What I really wanted to say was, *"I'm sorry I hurt your feelings. You don't have to wait until you hear from Dahlia to call me. I'll always want to hear from you."*

But Nathan, good old, ever-watchful Nathan, stood so close I could feel him literally breathing down my neck.

Instead, when Cyrus asked, "Is there anything else?" I replied, "No. Goodbye, Cyrus."

"That went well." Nathan's words would have seemed sharp and sarcastic if not for his soft tone. "Are you all right?"

I turned and pressed my face to the front of his T-shirt. His hard chest muffled my response. "No."

He laid a hand gently on my hair. "It couldn't have been that bad."

"He called me a monster." I looked up and shrugged. "Call me crazy, but it bothers me."

Nathan stepped back and turned away, but I caught the grimace he tried to hide. "Well, do you blame him?"

"Pardon me?" My hands came to my hips in a horrible cliché of an angry woman, and I forced them down.

"He's human now. We probably seem pretty damn intimidating to him." He calmly returned to the book, this time looking far more interested in it than he had before, when he'd been listening in on my private conversation.

"Excuse me! He ripped my heart out, not the other way around!" I conveniently glossed over the fact that I had killed him another way. Still, Nathan's attitude, that Cyrus was somehow right in lumping us together with the vampires who'd killed his girlfriend, chafed me. "You might be okay with calling yourself a monster, but I'm not!"

Nathan looked up, true concern on his face. "I had no idea this bothered you so much."

"Well, it does." I shook my head. "All of it does."

He returned to my side, this time a little more cautious. "Don't let him get to you. You're putting a lot of importance on what he thinks of you."

"I know." I wiped my eyes with the back of my hand. "And I know that has to worry you. 'Cause of what happened before."

"What do you mean?" Bless his heart, he honestly didn't understand.

"When I left and went to Cyrus." I looked away from the hurt in Nathan's eyes. "I wouldn't blame you if you thought I'd do it again."

His expression darkened. He seemed truly wounded that I would think *he* would think I was capable of that kind of betrayal twice. "Don't ask me to mistrust you. Carrie, you went to him because you were saving my life. I have no doubt that if you were put in that situation again, you'd do the same thing. It's one of the reasons I—"

My heart leaped up like a puppy begging for table scraps. It must have shown on my face, because he quickly cleared his throat and looked away.

"Well, that I trust you, anyway." He turned away and headed toward the door. "I'm going to get some blood. Want any?"

I patted my stomach a little too enthusiastically and injected syrupy cheer into my words. "Nope, made a pig of myself already."

"Okay," he answered, in a tone that clearly conveyed my cheerful act wasn't working. The door clicked shut behind him and I slumped on the bed.

It's not that I wished him to think I was going to go tearing back to Cyrus at any moment. I wanted Nathan to trust me. But another part of me wanted to protect him from myself. He was clinging to the belief I'd only gone to Cyrus before because Nathan's life was on the line. The truth was, I'd have ended up there, anyway.

Now, Cyrus was human. There wasn't anything left of the monster he had been. I'd been afraid of him then, but oddly in love with the bit of humanity I'd glimpsed beneath his surface. Now that he was all humanity, I couldn't trust myself where he was concerned, and I certainly didn't want Nathan to.

"Why do you want to go with me?" Bella asked.

Max ground his teeth. First Nathan wanted to keep him from heading east, now Bella? "Because you can't take care of yourself."

"I have the same assassin training as you," she pointed out.

"Is this national See How High Max Harrison's Blood Pressure Will Go day?" He slammed a wadded T-shirt into his duffel bag and turned back to his dresser. It helped him avoid the sight of Bella lounging on his bed. "If the Oracle gets inside your head again, do you think you'll be able to take care of it on your own?"

He jumped at the touch of her warm hands on his shoulders, unexpected, as he hadn't heard her leave the bed. "Stop worrying about something you cannot anticipate or change."

He didn't want to take comfort in her touch, but the sick, needy child in him forced his hand up to cover one of hers. "You're really going to exploit that whole I-can't-say-no-to-you thing, aren't you?"

Gently, she turned him to face her. Instead of answering, she rose on tiptoe and brushed her lips across the corner of his mouth.

"Don't." He pulled her hands away and forced them down.

She smiled, her practiced, seductive smile. "I thought you said you could not tell me no."

"I can on this." He swallowed to wet his suddenly dry throat, and turned away. "I can when it's for my own good."

When she moved, his suffering body felt the distance. He heard her flop down on his bed and sigh. "So, you will follow me to Boston and put yourself in danger, but you will not touch me?"

"Nothing personal. I just can't separate my emotions from my dick where you're concerned." He ducked the pillow she hurled at him.

"Do not be crude!" Her outrage couldn't cover her laughter, but even that had to fade, leaving nothing but uncomfortable silence. "Do you love me?"

Max grabbed a few more shirts and another pair of jeans and returned to the bed to cram them into his bag. He couldn't look at her, and waited as long as possible to respond. "I don't know. Maybe?"

"I told you that you did." Was that smug satisfaction in her voice?

"I said maybe." He sounded a bit more gruff than he'd intended, and it helped rebuild a little of the wall he'd let crumble where she was concerned. "So, what's the plan?"

"We will have to take your car." She shrugged. "As for everything else, I have no plan."

Max zipped his bag shut forcefully. "Let's go to Marcus's library and go online. We'll find directions and get driving."

"At night only." She raised her hands helplessly at his sharp glance. "I do not know how to drive. My people…we do not use cars."

No, you just hang out the passenger window with your tongue waving in the wind. Proud of his restraint for only thinking his latest dog joke instead of speaking it, he folded his arms across his chest. "Fine, we'll have to stay somewhere during daylight hours." Max eyed the cigar box on his nightstand. It held about two thousand dollars in cash. That would be enough to buy her food, bribe someone for extra blood if he ran out, and put them up. "Are you still packed?"

"I do not travel with much." A strange expression crossed her face, something between sadness and anger. She shook it off with a laugh. "I do not have much."

For some bizarre reason, he wanted to ask her why that was, why she didn't have a closet stuffed with clothes and enough makeup to whore up a whole brothel—not that she needed it—but he couldn't form the words. She'd made it clear to him they were separate entities and would remain so just about forever. That kind of distance didn't invite the free exchange of personal information.

Not that Max was interested in that touchy-feely crap,

anyway. They had a job to do, and it would be a lot easier if they both ignored the fact they'd made the dirty bad fun.

An unwanted image of her flushed, sweat-dampened face contorted in a grimace of pleasure filled his mind. He could almost taste the salt on her skin, feel her hips pushing up beneath him—

"I'd like to leave at sundown. After we talk to Nathan and Carrie," he blurted, to clear the vision from his mind. The last thing he needed was a sudden, reckless spate of sexual hallucinations.

"Yes, I am interested to hear how Cyrus has fared since I saw him last." Bella said these words as if Cyrus was a friend who'd recently moved out of town, not a soulless killing machine.

Max had never actually felt his eyes bug out before, and he hoped he would never feel it again. "Why the hell do you care?"

She frowned at him, as if he was the one being weird and irrational. "Because I have thought of him and worried about him. Is that so wrong?"

"Um, yeah," Max exploded. "He's a murderer!"

"Former murderer," she pointed out, rolling her eyes. "You sound very much like Nathan."

Max scowled at her. "Usually, that comment would get you decked. Luckily for you—"

"You do not hit women?" she finished for him.

He shook his head. "No. I was going to say, 'Luckily for you, I'm on Nathan's side on this one.' Ever compare me to him again and I'll pop you one."

"You are much too hard on him." She unzipped the

duffel bag and pulled out two T-shirts. "These look horrible on you."

"They do not." He stuffed them back in. "And Nathan is too hard on himself. I love the guy—not in a gay way or anything—and I hate to see him mired down in guilt. I mean, you were there for that ritual thing. He managed to get over killing his wife. What's left?"

Bella's shocked laugh illustrated her disbelief. "Nathan is by no means over his wife's death. He accepts that she forgives him, and allows her spirit to rest, but he holds himself responsible. And her death is not the only burden he bears."

"Yeah, I know, everyone has emotional scars." Max snorted. "Thanks for that, Oprah."

Bella didn't react to the barb. "Everyone has scars. It is how we heal them that matters. Nathan has worked to heal himself, and you would mock him?"

Not knowing how to respond, Max watched her walk toward the door. She paused, one hand on the door frame, and turned just slightly, not quite facing him. "Do not mock him for achieving what you cannot."

Before he could think up a smart-assed reply, she turned the corner and was gone.

Seven: Homecoming

"I think we should go back to Grand Rapids."

Nathan's voice dragged me, unwilling, from my sleep. We'd stayed up most of the day doing, well, what we usually did when we were alone with a convenient horizontal surface, and I was exhausted. I knew it was long past sundown, but my body protested the intrusion of consciousness. I muttered a groggy "What?" and struggled to stay awake for the answer.

He touched the side of my face, lifting a strand of my mussed hair and smoothing it against the pillow. "We would be just as safe there as here. And we'd have more research material at our disposal. Not to mention there's the store to run and I've got inventory scheduled for next week—"

"Stop," I mumbled. "Stop talking."

He paused. "What do you think?"

"I think you should stop talking and let me sleep." I turned away from him, onto my side, groaning when he leaned over me to snap on the bedside lamp. The light cut through my eyelids and I groggily sat up. "Don't you think it's a little silly to go back to the one place the Soul Eater knows to find you?"

"I think it's silly to let my fear run my business into the ground. It's not as if I have centuries of vast wealth to fall back on." There was a bitter note to his voice, and I knew he thought of his sire. "Besides, you'll have a better chance of manipulating Cyrus for information if you can see him face-to-face."

"Manipulate him?" I frowned. "You think I'm manipulative?"

Nathan smiled—no, half smiled—and dropped a kiss on my shoulder. "I think you're smart enough to do what you have to. Unless you don't think he'll be of use to us?"

I chewed my lip. Of course I thought Cyrus would be of use to us. Oh, I had doubts he was involved with his father, but he'd told me himself that he'd been seeing Dahlia. And if there was one thing Dahlia wanted, it was the kind of power the Soul Eater could offer her. If I had to use Cyrus to get to her, I would. "I think you're right. I think we should go back."

Later that evening, when Nathan, Bella, Max and I had done the requisite cell number confirmations and synchronizing of watches—okay, not really, but at times the three can lapse into their Movement regiment training—Nathan went to load up the van and Bella went with him to make sure she hadn't left anything behind. Max and I were left to our own devices in the foyer.

It only took a couple seconds before the realization that we'd been alone in this very room not long ago crashed through my brain like a rampaging wildebeest. At the exact same time, I saw an uncharacteristic flush color Max's face.

"So. This is weird." It was all I could think of to break the silence.

Max didn't appreciate it. "You know, sometimes it's better just not to talk."

I frowned at him. "Hey, so we made a mistake. It's not a big deal. At least, not a big enough one to ruin our friendship over."

"I know, I know." He went to the plastic console beside the door, which looked painfully anachronistic among the antique furnishings, and flipped it open. "But it wasn't a mistake. It's just that…"

"You've never had anyone you've gotten physical with stay in your life before," I finished for him.

He gave me an exasperated look, the one he often gives me when I'm a hundred percent sure I'm right. Turning back to the alarm console, he sighed. "And now I have two of them."

"Well, you'll only be saddled with one of them for the next couple of weeks, if that's any consolation." It was certainly better than having him shut up here any longer. All the memories of his late sire brought out a morose side of Max I'd never seen before and certainly didn't like. I wasn't sure it would do him any good to be stuck with Bella for an extended period of time—their mutual attraction was equaled only by their mutual desire to drive each other insane with rage—but at least the object of his unrequited love would be a living and breathing person.

"When we're talking about her, could you refrain from using words like *saddle?*" He punched in a few more codes and a loud, electronic beep sounded. "We're locked in."

I laughed. "Oh, good."

"It is good. It will buy us some time before she gets back, so you can give me some advice." Max motioned for me to follow him to the couch.

"Advice?" I sat at one end of the sofa and curled my feet under my legs so we didn't actually touch. Immature though it might seem, I couldn't get past what we'd almost done.

He nodded, his body posture as rigid and withdrawn as mine. "About Bella."

For a moment, I was confused. "I don't think she's going to have any lasting medical implications, if that's what you mean. Though she is a werewolf, and I can't claim to have a lot of experience treating them."

"No, nothing like that." Max looked around the room as if Bella were going to jump from behind a potted plant or something, and take us by surprise. "She's acting weird. You know. Like a woman."

I rolled my eyes. "Perish the thought."

Max didn't quite get my sarcasm. "It's making me crazy. One minute she acts like she wants to be with me and I'm the one rejecting *her*. The next, she's got this barbed wire fence and barking dogs around her, like I can't even ask her the simplest questions."

"And here I was assuming you didn't care about her."

Stabbing his fingers through his hair, he groaned. "I don't!"

"And you make it perfectly clear." Men. Idiots. "Did you ever think maybe she *has* had a change of heart, but she's afraid of your rejection?"

"I told her I wouldn't reject her!" He lowered his voice with obvious difficulty. Clearly, he wanted to scream the house down. "What else am I supposed to do?"

"I don't know." And I didn't. If I were the relationship guru, I wouldn't have spent the last four months stumbling through an equally bad situation. "Bella obviously doesn't have much experience communicating with the opposite sex. You don't have much experience communicating with the opposite sex without talking dirty. Maybe this trip will be good for both of you."

"Yeah, until I die of lack of oxygen to the brain caused by a permanent hard-on." He stood and paced. "What's taking them so long?"

"Maybe they're screwing in the back of the van," I suggested drolly.

"That's not funny!"

"No, but you are. You're completely out of your mind over her, you want her to be out of her mind over you and she probably is, but neither of you wants to make a move. It's so junior high, Max!" I stood and stalked to the door. "How do I get out of here?"

"Are you pissed at me?" Disbelief filled his voice, as if the idea was completely unfathomable.

"No. I'm just tired of watching you run in circles over someone when you're not committed enough to tell her how you feel." The second I said it, I realized how painfully his actions mirrored Nathan's. "Never mind."

But it was too late to take it back. He shut down immediately. "Listen, I'll call you from the road. If anything comes up. If you can be bothered to listen."

"Max!" My heart crumbled at his words. Maybe just at the realization of how selfish I'd been to cast him as the villain just because Nathan had hurt me in the past.

Max shook his head. "That was low. But you're going to have to talk to him sometime."

I know. Before I said it, however, someone pounded on the door. It was Nathan, uncharacteristically cheerful. "Hie ye hence to the van, wench, afore the sun comes up!"

"You really want to spend eternity with that guy?" Max's scowl bent into a reluctant smile.

"I'm having second thoughts."

In the garage, the four of us said our goodbyes. Nathan grudgingly shook Bella's hand—I could picture the word *toenails* flashing through his disgusted mind—and Max hugged me.

He whispered in my ear, squeezing me tighter as though it would help me comprehend. "Don't waste time on this, Carrie. The four of us might not have much left."

"Same to you," I whispered back.

Nathan and I had pulled out of the garage and onto Wabash Avenue before he asked me about the exchange. "So, what did Max say to you by the car?"

I could tell he was dying to know, but I couldn't share. To share would mean to explain, and to explain was to launch us into a confession I didn't want to make.

I smiled brightly, teasing, "It's a secret."

Nathan chuckled and turned back to the road.

* * *

At around midnight, Grand Rapids emerged from behind a curve as northbound I-96 turned into the Gerald R. Ford Freeway. When I was a child, I used to pass a few boring minutes in school pressing the heels of my hands into my eyes and watching the grid of sparkling lights flare up in the dark behind my eyelids. That was how the city looked at night, with my eyes opened.

"Are you awake?" Nathan asked gently from the driver's seat. He'd refused my offer of splitting the driving, citing my "long day" as reason for being rewarded with some extra sleep on the trip.

I nodded and smiled. I'd dozed a bit during the boring stretch of highway from I-94 to here, but I'd spent most of it watching Nathan. He'd hummed some of the time, occasionally singing soft lyrics from a song I didn't recognize, probably some relic-of-the-seventies classic rock monstrosity waxing poetic about *Lord of the Rings*. Every now and then he would smile and turn to look at me, and I'd close my eyes to feign sleep. I didn't often get a chance to observe him without his knowing, and I couldn't pass it up.

I put my hand on his knee, smiling when his leg jumped under my touch. "I was enjoying watching you be happy."

He glanced at me, his expression suddenly tender. "You're not used to it."

"You're right. When I left, you were grumpy, morose Nathan. It will take me some time to adjust to happy, humming Nathan." I swallowed the knot my sudden tears made in my throat. "But I like the change."

I reached for his right hand, resting on the gearshift, and

covered it with my own. We rode the rest of the way to the apartment in silence. Though I'd only been gone a few weeks, the sight of familiar neighborhood landmarks—*La Vitesse,* the courthouse, the veterans' memorial, heck, even the Brandywine Inn on the corner of our block—nearly had me dissolving in tears of relief. We parked down the street—all the convenient spots were full—and headed toward the building.

Nathan stopped me before he unlocked the outer door. "Listen, before you see the apartment—"

"It's a total nightmare of clutter and unwashed dishes?" I snorted. "Believe me, I've braced myself for this possibility before tonight."

"No, that's not it." He paused. "Well, it is a nightmare of clutter, but I washed the dishes. What I meant is, I made some changes. To your room."

"Oh." My heart sank. "What kind of changes?"

He scratched his forehead and looked down the street, as if the answer would drive up and rescue him. "Maybe it's better if you see it, and then you can scream at me. Or not."

I tried not to charge up the stairs once he got the door open, and I waited with unbelievable patience as he unlocked the one at the top. In the living room, books were scattered and stacked on every available surface. Despite his assertion that he'd washed dishes, I spotted four or five blood-crusted mugs he'd missed, and the couch seemed to have become some sort of holding pattern for laundry of indeterminate cleanliness. In the hallway, the door to my room stood open.

"Go look," he said quietly.

When I clicked on the light, the first thing I noticed was the new paint job. Somehow, Nathan had managed to cover with pale lavender the matte black walls Ziggy had preferred. My desk and computer were just as I'd left them, but a sheet of plastic speckled with paint and sawdust draped over them. Brand-new built-in bookcases lined the wall where my bed used to be.

I leaned against the doorjamb and tried to catch my breath, collect my thoughts, anything to help me comprehend without getting my hopes up too much.

"I know I was taking a chance, but I thought you needed a proper office. Or, at the very least, a place where you can get away from me when I drive you crazy." Nathan hovered behind me for a moment, then brushed past me to enter the room. He gestured to the bookcases. "I had the same contractor who fixed up the store work on this. Do you like it?"

"It's very nice, but…" The thought of the few research projects I'd begun with the intent to distribute the information to the vampire community reminded me of our current situation. Without the Movement, there was no communication network among vampires. It wasn't as if my metabolic studies and dissertations on vampire digestion were publishable in the *New England Journal of Medicine*. And they certainly weren't going to hit the bestseller fiction lists. "Nathan, I really don't have any reason left to continue my projects."

"Because of the Movement?" He fell silent, running his hand along the edge of a shelf. "That would be a stupid reason to give up all the work you've done."

There was admiration behind his words, and it seemed

somehow worth more coming from him. In my entire career as a human doctor, I'd tried to sustain myself on praise from my professors and bosses, to no avail. Nathan's unspoken praise was like water to a dying plant, and I was strangely moved.

My emotion waned a little as I stared at the place where my bed used to be. "Um…where's the bed?"

"Oh, I put it downstairs, in the back room of the shop." He thumped one of the shelves with his knuckles, as if testing for sturdiness. "Do you like the color? I thought it might be too girlie—"

The back room? The cement-walled, spider-infested utility room with the water heater and a single bulb for illumination? I glared at him. "Well, I definitely prefer it to lime stains from where the pipes drip!"

He frowned in confusion. "What are you talking about? Carrie, I don't want you to sleep down there, I just put your bed in storage."

I threw my hands up in frustration. "Well, what the hell do you expect me to do, sleep on the couch?"

"I expect you to sleep in my bed with me, like a proper girlfriend!" He stared at me, baffled for a moment, then laughed. "Christ, can't we get anything right?"

I stepped up to him and looped my arms around his neck. "We're not so bad at the naked, sweaty part."

He grinned at me, and I was struck all over again by how much taller he was than me. He leaned down to kiss me, breaking his motion to ask, "So, do you like it?"

"I like the office," I admitted. "I like just being home more."

"You're not going to like it tomorrow night," he warned. "Did you see all the books in the living room?"

"I did. I was trying to ignore them."

He brushed his lips against mine again and stepped back, motioning for me to follow him to the living room. "We're going to have to look through them for any mention of the ritual the Soul Eater was collecting the souls of his fledglings for, some information on the spell he was using to control me, and anything else that might come in handy for him now that he's got the Oracle on his side. It's going to take awhile. If you're not too tired—"

"I'm too tired," I interrupted, before he could suggest we begin work right away.

"Then I hope you're not too tired to get in that kitchen and cook your man some dinner." He affected a Midwestern accent to enhance the misogyny of the statement.

I rolled my eyes. "Oh, like a proper girlfriend?"

"You said it, not me." He had the nerve to smack my backside as I turned toward the kitchen.

"I'll chalk that up to the fact you're too tired to realize how very close to death you are," I called over my shoulder. In the kitchen I put the kettle on the stove and snagged a bag of blood from the refrigerator. "So, what have you found out so far?"

I expected to hear sounds of shuffling papers and opening books, but didn't. "Nathan?"

"Sorry." Judging from the tone of his voice, Nathan was a million miles away. "Yeah, Bella found two more versions of the spell she thinks I was under. The three we've got now are remarkably similar. What scares me is the number of variations that are probably out there."

I cut off the top of the bag with the kitchen shears and dumped the contents into the kettle, licking a smear of red off my thumb. Four months ago, I would have stopped to analyze that action. Now, consumption of blood was background noise.

In the foreground was my concern for Nathan and the realization we'd never actually talked about what had happened to him just weeks before.

I lit a burner and set the kettle over the low heat. Once it's warming, blood can't be left untended for long. I went to the doorway and looked into the living room. Nathan sat in his armchair, elbows on his knees, leaning forward and staring at the impossible pile of books on the coffee table.

"Do you think he'll try it again?" The possibility terrified me. When the Soul Eater had possessed Nathan, he'd driven him mad. Tormented by reliving the moment he'd killed Marianne, Nathan had become like a wounded animal, with no reason or control. Though Bella had managed to break the spell, it had been at a cost. Nathan had nearly killed me, and our relationship had been destroyed, as well. I wasn't about to accept those consequences again.

Nathan shrugged. "I don't know. But I didn't know he was going to do it last time."

I shifted uncomfortably. "Bella said that if you didn't feel guilty anymore, since Marianne forgave you—"

The teakettle gave a low, mournful whistle, and I hurried to remove it before our dinner burned.

"Well, that sounds simple enough. But it's not easy to forget that you've killed the woman you loved." His voice startled me. I hadn't heard him come into the kitchen.

More startling was the fact he'd said "loved," past tense. Though the look on his face made it clear he'd done so on purpose, I didn't know if he was trying to make me believe it, or himself. I took two mugs from the cupboard and poured the blood into them. "Maybe, since we're trying to make these great strides in our personal relationship, you could talk to me about it."

"I could." He took his mug and headed back to the living room.

I ground my teeth. "Well, are you going to?"

When I followed him, I found him sitting in his chair again, rubbing his eyes with the heels of his hands. "The Soul Eater is my sire. He knows everything about me."

"Through the blood tie?" It seemed so strange, that although Nathan and his sire were enemies, they were still bound. "Do you hear him?"

He looked up, his eyes rimmed in red from fatigue. "If he wants me to. And he can hear me. He knows how to hurt me. He did it with Marianne, and he could do it again."

"With your memories of Ziggy?" The thought hadn't crossed my mind until now. No wonder he was afraid. "Nathan, if that happens, we know how to stop it. You won't have to go through what you did before."

"When he put that spell on me, I didn't know it was a spell. I was reliving the night I killed Marianne, over and over. I could live with it, because it isn't as though I hadn't already lived it on my own every night. But Ziggy…" Nathan looked away. "Once was enough."

"The Soul Eater was only able to control you because you felt responsible for Marianne's death. You're not responsible for Ziggy dying," I pointed out.

He laughed bitterly. "Have you noticed my habit of blaming myself for things I can't control?"

I remembered the look in Nathan's eyes as he'd pleaded with me outside Cyrus's mansion to keep Ziggy safe, and the way he'd cradled his dying son in his arms when I failed. If Nathan was peripherally responsible for Ziggy's death, I was the central figure in his demise. I'd been the one who'd inadvertently marked him for death.

"You could blame me," I said quietly, but I added a smile in case Nathan was more comfortable interpreting it as a joke. "I had more of a stake in it than you did."

"If he'd been a vampire, that would have been a pun." Nathan's eyes crinkled as he smiled. "I don't want to blame you, Carrie. I just want to talk to you."

"I'm not going to complain. You kept everything in before." It is the central irony of my life that when I want something and end up getting it, it makes me profoundly uncomfortable.

Shaking his head, Nathan reached for one of the many books on the coffee table. "Grab a book and start reading."

"I said I was too tired," I protested.

"I know. Consider it payment for your new office." He settled back in his chair and turned his attention to the open page.

I grumbled, but complied. I'd only managed to halfheartedly scan two pages when the phone in the kitchen rang.

Nathan stood and went to answer it, taking his mug with him. "Want me to top you off while I'm in there?"

I shook my head and covered the rim of my mug with my palm.

On the page, the letters swirled and blurred before my tired eyes, and I had to double my concentration. I wasn't paying attention to the phone call, until I noticed the change in Nathan's tone.

"Fine. I'll tell her." He hung up without saying good-bye and returned to the living room. "That was Cyrus. Dahlia is going to be there tomorrow after sundown. You should go over at ten."

"You didn't let me talk to him." It was part accusation, part question.

Nathan shrugged. "He didn't ask for you."

I tried to not look as rejected as I, for some reason, felt. "Are you going with me?"

"I'd rather not." He resumed his position in the armchair and picked up his book. "You can take my cell phone if you're worried he'll try something."

"No, nothing like that." I waved my hand to dismiss the idea that Cyrus would try to harm me. "But you don't mind me going, do you?"

"Of course not," Nathan said, a little too confidently. "It's the reason we came back here."

Something in his tone said he wished we hadn't, but it didn't matter. Tomorrow, I was going to see Cyrus.

Eight: *A Bad Case of Nerves*

❧

Of all the horrible things Max could have envisioned happening on their trip, Bella being horrifically carsick every fifty miles was not one of them.

"You know, we could get a lot farther if I didn't have to stop and hose puke off the back seat four or five times a night," he grumbled, wiping his hands on coarse, gas station bathroom paper towels.

Bella lifted her head from the toilet seat—it was proof of her bravery, or stupidity, how close she let her face get to the damn thing—and tried to respond, only to let loose a spectacular arc of vomit.

"No more vending machine sandwiches for you." He crumpled the paper and tossed it on the pile spilling over the sides of the wastebasket. "Can you hold back the tide for a couple minutes so I can get us to a hotel?"

Her answer was the resounding echo of retching into the bowl.

Max leaned against the wall, then changed his mind and straightened quickly. "This place reeks."

"I am sorry I could not wait until the Ritz-Carlton," she spat, wiping her mouth with the back of her hand.

He grabbed a handful of paper toweling and offered it to her. "Don't get bent out of shape. Clean off your face and we'll hit the road."

Snatching it, she hissed, "A fine way to treat a sick person!"

"Carsick is not sick. It's an annoyance, but it's not sick." He met her glare head-on. Her eyes seemed duller, and dark circles ringed them. "Oh, shit."

"What?" Her face blanched. She looked around the bathroom as if planning an alternate escape route.

"You've got some weird dog disease, don't you?" He backed away.

Her panicked expression turned to anger. "I do not have a *dog disease*. I am a little under the weather. Most likely from being violated by one of your kind."

Max couldn't help his grin. "So, are you talking about the Oracle now, or—"

"Go to hell!" She turned back to the toilet and groaned with a painful-sounding dry heave.

He wet a paper towel and knelt beside her to press it to her forehead. "Take it easy. Getting pissed at me will only make things worse."

"Perhaps I should not go on this trip with you," she whispered. "I will not be useful if I am vomiting and ill. I certainly cannot fight in this condition."

"Who said you'd be doing any fighting?" The thought hadn't crossed his mind. Not that he didn't believe Bella could hold her own. He'd seen her fight plenty, and been on the receiving end of her ire. But lately she seemed more fragile, far too mortal for his tastes. Before, he wouldn't have cared if she'd gotten maimed or killed. In fact, when she'd had him pinned to the floor in Nathan's bedroom, ready to drive a stake through his heart, he would have laughed his ass off at her demise.

Sex, no matter how meaningless, changed things. Who was he kidding? If she got so much as a stubbed toe on this trip, he'd call the whole damn thing off, Oracle or no.

"I am a Movement trained assassin. I will do my part in a physical skirmish." She didn't sound confident about it. Probably because of all the vomiting.

"Come on. We'll find a Motel 6 or something and call it a night."

He helped her to the car with an arm around her shoulders. For someone who'd just been squatting on the floor of a gas station bathroom, she smelled fine.

"You throw up lilacs and perfume in there?" he joked, but her sense of humor, nearly nonexistent to begin with, had taken a nosedive since her unfortunate stomach bug.

"I do not feel like talking," she snapped as he opened the passenger door for her.

He slammed it closed behind her, and waited to retort until he'd rounded the car and dropped into the driver seat. "Good. Because every time you open your mouth, puke comes out."

He pulled out of the parking lot a little less gently than he normally would have, not because he wanted her to barf all over the dashboard, but it wouldn't hurt to put the fear of it into her.

By the time they checked into a motor lodge a few exits down the highway, Bella was sweating and pale again. She pushed past him and rushed through the shabby room to the bathroom.

In the light of the floor lamp, Max examined the two beds and took the rough, brown flannel blanket with the most suspicious stains and draped it over the window, tucking it behind the blinds rod. Hopefully, that would keep the sun out, once it rose.

In case it didn't do the trick, he stripped the bed the rest of the way and laid the sheets on the floor next to the bed farthest from the window. He'd be trapped between the wall and the platform box springs all day, a lot like lying in a coffin, but better that than being a human fire hazard.

More disgusting retching sounds came from the bathroom. It was amazing Bella had anything left to choke up, considering how her output had far surpassed her input. "I'm gonna go get our stuff out of the car. Will you be okay for a sec?"

More heaving, then a muffled, "I will be fine."

"Yeah. Okay."

The air outside seemed colder and newer. It could have been from leaving the musty stink of the motel room, but it smelled more like morning. The exact moment night clicked over to day had happened while he'd been inside.

He was sorry he'd missed it.

He pulled his duffel bag and the leather satchel containing Bella's things from the trunk. Out of paranoid instinct, he scanned the parking lot for vans, semis and hearses that could contain other vampires. There was no doubt in his mind the Oracle knew they were coming.

He also noted the length of the awnings over office and motel room doors. He did a quick mental calculation of the shadows they might cast, though the time of day would be an uncertain variable, and the space between each in case he and Bella needed to make a quick getaway.

He just hoped it wasn't at high noon. If so, Bella would have to finish the "mission" by herself.

Of course, there was a small chance they would escape detection altogether, tail the Oracle to wherever she was going, race in with metaphorical guns blazing and save the day. He was sure he had a better chance of winding up living in the suburbs with Bella and their furry kids, mowing the lawn on a sunny July day.

He didn't like the feeling of being adrift, not knowing exactly what to do or how things were going to go down. He never thought he would miss Movement briefings so much.

Cursing, he reached for his cell phone. Carrie and Nathan were probably busy wearing out their bedsprings, but Max felt no remorse at the thought of interrupting them.

"Hello?" Nathan answered, sounding tired, but awake.

"It's Harrison. You're still up?" He checked his watch.

"It's only midnight." Nathan paused. "Where are you?"

"Just crossed the Indiana border into Ohio. I thought you guys would hit the sack right after you got home." Max intentionally softened his suggestion of what he thought they'd be doing there. Ever since he and Carrie had done what they'd done in the foyer, things had seemed a little weird. More so now that Nathan knew about it.

"And I thought you guys were going to drive until dawn. What happened to that?"

"Well, I just like Ohio so much, I thought we would really be missing out if we didn't stop for the night in the purgatory of the Midwest." Max coughed to get rid of the tightness in his throat. "We had to stop. Bella's sick."

"Sick? Is it serious?" There was a rustling sound, indicating Nathan had put his hand over the receiver. It didn't mask his words when he said, to Carrie, Max presumed, "Max says Bella is sick."

"It's nothing serious." He raised his voice to recapture Nathan's attention. "She just doesn't do well in the car. I thought it would be better to air the vehicle out and try to make up the time tomorrow night."

There was muffled conferring on the other end before Nathan returned. "Carrie said try ginger ale to settle her stomach."

"An M.D. and that's the best she's got?" He supposed it beat cleaning up the car again. "I hope she didn't pay too much for med school."

"Yeah, well." Nathan's voice died out, then returned. "Was there anything else?"

"Ah, no. Just wanted to know if you've heard from any other Movement, if you had a heads-up for me, that kind of thing." What a lame excuse. It had been four hours since he'd seen them; what were the chances they knew anything else? He was as transparent as the windshield he'd had to clean at their last stop.

There was a noncommittal grunt from Nathan. "We haven't been at it long. Carrie will speak to Cyrus tomorrow, and I hope to know more then."

Max whistled. "She's going to see Cyrus? How do you feel about that?"

"The only way I can." What he meant, Max knew, was he couldn't elaborate because Carrie is within earshot.

"Give her a curfew." Not that Max didn't trust Carrie, but she had major boundary issues where her old sire was concerned. "I'll talk to you later."

"Yeah. Goodbye, Max."

Inside, Bella was still in the bathroom. Max went to the door and knocked softly. "Are you okay in there?"

Her answer may have been muffled by the door, but he still heard the tears in her voice. "I need to be alone."

The hell she did. "Carrie thought some ginger ale would help. Do you want me to go out and get you some? I mean, I've got time to kill. It's not going to be light for at least six hours."

"No. I will be fine. I just need to get myself…under control." There was a hesitant sniffle.

He leaned his forehead against the door. Part of him wanted to order her to stop being such a big baby. Another part wanted badly to comfort her. She wasn't a fragile, wilting flower. She was Bella, the ice princess, the stone cold assassin, the hottest, sexiest, meanest woman he'd ever had the great good fortune to fuck. She hadn't cried when he'd stitched up her slashed leg sans local anesthetic in Nathan's living room. Something had to be seriously bothering her to create such a reaction, and he had a feeling he knew exactly what that something was.

She didn't like being helpless. More specifically, she didn't like being *helped.*

Max knew the feeling well. People who spent their lives—or afterlives, as the case may be—alone liked to believe they were islands unto themselves. If they needed someone once, they might need someone again, and that someone might not be there a second time. Max had been through that pain. From the way she was acting, he knew Bella had, too.

Still, he couldn't leave her crying on the bathroom floor. "Do you want anything out of your bag? Pajamas or anything?"

Stupid thing to ask. All the question did was bring painfully arousing memories to mind. Bella didn't wear pajamas. It was almost unbelievable that she wore underwear.

"I do not have any." She gave another sniff. "May I borrow your shirt?"

Max threw a glance to his duffel bag on the bed. "Yeah, I'll get you one."

"No. May I have the one you are wearing?" she requested, timidly, if she could manage such a humble state.

He plucked the fabric between his thumb and forefinger and pulled it away from his chest, frowning at it. She was sick, he reminded himself, so it wasn't his place to argue. "Yeah, sure."

The door opened a crack as he peeled the garment over his head. Bella's naked arm snaked out to grab it, and the door closed again.

Shaking his head, Max went to his makeshift bed next

to the wall. He shucked his jeans and lay down, wincing as his muscles, cramped from the long drive, adjusted to the hard floor. He pulled the sheet over his lower half—no use having her think he was insensitive enough to proposition her after her barf-fest—and tried to convince his body that going to sleep at this early hour was a good idea. He'd need to be well rested once they reached the Oracle.

A click alerted him that Bella had emerged from the bathroom. Her hair, usually scraped back severely into a long braid, hung limply around her face. Max realized he'd never seen her with her hair down, even when they had slept together. She pushed a few dark strands behind her ears and folded her arms over her chest. She wore the shirt like a suit of armor, hugged it like a security blanket.

"It has your smell," she said quietly. "I have missed it."

"That's…" He closed his eyes. If he didn't look at her, if he couldn't see how vulnerable she was, he could stay mad at her for walking out of his life. "Creepy."

No, it wasn't that she had walked out; it was that she'd done it so easily. His anger was fading now that he knew it not to be true, and that was dangerous.

Her voice was uncharacteristically small. "You always make a joke."

His throat tightened. How did she manage to make him feel like shit with a few simple words? Did she practice? "It never bothered you before."

He felt her warmth as she knelt beside him. His leg jerked when she placed her palm on his knee.

When he opened his eyes, the look on her face made him

bolt upright. She was pale, paler than sickness should have made her, and her eyes were wide and scared.

"Christ, Bella, what's wrong?" He put his hand on her arm and she reached for it, entwining her fingers with his.

"Promise me," she begged, squeezing his hand. "Promise me whatever happens, whatever comes of the time we have left together, that when I am gone, you will do what is right in my memory."

As if touched by the hand of Death himself, Max felt a chill run up his spine. "What are you talking about?"

"You know I saw through the Oracle's eyes." She dipped her head, and a tear rolled down her nose.

"We don't know anything yet." He pulled her hand down, capturing the other and bringing them both to her lap. "Some of that stuff you're seeing might not be true."

"I know it to be true." Bella looked up, eyes blazing. It was a comforting sight. She appeared more like herself than she had before. "And I see horrible things. If I do not live, there will be things left to take care of. Promise me you will do what needs to be done."

"Fine. You want me to notify your next of kin, I will." He tried to laugh it off. "But I'm telling you, you'll be fine." He nearly bit his tongue to stop himself from adding, *"Because I won't let anything happen to you."*

She didn't argue, but he could see she wanted badly to tell him he was wrong.

He didn't want to hear it. "You're tired. You were sick. You're probably dehydrated. Go drink some water and get some sleep."

"I do not want water." She lifted one of his hands to her lips. "Sleep with me?"

"No offense, but watching you gag up two days' worth of chow isn't a big turn-on for me." He pulled his hand back. "Another time, maybe."

She smiled. "No. I meant, sleep beside me. Hold me."

"I can't tell you no." He pointed to the window and the dubious sun protection provided by the blanket. "But if that doesn't hold, I could be fried in a few hours."

"Then get up in a few hours and move." She clasped his hand as she rose, and tried to bodily haul him onto the bed, where they collapsed in a laughing heap. The playful moment didn't last nearly long enough for Max.

Later, when he thought she was asleep, and took the chance to wind a lock of her hair around his finger, she whispered, "I am afraid to die."

His heart squeezed painfully in his chest. There was no way he was letting her die, but a part of him warned he should stop this reckless closing of the gap between them, just in case.

But he was tired of constantly living on the defensive. He couldn't do it anymore, not where Bella was concerned. He pulled her tighter to his side, hoping he wasn't just making the most of the time they had left.

I tried not to make it obvious to Nathan, but I was climbing the walls as the time to meet Cyrus drew nearer. What would I say to him? What would he say to me? Would we fight? Would I pity him? Would I do something stupid, like I had the last time?

Would I find the place?

It hadn't occurred to me until then that I didn't know where Cyrus lived.

As soon as we'd crawled from bed, Nathan had gone right back to the books. I'd had to politely remind him to dress himself, he was so immersed in his research. After the dramatic grumbling and complaining he'd done then, I hated to bother him for anything else.

But this was kind of an important detail. "When you were on the phone with Cyrus, did he happen to give you directions?"

"Hmm?" Nathan looked up from the volume in his lap. "To do what?"

"Directions to his house." I rolled my eyes. "How am I supposed to get there if I don't know where it is?"

"You could call him. I'm sure he's awake." Nathan turned back to his book with a derisive sniff. "He *is* human now. He's probably eating dinner."

I looked at the clock. It was nine. Dahlia had probably been and gone by now. I dialed Cyrus's number.

When he answered, he sounded distracted and slightly out of breath. I didn't let myself dwell on the possible reasons why. "How do I find you?"

"Very well, thanks." He paused. "You mean, how do you find where I live?"

I groaned an affirmative.

With a sigh, he said, "I'd hoped it wouldn't come to this. Listen, I live very close to you. Why don't I meet you on the corner in front of the Brandywine?"

I frowned. Aggressive raindrops battered the windowpanes, and I'd heard a rumble of thunder not long before. Why was he being so difficult? "How about you just tell me where you live?"

"Fine." He gave another heavy sigh. "I live, you will be pleased to know, just down the street from you, in the big gray house with the rainbow-striped American flag out front."

In the spirit of friendship—no matter how weird and disordered—I held off a foghorn laugh and just snorted.

"Oh, it's terribly funny. It will please you more to hear that my apartment is in the basement. You have to go around the back and down the stairs." The bitterness in his voice tugged a little pity from me. "I assume it used to be a servants entrance, before the place was divided up."

"It can't be all bad," I began, but he cut me off.

"I have to go. I'll see you tonight." He hung up without saying goodbye.

At nine-thirty I kissed Nathan on the cheek to draw his attention out of his book.

"Leaving already?" He captured my hand and gave it a squeeze. Though he tried to block it from the blood tie, I felt his desperation.

Stop worrying. It's you I'm coming home to.

He smiled up at me. "I know, sweetheart."

"Then let me go, and don't worry about me." I didn't think he would follow my instructions, but it was worth a shot.

At least he pretended to be okay until I left. That was a huge step for him, and I was proud he could manage it. Besides, I couldn't feel guilty. This was what we'd come back for.

The house Cyrus described wasn't far. Despite the rain,

I walked. The wet had never bothered me, at least not since I'd learned in med school that it wasn't wet hair but a virus that caused the common cold. In fact, I kind of liked the rain.

As Cyrus instructed, I went to the back door, which opened onto a bare landing. My choice was up or down, and both passages were illuminated by lightbulbs swinging from cords.

"Snazzy," I whispered with a little amusement. Truly, it was a case of the mighty falling far.

At the bottom of the stairs was a laundry room with no door, and a single apartment marked B. I was about to knock on the door when it opened.

There was a weird second when my brain registered that it wasn't Cyrus standing there. My first thought was, *It's the wrong apartment.* My second was, *Oh shit.*

Dahlia seemed to be having the same thought process. Hers ended just a bit before mine. Her reflexes were better.

She grabbed me by the throat and pinned me to the wall.

Nine: In the Flesh

I had no time to react. Dahlia's face hovered centimeters from mine, and her hand at my throat tightened. The tips of her nails dug into my skin.

"What are you doing here?" She slammed my head into the wall. I felt the plaster crumble beneath my skull.

I pulled my feet up and kicked her, kangaroo style, so hard she bounced off the opposite wall. "I was invited, bitch!"

"Lucky you." She held up her hands and formed a flaming blue ball of energy. I lifted my arms to shield my face. Before she could release her spell, the door beside me flew open.

"Dahlia!" Cyrus strode into the hallway, a towel slung around his hips. I don't know if it was a reflex left over from her days as Cyrus's obedient pet, or if she was as overwhelmed as I was by his presence, but Dahlia condensed the murderous energy between her palms. When she opened her hands, it was gone.

"What the hell is she doing here?" she demanded, planting her fists on her wide hips in a bizarre imitation of an exasperated housewife. The gesture seemed all the weirder owing to her vampire face, which she made no move to cover.

In the tone Cyrus had used to placate me many, many times, he asked, "Why so jealous now? You know the history between us. She's an acquaintance, nothing more."

I made a point of ignoring his remark. I'd seen him wheedle Dahlia this way before, and it nauseated me. Not to mention the fact that I found myself slightly bothered by the label "acquaintance."

We'd been enemies. We'd been lovers. We'd been friends. Sometimes all at once. I loved Nathan, but a part of me wouldn't, would probably never, give up loving Cyrus.

Dahlia wasn't stupid. She knew this. It was why she glared at me, though her expression softened a bit. Her animosity gave me a frightening glimpse into the truth of Cyrus's feelings for me.

"Besides," he continued, "I've made it very clear to you that I'm not interested in having you around too often, haven't I?"

Her angry gaze jerked from me to him. "If I hadn't promised your father I wouldn't kill you, I would kill you."

I chuckled at her poorly worded threat. It was a mistake. She shoved Cyrus away and stalked toward me. "Do you have something to say to me?"

Shaking my head, I smiled. "No, I don't."

She turned back to Cyrus. "You better pray I don't tell your daddy I saw her here."

"My 'daddy' doesn't give a damn about me," Cyrus said with a shrug. "Tell him whatever you want. Just don't bother coming around here again, if you do."

Her manner changed immediately. "Sweetie, you know I'm just playing. Where's your sense of humor?"

"In my other pants, apparently." He kissed her forehead and gave her a shove toward the stairs. "See you next week?"

She glowered at me as she answered, "We'll see." Then she swept up the stairs, and the sound of the slamming door signaled her departure.

Cyrus turned to me with absolutely no humor in his expression. "You're early."

"I didn't realize she'd still be here." I followed him into his apartment. The bathroom was immediately to my right as we stepped through the door. I could see the shower, a bleak white stall, with the water still running.

"We lost track of time." Cyrus walked over—well, took a few steps, the bathroom was so tiny—and turned it off. With absolutely no pretense of modesty he dropped his towel and reached for the jeans slung over the towel rack.

I turned my back. "Whoa, a little warning would be nice."

"It's nothing you haven't seen before," he reminded me smugly. "Well, except for this damn soft stomach I'm getting."

I heard the smack of a hand against wet skin and rolled my eyes. "I always thought you could use a little meat on your bones. Your hips were always so sharp when…"

I let the sentence die. We both knew the when, and it made at least one of us profoundly uncomfortable. I wandered on into the apartment. A sofa bed, unfolded and in disarray from his tryst with Dahlia, took up most of the room. On the far wall were counters, cupboards, a sink, a stove, and a lime-green refrigerator that had probably existed long before my birth. A small bookcase held a few volumes, including a Bible. I looked over my shoulder to make sure he was still in the bathroom before I picked it up.

True to my luck, he came out the second I touched the cover.

"Snooping through my private things, exactly how I remembered you." He took the Bible from me and tossed it back on the shelf.

"I never pegged you for the religious type." I started to sit on the bed and thought better of it, considering who'd just left.

Cyrus gave me a withering glance, as if to say, *Oh, grow up.* He folded the mattress and replaced the cushions while I waited. "Maybe you've misjudged me. Again."

"I prefer to think you constantly surprise me." I shrugged. "I didn't mean anything by it."

He sighed heavily as he tossed two throw pillows onto the couch. "*She* wanted me to read it."

Of course. Cyrus's lost love, the other human hostage of the Fangs. "Oh."

"Don't we feel the tiniest bit insensitive now?" He flashed me a smile that was clearly meant to cover his lingering touchiness about the girl he'd called Mouse.

Changing the subject held the promise of alleviating this awkwardness. And I handled Cyrus a lot better when I was being a hard-ass and not a friend. "What was Dahlia here for?"

"Sex." He dropped onto the couch and leaned against the cushions. "So I hope you weren't looking for some. My mortal body is exhausted. And sore."

"I don't need to hear it." I held up my hand. "I know she

had a major hard-on for you before, but she was trying to become a vampire. Why would she want you now? You're just a grocery store clerk."

"Yes, make a joke, Carrie. You were always so *funny*." His inflection implied the word was used meant ironically.

I held up my hands in mock defenselessness. "Hey, you were the one who was supposed to be getting information. And I'm sorry, you can't possibly be buying it with sex. She's a vampire now. She could have anyone she wants."

"I *was* getting information. What little she'll give me," he grumbled. "I used to be one of the most powerful of our kind, now I'm just…" He let the statement die with a groan of disgust.

I sat down next to him. "Well, what *do* you know?"

"Apparently, Jacob is still working toward his demented goal of godhood. And he has an ally." Cyrus raised an eyebrow. "Anything you haven't heard before?"

I shook my head. "He's working with the Oracle. That we knew. She's been speaking through Bella."

How much should I tell Cyrus about the situation? Too much of his former nature had returned. Was it possible he played both sides?

As if he could read my mind, he leaned forward and put a hand on my knee. I jumped at the contact, and expected to see a smug grin spread across his face, but he remained deadly serious. "Carrie, do you think I want my father to succeed in this?"

"I don't know. Two months ago you were…broken down or something. Now it's like you're back to normal. But that's bad. I remember how you were." I closed my eyes. *I will not cry in front of him. I will not let him know how much what he did to me still hurts.*

"I'm not that person anymore." He touched my cheek, and when I opened my eyes, I saw his shone with tears. "I can't be. I know you think what happened between Mouse and me was all just the result of living in fear for our lives, but I can't believe that. If I did, I wouldn't be able to get out of bed in the morning. I loved her. I have to believe she loved me, because she told me. I never hid who I was from her, and she still loved me. I can't go back to being that monster. If I did, I would be letting her down."

I wiped at my eyes, not wanting to shed tears for him. It would seem weak, and a part of me feared he would laugh as if I'd fallen for an elaborate prank.

"Of course, I've had to do certain distasteful things to survive…." He trailed off. "But never mind about that."

I bristled at the quick way he'd changed the subject. But since he was on our side, I assumed I could trust him. "All we know is that the Oracle is heading to Boston. We don't know how to find the Soul Eater or how to fight either of them."

He nodded. "Dahlia said she was contacted by one of his men. They want her to do some spell to ferret out a weapon the Oracle prophesied."

"A weapon?"

"Apparently it's something she said centuries ago. There's some sort of weapon, and whatever side controls it will have the loyalty of every earthly vampire. 'A sword forged of the flesh of all vampires, bathed in the blood of the traitors.' If the Oracle is free, I'm sure he's worried that she remembers, and is simply trying to beat her to it. Or stay close to her to con her out of it." Cyrus inclined his head. "Actually, it is something my father has been working on for some time. Very complicated stuff."

I leaned forward, squashing my hopeful eagerness. "Do you remember what it was?"

"He didn't tell me." Cyrus rubbed his forehead. "Jacob gave me tasks and I obeyed. I never questioned."

I covered my face with my palms. "So, there's a weapon out there. And who will get it first is anyone's guess."

"It's an almost one hundred percent certainty that our side won't get it," he pointed out. "Since the Movement clearly isn't looking for it."

"Our side?" It seemed so strange that he'd attached himself to a cause that wasn't entirely self-serving.

He sent me another withering look. "The side that is not my father's. Anyone with half a brain should be on it, by now."

"Nathan and I will research this sword. Hopefully, we'll get a break before Max and Bella find the Oracle." The prospect of reading well into the daylight hours made me suddenly sleepy.

Cyrus tapped his lips thoughtfully with his forefinger. "I wonder if it is some kind of riddle. You said Bella has heard the Oracle's thoughts? What if that's indicative of some kind of power Bella has?"

"She *is* a werewolf. They specialize in magic." I rolled my eyes. "You know, the kind of magic spelled with a *k* at the end."

"The kind your boyfriend peddles in his shop," Cyrus pointed out. "The kind that pays your rent."

"Touché. I'll give Max a heads-up." Nathan's cell phone, tucked in my back pocket, began to sound a classical melody. "Yikes, that will be him. I have to go."

"Max?" Understanding caused a scowl to cross Cyrus's face. "Oh, the other him."

I ignored the ringing, though I knew I would play a game of twenty thousand questions when I got home. "Listen, don't give Dahlia the brush-off right away, if you can stand her for a bit longer. Any information you get would help us out."

"Oh, I think I can stand her."

"God, not only are you human, you're a fourteen-year-old boy." I shook my head. "Listen, find out what you can about Dahlia, but be safe."

"Do you honestly believe she'll harm me?" He laughed. "She was obsessed with me."

"Yeah, and she asked me to kill you. Besides, you have no idea where she's been. I haven't really looked into whether STDs can be transmitted from vampires to humans, but best play it safe for now." I didn't know what the appropriate goodbye gesture would be, so I held out my arm for an awkward handshake.

When he pulled away, he looked anywhere but at me. "I'll try to find out where Jacob is. I'm sure Dahlia must know. She's on his payroll."

"That would great. Thanks." I turned to go, and I'd reached the door when his voice stopped me.

"Thank you for not giving up on me, Carrie."

I glanced back and gave him a tremulous smile. "I don't know if I ever could."

When I reached the street I ran the short distance home,

invigorated by new hope and relief that something finally seemed to be going right.

Bella had slept for the rest of the night and all day, though she'd made valiant attempts to stay awake the few times she rose to get a drink or use the bathroom. Finally, just before sunset, Max had been forced to wake her.

She'd grumbled and shuffled around, getting ready, but hadn't gotten sick again, and as far as Max was concerned, that was all that mattered.

"I had the flu just before I was sired," he said, trying to sound sympathetic as they zoomed down the freeway. "It sucked."

She only nodded. "I do not have the flu. Are you sure you are driving the speed limit?"

Definitely not. "No one ever gets pulled over in Pennsylvania," he assured her.

"I would not know. I have never broken the law here before," she chided, leaning forward to fiddle with the dials on the radio. "Can we listen to something that is not so violent sounding?"

Max frowned. He'd had the classic rock station on since they'd crossed the Ohio border, but the signal had begun to fade. Still, he didn't want to end up listening to some late-night, lonely-hearts-sappy-dedication hour, either. "I wouldn't call Tom Petty violent sounding, but if you can find something else, go for it. Just no chick music."

"Chick music?" Amusement colored her voice, and when he took his eyes from the road for a second he saw a smile bend her mouth.

"Yeah, chick music. Alanis Morisette, Fiona Apple," he shuddered. "Tori Amos."

Bella laughed and turned her attention back to the radio.

This is nice, he decided. Driving along as though they were on a road trip, not a suicide mission. Teasing each other like old friends. Holding her as she drifted to sleep wearing his T-shirt.

This is too nice. What the hell was he doing, letting his defenses down so she could wedge herself into his life? What if she got hurt? What if she hurt him?

It was all the time he'd spent listening to Carrie's love woes over Nathan. Somehow, he'd let himself be talked into needing a *relationship.* God, the word used to hold as much appeal for him as *audit* or *classical music.* Now it caused an ache in his chest and a sudden need to touch Bella. It didn't matter how, as long as he could assure himself of her physical presence.

He cleared his throat. "There's some Carol King in the CD case under the seat. *Tapestry.* And if you tell anyone, I won't hesitate to kill you."

Bella laughed again. He heard her shuffling as she looked for the CDs, then the click of the disk as she put it in the portable player. She turned the volume down as "I Feel the Earth Move" started, and she placed her hand on his knee. "I like your chick music."

"With my bare hands," he warned playfully.

Without warning, her fingers dug into his flesh and her body spasmed. Max jerked the wheel and hit the brake, bringing the car to rest on the shoulder of the highway. Damn hard to do when it felt as if his knee was caught in a vise. His bones creaked under her hand, and when he got the car into park he tried frantically to dislodge her grip. He'd heard of people in the throes of a serious seizure injuring others. He didn't need to limp through the Midwest.

"I warned you to stay away!" The voice that hissed from Bella's mouth dismissed any notion she was having a simple mortal convulsion.

Max froze. "I'm…sorry?"

The Oracle crawled Bella's body forward with jerky motions, like a freaky puppet. Max flattened himself against the driver's door, feeling slightly ridiculous for being afraid of Bella.

That feeling fled when she twisted his knee. The bone and cartilage gave way with a sickening crunch, and he screamed.

"Every mile you come closer to me, the greater my power over you grows." As if to illustrate the point, Bella's body flew backward, her head striking the passenger window with a sickening thud.

Almost instantly, the Oracle's hold receded. Bella blinked, winced in pain, then wrapped her arms around her middle and cried out in panic. "Did it happen again? Did she do it again?"

Struggling to keep his head straight despite the pain, Max reached for her to offer whatever comfort he could give. He was afraid that if he opened his mouth he would start crying like a baby, from the pain of his knee or the fright that he was once again unable to protect her.

"What did she do to me?" Bella slapped away his hands, her voice escalating in pitch. "Did you see what she did?"

Her panic took him aback. "Bella, you're fine."

"I am not fine!" She pounded the dashboard, then raked her hands across her bound hair. Then repeated, more quietly, "I am not fine."

What was he supposed to do? He'd tried to hug her. That hadn't worked. Now she was crying softly and doing a fine job of withdrawing, leaving him in a damned awkward position.

And there was his knee. It was broken, no doubt about it. If Bella went all weepy and catatonic, he wouldn't be able to cart her to safety. Heck, he might not even be able to cart *himself* to safety.

And there was the Oracle's warning. It wasn't a threat he was going to take lightly.

A couple months ago, he would have hit the gas and laid on the horn to let the Oracle know they were coming. But with Bella in the car beside him, all he wanted to do was turn and run. *Funny how a person can grow on you.*

"Let's stop for the night. I thought I saw a motel at the last exit. I can turn around up there." He pointed to a gravel access lane across the median.

Pure disdain crinkled her brow above tear-filled eyes. "Was your brain damaged? We have gone perhaps two hundred miles tonight."

"I'm not brain damaged, I—" He sighed. "I just don't think it's a good idea to go any farther until we know more about what the Oracle might be up to."

"What?" All the fear fled from her expression. "You are afraid."

"I am *not* afraid." Of course, he would have to end up defending his bravery and probably his masculinity—

though she had no room to doubt that—when all he was trying to do was keep her from getting killed. "Listen, my knee is completely shot. You just had a scary experience. Let's find someplace where we can settle in. I'll have to heal for a few days, anyway."

"Your blood rations will run out," she argued. "And I will not let you feed from me."

He covered his frustration with an explosive laugh. "Oh, like I would want to. I prefer the taste of the human stuff. I've been known to stoop to cow, and I'll have to if I run out. But I've never eaten dog before."

A complete change came over her. The argumentative bitch disappeared, replaced by a mischievous girl. "Yes, you have."

That was all it took—her easy acknowledgment of the dirty, wonderful things they'd done together—and he couldn't be on the defensive anymore. "I don't want to go any farther, because the Oracle threatened you when you were...out."

"What did she say?" Bella's chin jutted bravely, and she looked as if she was forcing herself not to cry again.

There was no point in protecting her from the truth, especially since it was making it so damn hard to actually protect her. "She said she's going to get stronger the closer we come."

"She said that?" Bella shook her head. "That cannot be. I do not remember it."

"Do you remember anything from the last time she possessed you? Do you remember breaking my knee?" He hadn't planned on raising his voice, but he was too angry, too rattled by the whole experience, to keep his cool. "Bella, I was sitting right here."

They glared at each other in silence. He desperately wanted her to be the first to speak, but his stubbornness had frayed around the edges where she was concerned. "Listen, we can keep going and get you killed, or we can turn around and take a day or two to figure this out. At least give me the time to heal, so I have a fighting chance if you don't make it."

"Fine. We will stop tonight. But we cannot lose any more time. I do not think I can…" She waved a hand in the air. "I am tired. Speaking nonsense. You are right, we should turn around."

He started the car and pulled back onto the highway, grateful for the sparse traffic. He managed to cross the lanes to the median without having to play Frogger. Once they were headed safely in the opposite direction, he reached over and turned the music back on.

Fucking Carole King, he thought with a grimace.

They drove in silence for a while, with only *Tapestry* to distract him, until finally, releasing a tired sigh, Bella spoke.

"I saw something." Her shoulders sagged and a few strands of hair fell forward, obscuring her face from his view.

This uncharacteristically timid and bedraggled Bella was becoming far too common. He turned his attention back to the road. "Anything I should know?"

"The Oracle has arrived. She is in a place called Danvers. Have you ever heard of it?"

"Can't say I have. Not to make any prejudgments based on nerdiness, but I bet Nathan has a book with lots of arcane facts about it." Max reached toward the glove compartment, where his cell phone was stored.

Bella jumped, avoiding his hand. "I am sorry. I am still…guarded."

"I understand." But he didn't. He hated the Oracle more than ever, simply for putting this distance between them.

Bella reached into the compartment and retrieved his phone, but she didn't hand it over immediately. "There is more."

He didn't know how much more he could take. "Lay it on me."

"She has sent something via courier. A package." She hesitated. "It sounds crazy, but…I believe it could be her heart."

"What?" This just kept getting better and better. Max shifted in his seat, hoping he could use his left foot to push the gas and brake pedals and take the strain off his broken knee. "Do you know where she sent it?"

Bella waited far too long before answering. When he looked at her, she stared back with hard eyes. "Where do *you* think she sent it?"

Max turned back to the road and clenched the steering wheel tighter.

Ten: Sire

❧⟋⟍❧

"What? Is she okay?"

I looked up from the incredibly dull book in my lap—
no great sacrifice—at Nathan's startled exclamation. The
only time he ever sounded so worried was over something
evil-forces related, or when we were running low on beer.
Now, he stood in the kitchen, phone in hand, frown lines
creasing his brow.

He noticed me watching him, and turned his back so I
couldn't see his expression. Still, no matter how much he
lowered his voice, I could hear him.

"Not off the top of my head, I don't." The disdain in
Nathan's voice tipped me off. He was talking to Max.
"How should I… I don't know, get an atlas!"

I snorted. Nathan turned and gave me a sharp look, but
it faded into concern as he listened to Max. "I have no
idea what he would want with it. I know what I would do
if I had it."

I joined him in the kitchen. I didn't know what I could
do, other than stand beside him posing wordless questions

with facial expressions and hand gestures. But at least I felt like I was doing *something*.

"Well, keep an eye on her. And let me know what you decide." There was a long pause. "We'll find out. Just stay put. Give yourself time to heal. Let us know if you need any help."

Time to heal?

"What the hell happened?" I demanded when Nathan hung up the phone.

He rubbed his eyes. He was just as tired as I was. "The Oracle popped into Bella again. Used her to break Max's knee."

"Is she okay?" It was an unnecessary question. If something had happened to Bella, I'd have been able to hear Max screaming over the phone.

"She's fine. It was nowhere near as bad as the last time. Well, for her, that is." Nathan went to the cupboard over the sink and pulled down a bottle of Bailey's Irish Cream. "I'm going to make coffee. And I'm going to put a lot of alcohol in it. You want some?"

"Yeah, I could use some." I dropped into one of the kitchen chairs and plunged my fingers through my hair. It was only 2:00 a.m., but we'd spent the whole night inside and my internal clock was screwed. Even my scalp felt tired. "Well, we were expecting the Oracle to make another attack on them. They had to know it was coming, too. They're smart."

"Yeah, but Max isn't thinking logically. He wants to turn around and come back." Nathan slipped a filter into the coffeemaker and reached into the refrigerator for the can of coffee. "I almost wonder…"

"Wonder what?" Usually, if Nathan had a hunch, he was right.

He smiled and shook his head. "Nothing. I'm tired. My brain is misfiring."

Once the coffeemaker was merrily dripping away, he headed toward the living room. I grabbed his arm as he passed. "I can't face all those books without liquid fortification. Sit with me a minute, take a break."

Reluctantly, he took the other chair. "Bella did have more information for us. The Oracle is going to a place called Danvers. And she sent a care package to the Soul Eater. Bella thinks the Oracle sent him her heart."

"Why would she do something like that?" Truthfully, I was surprised she even had it. It seemed someone at the Movement would have taken it from her, in case she ever got loose. *Right now would have been fine.* But it wasn't the first time the Movement had dropped the ball. "Well, let's look at a map of Massachusetts, see if she picked Boston for a reason."

"You're right. That's the logical place to start." He exhaled noisily. "But you should call Cyrus, find out if he knows anything."

"He probably won't, but Dahlia will know. She's still working for the Soul Eater." I bit my lip, feeling somehow like Judas for what I was about to say. "I'm worried. That he might be…"

"A double agent?" Nathan tried to imitate a Sean Connery as James Bond accent and failed, Scottish though they both might be. "I'm sure this will come as no surprise to you, but I've considered it. Unfortunately, he's the only source we have."

I rested my chin on my hands. "Has your life ever been, you know, boring?"

"You mean, have I always been on the side of good, battling against the greatest evils known to vampire-kind?" He gave me a lazy grin. "No. I think that all came about when this bossy woman stepped into my shop about four months ago."

"And nearly had her head chopped off by your juvenile-delinquent son." Though I'd said it in jest, I wished I could unsay it. Not because I thought Nathan would take offense to my poking fun at Ziggy, but because we rarely, if ever, spoke of him. The pain was still too fresh.

Nathan laughed softly, lost in memory. I reached across the table to take his hand, but he stood and went to check on the coffee, which was doing fine on its own.

"Sorry," I offered lamely.

He shook his head. "Don't be. You're trying to acclimate me to talking about him. It's for my own good. There are times I forget he's gone, and talking about it, especially here…"

"Makes it more real." I knew exactly how he felt. When I'd first gotten the call about my parents' accident, I could have run across my college campus screaming, "My parents are dead, my parents are dead." But once I'd gone home for the funeral, I'd clammed up. For good.

I didn't want that to be the case with Nathan. "You can't just hold on to things forever. You tried that before. Look what it got you."

"I know." He stared at the liquid dripping into the carafe. We waited a long time in silence until the coffee was done. Then he poured out two mugs and spiked them both with the liquor. "Blood?"

"Please." I watched as he poured a little blood into each mug, and waited for him to bring them to the table. "Muddy pink. Just the way I like it."

He smiled. "Do you know how many times Ziggy accidentally drank human blood?"

I had to remember to smile encouragingly, lest Nathan clam up again. Gross, though.

"I used to trick him, too. You'd be amazed at how much corn syrup and red food coloring look like blood when you mix them together." Nathan got that faraway look on his face again. "Carrie, am I betraying him?"

That wasn't the question I expected. "How do you mean?"

He looked down at his mug. "Shouldn't I want to kill him? For what he did to Ziggy? A part of me is ashamed for not wanting retribution. But isn't it better, at least in the long run, that I don't feel that responsibility?"

"You're not betraying him." I took his hands in mine. "It hasn't been that long. I'm actually impressed that you've gotten beyond blaming yourself. It's much healthier that way. And besides…"

How much should I tell him? That Ziggy had actually grown to like Cyrus? That he'd respected him and trusted him in small ways? That it had been me who'd unwittingly killed him, regardless of whose fangs had been involved?

There was no way Nathan was ready to hear that. "Ziggy wasn't a vengeful kind of person. And he would understand that you're just doing what has to be done."

Nathan nodded. "Well, I'm not doing what needs to be done now, am I? I'm having coffee with you."

He stood and made a shooing motion toward the living

room. "So, what are your theories about this heart business? You'd be the foremost expert in losing one."

"You have no idea." I stood and kissed him. His mouth tasted like the coffee, sweet and coppery.

When I pulled back, he smiled. "You're not going to lure me away from research with sex. I like books too much."

I rolled my eyes, then collected my mug and followed him to the living room. How did he always see the ulterior motives behind my cunning actions? "Well, I suppose the Soul Eater could consume the Oracle's soul by eating the heart, couldn't he?"

"But why would the Oracle send it to him then?" Nathan groaned as he settled onto the couch. "God, this is uncomfortable."

My back protested as I sank into the armchair. "Well, if she didn't know he was going to eat her soul—"

Nathan gave me a withering look to point out my stupidity. Of course the Oracle would know what the Soul Eater intended to do with her heart. She could see into the future.

"What about this sword Cyrus mentioned?" I moved on quickly to avoid the inevitable taunting. "Maybe it's a metaphor, and her heart has something to do with it?"

Nathan took a sip from his mug. "Could be. We won't know until you talk to Cyrus. Do you think he's awake?"

I looked at the clock. "I don't know. He works third shift, so he's probably not even home."

"If he is, I won't lose too much sleep over disturbing his. Why don't you call him?"

I went to the kitchen and dialed Cyrus's number. After two rings, the answering machine picked up.

"Hi, Cyrus, it's me. Carrie." I winced at how lame I sounded. "Listen, we got more news about what the Oracle is up to. I could really use your connection to Dahlia right now. But be careful with her, okay? I mean, I don't want her to know that you're looking for the information, because she'll know that I know that she's working for the Soul Eater."

I hesitated a minute before I hung up the phone. It's a shame they didn't make answering machines with a "never mind, erase that" feature.

"And maybe after that, you two can go to the soda fountain and get a milk shake," Nathan said without looking up from his book.

I wished I had something to throw at him.

We spent the rest of the night thumbing through texts. I'd become a bit fed up with this hurry-up-and-wait scenario. The sun came up just about the time my eyes were too tired to keep reading. "I'm sorry, but I have to go to bed."

Nathan closed the book he'd been thumbing through, and rubbed his eyes. "I'm right behind you."

As we climbed into bed, I'd never been more appreciative of the too-soft mattress and worn sheets. "You can go ahead and let me sleep through tomorrow night."

He flopped against the pillows with a loud groan. "No way. If I'm going to suffer through another night like this, so are you."

I snuggled against him, rubbing my face against his T-shirt. It was thoroughly bizarre, going to sleep with him like a normal couple. We'd spent so long trying to maintain our independence from each other that the only way we'd ever wound up sleeping in the same spot was if we got naked and sweaty together. Sleeping beside each other, with no sex involved, clothed in sleepwear, seemed more intimate than lying together in a naked tangle of limbs.

He must have sensed part of my thoughts through the blood tie, because he chuckled. "Don't get used to this. Now that I can finally have you without the inevitable guilt that I'm using you, you're not going to leave this bed for days."

It took me a minute to decipher his words in his sleep-thickened accent. "You felt guilty about using me?" *I'd known he felt guilty.*

"Oh, aye. I'm a Catholic. We feel guilty all the time." He reached up and clicked off the bedside lamp, muttered something, then fell onto the pillows and was instantly asleep.

Though Nathan had no trouble sleeping through the day, I hovered stubbornly on the edge of unconsciousness, trying to stay alert for Cyrus's call. Every noise or creak of the apartment woke me, and once I even stumbled from bed before realizing that the phone I heard ring had just been a dream.

Finally, because I feared my tense state was disturbing Nathan's rest, I wrapped up in his bathrobe and padded to the living room.

The day was overcast, so I chanced a peek through the blinds. The startling brightness of late afternoon seared my retinas, and I blinked away blood tears. From the living room I could see the roof of Cyrus's house, if I craned my neck, but I couldn't see anything in detail. There was no sense going blind when I wouldn't learn anything new.

I glanced at the clock above the dinette table. Four-thirty. Why hadn't he called back?

I decided I would phone every half hour, until I got an answer. At sundown, if I still hadn't heard from him, I would go investigate. All I ever got were busy signals.

By the time Nathan woke, at six, I was already dressed and pacing the floor, waiting to be absolutely certain it was safe to go out.

"You're afraid Dahlia changed him," Nathan said over the rim of his breakfast mug.

I knew he'd picked that up through the blood tie. "He said he doesn't want to be a vampire again, and he's got a good reason not to be. But something's wrong, and I can't help but jump to conclusions."

"Maybe not." Nathan set his blood aside and came to stand behind me as I dialed the phone again. His big, strong hands kneaded my shoulders as I listened to the insistent busy tone.

"He could have a human girlfriend, or boyfriend, he's staying with. He might be grocery shopping or having lunch or doing any of the million things humans do every day. You remember those, don't you?" Nathan punctuated his question with a kiss on my neck, then added cheerfully, "Maybe he got arrested."

I knew Nathan was just trying to help, but I couldn't shake the feeling something was very, deeply wrong. I shrugged off his hands and stuck my arm behind the blinds to check the burn factor. *Getting lower.*

"Something is wrong. When he was in the desert, I could feel him sometimes. I don't know how it works or why it does, but I just have this… It's not the blood tie anymore, but it's intuition. I'm still connected to him, and I know something isn't right."

"Do you want me to go with you?" All the humor had left Nathan's tone.

I shook my head. "You should stay here, in case he calls. And if something has happened, if he's changed… I don't think he'll hurt me, but he would hurt you."

I tried the phone twice more before realizing I'd actually have to go to his house. I kissed Nathan goodbye, took the stake he gave me "just in case," and headed out the door in a sweatshirt with the hood pulled up to protect my face from the last rays of sun that gilded the clouds.

Cyrus didn't answer the buzzer rigged up near the back door, but a sliver of light showed through one of the basement windows. I forced the door—not a difficult feat even for someone without enhanced vampire strength—and clattered down the stairs in a rush.

What I saw at the bottom stopped me in my tracks. Cyrus's apartment door, open a crack.

I swallowed my fear and stepped forward, knocking timidly. The door creaked and swayed a little, and I choked as I called, "Is anybody in there?"

No answer. I gave the door a push. It opened wider. At least a body wasn't blocking it. The bathroom light was on, illuminating a wedge of the main room. The cupboards on the far wall hung open, their shelves bare. The dishes and nonperishable food were scattered on the floor. The cushions were thrown from the couch. A high-pitched, three-tone whine sounded from somewhere, followed by a muffled, "If you would like to make a call, please hang up and dial again" announcement. I spotted a loop of coiled phone cord poking out from beneath one shredded pillow on the unfolded sofa bed. I grabbed it and reeled in the phone and very broken answering machine.

My message.

A sob clawed its way up my throat as my brain reconstructed the events that must have led to the destruction around me. Of course, Dahlia would have heard the message. And of course, she would have flown into a rage and wrecked the place. But had she taken Cyrus with her when she'd gone? Had he staggered to the hospital or called the police for help?

I wrote the latter off. With my senses on hyperalert all day, I would have heard the sirens.

I paced the floor, breathing deeply, willing my blood to stop beating in my ears. Then I caught the coppery, warm scent of external blood. Maybe he'd left a trail. If it was fresh enough, I could follow it.

Two steps out the door, I remembered the one room I hadn't checked.

How I'd missed the bathroom, I would never know. The cracked tile floor was coated with blood. Scarlet handprints smeared the walls. It was like a scene out of a horror movie, and splayed right in the middle of the floor was Cyrus.

"No!" I knelt at his side in what seemed like way too much blood for one human being to lose and still be alive. My brain flashed back to the night I'd first seen him, in a bloody mess much worse than this. But he'd been a vampire then. I checked for a pulse, though it seemed futile. He must have lain here all day. Unbelievably, he was still alive.

His eyes slowly opened, slid from side to side before focusing on me. "Carrie?"

I laid one hand on his chest to gauge his shallow respiration. "I'm here."

My fingers were sticky with blood when I pulled them back. A dozen deep cuts scored his arms, to the bone in some places. Three long slashes banded his chest.

"I thought—" He struggled to breathe, wincing as the wounds on his torso parted with the motion. "I thought you were…Mouse."

My vision swam with tears. "No. No, you're not going to see her for a long time."

"Don't…lie. Carrie." Red bubbled past his lips. "Dahlia knows. Everything."

"I'm so sorry." I stroked his hair back from his forehead, not sure whether the action was too familiar or if I wasn't being tender enough. They taught comforting the dying in med school, but somehow it always got lost in memorizing muscle groups and dissecting cadavers.

Dying. Cyrus was dying. Right now, as I touched him, he faded more with each passing second. There was nothing I could do to stop it.

"I needed…to tell… I know where he is." He coughed and more blood spilled from his lips. I was amazed he had any left.

He couldn't speak anymore. Though he still breathed, his eyes rolled back in his head.

I was alone, with a dying human, in an unfamiliar place. My immortality felt false and traitorous. I might as well have been a fixture in this bathroom, for all my humanity.

I needed Nathan. Desperately needed him. I crawled to the phone in the other room, because it seemed I wasn't abandoning Cyrus as long as I didn't stand and walk away. My hands trembled as I punched in the numbers.

Nathan picked up on the first ring. "Carrie, what's going on?"

A calm wave flowed over me through the blood tie. He'd felt my shock and sorrow; he'd just waited for me to reach out to him for help.

"He's dead. Or almost." Tears spilled from my eyes and my breath caught on a hiccup as I tried to drag it in. I had the fleeting thought that I shouldn't grieve for Cyrus so openly to Nathan, considering their shared past. I dismissed it. No matter what I tried to show Nathan, he wouldn't be blind to my feelings. "Oh God, Nathan. He's going to die!"

"What happened? Can you do anything for him?" The earnestness in his voice brought more tears to my eyes. "Should I bring you the med kit?"

Staring down at my blood-drenched clothes, I felt bile rise in my throat. I closed my eyes. "There's nothing I can do." *Unless…*

There was an audible hitch in Nathan's breathing.

"Forget it, forget I thought that." My words tumbled out in a rush as I desperately tried to cover my mental ramblings.

"Carrie…" Nathan's voice held a pitiful note of pleading.

I wanted to slam the receiver back into the cradle and flee from the scene of my heinous crime. It would have been the sensible thing to do. Instead, I kept talking. "He knows something. He knows where the Soul Eater is, but he couldn't tell me."

"We can find another way—"

"He's going to die!" I gripped the phone so hard the plastic creaked.

The silence seemed endless. For all I knew, this could have been a pointless argument. Cyrus might already be dead.

"I'll be over in a minute with the med kit." Nathan's voice sounded tight, strained. The tension shattered with a guttural sob. "Please, don't do anything until I get there!"

But it was far too late. The seed of the evil notion had been planted, and I would see it through to harvest.

"I'm sorry, Nathan." I hung up the phone with shaking hands and slowly stood. Every step I took toward the bathroom seemed to require more effort than the last, as though I were wading into deeper and deeper water. When I finally reached Cyrus's side, I knew I couldn't hesitate. He was so close to death I could feel the angel in the room with us.

"Sorry to send you back empty-handed," I muttered, rolling up one of my sleeves. There was a cup with a toothbrush and a razor on the edge of the sink. My hands shook so badly I knocked it the floor when I reached for it.

The noise, coupled with my jostling of him while I groped for the razor, brought Cyrus back from the brink for a moment. His eyes searched my face, his mouth worked soundlessly as understanding cascaded over him.

He managed one word. "No."

I flicked the blade across my wrist. The pain surprised me. In the movies, it never looks as though it hurts. The blood didn't well up gracefully. It spurted, hot, wet jets from my torn veins.

He gathered enough strength to rise on his elbows and

pull back. His mouth clamped in a tight line, and I had to force his jaw open with my free hand.

"No," he begged, trying to spit out the blood that had already fallen on his lips. "Not this…"

I couldn't bear to hear it, to hear him say he would rather die than let me save him. I gripped his shoulder to pin him to the ground, and pressed my slashed wrist to his mouth to stifle his protests.

Cyrus had once warned me not to test his will. His might have been strong, but mine was stronger.

He stopped struggling, jaw going slack beneath my wrist, but he didn't draw the blood into his mouth willingly. It didn't matter. All he needed was to ingest some.

The process didn't appear to be working. I'd never changed someone, so I didn't know exactly what I was supposed to be feeling. There was no blood tie forming, though, no bond I could notice. All I felt was light-headed from lack of blood, and Cyrus seemed to fade faster and faster. His chest no longer moved with breath. His face turned blue.

What mistake had I made? My blood should have made him a vampire, the way his had made me when our blood had exchanged in the morgue.

Exchanged! Carrie, how could you be so stupid?

I needed to drink his blood—if there was any left—to complete the process. I just hoped it worked out of order. Pressing my lips to one of the gaping wounds on his chest, I gently touched my tongue to the gory, exposed muscle there. We'd accidentally exchanged blood when he'd turned me, so little I hadn't even noticed it. A few drops now *had* to do the trick. I sucked against the wound and a hot trickle slipped past my lips.

The change was immediate, unpleasant and violent. Cyrus's body bucked against the floor. Pain ripped through my chest, my head, my heart. I think I screamed. White-hot light flashed behind my eyes, and I collapsed on top of Cyrus's dead, yet somehow curiously alive, body.

A familiar, yet different channel opened in my head. It was Cyrus, and he was filled with hate, even as he drifted between the worlds of the living and dead.

He was my fledgling.

I was his sire.

Eleven: Fools Rush In

As much as Max hated being cooped up in the Prancing Pony Motor Inn, he was relieved that so far, the Oracle hadn't messed with Bella.

In fact, Bella seemed to actually enjoy their captivity. During the day she slept at his side, except for the few times she'd sneaked away to buy food from the gas station across the road. At night, she took almost domestic pleasure in caring for him, propping pillows beneath his injured knee and warming bags of blood in hot water from the tap.

"I think the diet of Twinkies and chips is agreeing with you," he said with a laugh when she brought him his breakfast on the third night.

She smiled and helped him sit up, fluffing the pillows behind his back as she did. "Perhaps. Perhaps I am just a nice person and you never gave me credit for that."

He shook his head. "You're not a nice person."

She slapped his injured knee lightly, and he yelped.

"Not nice at all," he grumbled, taking the bag of blood from her and biting off a corner.

He took a few long swallows and carefully lowered the bag, pinching off the opening between his fingers. Motel staff, no matter how low-rent the establishment, didn't tend to appreciate blood on their bedding. And Bella didn't have to look so damn disgusted when he ate.

"So, what's with you lately? Why are you so…happy?" He adjusted his wounded leg gingerly. It would be healed in a day or two more, but he planned to milk the injury for as long as he could, until he figured out what to do about the Oracle situation. In the time he'd wasted so far, he'd consulted an atlas and found a town called Danvers just north of Boston. Next to Salem, oh joy of joys, and he was sure it wasn't just a coincidence. The thought of coming up against a horde of witches like Dahlia made his whole body tense, but it wasn't as if Bella and he were helpless. When not puking her guts out, she had some fierce magical powers.

Unaware that he'd just counted her as a part of their arsenal, Bella reclined on the bed beside him, her head propped on her arms. "I am happy to be spending what could be our last days doing something useful."

It took a moment for her words to sink in. When they did, he had an overwhelming urge to push her off the bed. "You know, that's just great."

If he could have gotten up and stalked away from her, he would have, but if he could do that, he could drive the car, and she'd have them on the road in an hour.

She sat up, a heartbreaking, wounded look on her face. "I do not understand. Why are you angry?"

"Because you won't stop harping on this death shit!" He pounded the mattress with his fist. "You're not going to die."

"You do not know that," she insisted, her tone a little too reasonable. "Neither one of us knows when death will come for us."

"You don't know shit!" He sat up in turn. "And if you think you're going to die, you don't know much about me."

"You cannot prevent everything." She put her hand on his arm. "It could be out of your hands."

"Is this something the Oracle told you? Because she could be trying to trick you." How could Bella blindly believe anything that crazy bitch planted in her head?

"I have feared her since the moment I first saw her, the day I came to the Movement." Bella gave a soft laugh. "It is not unlikely she will be the death of me. Or you."

She knelt beside him and tenderly put her hands on his face, turning his head so she could look into his eyes. He didn't resist her.

"I am not lying. But she did show me something." A tear rolled down Bella's cheek. "A long time ago, when I first saw her. She showed me that I would find you."

Injured knee be damned. Max pulled Bella into his arms and kissed her, hard, as if the intensity of his physical actions could keep her safe from her own mortality.

"I thought you were hurt," she whispered against his cheek when his mouth moved from her lips to her jaw.

He smiled and brushed her ear with his lips. "Not so much as I let on."

Trying to ignore the gentle pressure against his chest, he kissed her mouth again. She turned her head.

"What's the matter?" he asked, leaning up on his elbows. But he already knew.

"Why would you lie?"

He groaned and flopped onto his back, sucking in a breath at the surprising pain that ripped up his leg. "I didn't lie. I really am hurt. Just not as badly as I let on."

"You pretended to be hurt more than you are. That is a lie," she said quietly, accusingly.

"No, it's not, really." How could he explain it to her? "I just didn't want to go any further on this trip before we got some concrete information. I don't want to rush headlong into something bad."

She shook her head. "We do not have to rush headlong. We simply need to get there. It is a long drive. How can you waste our time so?"

"I'm not wasting our time, I'm preserving your life!" He swore. If she wasn't going to let him protect her from the Oracle, he wasn't going to protect her from the truth. "She told me, through you, that the closer we come to her, the more power she has over us."

"I know this!" Bella sat up, uttering some angry words in Italian. "I swear you think I am a child, Max."

She rarely spoke his name, at least, not to him. He covered his face with his hands. "Bella, listen to me. You're afraid of the Oracle. You admit she's a danger to us."

Bella nodded.

"Maybe, just maybe then, if we don't go find her, we won't die." He bracketed her face with his palms. "We can get in the car and drive. It doesn't matter where we go, as long as it's away from her."

Bella's hands came up to cover his, to grip his arms and

gently force them down. "What about Nathan and Carrie? They are depending on us to help them."

"We can throw out the cell phone and forget them." He didn't know what shocked him more, the fact he suggested leaving his friends—and the world—at the mercy of the Oracle and the Soul Eater, or the desperation required to talk about it. Or what that desperation meant. "We can just forget everything. No one will ever find us."

"No." She lifted his hands to her lips and kissed them. "We would always be running from our pasts."

He shook his head. "I'm not going to take you to her. Not if you have this feeling of dread. Not if you're certain you're going to die. Never gonna happen."

"If you do not, I will find a way by myself!" Closing her eyes, clearly an attempt to calm herself, Bella asked, "Why does this bother you so? You used to want to kill me."

"Well, things have changed." He'd rather pull out his tongue than confess any more feelings for her, but he didn't want her to die, either. Maybe it would take some kind of grand gesture to knock some sense into her.

Maybe that was exactly what she was looking for.

He closed his own eyes, because if there was any mocking in her expression he wouldn't be able to stand it. "Bella, I—"

"I love you," she blurted, her voice hitching, as if she couldn't believe she'd said it, or she wanted to take it back.

Opening his eyes, he caught a glimpse of Bella as he'd never seen her before. Frightened, not of an enemy or unseen force, but of her own actions. Terrified of rejection. Ashamed that she'd displayed human feelings.

His chest constricted so painfully he wondered if it were possible for vampires to have heart attacks. He didn't know what to say, didn't have any words. What could he say when faced with such an unlikely reflection of himself?

Taking his silence for rejection, she looked down at her hands. "Now you will mock me."

"No." His voice was oddly hoarse. He cleared his throat. "At least, not for this."

"You are mocking me now." Her shoulders slumped. She didn't wear defeat well.

Having never been in love—at least, not this way—he found himself in wholly uncharted territory. It wasn't fair he had to feel so vulnerable.

"I'm not making fun of you." He slid two fingers under her chin to turn her face to his. "If I had said what you just did, would you have made fun of me?"

She lifted one eyebrow in a mocking expression, and for a second the Bella he knew was back. Just as quickly, though, she grew serious. "If you had said it to me, it would have been different. Because I would have wanted to hear it."

"I wanted to hear it." He dropped his hand and shook his head. "But something tells me you won't believe that."

"Why would I?" She laughed bitterly. "You wish me to believe that you do not love anyone. That you drown yourself in meaningless sex. That was fine, when it was what I wanted from you. But you wanted more from me than that, and I would not give it. And now, you will reject me as a punishment."

"I didn't want more then," he insisted, out of habit. "I mean…I used to do the meaningless sex thing. Because I did love someone, once. He died. And no, it wasn't a gay thing. He was my sire. I know you think the whole vampire thing is disgusting, and I know you're not going to believe this, but the blood tie…does something to you. And when he died… It was easier for me to think I wasn't lonely if I was going home with a different woman every night. Then things happened with you. And when I tried the meaningless sex thing again, it just didn't work."

He groaned and swung his legs over the side of the bed, sitting up. "I better stop talking. I'm just fucking this up more."

"You are not fucking up anything." Color rose in her cheeks. He realized he rarely heard her use profanity. "Max, we must talk about this or we will not be happy."

"We won't be happy anyway. We're going to die, remember?" The bitter retort rode a wave of bile up his throat, and he choked it back. "God, this is really happening to me again. I'm gonna fall for you and some horrible shit is going to happen."

She put her arms around his shoulders, rested her cheek against his. "Let's not think about that now."

He shook his head. "This isn't how I wanted it to happen."

"It is not how I wanted it to happen, either." Her voice was a whisper that tickled his ear.

His mouth went dry at the thought of the month he'd spent apart from her, a month he would never be able to reclaim. "We wasted so much time."

"Then let's not waste any more." She buried her face

against his neck and he felt the hot wetness of her tears. "Do you love me?"

He twisted slightly to face her. "What a stupid question. Of course I love you."

"Then let's not waste any more time," she repeated softly, pulling her shirt over her head.

If he had walked away from her, maybe he could have rebuilt some of his armor. Maybe he could have protected himself a little from the pain of her death.

But he couldn't walk away, and he wouldn't force himself to.

I don't know how much time passed between when I blacked out in Cyrus's bathroom until I woke up in Nathan's bed, but I felt as if I'd aged twenty years. My head throbbed and the faint light in the room seemed to have a personal grudge against me. My muscles were painfully tight, like I'd done a grueling workout without stretching properly. I groaned and my throat felt as though it would crack and bleed, it was so dry.

"You're awake. Thank God."

Nathan. I turned my head and tried to focus, but the light assaulted me. "Where's Cyrus?"

Nathan stroked the back of my hand. "He's on the couch. He woke up a few hours ago, but he's still healing from what she did to him."

"He lived." I took a deep breath, wincing at the soreness in my chest. "Well, that's something."

"Are you okay?" Nathan's voice held an edge of neediness that set my teeth grinding.

Pathetic as ever.

"That wasn't me." It was Cyrus's voice in my head, criticizing Nathan.

"What wasn't?" Nathan sat beside me on the bed. The mattress dipped and the axis of my world twisted.

"Nothing, nothing."

Tell him you can hear me. It will kill him.

I covered my ears. "You shut up!"

Gently, Nathan put his hands on my shoulders, but I barely felt it. "Calm down. It's just the blood tie. Take a deep breath."

This was the blood tie? Oh, I had plenty, and I mean *plenty* of experience with the fledgling end of things, hearing projected thoughts and viewing selected images, maybe even sharing a memory or two. And I'd instinctively shielded my thoughts from both my sires. I didn't realize how crystal clear they would have come through to them.

"Is this what you felt when you accidentally sired me?" I forced my eyes open so I could see Nathan as he answered. At the sight of him, a curl of disgust and shame wound through me. I couldn't tell if it was mine or Cyrus's.

Nathan nodded. "That's how I knew we'd formed a blood tie between us. Your babbling."

"I do not babble," I snapped, raking my hair back from my face.

"You did then." He pointed to the bedside table, where his pet fish had lived before its peaceful demise from old age. "A lot of it was about Shish's tiny goldfish memory span."

"Mmm. That was my pet metaphor for a while." I drew my knees up to my chest and rested my arms on them. "How long have I been out this time?"

"Probably not as long as you think. About twelve hours. And you weren't completely out. When I found you, I was able to rouse you enough to walk to the van. He wasn't as lucky." Nathan looked away. "Why did you do it?"

"I had to." At the memory of Cyrus's wounds, I felt my hands clench to fists. Nathan had saved me in the alley when I'd been damaged beyond repair, but he wouldn't understand this. If it were anyone else but Cyrus, he would know exactly why. "He has information about the Soul Eater."

Nathan shrugged. "We could have found him on our own. So, why?"

Tell him why.

"No." I clutched my pounding head, fingers digging into my skull like daggers.

But Cyrus was relentless. *Tell him I begged you not to. Tell him you took me when I was so close to death it almost killed you. Tell him you'd rather have me than him.*

"He's the same. He's exactly the same." I looked hopelessly to Nathan, but any trace of pity was gone from his face.

With cold resolve, he stood. "This isn't real, Carrie. But it's real enough that I won't sympathize with you over your bad choices."

"Not real?" I asked, hating the plaintive whine in my voice. But he stalked from the room.

I stood to follow him, but I couldn't find the door. That's when I realized I was dreaming. I stumbled, my legs twisting, and fell. Unable to catch myself, I hit the bare wood floor head-on, my face shattering like glass.

Then I woke up.

I gingerly felt my face. Still there, but I was alone. I eased out of bed, every muscle in my body protesting, and stumbled to the dresser for support.

"I packed your bags." Nathan stood in the doorway. His clothes were rumpled and dark circles ringed his eyes.

"Why were you in my dream?" I asked, hating the tremor in my voice.

"I could talk to you there without… Well, it was just safer to discuss what we had to in here." He tapped his temple with his forefinger, stopping midmotion. "I'm your sire. I have a duty to help you when you need it. And you're going to need it. But I didn't trust myself with you. I'm too angry."

My throat constricted. There were so many things I wanted to say, but there was no point. I'd known, I must have known, that Nathan wouldn't just blindly accept this. Cyrus had been a monster. The extent of his cruelty toward Nathan was such that even he didn't know the whole of it.

But I loved Nathan. Things had just become right between us, or at least close to right.

"You fucked it up, Carrie." He read my thoughts as easily as I'd heard Cyrus's in my dream.

Nathan jerked his thumb toward the hallway. "When you're ready, he's in there."

I looked toward my old bedroom. "Is he awake?"

"Has been for a while. I've got him tied down. He's been out of control." Nathan's tone implied he hadn't exactly appreciated having to deal with my problem.

"Thank you." I took a few, wobbling steps forward, forcing myself to ignore the shakiness in my limbs. My clothes, stiff with dried blood, rustled as I moved. I knew Nathan was behind me, and I made a conscious decision not to react when I saw Cyrus. That decision flew right out the window the second I stepped into my room.

Sometime in the night, Nathan had moved my bed up from storage. With the new bookshelves in place, the bed took up the entire floor space, except for a small square near the doorway. It was like a mausoleum crypt, and Cyrus lay on the bed, wide-awake, bungee cords and loops of duct tape securing him there like Hannibal Lecter on his little cart. All he needed was the muzzle.

I gave Nathan a brief, openmouthed look of dismay before rushing to my fledgling's side.

I'd heard that new mothers, after enduring the prolonged pain and exertion of labor, feel oddly detached from their offspring. I'd always thought there must be something profoundly screwed up in these people that they didn't feel an instant connection with the child they'd brought into the world. I could definitely sympathize with them as I knelt beside the bed. All my former notions of Cyrus—John Doe, my sire, a wounded, grieving human— fled. Though the blood tie connected us, he was a stranger. When his cold blue eyes raked over me, I shuddered.

"Why?" His demand scraped from an obviously dry throat.

Rather than answer Cyrus's accusation, I turned to Nathan with one of my own. "You didn't feed him?"

"You're lucky I didn't stake him."

"It's true," Cyrus stated in a voice that was at once chillingly familiar and repulsively alien. "He stood in the doorway for a good twenty minutes, trying to work up the nerve."

He's the same. He's exactly the same. My dream words mocked me with their truth.

"What did you expect, Carrie?" Nathan turned from me, disgusted. "I'll get him some blood. Stay clear of him, in case he breaks free."

"I can get it," I offered, backing away from the bed.

Nathan's tone warned me against arguing. "Stay clear of him."

Stay clear? There wasn't enough room to stay clear of anything. But his warning proved unnecessary. Cyrus didn't struggle. He lay perfectly docile, fixing me with an accusing stare.

I could remain silent only so long. "Listen, Cyrus, I'm—"

"Spare me your self-serving apologies." His voice was flat, emotionless.

Stunned and hurt, I brushed away unexpected tears. "If I hadn't done it, you would have died."

"That crossed my mind, yes." He looked away, up at the ceiling. "If I had died, I could have been with her again. I think I tried to tell you that. In fact, I distinctly remember trying to fight you off."

My stomach churned at the memory of his dying words. "I had to. Not for me. Only you can tell us where your father is." It sounded as lame as it had when I'd said it in my dream. Was that really the reason I'd forced my blood down his throat?

"A brothel in Nevada. Now give me my mortal self back," he snarled, baring his fangs.

I'd never really been afraid of Cyrus before now. When he'd been my sire, I'd feared my reactions to him and what he might manipulate me to do, but I'd never considered he'd physically harm me. He was different now. This Cyrus wouldn't seductively lead me to a destruction of my own making. He'd destroy me outright.

"You know I can't do that," I whispered, my tongue like lead in my mouth. I moved toward the bed, drawn by some strange instinct to be near him.

"Get away from him."

At Nathan's frighteningly calm warning, I turned. That was all it took. Cyrus tore free of his bindings. One arm, empowered by rage and reborn vampire strength, locked around my neck. The other grasped my forehead. He intended to break my neck.

Nathan didn't let it get that far. A stake flew from his hand. It missed Cyrus completely and embedded in the wall. He pulled another from his back pocket and flung it. This one struck Cyrus in the arm. With a sickening crack, the long bones of his forearm separated and he released his hold, screaming.

I dropped to the floor, my head spinning from shock and the force of Cyrus's hatred rocking through me. Nathan pinned him to the bed, a knee in his chest.

"Just like old times, Nolen?" Cyrus laughed. "I remember you liked it rough."

I squeezed my eyes shut tight. There was a thud, like someone dropping a side of beef onto wet pavement, and Cyrus was silent.

Nathan stood over me, nursing his sore fist. "Why did you do it?"

"I couldn't let him die." The admission came from numb lips. It hurt, but the pain was distant. "I still…"

Nathan was silent for a moment, considering. When he spoke again, I wished I hadn't heard him. "Get out."

"What?" The shock and hurt were almost overwhelming. But what had I expected? That he would welcome Cyrus into his home with open arms? "I don't have anywhere to go. You know that."

"And you knew it before you turned him. That means you made an informed decision." Nathan turned away from me, and when he did I felt the blood tie between us seal shut.

I tried a new tactic. "If we leave, where do you think he'll go? He's going to end up with his father again. Maybe I will, too."

Nathan seemed to consider this a moment. No matter how he tried to block it, I felt his panic and his primal need to protect me—his fledgling, not his pseudo girlfriend— from his sire. After a long moment, he sighed wearily and gestured to the stake jutting from Cyrus's arm. "Get me the medical kit. It's in the living room."

It certainly wasn't the reaction I was expecting from him. I stumbled out and retrieved the heavy red toolbox that contained our medical supplies.

When I brought it to Nathan, he didn't bother with so much as a thank-you. He focused solely on Cyrus, who twisted in pain on the bed as he slowly came to some watered-down form of consciousness. "You're going to be all right. Hold on a minute and we'll take care of the pain."

Throwing me a worried look, Nathan filled a syringe with a local anesthetic. "This is going to need stitching. Can you do it?"

I wanted to say, *Can you refrain from embedding more projectiles in my fledgling?* Instead, I folded my arms across my chest, tightening them to hold in my anger. "Do you have a needle driver?"

Nathan made a sustained suspense noise as he dug through the tool kit, then pulled out the shiny, scissorslike implement. "This?"

"Yes. I need to go wash my hands." When he rolled his eyes, I threw up my arms helplessly. "It's a habit. My parents didn't spend the better part of their stock earnings putting me through med school for me to just *forget* simple sanitary precautions."

It would also give me some time to get my head together. I'd expected Nathan to be difficult about this whole situation. I loved him, but I wasn't living under the delusion that he was abnormally selfless and cooperative. Still, a part of me had held out hope that this wouldn't destroy any slim chance we had together.

It couldn't be over. Not because of this.

And yet, did I really care? I had Cyrus.

I knew it.

Firmly, I shoved the thought—mine and his—from my mind. I didn't *have* Cyrus. He was my fledgling, and I had a duty to do by him, and that was it. At least I thought I had a duty toward him. I wasn't exactly sure what a sire was supposed to do. Cyrus had manipulated and tortured me. Nathan had given me a place to live and protection from the numerous dangers of an undead life. It seemed as if I should try and do the latter, not the former.

At the same time, I understood the seductive power I held. Cyrus had abused the blood tie, and now I had the opportunity for the sweetest kind of revenge—to give him a taste of what he'd done to me. And I understood, too, why he'd done it. Because he could. Because the ability was there.

I dried my hands and returned. Nathan stood silently outside the door: Cyrus lay on the bed, seemingly unaffected by the fact that he was bleeding all over the place. Nathan had a dark look on his face, but I ignored it and set to my task, still able to go on autopilot months after abandoning my medical career.

And oddly, as I worked, Nathan's feelings of anger subsided, giving way to…pity?

You pity him? What, I'm the big, mean sire and you're on his side now? I made a face and blocked the resentment I felt from flowing through our tie.

I'm not on his side. There aren't any sides.

I looked up at Nathan. He stepped into the room, his arms crossed as he watched me repair Cyrus's wounds.

Pursing my lips, I looked back to my work. *You act like you're more worried about him than I am.*

Right now, focusing on him is all that's keeping me from walking out of here. Nathan handed me a clean towel so I could wipe away some of the blood.

You're supposed to hate him. I clipped the thread and moved on to the next site that needed my attention.

I know what he's going through.

I didn't need to ask what Nathan meant. He'd become a vampire against his will, just as I'd made Cyrus a vampire against *his* will.

Nathan gave me a pointed look and went to his bedroom.

I finished my work in stony silence. Occasionally, I glanced at Cyrus, to find him staring with grim fascination at the needle sliding through his flesh. My arms broke out in goose bumps. I'd seen that expression on him before. In his vampire days, when pain—it didn't matter whose— gave him satisfaction unmatched by anything else in his life. I avoided looking at him again.

When Cyrus was patched up, I didn't bother to tie him again. He was angry, but not stupid, and he'd been a vampire long enough in the past to know his limits in the present. We heal, but it takes time. He wouldn't be able to effectively attack again tonight.

I washed up and went to Nathan's bedroom. He lay on the bed, a book in his hands, but his thoughts were so jumbled I knew he couldn't possibly be reading. "A little early to turn in, don't you think?" I tried to make my tone light. I failed miserably.

He looked up, said nothing, and returned his gaze to the page.

The argument hadn't even begun, and I *so* didn't want to be at the shrieking point yet, but I couldn't control myself. "He knows where the Soul Eater is! We need him!"

"Oh, come on, Carrie!" Nathan tossed the book angrily

aside and threw the covers back, swinging his feet to the floor. "We could have found the Soul Eater on our own and you know it!"

"No, I didn't!" I stalked toward the living room, then remembered Cyrus was in the apartment, and slammed the door instead. Lowering my voice so he wouldn't be able to hear me as easily, I advanced on Nathan, jabbing my finger at him accusingly. "We can't use your blood tie to find him, we've been over and over this! You could become possessed again. He could find you and then be one step closer to completing his ritual. As usual, I had to make the choice between doing something easy or doing something that was going to screw up my life! That's what it always comes down to, and I'm sick of it because it's not fair! But it's just how things happen."

With shocking speed, Nathan seized my wrist. "Not fair is having the guy who sodomized you and bled you dry, while your wife lay dying not two feet away, sleeping down the hall."

"Gee, and just a few minutes ago, you sympathized with him." I jerked against his hold. "Let go of me!"

Nathan growled a warning, his face flashing to vampire form, but he released my arm. I rubbed my wrist as he stalked toward the door. "Where are you going?"

"To the shop," he barked.

I glanced at the clock. It was only a few hours until sunup. "What for?"

He disappeared from view at the end of the hall, and I heard his keys jingle. "For the day."

The slam of the door punctuated his statement.

I spent the day in the bedroom with the door locked, but I wasn't able to sleep. Alternating between my anger toward Nathan and my fear that Cyrus would burst in and stake me while I slept, I watched the light behind the blinds grow stronger and brighter.

Once, a knock on the door startled me out of a light sleep. I threw back the covers and stood, calling, "Nathan?" before I realized he couldn't have come back upstairs without first walking through broad daylight.

"No." Cyrus's voice was uncharacteristically timid. "Are you all right?"

Let me in.

"I can hear your thoughts," I told him. "You know that." My palms itched to open the door, but I didn't know what his intent was. Why didn't I tie him back up? My reasoning that I would be safe and secure while he healed seemed insubstantial now.

"I know. I want to be near you." I heard him swallow a sound of disgust, even through the door. "Never mind."

A vision of Cyrus and me lying beside each other in bed, not in a sexual embrace but a comforting one, assembled in my mind. It took me a moment to realize I hadn't dreamed it up on my own. It came from him.

I listened to his footsteps retreat down the hall as I stood with my palm against the cool wood of the door, pretending I could feel him on the other side.

Twelve: Back to Not Normal

The nights after Cyrus's rebirth into vampire form were almost unbearable. After my first and only rejection of him, Cyrus became even more sullen and difficult. When he wasn't verbally antagonizing me, he abused the blood tie to his advantage, sending graphic visions of us performing lurid acts. The first few days I could tolerate it. After a while, the joke—and my resolve to resist him—wore thin.

Nathan came back to the apartment. I didn't kid myself that it was because he'd forgiven me. There wasn't a bed in the storage room of the bookshop anymore, and the floor probably wasn't very comfortable. We barely spoke, and with Cyrus equally frosty, I found the apartment a chilly place to be, indeed.

Not to mention the fact that, after countless hours of research, we hadn't gotten any more information about the Soul Eater and what he might be up to with the Oracle. I'd called the brothel the Soul Eater had supposedly been staying at. That is to say, I called the only brothel it made sense for him to be staying at. I wasn't entirely surprised to find that March's phone number no longer existed and her establishment had been removed from the list of licensed brothels in Nevada.

"They're not going to stay put, waiting for someone to come find them," Cyrus had said, an edge of taunting in his voice. "Unless you want to waste another week visiting the desert?"

And I didn't. Neither did Nathan. Though we agreed on little else, we knew that the Soul Eater moved around too much to justify going after him. And that he moved much faster than we could.

If the Soul Eater didn't want to be found, we wouldn't find him. And I had the distinct impression that when he wanted to, he would come to us.

"I've run out of ideas," I complained to Nathan as I sat beside him on his bed one morning. We hadn't made up after our fight, but for the time being we were politely ignoring the spat. It seemed he wouldn't be tempted to even consider making amends. It would probably be only a matter of time and defeating the Soul Eater before he kicked Cyrus and me onto the street.

Nathan laid his book on his chest—he would often read until I'd gone to bed, probably to avoid talking to me—and rubbed his eyes. "Don't worry about it now. It's been a long night."

"Well, I am worried about it, as we have a finite amount of time before Max and Bella find the Oracle."

Max had called that evening to update us on their status. They would reach Danvers by sunup, install themselves at a base of operations and begin networking.

Nathan agreed that it wouldn't be long before the Oracle's minions sought them out.

Nathan sighed. "I'm aware of the time issue, Carrie. But there's nothing we can do about it right now."

With a grunt of utter annoyance, I rolled onto my side so I wouldn't have to look at him. My mind wouldn't settle down, though, racing to every dead end it had already visited ad nauseum. "What about Dahlia?"

"What about her?" Nathan's voice held that weary, just-drop-it-already tone he'd perfected. "She'll kill you, and we certainly don't want her around Cyrus."

Stop talking about me like I'm not right down the hall.

I pushed Cyrus's thoughts out of my mind.

"I know. Maybe I could break in. Or something." To Cyrus, I asked, *Do you have any ideas?*

What about Clarence? Cyrus's voice echoed through my head. *He helped you betray me, and I know for a fact he cared even less for Dahlia. At least, he did when I was around.*

"That's a thought," I murmured out loud, accidentally.

"What's a thought?" Nathan tried to sound bored and disinterested, but I still had a blood tie to him, as well. His annoyance and his jealousy, which had been radiating off him in waves since I'd turned Cyrus, spiked.

"Nothing." I waved a hand dismissively, but a mean, antagonistic part of me added, "It was supposed to be mental."

He closed his eyes and his brow creased in frustration. For a second I expected an angry outburst. Cyrus must have felt my fear, because a deeply protective vibe thundered through the blood tie. The role reversal startled me. I never thought I'd see the day when Cyrus cared if I lived or died.

But Nathan didn't lose it. He opened his eyes and looked at me, really looked at me for the first time in days. "I hate this."

Before I could ask what he meant, he went on. "I hate that he's in your head again. Actually, I didn't really hate it before. But I do now."

For some reason, his admission stung. "You didn't care that he was my sire when we first met?"

Nathan shrugged. "No. It was a bit of a relief."

"Not for me. As I recall, you threatened to kill me." Some of the tension seemed to ease between us, but I tread carefully. "Why does it bother you now?"

"Because I know you loved him." He made it sound so definite, so matter-of-fact.

Even I couldn't have said it without immediately following it up with a qualifier like "in a way" or "sorta."

Is that true? Did you love me?

I put Cyrus off for a moment. "Do you think I chose him over you? Is that what all this is about?"

"How could it be about anything else?" Nathan smiled sadly. "I can't offer you unswerving devotion. I can't give you all of my heart. Not after this. But I don't want to lose you, either."

"Well, you can't really have me, can you? If you're not willing to give me something in return?" I wanted to reach out to him, to touch him, because that always seemed to make everything all better. But it would be a lie. "You're not going to lose me. Cyrus is…different now. He doesn't need me."

Don't be so sure….

"He doesn't need me," I repeated, for myself, for him.

"I think that was what made him so endearing before. Despite all the manipulation and torture, he really needed someone to love him. He's had that now, and he won't want the brand of love I can give him."

And what is that?

"And what brand is that?" Nathan echoed Cyrus's telepathic question.

I made sure to leave my link to my fledgling wide open as I spoke. "The false kind. The pitying kind."

Sweet girl.

Nathan smiled. "The type you think I'm giving you."

"Maybe it's what I'm giving you," I suggested, not unkindly. "In any case, he doesn't want me the way he did then, so he won't pursue me as he did before."

And I wouldn't be tempted the way I had been then, because I wouldn't want the secondhand, watered-down kind of love he could offer me, if he did see fit to do so.

I wouldn't be the next best thing to yet another lost love.

Nathan had heard the unspoken portion of my statement. "Then why do you want mine?"

Why did I? I'd been attracted to Nathan from the moment I'd met him. I'd been infatuated with his devotion to his mysterious dead wife and unofficially adopted son. Then he'd become my sire, and that brought its own kind of feeling. But why did I love Nathan?

I opened my mouth cautiously, not sure what would come out. "Because I see the way you loved Marianne. I see the way Cyrus loved Mouse. And I wonder…" My unexpected sob interrupted my words. "I wonder if someone could ever love me that way."

Wordlessly, he pulled me into his arms.

I couldn't stop crying. Although I considered myself pretty much in touch with my feelings, there was obviously one emotional area I'd boarded up. Now, all my frustration and pain crashed through the barrier I'd erected, and I couldn't hold it back any longer.

Someone could love you that way. I would have, if you'd given me the chance. Cyrus's thoughts stung me with a barrage of images, of moments that had never occurred between us. Lying with him in his big bed at the mansion, my lips curved in a contented smile as he held me. Cyrus watching me with pride as I moved gracefully across the ballroom, the picture of beauty and elegance in a couture gown. The same gown in a rumpled heap on the floor as I climbed into bed with an unidentified young man, then a flash of his dead eyes as I feasted from his throat.

Gagging, I sat up.

"Carrie, what's wrong?" Nathan went from comforting to urgently protective in a split second.

Tell him, Carrie. Tell him what's wrong.

Blood running in rivulets from my scarlet-stained mouth, flowing down my neck, between my breasts. Cyrus's cold hands on my shoulders, his rough tongue lapping the blood off my skin.

"No!" I clutched my head, desperate to make the visions stop, but terrified Nathan would guess the root of the problem and harm Cyrus in some way.

He did guess, but instead of tearing to the living room and ripping Cyrus to pieces, he gripped my shoulders and shook me gently. "Come on, Carrie, you can stop him. You're in control. Just concentrate and shut him out."

I'd had plenty of practice switching the blood tie between Nathan and me on and off. It turned out to be much easier from the sire's side of things. I took deep, metered breaths and mentally constructed a brick wall. Nathan had once suggested a bubble of white light, but I preferred my creative visualization more heavily fortified. I was relieved when Cyrus's barrage of hateful images faded, then disappeared altogether.

"What did he show to you?" Nathan's brow creased in concern, the kind he routinely exhibited before he completely lost his mind in anger.

There was no way I was going to admit to him what had happened, not when he'd almost chopped Cyrus apart in the past. "I'll take care of it tomorrow."

He gazed at me as though I might lose it again at any moment. "Are you sure?"

I nodded and gave what I hoped was a reassuring smile. "Yeah. Just…hold me?"

Nathan stroked my hair as we lay close together beneath the covers. Whether he thought I was asleep or not I couldn't be certain, but after a long, long time he kissed my ear and whispered, "I'm sorry we fought, sweetheart. That doesn't mean I'm not right, but I'm sorry we're in this again."

I drifted to sleep with a bittersweet smile on my face and my head blessedly empty of horrors.

I woke to hands on my breasts, my stomach, dipping between my legs. I smiled against lips that pressed to mine, and

I stretched, slowly and lazily, enjoying the attention. Winding my arms around Nathan's neck, I moved against him so his cold, firm body was flush to mine.

He guided my leg over his hip, his thick cock hard and eager against my sex. I was wet and ready for him, so he slipped into me easily, and I cried out at the intense pleasure of it. His fingers traced shivering trails down my arms, up my neck.

Another set of hands slid between our bodies. My eyes flew open and I shrieked in alarm.

Nathan smiled, seemingly unperturbed that another person was in bed with us. Cold flesh brushed my back, and I craned my neck to find Cyrus there, his body curved to mine. As he teased my intimate flesh with his hands, he gave me the same knowing smile I'd seen on Nathan's face. I leaned against Cyrus, eyes sliding closed with the pleasure.

This is wrong, my brain screamed. *This can't be happening.*

But it wasn't happening. It was a trick, a dream.

It felt so real.

I opened my eyes and glanced down to where Nathan slid in and out of me. Cyrus's fingers bracketed Nathan's cock, slick with my secretions, and Nathan buried his face in my neck with a groan. I felt his features change against my skin, and his fangs pricked me tentatively. Cyrus's erection prodded my backside as his fingers danced wickedly over my flesh. The pressure in my tortured body grew almost unbearable. I begged mindlessly, held Nathan's mouth to my neck. Cyrus guided his cock to my ass and pushed inside as Nathan's fangs pierced my neck.

I cried out in surprise at the discomfort and fullness of Cyrus's entry, but his skilled assault on my intimate flesh, coupled with Nathan's mouth drawing at my neck and his cock pumping inside me, drove me over the edge. Impaled between them, I screamed in release.

My eyes snapped open. Though I was alone in the bed, my body throbbed from the ecstasy of the dream, and the wetness between my legs testified to the very real physical effect it'd had on me. I rolled over, pushing sweat-damp hair from my forehead, and grabbed the note Nathan had left on his pillow: "Working. Nathan."

I went to the kitchen and put on the kettle, adding enough blood for Nathan and me. I would take it to him downstairs and lend him a hand in the shop, whether he needed it or not. Anything to strengthen the fragile peace between us and get me away from my perverted fledgling.

As the blood heated, I forced myself to ignore the contents of the dream. Of course, Cyrus had sent it, torturing me by day the way he assaulted me during the night. What had prompted this ruthless return of the man who'd tortured and abused me four months ago? He'd claimed his time with Mouse had saved him, yet he'd reverted to his old ways as if I'd flipped a switch when I'd changed him. Was it the simple state of being undead that made vampires go bad? Or was it just Cyrus?

Or was it me? When he'd been my sire, it had been his blood that tempted me to self-destruction. Was it *my* blood that brought out the worst in him now?

Wisps of steam had just begun to rise from the kettle's

spout when Cyrus ambled in from the living room, loose limbed and relaxed, clad in nothing but linen pajama bottoms. "That lovely mental interlude and breakfast? I'm flattered."

"It's not for you," I snapped, removing the kettle from the heat.

"So it's starvation then? Until I behave?" He stood behind me, too close, his lips brushing my ear as he spoke. "I'd rather hoped it would be a more physical form of punishment."

I elbowed him in the gut. He'd tensed for the blow, but still doubled over.

"Don't ever touch me again!" I grabbed the nearest available weapon, a barbecue fork, from the hanging rack on the cupboard door, and brandished it menacingly.

Instantly, the old Cyrus fled. Reformed, mortal Cyrus stood in his place, his hands up in a protective stance. "Carrie, I was only teasing."

"It's not just teasing. You invaded my mind, you put perverse thoughts in it—"

"*I* put perverse thoughts in it?" He shook his head. "No. I was the one woken this morning by *your* lewd fantasies."

Oh. No. "That's crazy. There is no way I would ever—"

He nodded patiently. "And do you think I would ever? Have I ever wanted to share you with him? Have I ever tolerated the thought of his hands on you? Do you think I would do it now?" Smiling a little cruelly, he wagged a finger at me in admonition. "I may be a bit twisted, but I can't be blamed for what's lurking in your head. You were the tormentor with that dream, not me."

Legs shaking, I stumbled to the kitchen table. Cyrus pulled out a chair for me and I sat, careful not to brush against him as I did so. "That's impossible. I would never…do those things."

"I know that's not true. You did some of it with me." I heard his intake of breath and he apologized hastily. "I'm sorry, I had no right—"

"You know what I meant," I interrupted, not wanting to dwell on the past, specifically the sordid things I'd done with him. "I would never ask Nathan to… I would just never."

Cyrus poured me a mug of blood and sat opposite me, looking genuinely sympathetic. "You don't need to explain. It's your subconscious doing this to you."

"I subconsciously want a three-way with you and Nathan?"

He rolled his eyes. "Listen, if you don't want my help, say so. But don't go on like this, angry with me for being in your dream. Against my will, I might add."

I sighed and dropped my head to the table. "Sorry. Stay."

He touched my hair hesitantly, cupping the back of my skull with his palm and flexing his fingers in a friendly, comforting motion. "Don't despair. I'm sure it's difficult, being blood tied to two men you've had relationships with."

I sat up, smoothing my hair back. "No matter how sick those relationships were."

"I'd drink to that, if I had anything to drink." He smiled as I slid my mug toward him. "Good to see you're not above sharing breakfast with me."

"What can I say? I've got a weak spot when it comes to you." I thought of Nathan in the shop, and worried he might have seen the dream, too.

Not to worry, Dotair, I tuned it out. His thoughts were uncomfortable, but not unkind. He apparently understood I had no control over my dreams, so why couldn't *I* get it?

"So, still planning to see Dahlia?" Cyrus swirled the mug a bit and dipped his pinkie in to pull out a still-congealed clot. "You could have left this on a bit longer."

I made a face and took my cup back. "We already know she has information we can use. Probably more than you've already gotten from her."

"Good luck getting it." He sounded weary, as though if he never heard her name again it would be too soon. "You'd almost have to learn to read minds. Or get her very drunk. She does ramble on when she's had too much to drink."

"The flaw in that plan is she's hardly going to go out bar hopping with me. Or you." I chewed my thumbnail as I thought.

"No," Cyrus agreed. "Our last rendezvous didn't go very well at all."

I drummed my fingers on the tabletop. "Do you think Clarence will help me if I asked?"

Cyrus blew out a long breath. "If you can find him, he might."

"Well, where did he go when he worked for you? What were his habits?" I vaguely remembered he was allowed to come and go from the mansion, but where exactly he went or came from I had no idea. "Did he buy groceries or something?"

"No. Food for the guards and pets was delivered by vendors." Cyrus's brow creased in thought. "I did send him to shop for my favorites and to get my chocolates. And all the little extras I might find myself in need of."

"I'd hate to ask." I took a sip of blood.

Cyrus shrugged. "Coercion items. Alcohol for the girls, indecent magazines for the boys."

"I *didn't* ask. I just said I would hate to." Pinching the bridge of my nose, I closed my eyes. "What would Dahlia have him do?"

"Dig up corpses for spare parts," Cyrus snorted.

"If that's all the help you're going to be—"

"Here's a thought," he interrupted. "Why not wait a discreet distance from the mansion and find out where he goes?"

It made sense. Cyrus didn't have to use such a smart-assed tone, but it made sense. "Fine." I glanced at the clock. "Well, there's no time like the present."

He followed me when I stood and took the mug to the sink. "Why don't you let me come with you?"

"Do you think that's wise?" I arched an eyebrow. "I mean, what with Clarence thinking you're dead and all?"

"Why wouldn't it be?" Cyrus looked as though he truly didn't understand the effect such a shock could have on a mortal human being. "Believe me, Carrie, he's familiar with the paranormal."

I considered. It probably did make more sense to take him with me than leave him behind with Nathan. God knew what could happen.

"Fine. But you're staying in the car."

I dressed and took Nathan his breakfast while Cyrus got ready—he took the longest showers of anyone I'd ever met—so I could discuss the plan with Nathan alone.

"Mmm, O negative," Nathan murmured appreciatively after a long sip. "To what do I owe this treat?"

I smiled, swallowing the sudden knot in my throat. "Cyrus and I are going to find Clarence."

"By yourselves?" From his tone of voice it was clear Nathan was trying to be nonchalant. He failed miserably.

I let him have his delusion of fooling me. "Is that a problem?"

"Maybe." He straightened when the bells above the door jingled, and gave a wave to the customer who entered.

I waited until the man disappeared behind a bookshelf to clear my throat and recapture Nathan's attention. "So, is it a problem?"

"A bit," he answered, keeping his eye on the shop. "That's a dangerous part of town."

It's not, I shot back mentally. *Nathan, stop treating me like a teenage girl who can't be trusted with her boyfriend.*

After your dream this morning? He glared at me as he thought it.

"Well, I'm not going alone," I reminded him, trying to keep my voice light for the sake of our charade. The customer's shoes scuffed on the floor. Humans might not be aware of the blood tie, but they were certainly aware of the tension it created. "I'll be going with Cyrus."

"Oh, that's right." *And who's going to protect you from him?*

I rolled my eyes. "That's right." *I don't need protecting from him. He's my fledgling. And I'm not going to do anything stupid.*

That doesn't mean he won't try *something stupid. At least take a stake with you.* "Have a good time."

I snorted. "Yeah, a good time."

The customer came to the register with a book on summoning spirits, and I quickly made my exit while Nathan was too busy to argue.

When I got upstairs, Cyrus was in his room, probably still getting ready. I considered what Nathan had said, that I should arm myself when alone with Cyrus. Though I doubted my fledgling—wow, that was still weird—would try anything, I admitted to myself it would be stupid to blindly trust him. I slid open the door to the closet that contained Nathan's weapons and pulled a crudely carved stake from the duffel bag on the floor.

"What are you doing?" Cyrus sounded curious and amused, but his face fell when his gaze dropped to the stake in my hand. "Oh."

"It's nothing p-personal," I stammered. Sighing, I dropped the stake back into the bag. "It is. I'm sorry. Nathan just thought…"

With a rueful chuckle, Cyrus nodded. "Of course."

I shifted my weight from foot to foot. The moment was painfully, stiflingly awkward. "It's just, when you were a vampire before—"

"Stop!" Through the blood tie, his shame and anger washed over me. "It will never be enough for you, will it?"

"What?" My fingers itched for the stake. Not that I

would be able to use it against him. The thought of killing my own blood sickened me. Still, it would have been a comfort to have some means of self-defense. "What will never be enough?"

"Anything I ever do. You're always going to see me as the monster who attacked you that night in the morgue, the vampire who manipulated and degraded you. But I was a man since then, Carrie, a good man. And now I'm your fledgling. Anything I'm capable of doing now, it's because of you." He clenched his fists impotently at his sides.

I looked away. "And if I did to you what you've done to me, you wouldn't trust me, either."

I heard his footfalls on the floor as he came closer. When I looked up, his face was a breath from mine. My heart pounded with uncertainty as he leaned closer. "If I wanted to kill you, I could do it anytime. We wouldn't have to be alone." His voice was a deadly whisper. "And you *did* do to me what I did to you."

He stepped around me, and I swallowed hard.

"I'll meet you in the van." His words were clipped and he left no room for another feeble apology from me, slamming the door resolutely to punctuate his sentence.

I sagged against the wall, willing all the tension from my body. Then I realized it wasn't *my* agitation, but Cyrus's. I closed my eyes, my chest aching with the knowledge that I'd hurt him.

Still, before I went to the car, I slipped a stake into my purse, just in case.

Thirteen: Triangle

"That's him, it has to be."

I ignored Cyrus's declaration of certainty. He'd spotted Clarence at least five times since we'd parked a discreet distance from the mansion.

"That's not him." I barely had to open my eyes to tell. "What is the matter with you? Did you never look at the man?"

"I looked at him," Cyrus admitted a little sheepishly. "But not often."

"Because you're a stuck-up, imperialistic bastard." I leaned my head back and closed my eyes. It wasn't because I hadn't had enough sleep. It just made it easier to ignore Cyrus if I could pretend to be unconscious.

The dream had really screwed up my head. Even he, shameless though he was, felt it. Now that I was blood tied to him again, the old attraction returned with a vengeance. But it hadn't ever really gone away. I suppose it had just lain dormant during his brief stint of humanity.

There was no chance of a return to that relationship. I

loved Nathan, and he almost loved me—at least he had until I'd fucked that up again. Even if we weren't on the best of terms, sleeping with Cyrus would be a slap in Nathan's face.

Cyrus looked more petulant by the minute. "Why not let me go in and speak with Dahlia on my own?"

"Because she filleted you the last time you were alone together and…" I blinked. "You're just trying to get sex from anyone, aren't you?"

"Well, someone has been bombarding me with pornographic dreams." He pointed down the street. "That's him!"

"It's not him. That man is six feet tall at least, and probably twenty years younger than Clarence."

"At least," Cyrus repeated, giving me an unreadable look. "I'm sorry, he just looked so similar."

"Why? Because he's black?" Of course I'd have to sire a white supremacist.

"Because it's dark and I can't see that well. Apparently, losing both eyes in a past incarnation has that effect." He raised his hands helplessly. "I'm as surprised as you."

"We should get you some glasses," I mused, scanning the sidewalk. "That's him!"

I could tell by the way the figure hunched over and kept close to the wall. His clothing was anachronistic to say the least—in the mansion, he didn't seem out of place when paired with antique furnishings, but on the street he looked positively Victorian—and he scurried like a spider toward the house.

"That *is* him," Cyrus observed. "I never realized how very strange he looked."

"You stay here," I commanded, pushing open the door. "I'll be back."

I didn't give him a chance to argue before I slammed the door. Clarence had nearly reached the gate to the servants' lodgings, and I had to jog to catch up with him.

"Clarence!" When I called his name, it was as if a shock went through him. He saw me, and for a moment I thought he would bolt. Something in his servant's nature seemed to stop him, and he waited patiently until I reached him.

"Doctor, what are you doing here? Are you trying to get killed?" He cast a worried glance at the house. "She's out of her head over something you did. I can't tell what, but she is not happy."

"That's why I'm here," I explained. "I need to speak to her."

Clarence's deep brown eyes widened. "Didn't you hear what I said? She'll kill you. She's been ranting and raving and doing God knows what. If you go into that house, you're dumber than I thought you were."

I ignored the implication that he'd apparently thought I was dumb before. "That's why I need your help."

"What kind of help?" He eyed me suspiciously. Then the meaning became clear as glass, and he started to turn away.

"No, I don't want you to kill her! Just waylay her a little bit. Cyrus said—"

"Cyrus?" His voice leaped with fear. "He died."

"He's back now." I wasn't supposed to let that slip. I might as well have let Cyrus spring out at Clarence in full vampire face. But then, maybe someone coming back from the dead wasn't that weird to him. After all, he did work for vampires. He'd probably seen worse.

"He can't come back *here*." Clarence shook his head as though his denial could stop it.

"I hope he doesn't." This could be a bargaining tool. If Clarence feared Cyrus… "It's really Cyrus who's sent me to do this. He wants to know how Dahlia is involved with the Soul Eater."

A visible shudder went through him. "They're tangled up. I don't know how."

"Maybe you could help me figure it out. It might keep Cyrus from coming back to find out for himself." I wielded the name like a weapon.

Clarence saw through the ploy. "You can't keep him from doing anything. Don't even try to play that hand."

I'd always underestimated this man. "How about the 'I'm your friend, you should help me' card?"

He laughed. "How about you ain't my friend and why don't you come back when you've got something to bargain with?"

He moved toward the gate, and I stepped forward as if to stop him with a hand on his shoulder.

Bad move.

He whirled before I could lay my palm on him, his eyes flashing rage. "Vampires don't ever get to touch me."

I remembered the second night I'd spent in Cyrus's house, when Clarence had displayed his scars from a past attack. I should have remembered.

He walked into the shadows between the stone columns, and the gate began to creak closed. I thought it was a lost cause, until his voice drifted back to me from the darkness. "I know how to take care of myself. And your friend up there. You come back tomorrow night, you'll get your answers."

I stood on the sidewalk, my mouth gaping like a carp's. "So, you'll help?"

"I won't repeat myself!" he snapped. I heard his quick steps up the paved drive, and turned toward the car.

Cyrus stood on the sidewalk, his arms folded arrogantly over his chest. "That went well."

"Get in the car before I run you over with it." What the hell did Clarence mean, that I'd get my answers?

Cyrus was quiet on the ride home, but he kept his smug smile. I parallel parked in front of the building, then turned to him to ask what his problem was. That was a big mistake. He lunged—no, more like launched himself—across the car, and I found myself pinned between the door and his body.

"What the hell are you—" My outrage was smothered beneath his lips. I was too shocked to fight him.

He pulled back and smoothed my hair from my face. "You still have feelings for me. You wouldn't have had that dream—"

"It was just a dream!" I insisted. "You know, those pictures in your head you can't control?"

"That come from your subconscious and betray your deepest desires?" He paused. "And fears. Do you still fear me, Carrie?"

A thrill of frightened excitement raced up my spine. "No. I don't fear you."

"You're lying."

He was coming in for another kiss when the door behind my back released. I tumbled onto the sidewalk in a heap. My head collided painfully with the concrete and bursts of light blurred my vision.

Before I could register what had happened, Cyrus exited the car as well, clearly not under his own power. I heard him offer up a feeble excuse—or was that an apology?—then he was silenced by the dull snap of flesh pounding flesh.

I struggled to my feet. I must have bitten my tongue in the fall, because I tasted blood. My vision cleared as I swayed in place, and I saw Cyrus pinned to the raw brick of the building, with Nathan's thick forearm across his throat. Nathan's fist connected with Cyrus's nose, and a sickening wet snap crack through the air.

I stood transfixed by the sight of Nathan losing control, lashing out. I'd never seen him like this, even when he'd been fighting Cyrus for my life. Cyrus's eyes rolled back in his head and he slumped in Nathan's grasp.

The pain in my head was unbearable. Cyrus's bleak thoughts entwined with my own dread, and I screamed at Nathan to stop. I hated the pleading in my tone, but I would have bargained, offered anything, to keep him from hurting Cyrus further.

On my knees, I wept and begged for his life. For Cyrus, the man who'd tortured and abused me, who'd wanted to kill me, who'd sent my heart like takeout to his deranged father.

A change came over Nathan. He released Cyrus, letting him slide to the ground, unconscious. Nathan's face held a mix of emotions, and for a second I thought he felt real remorse for his actions. It disappeared as he came nearer and seized my upper arm, his fingers digging into my flesh.

He dragged me toward the door and I resisted, unwilling to leave Cyrus behind. My legs twisted and I couldn't get on my feet as Nathan hauled me up the stairs, every step digging painfully into my back when I slipped and fell. I finally stopped resisting, letting him pull me into the bedroom. He shoved me through the door and slammed it shut. I yanked on the knob, but Nathan held it from the other side.

My reason fled. I needed to get to Cyrus. The certainty that if I didn't get to him, if I didn't protect him, he would die, consumed me. "Let me out!"

He didn't answer.

"Nathan, let me go to him! He'll die out there!"

"Let him burn!" I heard the floorboards creak as he settled with his back to the door.

I've never felt more helpless than I did at that moment. It was terrifying to me that my hands were tied while my fledgling lay defenseless on the street. My frustration exploded from me in a series of cruel accusations—that Nathan didn't care for me, that he was incapable of caring for anyone, that he would let Cyrus die the way he'd let Ziggy die, the way he'd let Marianne die.

Though I knew the effect my words would have on both of us, I couldn't stop them from coming. I couldn't even summon the strength to apologize for them. Until that moment, I'd thought I understood the power of the blood tie. I'd grossly underestimated it, and found myself destroying my relationship with my own sire in an effort to protect my fledgling. And there was no doubt in my mind that destruction was absolute.

Nathan remained silent on the other side of the door, but I could feel his rage as I gave one final, futile shove. There was no strength left in me, so I lay on the floor, drifting in and out of sleep, until I woke enough to realize time had passed. The door was open. Nathan was gone.

It was still dark out. I checked the clock in the kitchen and saw it wasn't long until sunup. There was still time for Cyrus. I jerked the door open and was about to tear down the stairs when I saw the note taped there for me to find: "Check your room."

There were no other words, no explanation of where Nathan was or what his intentions were. I went to my room and stood in the doorway. Cyrus lay on the bed, on top of the tangled covers, his bloodstained clothes twisted on his body. His face was wiped clean, but the damage Nathan had inflicted would take more than a day to heal.

Nathan had done this. He'd done it to hurt me, to hurt Cyrus. He'd done it to ease some murderous need for vengeance in himself, without thought for how it would affect anyone else. I was torn between rage and admiration. I'd been waiting for so long to see Nathan act on his volatile emotions after repressing them for so long. My only regret was that he'd acted out on my fledgling.

My only regret is that he isn't waiting on the corner for the sun to come out and burn him to a crisp. He has no moral compass. Cyrus opened one swollen eye in an attempt to punctuate his thought with a matching sarcastic expression, but the motion made him whimper. He was so pathetic, I couldn't help but pity him.

The part of me that was Cyrus's sire agreed with him. I

wanted to feel badly for the things I'd said to Nathan, but all I could think was how he'd separated me from my fledgling, and how would he feel if someone beat me and left me on the sidewalk to die? I eased into the small space between the door and the foot of the bed and knelt beside Cyrus.

I don't want your pity. His voice filled my head again.

I pulled off his shoes and socks, and he wiggled his toes gratefully. "I know you don't," I said with a smile. "But you're my fledgling. I've got to look out for you."

He reached for the button of his fly and I pushed his hands away to do it for him. "Let me take care of you, okay?"

Thank you. He clasped my hand briefly, then sagged against the pillows. I think he might have lost consciousness again.

I finished stripping him of his blood-stiffened clothes and drew the covers over both of us as I maneuvered myself beside him on the tiny bed. I kissed his forehead and stroked his hair, feeling nothing but absolute, unconditional love for him.

The floorboards in the hallway creaked, and I looked up to see Nathan watching us. He didn't apologize in words, but the look on his face told me everything I needed to know. He felt remorse for his actions, and that remorse sapped much of my anger.

He gestured toward Cyrus like someone swatting a fly. "That's how I feel about you, you know."

"No. I didn't." I turned back to Cyrus and let all my relief at his survival and my love toward him—some of it residual from the time I actually did love him—cross the blood tie to Nathan. "Because you never tell me."

I don't know if he hesitated from surprise at my words

or because he'd underestimated my feelings for my fledgling. When he spoke again, his voice was low and hoarse. "I feel all of that for you. More."

The uncertainty of the moment hung like a blanket of tension around my shoulders. Was this where we made up, or finally broke up?

Nathan's gaze held mine as he spoke. "And I would feel it even if you weren't my fledgling."

I moved as if to go to him, but Cyrus's mind invaded mine. *Please, stay with me.*

Understanding my reluctance, Nathan nodded. "He has you today. I've got you every day."

The gnawing guilt in my chest wouldn't let me turn my back on Nathan now. "All those things I said—"

"Don't apologize." He shook his head as if he could dissipate the hurt I'd caused him.

"Nathan, I—"

"Don't apologize," he repeated. "Because you meant everything you said."

"You know that's not true."

He held up a hand. "Don't. Carrie, you wanted to hurt me. If you hadn't meant those things, they wouldn't have hurt so much. So don't apologize."

Tears spilled from my eyes and a sob welled in my chest, blocking my words. I couldn't have spoken if he'd wanted me to.

Nathan straightened in the doorway and put his hands in his pockets. "I'll see you after sunset."

He turned to go and I found my voice. "Don't you want to know what happened with Clarence?"

I saw the muscles beneath Nathan's T-shirt bunch. I knew he felt my hope and, admittedly, pride at how well things had gone at the mansion. In other words, he knew that I was about to tell him exactly how I would proceed to put myself into danger in phase two of my plan. "Fine. How did it go?"

"It was okay. He agreed to help us." I wished I had some details to give him, now that I'd brought it up.

"Help doing what?" There was a note of amusement in Nathan's voice now. An easy, friendly tone that warmed me from the inside.

"Don't know. I have to go back tonight."

He took a deep breath, to stem the tide of warnings that would come flowing from his mouth if he let them. "We'll talk about it tonight."

I watched as he turned to the corner toward his bedroom. "I'm going, you know," I called after him.

He echoed back, "We'll talk about it tonight."

Fourteen: Clarence

$\sim$ c $\sim$

In the end, Nathan agreed that it should be me meeting Clarence, because I'd made the arrangement and because the butler would likely try to kill Cyrus if he set foot on the grounds.

"Or you, for that matter," I'd tacked on. "Clarence doesn't like vampires."

Nathan had smiled at that. "Funny how his line of work always seems to lead him to them, huh?"

It had felt much too easy, his acceptance of my "I'm going and you're not" decree, and I'd wondered if he was actually still mad at me and hoping Dahlia would finish me off. Then I'd wondered if he was still mad at Cyrus, and what he would do to him when I left.

He'd felt my doubt and it had clearly hurt him. "You're my fledgling. Do you think I would cause you that sort of pain?"

Without waiting to think about it, I'd snapped, "You were going to this morning."

We'd parted on less than warm terms, with Nathan trying to act as though he wasn't angry with me and me pretending the whole exchange had never happened. Still, before I'd left, he'd reassured me again that he wouldn't harm Cyrus, and it was all I had to comfort me on the walk to the mansion.

I refused to think of the place as Dahlia's house. When I'd first entered the grounds it had been Cyrus's home, and he had been my sire. He'd wanted me to consider it my home, as well, though I'd never been truly comfortable in the palatial rooms full of armed bodyguards. So I must admit it was a shock when, upon meeting Clarence at the back gate, I found no watchful, black-clad men with walkie-talkies and grim faces. Clarence looked behind him, to where my gaze sought any sign of a trap, and he shook his head. "She ate them. Or fired them. Mostly ate them. I got to keep their building, though. More room than I had in the house, and I can get away from her for a few minutes if I want."

"Is she treating you well?" I asked as I followed him up the path toward the house.

He stopped and gave me that "stupid vampire" look. "Of course she is. Didn't I just say she gave me a house? And she's been giving me days off. Not just one a year like your old man did."

My old man. I snickered at the thought of Cyrus being in any way fatherly to me. Then I remembered my grim purpose for being there, and sobered. "If she's so great, why are you helping me break into her house?"

Clarence stiffened at that, pulling his noble dignity around him like a suit of armor against my scurrilous accusations.

"What you're doing tonight isn't going to hurt her. It's going to hurt the big man. I've got no love for him."

"So, what's going on? Did you send her out so I could snoop, or what?"

He shushed me urgently. "I drugged her, but I don't know if it took yet. She's got a resistance to most things."

"Try to poison her often?" Clarence had definitely had no love for Cyrus, but as far as I know, he'd never tried to kill him. And if he was so damn fond of Dahlia, he wouldn't have tried to kill her.

He shook his head, a look of sadness on his creased face. "No. She's tried to kill herself, though. It's a shame, she wasn't a bad girl. She wasn't a nice girl, but nobody should want to take their own life."

Dahlia had tried to commit suicide? Color me surprised. "Well, how will we know if she's drugged or not?"

"You'll know if she doesn't kill you when you go in there." We'd come to the terrace, and I found myself looking guiltily over the flagstones, wondering if there would still be a stain from the night Ziggy had been killed. I'd been back to this house once after he'd died, but I'd been too preoccupied with my status as noble human sacrifice to think of looking. To my relief—and oddly enough, disappointment—the stone was clean, and I waited patiently for Clarence to unlock the French doors to the foyer.

I'd wondered if Dahlia would have redecorated when Cyrus was gone. She hadn't changed much, except to add potted plants and a simple wrought-iron café table and chairs to the foyer. The doors to the study were closed, but for the strangest instant I wanted to rush to them and throw them open, to find Cyrus there, the old Cyrus, waiting for me.

"She's upstairs," Clarence said, correcting what he thought was my presumption that I would find Dahlia in the study. He pointed to the curving staircase. From the foyer I could see that the second level was dark. "You know the way."

I started up the steps. Clarence made no move to follow me. My heart leaped farther up in my throat with each step I took. I'd never been back to the rooms where I'd lived with Cyrus, where I'd made love to him—no, had sex with him; I had to keep *that* straight, at least. Where I'd bargained for Ziggy's life. I ached for those months. I don't know why. When I was living them, I'd been in hell. But things hadn't improved too much since, and I realized with a shock that maybe I had loved Cyrus then more than I loved Nathan now.

There wasn't time to mull over my relationship problems, though. The huge double doors to Cyrus's room loomed ahead. As I passed my former quarters, my fingers itched to touch the door handle, and I indulged myself. I had no doubt my things had probably all been thrown away, but I had to go back, just for a moment.

I hadn't changed the decor of the room when I'd inherited it from Dahlia, so it was no surprise to see it remained exactly as I had left it. In fact, a light film of dust on everything suggested it hadn't been inhabited for quite some time, either.

I paced quietly around the furniture in the parlor. There was the sofa Ziggy had slept on. There was the chair Cyrus had thrown me into in a fit of rage.

And there was the secret door he'd used to spy on me and intrude into my space. The hutch in the corner remained as it had been, but a tiny latch was installed now. I wondered if that had been during Dahlia's post-Carrie return to power, brief though it had been.

From the window I caught a glimpse of the rusty, unused gate where Nathan and I had met to plot Ziggy's freedom. A lump formed in my throat. I would have given anything then to be with him, away from Cyrus. Why was I so torn now?

Memories of my captivity—my willing captivity—crashed over me. The humiliation I'd faced at Cyrus's hands, the power he'd exerted over me to make me act against my nature. I'd forgiven him of all these things and effectively erased them from my consciousness. But they would never be gone from my heart. God, how I'd taken Nathan for granted since he'd freed me.

The door to my old bedroom was closed. I stalked to it, flung it open and crossed to the mammoth bed. With one hard shove, I managed to move the frame, and heard the unmistakable whisper of paper slipping. I felt in the gap blindly until I found what I was looking for. The drawing Nathan had made of me, the one I'd carried with me when I left him for Cyrus.

The paper was as crisp as the day I'd hid it. I unfolded it and looked down at the woman Nathan had seen standing in his shop. It was by no means accurate. For one, I rarely wore my hair down. And my eyes weren't quite as big and innocent-looking as he'd made them. And I was older now. Sure, I hadn't aged physically, but sometimes, like now, I wanted to get in a time machine and go back and give the younger me a good hard slap.

Of course, this was presuming I'd learned anything at all. In another six months, would I want to come back to *this* moment and slap myself, too?

The clock on the mantel in the parlor chimed, and I remembered I wasn't here to sightsee. This wasn't my room anymore, this wasn't Cyrus's house. And I had a job to do.

I went to the hutch and lifted the latch—how she thought something this flimsy would have kept Cyrus out, I had no clue—and ducked through the secret door.

The anteroom was the only part of Cyrus's suite I'd been in, besides his bedroom. I'm sure there were more secret doors, but I'd never seen them or known where they led. My suspicions were raised solely by the seemingly effortless way the guards and Clarence could be summoned. The door to the bedroom was open, though, so I slipped through it.

I was expecting a more visceral response to the sight of the bed where Cyrus and I had shared our intimate times. I didn't know it then, but he'd let his guard down with me. When he'd asked if I loved him, he'd opened himself up, despite his past hurts. No wonder my rejection had sent him over the edge.

Still, I didn't freeze up or break down once I was back in this room that had terrified and excited me before. It looked different, for one thing. The walls were still white, the carpet still ivory, but she'd hung posters up, and it appeared she'd raided Pier One Imports of every remotely gothic wall sconce they carried. The room was way too much of a fire hazard for hyperflammable little me, but I supposed if she wanted to sleep in a death trap, I couldn't complain.

Dahlia lay on the bed, dressed as though she'd been ready to go out for the night. On the bedside table, in front of a metal tree sculpture with twisting branches, from which hung a dozen or more necklaces, spiked collars and chokers, was an empty glass with bloody residue. I lifted it and sniffed. Whatever drug Clarence had used to render her unconscious, he'd wisely picked one that didn't leave a scent.

From her shallow breathing, I could tell Dahlia truly was asleep. So I had her where I wanted her, I guessed. But what the hell was I going to do with her?

I paced the room, from the fireplace to the writing desk. I thought of Cyrus sitting there the night I'd come to him. Dahlia's laptop was there now, but the gold-plated desk set was, too, albeit covered in a layer of dust. I pulled out the letter opener and wiped the blade on my shirt, not entirely sure what I intended until my gaze rested on the empty glass at the bedside.

If I had seen Cyrus's and Nathan's pasts in their blood, could I see Dahlia's? Or did it only work if there was a blood tie? I supposed there was no time like the present to find out.

I wouldn't drink directly from her. It would be too weird, considering she was the first person I'd ever fed from, and now we were enemies. Plus, things hadn't gone so well for me that first time. I wanted to escape this with as few stab wounds as possible.

I wiped the inside of the glass with my shirttail, hoping the residue of the drug wouldn't knock me out, and I rolled back the rubber bracelets on Dahlia's wrist. I took a deep breath, closed my eyes, and stabbed the point of the letter opener into her arm.

Blood squirted out, and I wiped some from my face, gagging, before I managed to direct the flow into the cup. When it was full enough for a few swallows, I set it aside. I ripped a strip from the sheets and wrapped it tight around her wound.

Lifting the cup to my lips, I caught the scent of her blood. It had changed, just as she had, from human to vampire, but beneath the stale, dead scent of vampire blood I caught the smell I remembered from the night I'd fed off her. You never forget your first time.

I swallowed the blood quickly, concentrating on the taste of it, willing myself to access the cellular memory it might carry. The room spun as if I were drunk, and I slid to the floor, my head lolling back to rest on the mattress. Slowly, my vision blurred and a rushing sound built in my ears. Dahlia's memories seeped into my consciousness without any goading from me.

Was this something that happened with all vampires? Human blood didn't affect me this way, at least not often. It had happened when I'd fed from Ziggy, but he'd been trying to communicate with me then, I think. Was Dahlia conscious enough to manipulate my brain now?

I became too absorbed in the pictures flashing through my mind to think further on it. Dahlia's thoughts were concerned mainly with Cyrus, a fact that didn't surprise me. A noisy club packed with writhing bodies—the club where I'd met Dahlia?—seethed around me; the monotonous pounding of industrial music filled my ears. The crowd parted like something out of a movie—perhaps Dahlia embellished this part—and she caught sight of Cyrus across the crowded room.

This was the first time she'd seen him. And she'd wanted him at first sight. She approached him purposefully, and when he noticed her, I recognized his expression. Hunger, and deviant lust. He'd wanted her, too.

It made me oddly jealous to know he'd felt this way for her. I wanted to believe she'd been more passionate for him than he had been for her, but there was no mistaking his intent as he rose, took her hand and lifted it to his lips.

"I'm Cyrus. And you are?" he asked, and she had to strain to hear him, as he didn't raise his voice over the loud music.

"Going home with you tonight," she responded boldly. Then I was rushing forward in time, to the car where Dahlia sat in Cyrus's lap as he tugged her head back by her hair and bit her neck, not to feed but to arouse. Then to his room, where he pinned her to the bed and showed her his true face. She feared him, but she didn't show it, and he liked that. That's why he didn't kill her like the other girls. That, and when he held her down and fed from her while he fucked her, she invaded his mind and gave him a sense of her true power. If there was one thing Cyrus hadn't been able to resist in his former life, it was the promise of power.

I lost track of time as I watched her short life unfold from that moment. It was like watching a movie on a broken projector. Sometimes the images moved too fast to comprehend, sometimes so slowly it seemed they would burn up. Still, I wasn't frightened. I felt I could pull myself out at any time, though I couldn't control what I saw or heard.

Then I saw Max, standing in the parlor of what used to

be my room, and I jolted. This must have been the night we came to kill Cyrus. I knew he'd been delivered to Dahlia's room. But why would she remember him? That had been months ago, and as I'd witnessed, Dahlia was fairly Cyrus-centered then.

The guards who'd wrestled him up the stairs pushed him through the door and slammed it behind him. In true Max fashion, he flashed a huge grin despite the fact his arms were bound behind his back and he was completely vulnerable at the hands of his enemy.

Dahlia didn't waste much time looking at him. She turned back to whatever she had been doing, which involved a mortar and pestle, a Bunsen burner and a beaker, and a huge, leather-bound book with handwritten lines. She took a carafe of blood that rested to her right and poured a glass, then removed the beaker from the heat and mixed the contents with the blood. The scent of burned cloves stung my nostrils, and my stomach clenched with dread.

With little ceremony, Dahlia picked up the knife—an athame, as she thought of it—and the blood, and approached Max. She cut the plastic tie holding his hands and gave him the glass. "Drink."

"Yeah, honey, I wasn't really looking forward to turning into a toad tonight." He tried to hand the glass back. "I mean, I'm sure you're a wonderful cook and all—"

"Drink it or I'll kill you." She went back to her book, but I couldn't read the writing before she snapped it shut. "I was saving it for Cyrus, but he doesn't seem to have any interest in helping the cause."

"Helping the—" Max began, only to be cut off again by Dahlia.

"Drink it or I'll kill you." She turned to watch him finish off the glass, then strode forward and wrapped her arms around his neck. He resisted her a little, but she rose on her tiptoes to kiss him. "Now fuck me."

Max obliged with relish, and Dahlia was no slouch, either. We were going to have to have a serious talk when I saw him next. He'd never mentioned any of this to Nathan or me. Normally, I wouldn't care to hear details of Max's sex life, but Dahlia was the enemy. He should have at least mentioned that he'd had sex with her.

When they were done—her memory skipped mercifully ahead—she ordered him to get dressed, and pushed him toward the door. The rushing sound started in my ears again, and I was pulled out of the scene. I was back in Dahlia's room, sprawled on the floor, with a wicked hangover.

"See everything you needed to?"

The voice startled me enough that I sat up despite the splitting pain in my skull. Dahlia glared at me, her eyes accusing slits, but she did not move. "Get out."

"Tell me what 'the cause' is, and I'll consider it." I reached into my back pocket for the stake I'd brought for protection.

"I'm not going to tell you anything." Even her voice sounded tired. "I want you out."

"Are you going to make me leave? You don't seem to be in any position to fight me off." I climbed on the bed and pressed the point of the stake into her chest, making sure she could feel it through her clothes. "What's 'the cause'?"

Her eyes narrowed. "Fuck you!"

"You leave me very little choice." I raised the stake as though I was going to plunge it through her heart, hoping she would change her mind and tell me.

I should have known better. She just glared at me while I hesitated with the stake in midair. Then I felt something at my back, and turned to see Clarence there, brandishing a crossbow.

I dropped the stake. "Clarence, what are you doing?"

"I'm sorry, miss. But I can't let you kill her." He kept the bow leveled at my chest to show he was serious. "I think it's about time you leave now."

"Wait, wait." I shook my head. "She knows you drugged her. She knows you worked with me. She'll kill you once it wears off."

Dahlia laughed behind me. "Damn straight I will."

"She can't kill me," Clarence said, and he sounded as if he truly believed it.

"Think about what you're doing. She's a vampire." I raised my hands, my gaze flitting between the point of the bolt aimed at me and his face. "Besides, you can't kill me, either. I don't have a heart in my chest."

He shook his head. "Oh, I might not kill you outright, but I can put you out long enough to stoke up that fireplace and toss you in."

"Fair enough." I looked at Dahlia, then back to Clarence. "Fine. I'll go."

"You know your way out," he said. "I won't be seeing you around here again."

"No, you won't." I paused at the door. "Why are you protecting her?"

"Because I come with the house. And she's better than some of them that's been here." He nodded in the direction of the door. "Like the old master and his father."

The Soul Eater? I wanted to ask more, but he dropped the bow and turned to tend his mistress. I didn't want to make him any more of an enemy that I already had, so I left.

Exactly how old was Clarence, and how long had he worked in the house? I knew he had a peculiar affection for it, so much so that he would not escape his vampire employers even when he had a chance. It was a riddle I would probably never know the answer to.

I was crossing the foyer to the front door when I stopped. The doors to the study were closed, but I knew they would not be locked. I don't know how I knew this, but I moved toward them automatically and pushed them open.

Maybe it was the lingering influence of Dahlia's blood in mine, maybe it was my own memory, maybe it was just instinct, but when I opened the doors, the first thing my gaze rested on was the spot where I'd killed Cyrus. The pain and sorrow of that night rushed through me, as fresh as the moment it had happened. I'd kissed him and plunged a knife through his heart. How could I have done such a thing? It was the blood tie between us now that caused me pain. Then, I'd understood what had to be done; now I was horrified by it.

I tore my gaze away and there it was. Lying on the leather sofa, beside a *Cosmopolitan* magazine, of all things, was the leather-bound book I'd seen Dahlia reading on the night she'd given Max the mysterious elixir.

I looked over my shoulder. Clarence must have still

been upstairs. I clutched the book to my chest, gave one last scan of the room, and tore into the foyer and out the door.

I didn't stop running until I reached the street, then doubled over, panting. I slipped the book beneath my shirt and hugged it tight all the way back to the apartment, certain at any moment I'd turn and Clarence would be there, ready to kill me for stealing from his mistress.

But I was equally certain that whatever was in the book was the missing piece that would make all the others fit.

Fifteen: The Cause

Nathan wasted no time at all delving into Dahlia's hand-written notes.

"This is amazing," he murmured, his dark head bent over the pages as he sat at the kitchen table. Cyrus and I stood in the doorway, watching in tense silence. Sometimes, when lovers fight, the guilty party will bring flowers home. To appease Nathan, all I had to bring home was the notebook of a notorious witch. I wondered how I'd top it the next time he nearly kicked me out.

"Just amazing," he repeated, turning a page.

Cyrus was the first to snap. Thank God, because I'd been on pins and needles, but I hadn't wanted to be the one to break Nathan's reverie. Cyrus, however, had no problem doing so. "Well, what is it?"

Nathan looked up and gave a weary sigh. "It's a grimoire. A spell book. Haven't you seen this before?"

"No," Cyrus sniffed. "I didn't really take much of an interest in what Dahlia did."

"You should have," Nathan said, a little smugly, as he

looked back to the book. "There are things in here that would interest you."

Now Cyrus looked at the pages. "Like what?"

"Aphrodisiacs, love potions, all things she apparently used on you." Nathan snorted and read aloud, "'Tried this and he couldn't get it up.'"

"I was probably very tired!" Cyrus snapped.

"I'm sure you were." I patted his head condescendingly. "What do you know about 'the cause'?"

Cyrus ducked my hand and smoothed his hair with an annoyed glare. "What cause?"

I shrugged. "Dahlia said it. It's why she had sex with Max."

Nathan looked up sharply. "She had sex with Max?"

"Believe me, I was as surprised as you are." I suppressed a shudder of revulsion. "I thought he had better taste."

Cyrus reached for the book. "Did she tell you anything else?"

As I tried to remember, pain ripped through my head, either from the blood or the poison. "She was making something…a potion. It smelled like burned cloves…."

From somewhere faraway, I heard Nathan say, "Grab her, she's going to fall." When I opened my eyes I was on the couch, and it felt as if someone had hurled an ax into my head. Nathan leaned over me, his face full of concern.

And anger.

"How did you get this information from Dahlia?" His stare seemed to cut through me and blanket me in his worry all at once.

"She…told me?" I wasn't a good liar on my best day. Nathan saw through my words easily.

He laughed, a tight, humorless sound, and I got the distinct feeling he was close to losing it. "She told you? You walked into the mansion, sat down over tea and she said, 'By the way, I had sex with your friend and I'm working on a shadowy purpose I'll only call 'the cause'? Now, please leave my home unhindered so you can tell all your friends?"

"Of course not," I snapped, trying to sit up. I caught sight of Cyrus through the kitchen doorway, his fair head bent over the spell book. His lips moved silently as he read, making him look more boyish than I'd ever seen him, and my heart swelled at the sight.

"Carrie, focus." Nathan sounded tired and irritable, and I realized I hadn't shielded him from my feelings for Cyrus.

I wanted to reach out to Nathan and assure him I still loved him best, but something in his stiff, annoyed demeanor suggested that would be a bad idea.

"You knew Clarence was helping me," I hedged. Then I sighed, my brain too fuzzy to keep up a convincing lie. "He drugged her, and I drank her blood."

Nathan recoiled in horror. "Why would you do something like that?"

"Nostalgia?" Cyrus suggested blandly from the kitchen. Nathan ignored him. "Carrie?"

"I drank your blood, mixed with Cyrus's, and I saw your…history. I thought if I drank her blood…" How could I have been so stupid? If I drank her blood, and she had been drugged, I'd ingested the drug myself. "It's hard to believe I ever passed the MCATs."

"It's hard to believe you lived past the age of ten!" Nathan stood and stalked away, then turned and paced back to the couch. "For someone smart enough to be a doctor, you have remarkably little common sense!"

"Well, it seemed like a good idea at the time!" Why did those words always follow an abysmally stupid action? "Besides, it bought us some information!"

"That might be false!" Nathan paused in his agitated pacing and sat at the end of the couch, elbows braced on his spread knees. "When you drank our blood, you saw what you did because we'd both been blood tied to you. We couldn't lie to you because we didn't have the capacity to control what you saw. But Dahlia has no tie to you. She could have shown you anything she wanted."

I cast a sidelong glance at Cyrus, remembering his face as he loomed over Dahlia in his bed. "She was drugged. How could she have planted things in my head if she was unconscious?"

"She might not have made them up," Nathan conceded. "But she may have left out crucial details that would have changed the order or meaning of what you saw."

"She's crazy, don't forget. Some of what you witnessed might not ever have happened, even if she believes it did." Cyrus interjected his comment in an offhand way. He was still absorbed in the book, probably wondering what exactly his ex-girlfriend had tried on him.

"There's that, too." Nathan seemed loath to admit Cyrus had said something helpful. "The point is, we still don't know anything. We just have this book, and her convoluted memories. It wasn't worth the risk you took."

Underneath his anger, I felt his love. He worried about me. I reached for his hand, and he took mine willingly, giving a gentle squeeze.

"I'm sorry, I wasn't thinking. I was just so consumed with wanting to find something, any sort of break to help us." I shook my head. "It was so easy before."

Nathan sighed. "You didn't fail. You got us this book. That's something."

He leaned down to kiss me, and jealousy surged through me from Cyrus's direction. I heard him push back his chair, then his footsteps as he came into the living room.

"Really, the only thing we need to know is where my father is going next. He won't stay in one place too long. It isn't his way." Cyrus sat on the floor beside the couch, and I couldn't help but lay my hand on his head. He leaned back, into my touch, and Nathan looked away.

I couldn't take much more of this. Being the object two men competed for wasn't as glamorous as it sounded in the movies. The two men who both wanted one hundred percent of *my* time weren't dashing, international playboys. They were undead and surprisingly immature, considering the youngest was just over a hundred years old.

Oblivious to my distress, Cyrus went on. "That might be easier to find out than just charging into the mansion and drinking people's blood."

"Oh?" Nathan's annoyance was practically tangible. "Why didn't you mention this before Carrie risked her life?"

"Because you wouldn't listen to me unless it was your very last option," Cyrus retorted. "And you didn't take the time to ask me when you were pummeling me the other night."

"I'm sorry about that," Nathan said quietly, and though there was a bitter edge to it, his apology sounded genuine. "What's your idea?"

"My father travels rather conspicuously. A full retinue of armed guards, black sedans, a hearse. Do you think those things are easy to ship?" He raised an eyebrow, as if in challenge.

Nathan and I both shook our heads.

With a satisfied smile, Cyrus continued. "Do you know of many places you can *rent* a hearse? All we have to do is look up records for hearse sales in the last few days."

"What?" I thought I could feel my eyes bugging out of my head at his suggestion. "How do you expect us to do that?"

"I don't know," he said with a shrug. "They do it in the movies all the time. Someone always conveniently knows someone who can get the information."

I smacked the back of his head and rolled my eyes. "I'm so glad we've reached the but-they-do-it-in-the-movies phase of desperation. It inspires a lot of confidence."

There was a long moment of silence before Nathan spoke. "I know a way."

"Whether you know a way or not, it's stupid and we're still screwed." I shook my head. "It's impossible."

"I believe Nathan is alluding to another solution. One we have denied from the very start." Ominous silence followed Cyrus's statement.

Then Nathan turned to Cyrus, his eyes hard. He spoke, and his voice was as raw as the pain I felt through our blood tie. "Believe me, I've considered it."

Cyrus contemplated him for a moment, then shrugged.

"I'm merely stating the obvious. You're all too eager to send Carrie out to do your spying, but when it comes to something that might endanger you—"

"Oh? I should expose her to the danger I pose when I'm under his influence?" Nathan shouted.

His sudden change of tone startled me, and the motion sent another pain ripping through my head. Whatever Clarence had given Dahlia, I pitied the hangover she would have when she fully recovered. "Cyrus, he can't open up the connection to the Soul Eater. He was possessed—"

"By a spell. A spell Dahlia probably cast." When I didn't immediately agree, Cyrus point toward the kitchen. "It's in the book. You can see for yourself."

With considerable determination, I pushed myself up and staggered to the kitchen. There, on the page he'd left open, were the symbols I'd seen carved into Nathan's skin, some of which he still bore as nasty scars. Next to the neatly printed sigils, Dahlia's handwriting proclaimed, "Cannibalized from various sources. My version works better."

I should have staked her when I had the chance, the smug bitch.

"My father isn't capable of something like this," Cyrus said quietly. "Dahlia did it. In fact, if you look closely at this book, you'll see she's been behind most of the magic done on my father's behalf. She even wrote the spell that brought me back from the dead. It's all there. And I suggest we anticipate my father's next move, as there are far nastier spells that she's come up with."

"Nathan?" I asked tentatively. "Nathan, do you want to come look at this?"

He gave a barely perceptible shake of his head.

"We've had the best tool for tracking my father right here the whole time," Cyrus continued. "He just won't use it, Carrie."

What was I supposed to feel? In my heart, I understood Nathan's reluctance to open up to his sire. The man had taken his wife from him, tried to take his soul. Nathan's life, faith and dignity had been destroyed. Why on earth would he want to feel anything his sire wanted to give him?

Another part of me, though, was angry. Nathan had sent me into danger. Sure, he'd worried about me, but he'd been more worried about himself, about what would be easiest for him. I tried hard to keep my bitter feelings from the blood tie, but he felt them.

"That's not it at all, Carrie." He stood and walked toward the bedroom, adding a mental, *You should know me better than that.*

I looked helplessly at Cyrus. He touched my face, his fingertips skimming my cheek. "Talk to him."

When I went to the bedroom, I found Nathan sitting on the edge of the bed, staring bleakly at the wall. But I knew he didn't see it. He was in another time, another place entirely.

I knelt beside him on the bed.

"You think I was being selfish." His voice sounded hollow.

I considered. "Yes. Out of self-preservation. You don't know what he's going to do to you."

"I shouldn't have let you go to that house tonight." He scrubbed his hands over his face. His eyes were raw looking. "I have the perfect weapon, and I'm too cowardly to use it."

"It's not cowardly. He has incredible power over you." When Nathan scoffed at that, I took his palm and laid it over the place where my heart used to be. "Like you have power over me."

"What power, Carrie?" He threw up his hands. "I can't make you do anything you don't want to."

Alarms went off in my head at that. "Why would you want to force me to do something I didn't want to?"

"To keep you away from him," he sputtered. "To keep you from constantly running to him for solutions, for comfort. To keep you from loving him."

"I love *you*." Stunned as I was by this unprovoked outpouring, it took me a minute to comprise a more intelligent statement. "I feel for him what I presume all sires feel for their fledglings. Am I wrong?"

Nathan's gaze was so intense it could burn. "And what do you think that feeling is?"

He'd never come so close to saying the words. I was speechless for a moment. He took advantage of my state to continue. "If I open myself up to my sire, I don't know what will happen. Maybe he'll ignore me. Maybe we'll learn everything we need to. But maybe I'll get lost again, and this time you won't need me enough to get me back."

I pulled him to me, wanting to draw some of his fear into me, to relieve him of the burden of it. "How could you think that? I love you. When you were under his control before,

I risked my life and my soul to save you. I would do that a hundred times more if I had to."

"But I wouldn't." His throat moved as he swallowed. "I couldn't go through that again. Not with what he has to use against me."

Ziggy. "Nathan, he can only use it to control you if you still feel guilty. And what happened to Ziggy wasn't your fault."

"Wasn't it?" he snapped, as if angry that I would even suggest otherwise. "I kicked him out—"

"He ran away."

"Well, I didn't try to stop him!" Nathan stood and paced, and I eased back a little farther on the bed. Not that I thought he would hurt me, but I'm always uneasy around people in such an agitated state.

"Nathan, this is your problem. You push everything down until you're forced to deal with it, and when that time comes, you can't. This guilt is like…it's like gangrene. If you don't treat it, it eats you up."

"That's a fine example, but the only procedure I know for treating a morbid limb is amputation. I'll be damned if I'm going to cut off my memories of my son." He sat again, as if it was too much effort to bear the weight of standing and the weight of his grief at once. "But it's not just for myself I'm worried."

He took my hands in his and lifted them to his lips, kissing my palms, then my fingertips. Nathan rarely indulged in such intense physical contact unless it would lead to sex, but through the blood tie I felt only desperation. When he looked at me, I saw the meaning behind his fear before he spoke the words.

"He's taken everything from me," he whispered, squeezing my hands almost too tightly. "Marianne. Ziggy. He'll take you, too."

I tried to stammer out a generic reassurance, but he would have none of it. "Don't argue, Carrie. You don't know him. He wants. That's all he is, a creature made of want. If you thought Cyrus was bad, he is just a watered down version of his father. He'll take me back, and you with me. I can't have that happen to you."

"I'm not going anywhere." I jerked my hands from his, clenching them to fists. "You really underestimate me, don't you? I'm not property. I can't be owned or taken. Not by Cyrus, not by you, and definitely not by the Soul Eater."

I eased my defensive posture. "You said yourself we have the perfect weapon. That you're too afraid to use it. That's him. Don't you get that? Your fear of him is how he's controlling you."

"I know that." Nathan looked as though I'd slapped him. "I've known that for years. Why do you think I was alone for so long? Why do you think I had only Ziggy in my life when I met you? I know my sire controls me. He keeps me isolated. I can shut him out, Carrie, but not permanently, and not forever. Eventually, I'm going to hear him again."

"So, why not today?" I'd spoken the question without thinking about it, but I'm glad I did. I might not have said it otherwise.

For a moment, he wavered between emotional breakdown and an outburst of righteous indignation. Then his shoulders sagged and he rubbed the bridge of his nose, eyes closed in fatigue. "Fine."

"What?" I couldn't possibly have heard him correctly.

He lay back on the bed, staring at—no, through—the ceiling. "You're right. I should just get it over with. We're sunk otherwise. We don't have any other weapons available, and I'm just being cowardly."

He closed his eyes and took a deep breath. I grabbed his wrist, snapping him back to attention. "You're not going to do it right now, are you?"

"No time like the present."

I waited, not daring to move, barely breathing, my gaze trained on his face. Would he go all screwy and possessed again? Would I have to run for my life? I mentally calculated the time it would take me to stand after kneeling so long, weighed it against my speed on legs that had fallen asleep, and realized if he did go into mindless-monster mode, I was pretty much a goner.

When his eyes snapped open not a full minute later, I jumped back and gasped.

"Christ, woman, you scared me!" He pressed a hand to his chest. "Were you just staring at me the whole time?"

"No," I lied. "Kind of. In case. You know."

He smiled. "Sorry to disappoint you."

"So, it didn't work?" It couldn't have, in that short a time, could it?

He blinked, as if clearing his vision. "Oh, it worked. He's headed to the mansion, to pick up Dahlia. And to move back in."

"Wait… I thought the mansion belonged to…" I rose

and wandered to the living room. Cyrus was in the kitchen still, reading through Dahlia's notes. I took the chair across from him.

"Cyrus, who owns your mansion?" I watched his face for any flicker of emotion, but none showed.

"My mansion? If I had a mansion, would I be staying here?" He turned a page casually.

I rolled my eyes. "You know what I'm talking about. The house on Plymouth Street. Who owns it?"

"My father." He touched his tongue to his forefinger and turned another page. "Why do you ask?"

"So Clarence, then, he works for your father?"

Cyrus nodded. "He comes with the house."

"How long has your father owned that house, Cyrus?" I had the strangest feeling I'd overlooked something important. "Twenty years? Thirty?"

"One hundred and fifty." He stretched his arms over his head and yawned. "He liked Michigan because it had a lot in common with England, climatewise.

I leaned on the table and scanned the page in front of me. "Is there some connection, then, between this area and the Oracle?"

Cyrus shook his head. "No. He wasn't interest in her then. I don't know why he's interested in her now. He just liked the weather."

I glanced behind me to where Nathan stood in the doorway, his face grim. I turned back to Cyrus. "So, how can Clarence come with the house, then? He's old, but not a hundred and fifty years old."

Cyrus looked at me as if I'd gone out of my mind. "You

don't think he's alive, do you?" He started to laugh, a chuckle that grew to full-out laughter such as I'd never seen from him, until he pounded his knee with his fist and wiped tears of mirth from his eyes. "Oh, that's priceless."

"So, he's a vampire then?" I snapped, not nearly as amused as Cyrus. "He's working for your father?"

"He's a ghost, Carrie." Cyrus gave one last, soundless hitch of laughter. "I can't believe you didn't know that."

"That's not possible," I scoffed. "There are no such things as ghosts."

"You said the same thing about vampires," Nathan reminded me. "And werewolves."

"Yeah, but—"

"I watched one of my father's minions do it," Cyrus interrupted calmly. "Do you remember when I cut your heart out?"

I glared at him. "That's a stupid question. Of course I do."

"Do you remember what it was like to die?" He paused, waiting so I could think it over.

Not that I needed to search my memory. Dying, and what happened after, was never far from my mind. It wasn't that I was a morbid person, but the memory of leaving my body and floating among a bunch of faceless, vaguely similar ghost people was all the motivation I needed to keep myself from danger.

"But it must be different for humans." I flinched at the word. I still hated to think of myself as somehow apart from my birth species. "They have souls."

"Do you think we don't have souls, Carrie?" Nathan

asked softly, putting his hands on my shoulders. "Do you think you don't have a soul?"

"That's not what I meant. Not a soul in the philosophical sense. I meant in the Judeo-Christian sense. That there's something in a person that goes to heaven. Obviously, we don't go there. We go to the weird blue shadow world." I shuddered at the thought of it. Drifting with no sense of time or identity, and worse, not caring that you were.

"Well, I won't argue. But wherever he was expected after death, Clarence didn't go. Oh, we made a great game of cornering him in the dining room and chasing him around the table. He even did that feint where it seemed he'd go one way, but then turned and went another." Cyrus smiled, lost in reminiscing, and the hairs stood up on the back of my neck. He looked first at me, then Nathan, and a guilty expression came over his face. "Well, at any rate, Geoffrey caught him, drained him and left his corpse on the floor. Father was livid. You know how they say it's hard to find good help? The same was true then. He was raving, ranting, tearing through his parlor like a man possessed—you remember the parlor in my suite, Carrie?—until he finally calmed down enough to kill Geoffrey as punishment. Imagine his surprise when, just as Geoffrey's body burned down to ash, Clarence walked in and politely asked if we required him to clean up the mess!"

As neither Nathan nor I were laughing, Cyrus wisely swallowed his amusement.

"What I don't understand is, if Clarence is tied to the house, and he's working for the owner, how was he able to help me against you and Dahlia?" I tapped the nail of my index finger on my teeth as I stared at the book.

"Well, Dahlia and I didn't own the house. My father's name has always been on the deed, in one form or another." He turned another page and started reading. "So, my father wanted me dead, and wanted you to find this."

"But why?" As I pondered the question silently, Cyrus turned back to the spell book, apparently unconcerned with the fact his father had wanted to kill him. It seemed so bizarre, to want to kill your own flesh and blood. And Dahlia…she'd been human once. What would the Soul Eater want with her?

"Oh, God." I heard Nathan's quiet exclamation and looked up. Cyrus had pulled his hands back from the book as if it had burned him. I turned to Nathan. He stared, wide-eyed in horror, at the spell book.

I looked down, finally coming to the party, albeit late. Scrawled in Dahlia's hand was the heading "Vitality Elixir," and, after a lengthy list of ingredients and incantations, "used on that Movement guy. Didn't work."

"What the hell could that mean?" I guessed "that Movement guy" could have been Max, but "Vitality"?

Nathan took the book, his eyes moving so fast as he scanned the words I wasn't sure he could possibly be processing the information. "This is… What the hell was she trying to do?"

He strode to the living room and grabbed a notebook. On a page he drew three columns. "There are so many different components…. I don't know them all. I'll divide up the ingredients list by three. I'm going to have to contact one of my customers versed in Roman magic and curses for the incantations."

"Don't bother," Cyrus said, finding his voice. "Look."

Nathan glanced up from his notebook and I leaned over the spell book. In the margin, in cramped, tiny handwriting, Dahlia had added: "For forging the 'sword' (born vampire). Used on Cyrus. No effect. Used on blond vampire. No effect. Needs work."

"What is it?" Nathan asked, coming to stand in the doorway. Nausea gripped my stomach as I continued to read.

"Perhaps it will work in cross-species breeding, human-to-vampire or vampire-to-werewolf."

Cyrus's voice was hoarse. "She used this on me?"

Nathan frowned at the writing, scrubbing a hand over his face. "There are definite fertility elements to the spell. It looks like she was trying to make exactly what it says, a born vampire."

"She used it on Cyrus. The other vampire… I bet that was Max." My thoughts spun faster and faster, rushing to a horrible conclusion I knew I didn't want to reach.

Nathan shook his head, forehead still creased in concentration. "It says here it didn't work. But…oh."

Bile rose in my throat. "It didn't work because she was a vampire, too. But she gave it to Max."

Max. Bella. Her unexplained fatigue and carsickness.

But it wasn't carsickness at all.

Bella was pregnant.

Sixteen: Vitality

⎯⎯⎯∽⊙⊱⊙∽⎯⎯⎯

They arrived in Danvers the night before the full moon.

"You're not going to go all, you know—" he gave a mocking, horror movie version of a wolf's howl "—are you?"

"Max, imagine if I behaved that way toward your customs and traditions," Bella admonished, grabbing her bag from the car.

"You do! You hate vampires." He slammed the trunk closed and followed her inside. The place was pretty standard—two beds, a television with bolted-down remote, a sink outside the bathroom for no reason that made sense. But if anything could be said for the East Coast, at least their cheap roadside motels were clean.

Bella began unpacking. He'd only ever seen her remove clean underwear and a toothbrush from her bag, but apparently it held all manner of interesting things. Like a studded collar and wire cable leash.

"Nice," he said, following it up with a whistle. "So, am I the submissive or…"

"It is not for sex." She looped the lead through a double ring on the front of the collar. "It is to keep me restrained tomorrow night."

"I thought you could force yourself not to change. That it was some sort of code of your…people." Still, he found himself scanning the room for a place to hook the leash.

After a long moment, she answered. "It is our code not to harm humans. But there are other factors. I may not be able to keep from changing. I am under much stress."

"I get it." Max cut her off. He didn't want to hear her tell him again that they were as good as dead. "So, will you recognize me or will you rip me to shreds?"

"I do not know." She lifted one shoulder in an elegant shrug. "If I did attack you, I would not eat you. Vampires taste terrible."

"That's a comfort." If being maimed could be considered a comfort.

She reached into the bag and withdrew a vial. "Just in case I am unmanageable, you can use this."

He took the bottle, examining the shimmering blue liquid inside. "A sedative?"

"Something like that." She gripped the radiator and gave it a tug. When it creaked, she shook her head. "Perhaps I should attach this to the leg of the bed. I will probably succeed in moving it, but it will not cause structural damage we would have to pay for."

"There's another comfort." He slipped the vial into his front pocket. "In the event I do need to give you the night-night drug, how do I get it into you? I mean, are you going stop being a crazed werewolf long enough to swallow it?"

She knelt on the floor and slipped the bar of a thick padlock around the leg of the bed. Attaching the looped end of the cable, she snapped the lock shut with an ominous click. "No. You will have to feed it to me in something."

"Like giving a dog a pill in a piece of cheese." He smiled, to show he was half joking.

"I do not like cheese. I am fond of orange juice." She paused for a moment, her palms coming to rest on the front of her jacket, but she forced them down. Her expression grave, she put her hands into his. "Promise you will only use it if I become a danger. I am a very calm wolf, but we all have the potential for fury. Especially under the circumstances. The potion is very powerful, and I do not want to be incapacitated by an overdose."

"Fair enough." He eyed the lead in his hand. "You know, since you might be a wolf for, what? Is it three nights with you guys? We should put this to good use."

With a low, playful growl, she moved closer to him. Then she stopped. Her body tensed.

"Bella?" *Oh God. Not again.*

Before he could complete the thought, Max flew backward, propelled by an evil wind that seemed to come through the walls. Nothing else moved—the curtains didn't even stir—but Bella rose slowly from the floor, her head tipping back. Her mouth fell open, blood dribbling from her lips as the Oracle spoke through her. "Bring the weapon to me!"

"You want a weapon? I'll bring you a weapon, you crazy bitch!" He reached into his back pocket for the stake there, then remembered it was Bella, not the Oracle, he would kill if he used it. *How did she get so far into my head?* The thought of what he'd been about to do sickened him, but there was no way to retaliate against the power that was destroying Bella.

"Bring the weapon to me!" the voice raged from Bella's throat. Then, as quickly as it had come over her, the Oracle's power was gone. Bella dropped in a heap on the floor, lay still for a moment, then snapped up, her eyes cold with hatred.

Max stepped warily toward her. "Bella, is that you?"

"It is me," she gasped, choking up more blood. "She is here. She has people here. They know we are coming."

He scrubbed a hand over his face, hating that his hand was trembling. "You rest. I'll keep watch. And I'll call Nathan, see if he got any information on reinforcements."

"No." She shook her head, drawing herself up slowly. "No. I will not wait for them to come after us. Get back in the car."

"Bella," he began, ready for a fight. He walked toward her, and she was on her feet before he reached her, brandishing a stake.

She leveled the point in front of his chest. "Get back in the car."

Max kept one eye on the road and one on Bella as she leaned out the car window, scenting the air. For the first time, he was tempted to snap at a passenger for not wearing a seat belt. She was hanging way too far out.

When had he become so like Marcus? If this was what love did to someone, no wonder Max had avoided it for so long.

"Are you getting anything?" he asked, gripping the steering wheel tighter, as if that would hold her in. If she fell and broke her neck, he'd kill her.

She slipped into her seat again, thank God, but didn't buckle up. "Turn at the next available right."

"The next available right is a dirt two track." He leaned forward. "Or less."

"That is where you must go." She wrinkled her nose. "I smell vampires."

"How many?" The last thing he needed was to drive into an ambush, though it seemed too late for regrets as he steered the car onto the dirt path. "There are things I need to know before we get there."

She shrugged. "There were many. Now, there is only one distinct scent. Two, three at most."

"One is still a possibility?" He downshifted, wincing at the scrape of the rutted road against the undercarriage of the vehicle.

"Of course. Better to be prepared for more, though." She reached into the back seat and pulled two stakes from Max's supply. "May I?"

"Help yourself. What happened to yours?" Max leaned forward. The windshield had begun to fog, a phenomenon he hadn't had to deal with since he'd become a vampire. Mortal passengers were such a pain in the ass. He rubbed the glass clear with his forearm.

"They are in the trunk. I have everything else. Holy water, my crossbow—"

He shushed her. "Is that it?"

Ahead, a ramshackle cabin with two windows and a

bowed porch stood at the place where the track ended. Bella rolled down the window and sniffed, then gave a short nod.

Max raised his hand and lifted three fingers. She shook her head and replied with one finger. One vampire. *No problem.* Breathing a sigh of relief, Max eased the car door open. He didn't close it once he was outside. No sense in letting the poor sap know they were there.

Bella retrieved her weapons from the back seat and followed suit, waving to signal he should follow her.

Like hell he was going to let her charge in there unprotected. He jogged ahead, grabbed her shoulder and used her moment of surprise to push her behind him. He heard her cluck her tongue in annoyance, and he held up his hand for quiet.

The steps to the cabin were damp and broken, and probably prone to squeaking. Max placed one foot on the first step, his face frozen in a preemptive wince as he anticipated a loud creak, or worse, the whole thing splintering under his weight.

When it didn't, he motioned Bella forward.

The porch was only about four feet wide. The sagging roof didn't allow for much vertical clearance, and Max had to stoop. The door to the cabin didn't even have a handle. A beam of light projected from the hole where the knob used to be.

Are they making it easy on purpose? He pushed aside the feeling he and Bella were walking into a trap, and gave her a thumbs-up. When she replied in kind, he kicked the door in.

If he'd had any doubts they'd found the right place, they vanished the second they stepped inside. The furniture in the tiny room consisted of a kitchen table, a rusty utility sink, a minirefrigerator and a dirty cot with a stained pillow. A lone figure sat at the table, hunched over with his head in his hands.

"I knew you were coming." He lifted his bald head, and Max saw the man's eyes were ringed with dark circles.

"Are you a vampire?" Max asked calmly, pulling a stake from his back pocket.

The man nodded.

"What's your name?" He weighed the wood in his palm. The tiny voice in the back of his head that always popped up during moments like this sing-songed *That could be you.*

The vampire at the table resumed his slouched posture. "Ford Prefect."

"Ford Prefect?" *Odd name.* "Well, then, Ford Prefect, by order of the Voluntary Vampire Extinction Movement—"

"That is not his name," Bella said quietly from behind him. When he gave her a questioning glance, she shrugged. "It is the name of a character from *The Hitchhiker's Guide to the Galaxy.*" As if in defense, she added, "I like to read."

It took him a minute to get the flow back, but Max managed. "Oh, I get it, you think you're going to smart off to me and go out like a real badass, huh?"

"More or less." The vampire leaned back in his chair, trying—and failing—to affect nonchalance. He had a ring through the center part of his nose and he toyed with it, sliding it back and forth between his fingers.

"Well, nice try, but—" The thunk of the crossbow releasing a bolt cut Max off. The projectile sliced through the air, sinking deep into the vampire's shoulder.

He screamed, and Max rounded on Bella. "What the hell was that?"

"A clean shot with the intent to maim." She reached to the quiver at her back and pulled out another bolt, snapping it in place and cranking the handle as if nothing was amiss.

"We're supposed to get information from him, not kill him outright!" Max grabbed the bow and jerked it from her grasp, and the bolt snapped free, whizzing past his ear to embed in the dirty wall.

"I will get our information," Bella said, rolling her eyes. "Perhaps you should try to not kill *yourself* outright."

"Oh, I'll try not to kill myself outright." Somehow, repeating her remark with added sarcasm didn't come off with the bite he'd hoped it would. He tossed the bow aside, cursing himself as she stalked toward their prey, her braid snapping lethally behind her.

She leaned over the groaning vampire and grasped the end of the arrow, giving it a sharp tug. When he howled, she said, "Oh, I am sorry. Did that hurt?"

"Fuck you, bitch!" He spat at her, but she dodged it.

With a twist of her wrist, the vampire was screaming again. "You should be more polite to the person holding your life in her hands. Will you be more polite?"

There was a litany of curses, and she responded with a downward jerk of the arrow. "It would not be in your best interests to bring this wood closer to your heart."

The vampire went deathly still. He raised his hands. "I don't know anything. Why would I know anything? Do I look connected? I don't even have a phone."

Bella's eyes darted around the room. They widened

and she nodded toward the minifridge. "But you do have duct tape."

She didn't have to say it twice. Max grabbed the dusty roll of tape from the top of the refrigerator, stepped forward and started immobilizing their friend.

"Leave one of his arms free. Tape that hand to the table, palm down." She jerked the bolt from his shoulder, and blood gushed out, first a strong pulse, then a trickle.

"You're not going to let him bleed to death, are you?" Max pulled a strip of the tape free and morphed his face, using his fangs to bite through the heavy material.

Bella laughed at him. "No, but he will wish for death when we are finished."

"I told you, I don't know anything." The vampire let them lay his arm across the table, too distracted by their threats to put up any resistance.

Max had seen this too many times. The realization hit him like a ton of bricks, and he paused in his bondage duties to absorb the blow. He'd gone soft somewhere between his last job and this. He didn't want to cause pain and death anymore. He didn't want any part of this.

Most of all, he didn't want to see Bella do these things. He wanted to pull her from this cabin and drag her to the car, start driving somewhere else and never look back.

"Max?" Bella frowned at him. How long she'd been doing so he had no clue. When his gaze met hers, her eyes flared, then narrowed in silent understanding. She pursed her lips and nodded toward the tape in his hand. "Keep going."

If asked to describe Bella's methods of torture, the

words *cruel efficiency* would have been the only appropriate answer. She didn't bother with a lot of talk once her victim was secured.

"What is your name?" she asked him.

When he answered, "Arthur Dent," she stabbed the arrow that had previously been lodged in his shoulder straight through his hand.

"I take it that's another fake one, huh?" Max asked, raising his voice to be heard over the vampire's screams.

She wrenched the bolt free and repeated her question. "What is your name?"

"Patrick! It's Patrick!" he howled, straining against his bonds.

To Max's surprise, they didn't break. All that stuff they said about duct tape was true.

"Patrick, do you work for the Oracle?" She twirled the arrow through her fingers and held it poised above his already healing hand. The speed with which the injury closed was an indication of Patrick's age. And power.

Careful with this one, baby. As soon as he'd thought it, Max saw her eye the wound. She took a step back, her retreat so subtle Patrick would never notice. She motioned Max in with a tilt of her head.

He pulled a leather glove from his back pocket and slipped a small vial of holy water from one of the fingers. He set the vial on the table in plain view while he pulled on the glove, then retrieved it and unscrewed the top. "We're waiting, Patrick."

"I w-work for the Soul Eater," he stammered, eyeing the liquid.

"The Soul Eater?" Bella gave Max an arch look. "What are you doing here then?"

"Yeah, the Soul Eater is in San Francisco." It was a lie, but to Max's relief, Bella played along.

So did Patrick. "San Francisco?"

The vampire's outrage spurred Max's story along. "Yeah, didn't you know? Man, they keep you way out of the loop."

"Bullshit!" Patrick tried to raise his hand. "If they're in San Francisco, why would they send me up here?"

Max snorted. "That's what we want to know. What is the Soul Eater up to with the Oracle?"

Suddenly brave again, Patrick spat once more at Bella. "I'm not telling you shit!"

She nodded to Max. He let a drop of holy water fall onto the freshly healed skin of Patrick's hand. A cloud of foul steam rose from the wound as the skin scalded away under the droplet.

"Plenty more where that came from, sport." Max tilted the vial theatrically.

Patrick stopped his howling long enough to dissuade him. "Okay, okay. I'll tell you."

When he didn't answer fast enough, Bella nodded to Max.

"No! No!" Patrick begged. "I'm here to pick something up."

Now they were getting somewhere. Max pulled the vial back a few inches. "Pick what up?"

Patrick calmed a little once he saw he was out of immediate danger of scorching. "A weapon. I don't know what it is."

"This weapon… You will take it to the Soul Eater?" Bella's voice sounded strange and tight.

Max didn't register that until it was too late. Patrick lunged in his chair, not quite breaking his bonds, but twisting enough to flip the table and tear his hand free. Max fell back just as the other vampire lurched awkwardly to his feet. He swung the chair still taped to his back against the wall, shattering it. With a cry of fury, he ripped a piece of the splintered chair from the tape that still dangled from his elbow. He advanced on Bella, brandishing his makeshift stake.

"Hey, no!" Max climbed to his feet, pulling a stake from his pocket.

Though she wasn't a vampire, Bella *was* mortal, and she would have been stupid to ignore the consequences of having something plunged through her heart. With lightning fast reflexes, she grasped her assailant's forearms. Her face contorted in fighting rage as she tried to subdue him, but she wasn't strong enough. He threw her off and she fell, bringing her legs up to connect with his chest as he lunged toward her.

Max jumped across the overturned table, knocking Patrick off of Bella. He had him pinned to the floor with a foot against his throat before she got to her feet.

"Where's the Oracle?" Max dug the point of the stake into Patrick's chest.

The vampire laughed. "I could take you to her."

"Fuck you! Where is she?" Max pushed harder and saw blood well around the edges of the stake. "Where the fuck is she?"

"Max! You will kill him!" Bella's voice cut through the red haze of Max's anger. This asshole had tried to kill her.

He'd tried to push a stake through her heart. He'd put his hands on her in anger.

"Max, please, we will not get any information from him this way." Bella grasped his arm.

Relenting with the stake, just a little, Max twisted his foot. Patrick's face went purple.

"You're going to die. You can tell us where to find the Oracle and I'll send you out fast, or you can hold out. I could make this last all night. What do you say?"

Patrick grasped Max's ankle, trying to dislodge his foot, but when it didn't work, he settled for giving him the finger.

"Get the holy water," Max growled. He dropped to a knee on the vampire's chest and gripped his jaw, forcing his mouth open.

Patrick's loud, angry sounds of protest changed in pitch to frenzied panic when he saw the vial in Bella's fist.

"You gonna talk?" Max reached toward Bella for the vial, but something in the way she clutched it tighter warned him off.

It didn't translate to Patrick. "Fine, fine. I don't know exactly where. Her people came here the other night."

"Are they coming back?" Max struggled to keep a grip on the stake. Why were his hands suddenly sweaty?

"In two nights." The whites of Patrick's eyes were becoming a spiderweb of broken vessels. "They'll be here right at sundown. They're supposed to take me to the Oracle. She'll have what she wants by then. She thinks…she thinks I've got a message from the Soul Eater that can only be delivered to her."

"It is never the same ones twice," Bella interjected with

a delicate sniff. "Many have been here since you arrived…two weeks ago."

"You're good," Patrick said, with a sneer to show he didn't appreciate it. "Another guy was here before me. One of the Soul Eater's own babies."

Max applied a little more weight to his knee. "What's the message?"

"No message," the vampire groaned. "It's a sham. I'm supposed to go in and get what the Soul Eater wants. The other guy has his own instructions."

"What's that?" Max asked, something cold clenching in his guts.

Patrick looked at Bella, a crazed light coming to his eyes. His mouth parted in a sickening smile. "You're going to die. You know it. You should have let me stake you."

"Shut up." Max pressed the stake into Patrick's chest.

He didn't pay any attention to his imminent demise, his eyes still trained intensely on Bella. "You'll suffer. And you'll die. And you'll know you are powerless to protect your child."

"What?" Max looked to Bella for a denial. She backed away with her hand over her mouth.

This can't be happening. The last few weeks unspooled in his mind. The riddle was so obvious now that he knew the answer.

The vampire beneath him laughed. "You didn't know?"

He burned before he could scream.

Max grabbed Bella's arm and jerked her from the cottage, oblivious to her protests. He knew he should have investigated the room for more evidence. No, he didn't care they'd come all this way for nothing.

Once they were in the car, driving way too fast down the dirt road, he exploded.

"What the hell was he talking about? A kid? It sure as hell can't be mine!" The vehicle went airborne for a minute when they reached the road. For a second, he wasn't sure they wouldn't sail into the ditch.

Bella sobbed silently beside him. "It has to be! I have not been with anyone except you."

"Hate to burst your little lie bubble, but vampires aren't exactly fertile!" He gunned the engine to make it through a yellow light. "Meaning that can't be mine!"

"Well, how else would you explain it?" She pounded the dash with her fist. "I do not know how it happened. But it happened! And now the Oracle will take our child!"

"There is no child!" He clenched the steering wheel almost hard enough to snap it. "We're going back to Chicago. We'll get this all sorted out there."

She nodded, for once being reasonable. "You are right. We will leave. We will leave."

"Finally, something you say makes sense." They'd get as far away from the Oracle as Max could get them. As for Bella's story of how she got knocked up…well, they could figure that one out later.

He relaxed a little, settling back in his seat. Things would work out. Bella wouldn't die, they'd be finished with this Oracle business and everything would work out.

He saw the headlights of the car just before it hit them, crumpling the passenger side and spinning them into a ditch.

Seventeen: Mother

"That's not possible," Nathan insisted, shaking his head. "If Bella were pregnant, wouldn't the baby end up—"

"A lupin." Cyrus shook his own head. "But that wasn't her intention. Dahlia assumed she'd be the one impregnated, obviously, or she wouldn't have used it on me."

"A lupin is just a werewolf who aligns with technology instead of magic." Nathan's definition didn't sound as confident as it might have in the past.

"That's what your precious Movement tells you. The wolves know better. Among them, lupin is a blanket term for any vampire who's been bitten by a werewolf, or a werewolf who's exchanged blood with a vampire. They might retain all of the distinct powers from both species, or just take on a few key characteristics." Cyrus didn't cover up his smirk. "Our side has known for years."

Still reeling, I reached for the book. "How long was Dahlia working on this?"

"Your guess is as good as mine. I remember drinking

a potion, but she was always giving me potions." He wouldn't look me in the eye. "For various…sexual reasons."

"And you never wondered what they were for?" Nathan asked, arms folded, expression incredulous.

Sheepishly, Cyrus looked at us. "No. The first few times I did, of course. But they were always herbal concoctions. To enhance the act. She took them as well, so I assumed they were safe."

Nathan snorted. "You know what assuming does. It makes an—"

"That's not constructive," I snapped. A wave of sickness rose in my throat. Memories of the first time I'd been with Cyrus overwhelmed me. It had been tense, violent, deviant…and I had no doubt he'd treated Dahlia the same. She'd done those sick things to conceive a child?

"Why would she want a baby? Did she think it would make you turn her? Stay with her?" Nathan didn't so much ask us these questions as throw them out for brainstorming.

"Well, it's obvious she thought a natural-born vampire would have something to do with the Oracle's prophecy about the weapon." I tried not to imagine what the baby would be used for.

"Or it *is* the weapon." Nathan's words gave form to my dread. He lifted the book and scanned the page. "Though it seems unlikely to me that she could have achieved all this in the time between the Vampire New Year and the time we killed you. I wish she would have dated this."

"No, she didn't start after the Vampire New Year. That's why I can't imagine her purpose. But she gave me the potion the first night I was with you." Cyrus realized too late the effect his words had on me.

I stumbled into the living room, breathing hard. I heard Nathan mutter something, and the scrape of a chair. But it was Cyrus who came to stand awkwardly behind me. "Carrie?"

"Don't!" I marched down the hall, raging with the things I wanted to scream at him. The fact his little "pet" had tried to take away my reproductive freedom—albeit freedom I didn't really know I'd had—should have been at the top of the list. How could he have not suspected? She'd never hidden her ambitions, from him or anyone else. So how could he have not known? And what would have happened to the child we might have created?

Another, more haunting possibility—that we could have had a child together, that I could have been a mother—tore my heart. But what kind of child would it have been? An unholy monster, like its father? Would I have lost all my humanity in protecting and caring for it?

To his credit, Cyrus didn't try to give me space. He followed me to my room and sat on the end of the bed after I flung myself across it. Two tear tracks, tainted pink with blood, wet his face as he looked at me. "I didn't know. Carrie, I swear to you, I didn't know."

He pulled his legs into the small space at the end of the bed and closed the door, shutting us in the dark. He didn't turn on the light.

"How could you not know?" But that wasn't what I wanted to ask him, and he knew it.

"You mean, 'how could you take potions from her?'" His voice was thick with emotion. "'How could Dahlia have done something you weren't aware of, when you were the person closest to her? Didn't you care about her? Didn't you take an interest in her beyond what she could do for you?' I wish I could tell you that I was forced. I wasn't. I took what she gave me, like a common drug addict. I can't lie and tell you that I knew all about it, or that I cared about her, or that I ever asked her a single question that wasn't a proposition. I don't even know her last name."

"How could you be that way?" I hated how my voice trembled when I cried. I sounded like a seventeen-year-old breaking up with her boyfriend. "How could you treat her like that?"

"I don't know. I'm ashamed of myself. Not because you want to hear it, but because I am. And you know I've changed. But I can't change the past, no matter how much I wish it."

We sat in silence for a long time. I measured the seconds by the beating of his heart, which sounded as loud as my own in the silence of the room.

"It would have been a lovely child," he said finally. "We're not unattractive people."

I smiled, in spite of the pain that twisted in my chest. "Nursing a vampire baby might have proved problematic."

He chuckled, then there was more silence.

"Why did she do it?" I asked, though I knew what the answer would be.

"Because my father asked it of her." Cyrus sounded miserable, and lost. "I've no doubt of that."

"But she did it before the Vampire New Year," I reminded him.

He shook his head sadly. "I wouldn't be surprised at all if my father had arranged my meeting her from the start. He has that kind of power. He can make anyone do anything."

It was true. Cyrus had been so desperate for the Soul Eater's love and approval he'd killed his own brother to become their father's fledgling. He'd sacrificed his own happiness, his humanity. He'd even admitted he would have given Jacob Seymour his very soul if he'd required it. But why? I'd seen the Soul Eater. It certainly wasn't his good looks and charming demeanor that commanded such suicidal loyalty.

Sensing my thoughts, Cyrus tensed beside me. "He wasn't always like that, Carrie. You saw him at the end of a yearlong fast. He's little more than a glorified corpse at that time. My father…my father is selfish, but he tricks you into thinking he deserves all you do for him. And he acts grateful. That gratitude is like a drug for people like Dahlia and me. For anyone who's lived a life like mine."

Cyrus seemed to struggle with something. His confusion and pain were evident through the blood tie. Images of Mouse, interlaced with images of a time long ago, flashed in his thoughts.

I took his hand in mine. "Tell me."

With a sad, quirked smile, he lifted my hand to his lips. "I'll show you."

It was an intimate thing between us, the sharing of memories. We'd done it before, when he was the sire and I was the fledgling. Though our roles had reversed, it felt as natural as before, and comfortingly familiar. It was something I'd never dared to do with Nathan. He'd seen flashes of memories through the blood tie, and the few times he'd tasted my blood, but I'd never invited him into my head the way I had Cyrus. Maybe I didn't trust him. Maybe I thought he would judge me for what he saw. Maybe I was trying to protect him from seeing something that might hurt him.

With Cyrus, I didn't care. Nothing I had ever done had been more shameful than the things I knew from his past. And nothing he saw could hurt him. He knew the extent of my betrayal. He knew me better than Nathan did. Probably better than I knew myself, since he'd seen and reveled in the dark side of my personality that I denied.

We lay together on my tiny bed, our hands still twisted together. "Are you sure?"

"What do I have to lose?" he asked, drawing in a shaking breath. And then I was rushing forward, through absolute blackness, through emotions too numerous to feel, let alone name.

On the other side of the blackness, I saw a woman. For a moment, I thought she must be very tall. She towered over me, her hip bones at my eye level as we faced each other. Then I remembered I was not myself, but was looking through Cyrus's eyes. Cyrus as a child.

The very thought of it, that somewhere, before the scheming and murder, he'd been, well, as innocent as a baby, would have choked me up, if I'd been in my body.

I took advantage of the moment to study the woman. She wasn't an adult so much as a girl. Rail thin, with limp, dirty blond hair and dark circles under her eyes, she looked like she would drop from exhaustion as she stirred the huge iron cauldron that hung over the hearth. A chubby hand tugged on her skirts, and she looked down. A genuine smile lit her tired face, then a look of alarm replaced it. "Simon, no! Very hot. You'll burn yourself, mark me!"

It was something young Cyrus heard often. She was terrified of the children burning themselves. Lifting him up, she kissed his forehead and wiped his nose with her apron. Setting him on his feet, she handed him a wooden bucket. It was heavy, and the rope handle made his palms itch, but he was a good boy. He knew how to get the water and bring it back for his stepmother.

"Out with you," she said, giving his backside a pat. From his halting gait, I imagined he was three or four years old. He stumbled through the oiled canvas flap over the doorway, tripping a bit on the hard-packed earth, and I was rushing forward again, to the spot where Cyrus, with no way to brace himself from the impact, smacked his forehead on the ground.

Young Simon Seymour was a hardy child, despite his surroundings. He stood, brushed off his scraped knees and took a few steps before he heard his stepmother's voice.

"Simon? Are you all right?"

Dropping his bucket, he plopped down in the dirt and summoned the best fake tears a three-year-old could produce. When the girl ran from the broken-down cottage, her face showed only concern. No annoyance that her work had been interrupted, no resentment that she had to tend a child that was not her own. She scooped him up, holding his probably dirty face close to her own, kissed him and murmured reassurances that he'd be all right.

I was touched to the core to see that, no matter how the

rest of his life had gone, he'd had at least one person who'd loved him unconditionally.

The scene changed. Cyrus was still a child, perhaps a few years older. His footing was surer, his thoughts more sophisticated. He carried a wooden bucket, probably the same one from the earlier memory, toward the river. It was hot, and the water level was low. He'd have to climb down the bank to get any at all.

He'd set the bucket down carefully and was about to begin his descent when he heard the screams. It wasn't uncommon to hear a woman shouting in the village. Women screamed at their children, screamed when giving birth, screamed when they were being beaten. Women screamed all the time over the smallest things, in his opinion. Except his mother.

That's why he didn't recognize her voice right away.

He realized it was her when she burst onto the lane, wailing in pain and terror. Flames consumed her clothes, burned away her hair. She beat at her blazing skirts with bloody hands. The skin fell away in huge chunks.

She was trying to get to the river, he realized, his small heart beating furiously in his chest. She needed water, needed help. Without a thought for the sharp rocks and protruding roots, he grabbed the bucket and slid down the bank.

It seemed to take forever, while the screaming went on and on. The bucket filled slowly, as if with tar instead of water. The weight was insubstantial, though, and he bounded up the slippery bank faster than he'd ever managed before. His legs and arms should have ached from the exertion, but he gained the top and raced to where his mother had fallen, her body still smoldering, blackened skin indistinguishable from her burned garments. When he threw the water over her, steam rose.

She didn't move. She made no sound. Made no sound, but he couldn't stop the screams in his head.

Men and women from the village had crowded around. More ran toward them. And there was his father, fists clenched so hard blood ran from where his nails bit into his palms, though his face was an impassive mask. "Go home, Simon. Finish making supper."

In an agonizing second, like pulling off a Band-Aid, I returned to the present. Cyrus looked at me with pity. After what I'd seen him go through, he pitied me?

"For having seen it." He stroked the side of my face, and I realized it was wet with tears.

Sniffling against the threat of more, I asked, "How old were you?"

"Seven, as far as I know. I'm not sure when I was born." His hand stilled, coming to rest on my hair. "She was my father's third wife. He didn't love her, but… I think it was the horror of it. It changed him. Very shortly after that he met the man who would sire him. The man bought our bond and we moved away from the village to live in fealty to him. Father told us to forget everything before. It was a new start."

"How did it happen?" If someone had told me even an hour ago that I would feel something other than hatred for the Soul Eater, I wouldn't have believed it. But the look I'd seen on his face, the suppression of emotion that was clearly intended to hide his pain from his son…

"She was hanging the pot over the fire, and her skirt

brushed the embers. That's all it took." Cyrus cleared his throat. "It wasn't uncommon, then."

"Whether common or not, it was horrible." I couldn't stand it anymore. I put my arms around him. "For you and your father."

It didn't absolve Jacob Seymour of all the sins he'd committed, but it did explain them a bit. It also explained why Cyrus was so desperate for affection from any female at all, regardless of whether she was willing to love him in return, or was even capable of doing so.

Our eyes met. His were red, from unshed tears. "The only women who ever loved me were taken from me. Once by fate, the rest by my father. I can't forgive him that."

"You shouldn't have to." I wanted badly to tell him how much I'd loved him, but it would have been a lie.

"You didn't love me." Even though he was now on the opposite side of the blood tie, my emotions were still transparent to Cyrus. "But I believe you wanted to."

"I did." I couldn't hold back my tears. Not over this. "I did."

"If it makes you feel any better, it's a credit to your character that you couldn't." He smiled a little, but it faded quickly. "I know that now."

"You hated me for it." I leaned my forehead against his. Our lips were so close to touching. My mouth went dry. I touched my tongue to my lips, and he was on top of me, smothering my mouth and crushing my body beneath his.

I still do. But his thought was swallowed up in a tidal wave of longing and…fear?

Cyrus leaned back and gave a curt nod to the door. "The last time I did this, your boyfriend beat me up."

"He's not my boyfriend." I paused at the sound of the door in the living room closing. "And I don't want to talk about it."

I did, just not to Cyrus. *It's just a kiss,* I projected to Nathan through the blood tie. The cold that met my thought from the other end forced a tangible shiver down my spine.

"Forget him, Carrie." Cyrus's arms tightened around my back. "You've given him so many chances."

"What is it to you how many chances I give him?" I snapped, pulling away.

"It doesn't mean anything to me." There wasn't malice in his words. "I know you're mine, whether I want you or not."

"What's that supposed to mean?" This was a side of him I hadn't missed, the possessive, arrogant side.

He sat up, but not beside me. "Let's look at this reasonably. After I attacked you, when you knew I was a monster, you sought me out."

"Because of the blood tie," I reminded him.

"Fair enough." He shrugged. "After that, when you needed help with Nathan, you turned to me."

"I needed your pet to undo what she'd done to him."

He sighed. "You're rationalizing. In the end, you kept coming back to me. Even to kill me, you wanted it to be between us alone."

He was right. There was no arguing that. When something concerned Cyrus, I wanted to be the only one involved. Whether I was fighting him or rescuing him.

"I'm not laying claim to you, Carrie." His elegant hands kneaded my shoulders. "But it seems you've already laid claim to me."

I turned and leaned into him when he curved his body around me. "But you let me."

"I did." His lips brushed my jaw, my ear. His mouth came to rest on my throat, the opposite side from where the scar of his first attack still marked me. "I suppose it's meant to be, then."

His fangs pricked my skin, threatening to break through and asking permission all at once. "What about Mouse?" I asked, stopping him.

"What about Nathan?" he retorted, lifting his mouth. "There is a part of me that is still in the desert with her. While I was there, a part of me was still with you."

"I seem to have a gift for falling in love with men who are in love with their pasts."

My admission seemed to freeze him in place. I didn't apologize for it or explain it away. I'd been in denial for far too long.

He faltered a little when he tried to speak, cleared his throat, then started over. "Well, that may be true. But I'm no fool. I know who's here now."

In the past, I might have looked for a trick or a trap in his words. Now, they brought tears of relief to my eyes.

This time, when he asked me if I loved him, I could say the words without fear of what I would become.

Eighteen: Crash

"Get them inside and get them restrained!"

The words came to Max as through water, garbled and hard to decode. When he understood them, he struggled. Nothing held him down, but something definitely pinned him from the sides. Canvas, if his eyes weren't fooling him.

"Bella!" He thrashed in his hammocklike prison, but he couldn't quite get his arms free. "Bella!"

"We've got her. You're going to be okay." A pale face peered over the edge of the litter. "What's your name?"

"She's pregnant. Is she okay? She's pregnant." He closed his eyes, willing himself to focus on the noise around him. If he could just hear her voice… "Bella!"

"She's fine. What's your name?" the medic repeated.

What the hell had happened? Where was he? What were these people doing?

The car. Rolling down the embankment. Blood. Everywhere, there had been blood.

Oh, God, he wasn't with the paramedics, was he?

They could put him in the hospital, sedate him, stick him in a nice, sunny room with an eastern exposure....

"I'm allergic to sunlight!" he shouted, finally freeing his hand to reach for the face before him. "I can't be in the daylight!"

The woman's face twisted into a demonic vision. Max had never been so happy to see something so nightmarish in his entire life.

"We know," she said with curt efficiency. "What's your name?"

"Max Harrison. I'm—" He'd almost blurted, "I'm Movement." *That would have been smooth.*

What the vampire said next was music to his ears. "Max Harrison, by authority of the Voluntary Vampire Extinction Movement, I'm placing you under arrest."

"I'm Movement." He gave a tired laugh. It was increasingly difficult to stay awake. "When there was one."

"What?" The woman's pale face went paler. "What did you say?"

"Leave him alone, he's not in any shape for interrogation," another voice admonished. "Get him into the van."

"Bella. Where's Bella?" Max's stomach turned. Why wouldn't they tell him anything? "I need her. I need to see Bella."

"You will," the male vampire assured him. "You will."

Something pricked Max's arm. Sleepy warmth spread through his veins, and everything went dark.

When Max woke again, he was in a hospital bed. He started, scanning the room frantically for a window. When he didn't find one, fragmented memories came back to him. He was with Movement. He was fine.

He tried to sit up. His arms were tied to the bed rails.

With a frustrated groan, he tugged futilely at his restraints. Leather. Not too shabby. Nothing he couldn't break free from on a good day, but this was definitely not a good day.

"Anybody out there?" No one answered his call. "Hey, can somebody hear me?"

"I hear ya, I hear ya." Heavy footsteps thudded toward the bed. Max turned his head. The vampire who stalked toward him probably weighed in at three hundred and fifty pounds of intimidating bulk stacked seven feet tall. His bushy red beard and beady black eyes looked more suited to a plaid shirt and overalls than the white doctor's coat he wore.

"Paul Bunyan?" Max said before he could stop himself.

The doctor didn't find it very humorous. "What do ya need? Keep in mind, I ain't lettin' you up, not 'til your Movement cred is established."

"Bella," Max wheezed. His chest ached with uncertainty. "Where is she?"

"She's over there." Dr. Lumberjack indicated a curtained-off cubicle not far from where Max lay. Fluorescent lights within cast ominous shadows of large medical machines.

At least Max could hear the steady beeping of a heart monitor. "Is she okay?"

"She's fine. We've got her sedated to keep her from moving around and opening her stitches, but she's gonna pull through."

"And the baby?" He wet his lips. "I mean, you knew she was pregnant?"

"We figured it out." The doctor raised an eyebrow. "Got a personal stake in it?"

"What do you think?" Max snapped. Then he softened. "I'm just looking out for her."

"The baby is fine. We did an ultrasound for her file. Do you wanna see?" Before Max could answer, Dr. Bunyan flipped open a chart.

The picture he held over Max's face didn't look like anything at all, at first. Just a weird swoop of grayish lines against blue-black. Only when the doctor tapped the printout and said, "That's the kid, right there," did Max understand what he was seeing. Within a dark area shaped like a jelly bean was a grayish object that bore an uncanny resemblance to a shrimp.

"That's the baby?" Max asked, looking from the image long enough to see the doctor nod. Max's chest constricted as if his ribs were in a vise. "That's…amazing."

"Is there something you wanna tell us?" the doctor asked, whisking the picture into the chart.

Max shook his head. "I told you everything I know."

The big man grunted in disbelief, but let the subject drop.

"Can I see her?" The fact she hadn't spoken yet troubled Max. He didn't think there was a sedative on earth that would shut her up.

"Sorry, can't let you up yet." The doctor tapped the chart in his hands cheerfully. "We'll let you know when your Movement cred checks out, and then we'll talk. But you can push this button—" he pressed a plastic control into Max's palm "—if you want to talk to someone before then."

"You mean if I want to spill something about the baby?" Max narrowed his eyes at him.

"Not necessarily." Whistling, the doctor walked away.

The sound of a door closing echoed in the space. Max was alone. "Bella?" he whispered. When she didn't answer, he dropped his head to the pillow and stared at the exposed pipes on the ceiling.

He had no idea how long he'd been asleep when Bella woke him.

"Max?" She sounded terrified. "Max!"

"I'm here, baby." He tested the restraints. Still strapped in. "Keep your voice down, or they'll come back."

"They?" Her voice quivered. "Max, where are we?"

He studied the concrete ceiling and exposed ventilation system. "A warehouse, apparently. We've been arrested by the Movement."

There was a pause in which Max heard her release a long, slow breath. When she spoke, she sounded much calmer. "Thank God."

He hated to get her worked up again, but he'd never coddled her before and he wouldn't start now. "Don't be thanking him yet. They know about the baby."

She paused again. "Oh?"

"Yeah, and I think they know where it came from." He craned his head to look for any sign of recording devices. Though he didn't see any, he wasn't sure they were a hundred percent in the clear. "Though I'm not entirely certain, myself."

She sniffled. Damn it, he'd made her cry.

"Don't do that. I'm sorry." When she didn't let up, he said, as brightly as he could manage, "Hey, they showed me an ultrasound of it."

"It survived?" The hope in her voice was tremulous. She was holding back, in case he answered in the negative.

He kept his voice intentionally light. "Oh, yeah, everything is fine. Looks like a shrimp, but seems fine."

She laughed tearfully. "Thank you, Max."

"I'm the last person you need to be thanking." He closed his eyes, resisting the urge to bang his head against the bed rails. It was his fault they were here. If he'd just calmed down, slowed down…

They'd probably have been captured by the Oracle. Brilliant.

"How did they find us?" Bella had dredged up her business voice. "No one knew we were there."

"I don't know. I suppose they'll tell us, once they figure out we're not working for the Oracle." He thought about pressing the button to call someone in so he could demand some answers.

As if reading his mind, Bella protested. "No. Let them come to us in their own time. I want to be with you right now. Even if we cannot see each other."

A reluctant smile tugged at his lips. "You know, I've always wanted to try bondage. I guess it works better when one person is untied."

"I would prefer that person to be me." She laughed, and when it died away, turned serious again. "Do you think they will harm the baby?"

"I think if they try, I'll be busting some heads." He said

it extra loud, so if their captors were listening, they'd hear. Then, more quietly, only for Bella's ears, he added, "You know I won't let that happen."

"Thank you," she replied. "Max?"

"Yeah?" God, he wanted to have her right there next to him. Seeing the ultrasound had made the idea of the baby oddly real. He wanted to put his arms around her, to lay his hands protectively over her stomach. Did a baby move when it was just a tadpole-looking thing? Would he be able to feel it?

Bella's voice trembled when she spoke. "I love you. You are the only one I love."

Or have loved, was the unspoken part of her statement, Max knew. She was still worried he thought he wasn't the father.

Well, was he? It seemed impossible, but there it had been, photographic proof. And Bella had said before that wolves were different when it came to sex. Even the most sexually active werewolf wouldn't have more than one partner in an entire lifetime. It probably wasn't as if she'd been banging some human guy in the busy month they'd been separated. She'd told Max as much, and as unbelievable as the whole situation seemed, he believed it.

"Yeah, I know. Don't you worry about that." He hoped that was enough. "And I love you."

After a long silence, he realized she was sleeping again.

"Max, wake up!"

The room was pitch-dark. Someone had come in—day

or night? he'd lost all sense of time—and turned off the overhead fluorescents.

"Max! Did they drug you or something?"

"Probably," he rasped. That voice was so familiar.

"Open your eyes, you dork."

He did. Anne, the eternally teenaged receptionist from Movement headquarters, stood over him, her porcelain-doll face etched with worry.

Max sighed in relief. "Oh, good. Can you go tell them I'm Movement so they'll let me up? Or feed me?" Then he blinked, crucial details rising to the surface of his groggy mind. "Wait, you're dead."

"Um, obviously I'm not, 'cause I'm standing right here." She leaned over him, squinting in annoyance at his restraints. "We've got to get you out of here."

"What?" He raised his head as far as he could from the pillow. "They're Movement."

"They're not Movement." She slipped a bobby pin from her hair, which she'd pulled back in a tight configuration of dark coils. A thin black feather floated down from the marabou trim of her leather coat to tickle his nose as she leaned close. "Hold still."

Max watched with grim amusement as she slipped the pin into the small brass padlock that secured the restraints around his left arm. Within seconds, his hand was free and she'd set to work on the other one.

"Okay, Velma, if they're not Movement, who are they?" When his right arm came free, he rubbed his wrists with a grimace. Leather would never sound sexy again.

"They're the Soul Eater's people." She grinned in triumph as she freed his right leg. "You have no idea what I've had to do to get in here."

"How did they know where we were?" He sat up, finding it hard to be still while she worked to unlock his left leg.

She shrugged. "They knew you were at the cabin in the woods. They've been watching that place like crazy. So were we. I hear you really tore it up."

"I had help." It had never felt so good to be *out* of bed before. "Thanks, Care Bear."

"You're welcome." She motioned toward the curtained area where Bella lay. "Now let's get her."

Max pulled back the drape and froze.

He hadn't seen Bella since before the accident. Well, during the accident, really. The stitched-closed gashes on her head and face came courtesy of the passenger window. Or the former passenger window, if he wanted to be technical. The shards had rained over them, and he'd seen her blood hang suspended in the air for a split second before it splattered across the dash. The bruise across her neck and upper chest bore an uncanny resemblance to a seat belt. He didn't want to think about what the lap belt had done to her. The black eyes were unexplainable, but probably had something to do with her smashed, slightly out of shape nose and the tape across the bridge of it. Her right leg—the one closest to the point of impact—was bracketed by some weird metal contraption.

"It's an external fixator," Anne cheerfully explained as she lowered the side rails. "That takes me back to my last assignment. I fell the equivalent of sixteen stories out of a hot air balloon. Ended up with metal screws in my pelvis.

Good old Movement medicine. They were thinking up things like that long before real MDs were."

"How are we going to get her out of here?" There was an IV in her right arm and a catheter tube taped to her leg.

"I have a wheelchair in the car. You'll have to carry her that far, if you can." Anne untied the catheter bag from the rail and grabbed the IV bag from the pole. She tossed them onto the bed between Bella's legs and pulled the bottom sheet free. "I guess scoop her up and carry her. That's probably our best bet."

"I think you're right." He leaned over Bella and pressed his lips to her forehead, trying not to smell the blood in the cut over her eyebrow. "Wake up, baby. We gotta go."

"Go where?" she mumbled sleepily, a smile slowly spreading across her face. Her drowsy eyes shot open as she remembered their circumstances. "How did you get free?"

Anne stepped closer, touching Bella's arm. "You're not safe here."

"With the Movement? Do not be absurd." She looked to Max. "Tell her. Tell her what is going on."

"She knows what's going on." He checked over his shoulder, sure that at any moment Grizzly Adams, M.D., would come in and shut down their whole operation. "These people are not Movement. They're the Soul Eater's guys. They were watching the cabin."

There was a noise at the door. "They're coming. I barred it from the inside, but they will get through," Anne warned.

"Let's go." Max scooped Bella up as carefully as he could, though she cried out when he jostled her leg. "I'm so sorry, baby."

"There's another door." Anne gestured to the side of the room, which had been blocked by the curtains. "Come on!"

They charged through the door, into a maze of industrial shelves coated in a thick layer of dust. At the other end—they had to run about the length of a football field with Bella crying out at each step—an illuminated exit sign glowed an eerie red.

It wasn't a shaft of heavenly light, but he'd take it.

Anne ran ahead and kicked the door down.

"Was it locked?" he called over his shoulder as she let him pass through.

"I don't know. The car's over there!" She ran ahead again, sliding over the gravel in her platform combat boots.

"Easy, baby," he soothed against Bella's damp hair as he leaned down to put her in the back of the car. "Why the hell does the Soul Eater want us?"

"You know why!" Anne closed the door as soon as he slid inside beside Bella. The locks popped into place automatically.

There were no handles.

"Anne?" He pounded the window with his fist. The glass thumped dully. Bulletproof. Break proof.

Outside, three vampires ran from the building. Anne pulled three slim stakes from the waistband of her black plastic pants and threw them one after another without pausing to check her strikes. She didn't have to. As she dropped into the driver's seat, the vampires burst into flame.

"It doesn't matter what the Soul Eater wants with her," she managed through rapid breaths as she started the car. She turned toward him, leaning over the seat.

Max didn't see the hypodermic until she stuck him with it. His vision swam and went dark. The last thing he heard before he blacked out was Anne saying smugly, "Because the Oracle wants her more."

Nineteen: Hocus Pocus

I was still asleep when Nathan burst into the room. So, apparently, was Cyrus. He sat up beside me, glowering and squinting against the illumination from the overhead light.

Nathan looked from Cyrus to me, then scowled. "Get up. We've got problems."

He slammed the door so hard a light rain of plaster fell from the ceiling.

"Well, that is a somewhat less pleasant wake-up call than I'd hoped for." Cyrus eased from the bed, wincing as he stood. "And I think I'll go back to sleeping on the couch."

"Yeah, and he'll stake you as soon as you fall asleep." My muscles protested as I sat up. "Oh, it's going to be a long night."

"It was a long day. I'd forgotten how much you snored. And drooled," Cyrus said, casting me a sidelong glare.

"I forgot how much you exaggerated." I rubbed the corner of my mouth anyway, just in case he was right about the drool.

We limped out to the living room. Nathan looked like a

man who'd rather be breaking someone's legs with a golf club. It *was* going to be a long night.

"What's going on?" I asked, sitting on the couch. When Cyrus sat beside me, I scooted away.

It didn't go unnoticed, by either of them. Jealousy hit me from both sides of the blood tie, for different reasons, and I had to consciously divert my focus to the task at hand.

To my relief, Nathan cut me off from the tie on his end. "I got a call from some Movement vampires in Canada. It seems Max and Bella were in a car accident. Max was okay, but Bella was in bad shape."

"Was?" Cyrus put his hand on my knee. Not possessively, though Nathan would probably see it that way.

I didn't brush it aside. "But they survived the crash?"

Nathan nodded. "As far as they knew. But they're not there anymore. They killed three Movement doctors and escaped. He left everything behind. Money, car, phone… there's no way to contact him."

"Why would they run from the Movement?" It didn't make any sense. Max was still an active member. He didn't have a mark on his head, like Nathan did. He wasn't even hanging out on the fringe like I was, waiting for someone to get the notion to pick off some nonthreatening vampires.

Nathan considered a moment, then held up his hands. "I don't know. They think they had help."

"Help against the Movement? That doesn't sound promising. Who would help them against the Movement?" Cyrus said this without his trademark sarcasm. It was a good thing. Neither Nathan nor I would have appreciated it.

"They could have been kidnapped," I offered helpfully. "Like, maybe somebody took them?"

Nathan shook his head. "Who would be able to get a vampire and a half-crippled, pregnant werewolf out of a warehouse under heavy Movement guard?"

"Someone they trust," Cyrus said quietly, not looking at either of us.

"Excuse me?" Barely leashed rage swam beneath the surface of Nathan's too polite inquiry.

Cyrus looked up, first at him, then me, then back to Nathan. "If someone in the Movement that they trusted helped them, they might not have resisted."

"It's impossible." Nathan stood and turned away, raking a hand over his stubbled jaw. He looked as though he hadn't slept. "No, it's not possible."

"Consider the situation," Cyrus continued calmly. "You said they were heavily guarded. If someone wanted to get in or out, they would have to kill a lot more than three people."

"The only person who could pull it off would have been an assassin," I interjected. "Someone who could take on three vampires at the same time."

Cyrus made an affirmative sound. "And convince your friends to go with them."

"What are you talking about?" Nathan whirled, his face twisted with rage. He stabbed his finger through the air in Cyrus's direction. "First of all, you've never been part of the Movement, so you don't know anything about how we operate."

"I know how we infiltrated and subverted it time and again," Cyrus replied calmly.

"He has a point." Why did I suddenly feel as if we were ganging up on Nathan?

A moment later, I didn't care. Nathan glared at me, his eyes cold. "You certainly wouldn't have any clue about the Movement works. It's a group of vampires loyal to a common ideal. The key word being *loyal.*"

The bottom dropped out of my stomach. "What did you say to me?"

"You heard me." Across the blood tie I felt a wave of shame at the way he was acting, but his anger was too great to suppress.

"That is enough!" Cyrus shot to his feet, and for a moment I thought he would try something stupid, like punching Nathan. Instead, he swallowed audibly, unclenched his fists and spoke in a calmer tone. "We are not in an ideal situation. I will seek to rectify that as soon as I can get my house back from my formerly human former girlfriend. But we have larger problems at hand than the issue of your romance with Carrie."

My heart ached at his words. I did love Cyrus, now that I was morally free to do so. But I loved Nathan, as well, and I hated causing him pain after all he'd been through for me.

Cyrus shot me a cold look. *You'll never know what you want. Now is not the time.*

Nathan looked from Cyrus to me and sighed. "What's our next step, then, oh wise one?"

Thankfully, Cyrus let the jibe slide. "We go back to our only source of information. My father."

"Oh yes. Your father. The one who controlled you for

how many centuries? Let me drive you right over there."
Nathan laughed.

"Nathan!" I clutched my head, unable to bear another
moment of this pointless bickering. "Max and Bella are
clearly in danger. We need to find out where they are, so
we can keep the Soul Eater from getting his hands on the
baby. We know him well enough to know whatever he
wants with it probably isn't good. And what he'd do to
Bella and Max wouldn't be good, either. Can we all at least
agree on that?"

"Of course we can," Nathan grumbled. "But I'm sick of
sitting around talking about it. We've been stuck here for
days just reading and researching and waiting, while
they're off getting killed."

"That was what we agreed on." But I could definitely
sympathize. I'd felt helpless for the past few days, as well.
It was hard, after being so active in our past dramas, to be a
bit player in this one. "We don't have anything else to go on.
We don't know where the Soul Eater is. We don't know
where Max and Bella are. All we can do is wait."

"You're half-right." Nathan looked as tired as he
sounded. "I know where Jacob—" He stopped himself, gri-
macing. "I know where the Soul Eater is. He's coming
back. For Dahlia."

Her name forced my hands into fists. Jealousy and anger
burned through me. Yes, I was still jealous of her, after all
this time. "Fine. I'll go and find out what we need to know."

"Are you insane?" Cyrus actually laughed at me. "My
father will kill you. Dahlia will kill you before he gets
the chance."

I shook my head. "Clarence will help me. He talks a tough game, but he hates vampires. He'll do anything to get them out of the house."

"He can't help you, Carrie. As long as my father's name is on the deed, Clarence can't do anything that will directly harm him. He—"

"Comes with the house, I know, Cyrus," I interrupted. "But I have to try. I'm the only one who isn't blood tied to him, vampirewise or through genetics."

"Absolutely not!" Nathan shook his head vehemently. "It's ridiculous and dangerous."

I tossed up my hands, though I knew I didn't sound one hundred percent reasonable. "We have a chance here to do something. I'm the only one in this room who hasn't been manipulated or enslaved by the Soul Eater. We think he wants Bella, for the baby. So, why don't we do more? Why don't we go over there, to the mansion, and find out what he's up to? Why don't we do something—"

"Something suicidal!"

"But *something!*" I shouted, jumping to my feet. "I'm sorry if I can't think of exactly what you want to do, but we have to do something!"

Nathan's hands clenched to fists at his sides. "You're sorry? Since when do you care about what I want?"

I drew a deep breath, willing myself to calm down. It took great effort. "You're right. I've never done anything with your best interests at heart. I never traded your life for mine. I never risked myself to protect your son. Never let your dead wife's soul invade my body to free you from an evil spell."

"Not without throwing the facts back at me over and over," he snapped. "If you want to go get yourself killed, fine."

"Who says we're going to get ourselves killed?" Cyrus asked, leaning to pick up Dahlia's grimoire from the table. "I'm sure she has something in here we can use as protection."

Nathan regarded him for a moment with icy contempt. He softened a bit as he took the book from him. "These spells are far too advanced for a beginner. There's no way you'll pull it off."

"What about you?" Cyrus demanded. "You own that shop downstairs. Do you mean to tell me you don't know any…hocus-pokery?"

I snorted, despite the tension in the air. Both men glared at me.

Nathan shook his head. "I don't actually practice witchcraft. I'm only in the New Age business to take advantage of the rampant consumerism."

I looked at the book in Nathan's hands as though it were a deadly viper. "Well, what could it hurt? I mean, we've looked through it. She has all sorts of things we could try."

"Hexes, counterhexes, invisibility spells." Cyrus rattled off the list. "That last isn't a bad idea. I know she had one."

"Invisibility spells are rarely literal," Nathan protested. "Often, they're just to help keep a low profile."

Cyrus stepped forward and took the book back, flipping pages with a frown. "Ah!" He jabbed his finger at the top of one page and held it up so we could see "Invisibility Spell (Literally)" scribbled across the top.

There was a long moment where no one spoke. I have

no doubt we were all considering the implications. It would take a lot of nerve to try and sneak into a witch's house cloaked by an invisibility spell, if it even worked. It would be dangerous.

Of course, no more dangerous than what I'd already done. "I'll do it."

They looked at me as if I'd suggested I would make the Statue of Liberty disappear.

"How?" Nathan folded his arms across his chest as if daring me to prove him wrong. "Do you even know the basics of spell work?"

"No," I reluctantly admitted. "But I did participate in the ritual to get you back from the scary side. And I used to play that light-as-a-feather game at slumber parties."

Nathan actually smiled a little at that. "I quiver in fear."

"From what I understand, our options are fairly limited. We can either charge in, guns blazing, so to speak, or try and sneak in to gather the information and then go rescue your friends." Cyrus tapped the book. "I think we should try the one where my father doesn't kill us all, and we have a chance to save their lives as well."

Nathan watched us, his expression tight. "What about me?"

"What about you?" Cyrus asked offhandedly.

He rolled his eyes. "I have a blood tie to your father, you stupid bastard! He'll know we're coming!"

"There's no need for name calling," I interrupted. "You've closed him off for years. He won't suspect anything."

"That's not true," Cyrus said quietly. "Nathan's absolutely right."

I turned to Cyrus. "So, it's just you and me, then?"

"The hell it is!" Nathan roared. "I'm not letting you go in there with him!"

"If she can't go with me, she has to go alone. You've already made it clear you don't like that option, either." Cyrus sighed. "Neither do I. But it is our best option."

"Cyrus—" I began, but he cut me off.

"I'm still susceptible to him." He looked down, as if ashamed. "He's a very…charismatic man."

"She managed to fight off your charms for a while, anyway. Maybe she has a chance against him." Nathan sounded resigned and very, very unhappy. "I've got to go downstairs and open the shop. If you promise not to be trouble, the two of you can come down and help me find the ingredients for these spells. Carrie, you'll have to practice."

He sounded like a music instructor. Practice! As if I could practice for something so dangerous. In fact, the less I thought about it, the less likely it would be that I would back out.

"Fine. You two see what you can do. I'll rejoin you shortly." Cyrus issued his proclamation with the air of someone who knew exactly how to order people around.

"What are you going to do? Wish us luck?" I planted my hands on my hips.

"No, I'm going to take a shower. Unlike others in this apartment, I don't let personal hygiene fall by the wayside when catastrophe strikes." He nodded to Nathan and me and disappeared down the hallway.

Nathan said very little as we walked down to the shop. He unlocked the door, and I stepped inside and waited for him to turn on the lights. I never touched the switches behind the counter. They always gave me static shocks.

The banks of fluorescents clicked and buzzed, illuminating the store from the back to the front. I blinked against the changing light and headed toward the counter.

On the floor behind the glass display cases containing gaudy pentacles and ridiculously expensive crystal wands, I spied a sleeping bag. Nathan stooped down and began rolling it up. I watched for a moment, until he glanced up and asked, "Well, are you going to give that spell a look?"

"You've been sleeping *here?*" I winced, imagining what the hard wooden floor would have done to my back had I been in his place.

He zipped the sleeping bag with great purpose. "It's not permanent. I'm not going to just hand my apartment over to you."

"I would never ask you to." My fingers flexed on the edge of the countertop. "I never asked you to."

There was a long silence. When Nathan looked at me again, his eyes were rimmed with red. "Why him, Carrie?"

My voice caught in my throat. "Would it have been better if it was someone else?"

"No." He didn't turn away, just kept staring at me with an intensity that burned. "No, it wouldn't have been."

I glanced down to hide the tears in my eyes. "He loves me. Or, he wanted me to love him once, and now that's just…enough."

"You wanted to love me once, too," Nathan reminded me.

I nodded and swallowed against my tears. "He's different now. When he was my sire, I wanted so badly to give in to him. To let my humanity go just so I could be with him. But I couldn't. I don't know why."

"Because you're a good person." He smiled sadly. "So, you love him now because he deserves it?"

"Nathan, I would never want to hurt you. But…" I closed my eyes. "But no matter what, I'm going to be with someone who doesn't love me more than he loves a memory. He's my fledgling. I do feel like…like I owe him my affection."

"I know exactly how that feels." Nathan's words sent a dagger through her. "Except for the bit about owing my affection. You see, I never felt I owed you anything. What little I could give you, I gave freely."

My chest constricted, and I couldn't hold back my sob. "Nathan—"

"No." He turned away. "No, I get the last word in this one, Carrie. Read the spell. I'll go look for a book on basic magic."

I slumped over the counter, resting my forehead on my palms. It would have been so nice to break down, to sob my eyes out at the unfairness of it all. Once again, I was pulled between the same two men. Once again, I would never be certain I'd made the right choice.

But there was no time for self-pity. Wiping my eyes, I willed myself to stop crying. Time to get down to business.

The spell was broken down into two parts, an ingredients list and various directions, numbered, renumbered, crossed out and scribbled over.

"We need heliotrope," I called.

"The herb or the stone?" Cupboard doors scraped open somewhere in the back of the shop.

"Both, actually." I scanned the ingredients. "And a blue

candle. And a bunch of stuff that is, like, way too disgusting to even consider."

Nathan returned and leaned over my shoulder. His closeness did nothing to calm my strained nerves. "Why would she include these things?" he mumbled, his finger pausing near the item "baby teeth."

"Maybe to get someone off track?" It came to me in a flash of inspiration. "If I were to look at this spell, I would think all this weird, exotic stuff was the most important."

The bells above the door jingled, and Cyrus strolled in casually, a carefully composed expression on his face. "So, what have I missed?" He stopped at my side, one hand possessively on the small of my back, and leaned over the book. "Do you really have all these ingredients?"

"That's what we were just discussing," Nathan explained. "We have the heliotrope. Not much else."

"Mmm." Cyrus squinted at the list. "Well, we're sunk. The calf's heart we can get from a butcher, but human toenails... I'd give mine up, only they're not human anymore."

"See?" I smiled triumphantly. "I bet these are all a distraction. Whoever attempts the spell will break their back finding all these morbid components, and leave out one or two small details. Only, the small details are the only truly important ones."

"I have to admit, I'm impressed." Nathan rubbed a hand over his jaw. "How did you know that?"

"Recipes. My mother used to complain that her mother-in-law always left something important out, or labeled it optional. It was like cracking a code." I turned my attention to the actual instructions for the spell.

"Women are devious," Cyrus observed, as if realizing it for the first time.

I pointed to the page. "See here, she has you anoint the heliotrope stone with oil of heliotrope, but everything else gets thrown in a cauldron and burned."

Cyrus sniffed in distaste. "Imagine the stench."

"I'd rather not." Nathan shook up the small bottle of oil. "Let's hope this is the real stuff, not a synthetic. I'm paying enough for the real deal, but suppliers can be a bit shady."

"Oh, I've heard the herb trade is brutal," Cyrus quipped.

I elbowed him. "If you're not going to help, there's a sinkful of dishes upstairs."

"Are you ready to try this?" Nathan asked, lifting the rock so I could see it.

It was green, with subtle red flecks the color of dried blood.

"Also known as bloodstone," Nathan said, turning it so the red flecks sparked in the light. "An obvious choice for a vampire."

I held out my palm and he dropped the stone there. It seemed to burn my skin. "What do I have to do?"

"Anoint the stone with the oil, apparently," Cyrus observed with a bit of amusement. "And carry it with you to remain invisible."

An involuntary shiver went up my back. I'd volunteered to do it, but now I wasn't so sure I liked the idea of being invisible. So much of the human psyche is tied to the physical body…. I wondered what effect it would have on a person to be unincorporated, for lack of a better term.

Nathan put a reassuring hand on my arm. "Likely, it

won't make you physically invisible. Most of these spells just cause anyone who sees you to not notice you."

I closed my fingers over the stone. "Okay, here goes nothing."

Nathan unscrewed the cap of the oil bottle and held it tentatively toward me. "Now, this isn't the whole of the spell. What makes it work is your intent. Focus your mind, all of your energy, on becoming invisible."

I'd certainly had enough experience with that. Calmly, I set the stone on the counter, imagining shrinking down in my chair in my high school English class when the teacher asked a question. I thought of walking through a bad part of town at night, keeping close to the buildings, sticking to the shadows.

I thought of sneaking across the lawn behind Cyrus's mansion to meet with Nathan at the gate, and pictured the guards looking at me and seeing nothing.

Then I realized I was already an expert at invisibility. No one had seen me without me wanting them to for years. My face, my build, even my hair color were so nondescript I could rob a bank without anyone identifying me. This would be a piece of cake.

At the same time I thought it, another wave of confidence rose within me. It was darker, ego driven and wild. Crazy.

It was Dahlia.

"I drank her blood," I heard myself saying, as if from far away. "I think it's doing something to me."

Cyrus stepped back. Even Nathan seemed frightened.

I am invisible, I chanted in my head as I wiped the oil on the stone. The flowery scent calmed me, even as the stone seemed to burn from my concentrated energy. All my thoughts and visualizations flowed from my body through the fingertips of my right hand, into the stone.

Then, just as abruptly as the sensations came, they stopped. The dark energy left over from Dahlia's blood soaked into the stone, leaching some of me with it, and I jerked my hand back.

"She did it," Cyrus said, almost breathlessly. "I can't believe she really did it."

"What? What did I do?" Before they could answer, I picked up the stone, so cold it burned, and gasped as my hand, then my wrist, then my arm vanished as though dissolving. I looked at my feet, only to see the floor they should be standing on. I waved my fingers in front of my face, but they weren't there anymore.

The room spun around me. Without visual confirmation of my body in its own space, I lost my sense of balance for a moment, stumbling against the counter.

"Grab her!" Nathan shouted.

"How? I can't see her!" Cyrus reached out uncertainly and I grasped his arms. The second the stone touched him, he vanished as well.

We stood perfectly still, holding each other for balance. I would have paid anything to see the expression on Cyrus's face.

"Well, we know it's not just figurative invisibility now, don't we?" he said with a rueful laugh, and I laughed with him.

Something was finally working to our advantage.

Twenty: Origins

Sitting up, Max blinked in an effort to bring his vision into focus. When he tried to rub his eyes, chains rattled and his arms met with marked resistance. *Waking up in another dark, strange place, restrained.*

Perfect.

"I wondered when you would wake."

Bella. He wished he could see her. "Did she hurt you?"

There was a squeak. Something nudged his foot. When he looked up, he saw her face.

"The drugs will make it hard to see for a while. Relax, and let it pass." Her fingertips brushed his face. She wasn't bound.

"Did they hurt you?" he repeated. His tongue felt as if it were covered in fur. He'd kill for a drink.

The scent of her blood assaulted him, and he involuntarily lunged toward her. He heard her startled intake of breath, felt her withdraw a bit. He'd scared her. "Sorry, can't help it."

"I know." She placed her cool palm against his forehead. "No, they did not hurt me. They tended me better than the Movement did. At first, I did not know why, but…"

"Why didn't they tie you up?" Not that he wanted her restrained. He just wondered why she was free and hadn't tried to make a break for it yet.

"I could not go far. I am…in a wheelchair." She whispered the word like a curse. "I am crippled."

He closed his eyes, though he couldn't see worth a damn, anyway. "I'm so sorry, baby."

"Do not be sorry. They followed us from the cabin. You could not have prevented it." She moved away, and he wondered why he hadn't recognized the sound of the wheelchair as it moved across the dirt floor of the room.

"You sound awfully calm." Too calm. Something was wrong. He couldn't put his finger on what.

Anne. That bitch had sold them out. When he got his hands on her, he'd rip her black little heart right out of her chest.

"I have had time to think." Bella returned with a bag full of blood. He didn't know where it came from, and he didn't care. She held it to his mouth and he tore into it, not caring that some of the contents probably ran down his chin and stained his shirt. Only when he'd drunk half of it did he consider it might have been drugged. He jerked away, the remains of his meal sloshing onto his lap.

Bella shrieked and jumped back. "You should have drunk all of it!"

"Why?" He struggled against his shackles. "Are you in on this? What do they have planned?"

"I did not know. Not before Anne brought us here." Her voice dropped to almost a whisper. "I was never involved in this in any way. Until we were brought here, I knew only what you knew. You must believe me."

She flung her arms around his neck despite his bloody clothes. He wished he could put his arms around her. It had been too long since he'd been able to. "I believe you, baby. But tell me what's going on."

"It was a setup," she sobbed against his shoulder. "The cabin, the car accident. The Movement got there before the Oracle's people could collect us, but when we went with Anne… She is not on our side.

"I woke in the car. You were drugged. When we arrived here, they took me to a medical facility. I do not know what they did to me. When I woke again, they did not argue when I asked to be brought to you."

"They treated you okay?" That didn't bode well for her, somehow. "What about the baby? Is it okay?"

"Yes," she said quietly. "That is what they want."

If ever there was a moment he could imagine busting iron chains, now should be it. Max roared, his face shifting as he struggled against the shackles.

"Calm yourself," Bella soothed, laying a hand on his brow. With a heavy sigh, she withdrew. "I think perhaps it is time to tell you something very few of your kind know."

He swallowed thickly. "Is it anything I want to know?"

"It is something you must know, now." She hesitated for a moment, then, with a deep breath, plunged in. "You know of the division between werewolves and lupins?"

It wasn't the question he expected. "Yeah. It's something the Movement teaches. Werewolves are into the earth spirituality, and using magic to control their change, while lupins figured out a way to do it medically, and think they're all better than you."

"No," Bella said with a note of sadness in her voice. "They have been lying to you for years."

The Movement lied? It should have come as more of a surprise to him, but lately it was hard to disbelieve any nasty thing someone had to say about them. "Is that so?"

His vision had cleared enough that he made out her emphatic nod. "The real cause for our division is… Perhaps I should start from the beginning.

"You recall what I told you about the blood debt that can never be repaid? The curse that is branded on my body?"

"Sure." Max searched the corners of his still-foggy brain. "Something about all werewolves being descended from Pontius Pilate and that's why you're all cursed, right?"

"The division between werewolves and lupins started there, though both factions kept it quiet until lately. When the children of Pontius Pilate, and their children, became aware of their affliction, naturally, they hid it. It was a superstitious time, and they were surrounded by godly people. Some of them returned to Rome, where their animal state was worshipped as a gift from the gods, an allusion to Romulus and Remus, who founded the city.

"But the ones who stayed behind in the land of the Hebrews learned quickly to control their change. They lived their lives as quietly as possible, though some began to piece together the reason for their curse. It took generations. In time, the gospel of the carpenter messiah was preached even in Rome. The werewolves there were persecuted, as were followers of the old gods. I pity them, in spite of their later alliance. They were if not divinity, then royalty in the Roman Empire. They fled, their numbers now rivaling Rome's most populous legion, to their roots in the Holy Land.

"Though their brother wolves welcomed them with open arms, it was not long before the falling out occurred. You see, the werewolves in Jerusalem now understood the nature of their curse. This knowledge was not accepted by the Roman wolves. Already bitter at the rise of Christianity, which had stolen their prosperity in Rome, they were not about to die to repay the blood of a Hebrew carpenter.

"What happened next is not entirely clear. There are too many versions of the story to say that the one I tell you is the absolute truth, but it was taught to me as a child and it is the version I know best. There was a Roman noblewoman, Julia, living in Jerusalem. Her husband had been a prefect there, and when he died she had become stranded, without money enough to return to Rome. How she continued to survive was a great debate, but it was said that men could be seen entering her house during the night, and she always had enough coin to pay for bread. She never left her house, not by day or by night, but she sent many letters and entertained guests from far-off lands.

"Somehow, she became aware of the werewolves in the city and their situation. She sent for three of the Roman expatriates, Titus, Cicero and Lucius, and held a dinner in their honor. After the rest of the guests had left, she met with the wolves in private, and here is where the story of the lupins and werewolves becomes a tale of feud. After the meeting with Julia, the werewolves were never the same. They were cursed with an insatiable blood hunger. They transformed at will, no longer enslaved by the full moon. You see, Julia was a vampire, and out of boredom or for her own evil ends, she turned them. They were the first lupins."

"Oh, fuck," Max whispered, almost unaware he'd spoken.

Bella didn't admonish him for interrupting. "Of the three, Titus was the least pleased with his change. He had begun to accept the blood debt we inherited from Pontius Pilate, and had secretly been studying the gospels with another pack of werewolves. When he revealed his new nature to them, they shunned him. Word spread quickly through the Jerusalem faction. They grew mistrustful of all Roman wolves and declared war on them. The Roman wolves scattered again, but they vowed to destroy the werewolves. One by one, they were turned, either by Cicero or Lucius. Titus disappeared, though a rumor surfaces every now and then that he runs a monastic sanctuary for lupins who have changed their ways and wish to repay the blood debt."

"By killing other lupins." It was all becoming too clear. Horrifyingly clear.

Bella nodded.

"And Julia? The noblewoman who started it all?" Max asked, dreading the answer.

"Why do you think the Movement did not share this information with you? She is the Oracle, whom you helped hold captive all those years." There was no mocking in her tone, but Max still felt like a fool.

"Sons of bitches. They knew all along what the lupins were and they never told us? Why?"

"I do not know. When the Order of the Brethren formed, they attempted to apply their code to lupins. The lupins were…not pleased. That is why the Brethren turned to the werewolves, instead. They offered help in exterminating lupins as long as werewolves—"

"Kept their mouths shut and killed some vampires, and lupins, which should have paid the blood debt." It seemed all too clear now. But why had they kept the Oracle? She'd made powerful predictions, but they were often too abstract to really understand until after the foretold event had taken place.

As if reading his mind, Bella said, "The Oracle was an insurance policy. We knew we could not win the fight if they had her on their side. After the Movement captured her, they kept us under their control with the constant threat of her release."

"Wonderful. I'm glad it worked out so well for them." Max yanked at his restraints. "So, lupins are half werewolf, half vampire. Stands to reason that our baby—"

"Is a natural-born lupin," she answered sadly. "The only one of its kind."

"Which is why the Oracle wants her." *Just great.* He'd never wanted kids until he found out he was going to get one whether he wanted it or not, and now she was going to be taken from him.

"Her?" Bella asked, her amusement audible. "I thought you said it looked like a shrimp."

"It did. I just…" He hung his head. "We've got to get out of here."

She looked away. "They told me, after they brought me here…you are to be an example."

"And example of what? The most stupid vampire on

earth?" He flopped back on the cot, wincing as the cuffs bit into his wrists.

"They have some Movement holdouts as prisoners. They are going to…torture you, and kill you. To frighten them into changing sides." Bella sobbed openly now.

It made him feel a little better to know she was upset at the prospect of his imminent death, even if he couldn't be. He was, stupidly, more worried about her. "Well, I always did want to go out in a *Braveheart* kind of way. I'll just have to think of something cool to yell before they cut my head off."

His attempt at humor failed to lighten the mood, and he swore. "Come over here, Bella. If I'm gonna die, I at least want to spend my last hours with you."

She rolled her chair to his side. Groping blindly, he found her hand. Their fingers entwined as she lay her head on his chest.

"Don't count me out yet, baby," he murmured reassuringly. "We're all coming out of this one alive."

He just hoped it wasn't a lie.

When we turned in for the morning, all three of us agreed: I would go to the Soul Eater's mansion at dusk.

With all the nervous tension coiling in my stomach, I couldn't sleep. It didn't help that my bed was barely large enough to sleep one person comfortably, let alone both Cyrus and me.

"If you don't stop tossing around, I'm going to tie you down," he warned sleepily. "And not in a sexy way."

I burrowed my face against his cold chest. "I'm sorry. I can't sleep."

"Really? If you hadn't said so I might not have noticed." He pulled me closer and I wriggled to face away from him. His arm relaxed where it lay over my stomach, and I thought he'd fallen asleep again when he spoke. "Carrie, don't go."

"What?" I half sat up.

"Don't go," he repeated. "Let's pack up right now, steal the van and just drive."

"You know we can't." But my heart shouted, *Go!* I would listen to my mind this time, I decided firmly. So many decisions I'd made lately based on my feelings had turned out horribly wrong.

"We can! We won't have to face my father. We'll find someplace nice—well, maybe not nice, but a place to stay, nonetheless—and we'll hide until all of this nonsense is over," he insisted, his tone pleading.

I wanted to give in to him. The look of utter desperation on his face nearly overwhelmed me. Then I thought of Nathan in the next room. I imagined him waking to find I'd gone, and realizing he had to fight his sire alone.

"I can't lose you, Carrie. I just can't." Cyrus pulled me tight to him, his fingers digging into my back. Had he always been this fragile, even when he was a monster?

"You won't lose me," I soothed, freeing a hand to stroke his hair. "But if we don't go after your father, who will? Nathan? Is he going to sneak into the mansion? Is he going to rescue Bella and Max?"

There was no way he'd be capable of it. Resisting his sire's will alone was a dicey proposition. But to expect him to pull it off and free Max and Bella was ridiculous wishful thinking.

"I'm not going to leave Nathan behind." I repeated, "You won't lose me." Then I realized I'd never even imagined I might lose him, or Nathan.

Suddenly, I understood too well where Cyrus was coming from.

We were mostly silent as we prepared for the night. Nathan dug out his old Movement uniform for himself and a matching set for Cyrus. I thought of making a joke about the Doublemint twins, but figured it would go over like a lead balloon.

I dressed for comfort—I was going to be invisible anyway, I argued when they objected to my decidedly non-blacked-out attire—and armed myself simply. A few stakes and a couple vials of holy water were the weapons I hoped I wouldn't need. If all went according to plan, I would get into the mansion, poke around until I found what I was after, and slip back out without a fight.

Of course, when had things ever gone according to plan? The gods of physical humor seemed inclined to watch me try to fight as often as possible.

Nathan, on the other hand, had a pile of weapons beside him as he sat in the armchair inspecting his crossbow.

"Is that all you're taking?" I asked sarcastically, dropping onto the couch.

He smiled wryly. "Where's Cyrus?"

"Showering and changing into his spiffy new Movement attire."

Nathan raised an eyebrow.

"He says if he's going to die again, he's going to die

clean." I surreptitiously sniffed my armpit. I didn't want to be the one who died with B.O.

"No one is going to die," Nathan assured me in the gruff, detached way he always spoke when his hands and eyes were otherwise occupied. "This is probably the easiest thing we've ever done, on account of your unexpected talent for the occult."

"I told you, that was Dahlia's blood doing it. Let's hope she doesn't pick up on the trick while I'm in there." I looked around the apartment. All the furniture was visible. "Where's the stone?"

"It's in the shop, on the table when you first come through the door, so don't walk into it." He set the crossbow aside with a heavy exhalation. "I want you to be extremely careful tonight."

How like him, to turn an inconsequential moment into a too-serious-for-comfort pep talk. I put on my brave face for him. "You know I will be. When have I ever marched into danger recklessly before?"

Another sardonically arched brow.

"Okay, but those times were life-and-death. And once, it was your life on the line, so you can't really complain." On impulse, I stood and went to his chair, knelt beside him and laid my head on his knee.

I think he was too startled to say anything at first, but after a moment he put his hand on my head. "I love you, Carrie."

If he had hit me in the chest with a sledgehammer, it would have had about the same effect. I couldn't breathe. It was like he'd knocked the wind out of me.

I wanted to ask what he meant by that. Did he love me

the way a sire is supposed to love his fledgling? Or did he love me like a man is supposed to love a woman when there isn't a bunch of screwed up emotional baggage and vampire history thrown in the mix? And why now? Why wait until we were about to do something dangerous to confess his love? Did he think one of us wouldn't survive to feel awkward about this later?

But I didn't ask any of the questions I was dying to have answered. I'd finally heard what I'd wanted to for so long. I just took it for what it was, for now.

"I listened to my blood tie with the Soul Eater last night," Nathan said, changing the subject as naturally as if he'd just said, "The weather's been fine, hasn't it?"

I did not recover so easily. My "Oh?" was forced and transparent.

He nodded. "He has the Oracle's heart."

This time my "Oh?" was surprised and strangled.

"Yes. He is planning on devouring it, and with it, the Oracle's soul. Do you want to hear what I think?"

I knew it was a rhetorical question, so I didn't answer. He'd tell me anyway.

And I was right. A spark that had been missing for so long lit Nathan's eyes. "I think we should change our objective a little. Are you up to finding the Oracle's heart and destroying it?"

I laughed a little to cover my shock. I'm sure it worked about as well as all my attempts to cover my emotions. "Well, um. I suppose so."

"The way I see it, we'd kill two birds with one stone." He smiled. "Or you would. If the Oracle has Max and

Bella—hell, even if it's the Soul Eater's people who have them—the death of the Oracle is going to throw things into a tailspin. It'll be easier for them to get away, and it cleans up our problem with her forever."

"It will also ruin the Soul Eater's current plans and buy us more time to regroup." I nodded. "Okay. I'll do it. If father is anything like son, I have a feeling it won't be too difficult."

"Father is indeed like son." Nathan suddenly turned serious. "They are very much alike, Carrie. If something happens, if things go wrong…if you're forced to confront him, don't underestimate him. He is very manipulative and seductive."

Seductive? I'd seen the Soul Eater a total of one time in the flesh. He'd been half-decayed and reeking of death, calling out for blood and souls in an inhuman chorus of horror. I'd seen him in memories, but he'd been a filthy peasant then, and dung is not a look I find attractive on a man. "I'll try to resist his charms."

Nathan didn't laugh with me. "It isn't a joking matter, Carrie."

For the first time, he purposely forced his own memory into my mind. At first, I didn't realize what was happening. I was used to the feeling of sharing memories with Cyrus, and seeing them through blood. I'd even seen Nathan's memories via his dead wife's soul, but I'd never, in all the time I'd known him, actually seen something Nathan had chosen to show me.

In an unpleasant flash, I went from sitting calmly on the living room floor to running half-naked across a vast lawn.

The rain slashed Nathan's face and his feet slipped on the grass. Behind him, the sound of barking dogs increased as they gained ground. The tall iron fence, impossibly faraway, mocked him with the chance of freedom. He was doomed.

The dogs were at his heels now. He turned, flashing his fangs at them, feeling guilty and absurd at having to use the tools that monster had given him. More guilty at the thought that he could kill one of these animals and feed. Hunger gnawed his guts, the intensity mounting as his steps slowed and he admitted defeat on the cold, wet lawn. Despair crashed over him. He would never survive here.

Not that he wanted to. Not after what he'd done to Marianne. He thought of her body, still lying in the ballroom, and he fell to the grass weeping, heedless of the dogs that tore at his flesh. They wouldn't bite for long. They didn't like the taste.

Rough hands dragged him to his feet. "Take him in to the master," a voice ordered. Nathan knew they were tiring of his constant escape attempts.

He didn't resist as they dragged him across the lawn, up to the house. I didn't recognize the place, but I assumed it was still the house in Brazil. The palm trees lining the walk gave it away.

Inside, they took him to a large parlor. A man in a deep red robe stood at the fireplace. I couldn't see his face, but his white hair hung in a long braid down his back. I recognized Cyrus, lounging in a chair beside the fire. Annoyance crossed his face at the sight of Nathan. I'd expected a more volatile reaction, considering his wife had been killed as a sacrifice to the Soul Eater's hunger in Nathan's place. Then Nathan's gaze fell to the sling that cradled Cyrus's arm, and the bruises that marred the shadowed side of his face. Apparently, Nathan had already exacted some revenge.

"Kneel before the master," the guard holding him commanded, shoving him toward the man in red. Nathan stood his ground.

"Kneel!" Cyrus kicked him, an agonizing blow to the kidneys, dead and useless though they might be. Nathan crumpled to the floor.

"Enough!" The man in red turned, his eyes furious as he regarded his son. Jacob Seymour, his body refreshed from feasting on his daughter-in-law, turned his gaze to his new fledgling. His sharp, regal features softened. "Nolen. Nolen, Nolen. Why are we still running?"

Nathan hung his head. Shame filled him, absurd though it seemed. He hated this monster who'd taken Marianne and taken his mortal life. He hated that he could still taste Jacob's blood on his mouth, that he craved more. And he hated the part of himself that kept him from escaping.

It shouldn't be impossible to leave this house, but it was. There was pain, physical pain when he was separated from his *sire*. The word burned like a brand through his mind, which was also under this man's control.

The Soul Eater stooped, elegantly somehow, his moves fluid and spiderlike. "You haven't fed in so long. You look positively worn-out."

His hands on Nathan's shoulder's took away some of the pain and longing. It sickened Nathan and comforted him at the same time.

I could see now what he meant by "seductive." The lines were blurring in Nathan's mind, crucial lines between torment and relief, what he wanted and what he was forced to do.

"Bring him something," the Soul Eater commanded one of his guards, straightening. "Something…pretty."

"And that screams," Cyrus added cruelly.

Nathan struggled to stand, but he'd expended the last of his energy trying to flee.

Jacob straightened, bringing Nathan gently to his feet as he did so. "Why do you do this to yourself? Why do you deny yourself the satisfaction of feeding?"

"I don't know," Nathan half sobbed. He shook from cold and exhaustion.

The Soul Eater wrapped Nathan in his arms, cradling him against his cold chest. "It hurts me that you would rather die than stay with me. You're like a son. My son."

Cyrus scoffed. "Lucky him."

Contempt radiated off Jacob Seymour like a wave. It even reached Nathan through the blood tie, though it wasn't directed at him. "Better than a son, in some ways."

The guard returned, pushing a girl through the doors. Nathan turned, instantly aware of the scent of fear and blood.

The girl wrestled with the guard who held her captive. Her arms were bound behind her back. The buttons of her dress were fastened out of order and the thin fabric hung, limp and dirty, around her body. Her feet were bare, and bloody with scratches.

"This one has tried to escape a few times, as well," the Soul Eater said, stroking Nathan's hair. "It's your right, you know. You're not like them anymore."

Above the strip of cloth that gagged her, the girl's eyes widened. Her hair was dark, like Marianne's.

"Do what you will with her. She is yours." The Soul Eater stepped back, and Nathan turned, looking for reassurance, an absolution, maybe.

The girl screamed, and he ran. He was on her in an instant, holding her down, whispering apologies that weren't meant for her, before he tore into her throat.

And I was in the apartment again, shivering.

"You know I would never do those things, not on my own," Nathan said, his voice pleading. "But that is what he's like. He finds your weakness and he chips away…. You don't know he's doing it."

"I'll be careful." But I couldn't stop shaking, and I couldn't get the sound of the girl's screams out of my head. Or the touch of the Soul Eater. Though his hands had been on Nathan, they might as well have been clutching me.

And I feared they soon would be.

Twenty-One: From Bad...

~~~~~~~

They came for them, eventually. Max had no idea what time it was. Since the accident, time seemed to be constantly slipping away.

When the door opened, Bella woke with a start, her face creased in confusion. Then she seemed to take in her surroundings, and horror replaced it. "No!"

"Hey, you stop that," he admonished. "Have I ever died before?"

Really, it was going to be hard enough to get tortured without having to remember her sobbing and wailing as they dragged him from this room. He'd much rather hold the image of ice-cold-bitch Bella making fun of him for being a pussy, while they did God knew what to him.

"Good morning, good morning," a mocking voice called from the door. A vampire stepped in, cocky smile pasted on his face.

The smile that usually preceded a gory, horrible death for the smiler. Things were looking up.

Two more vampires followed him, both carrying crossbows. They had stakes in holsters at their hips, like gun-slingers-in-training, and they acted bored with their work, a sure sign they were overconfident.

Bella noticed, too. Her despair turned at once to flinty resolve. She mouthed, "The one on the right first," kissed Max and wheeled herself out of the way.

The one on the right. A nervous guy about an inch shorter than Max, with his finger already itching to pull the trigger and send a bolt into Max's heart. He would be a problem. *New guys.*

The first one who'd entered unlocked Max's shackles. "Get on your feet."

He then marched him to the door, a little more roughly than necessary. Oh yeah, he was begging for death.

"I love you, baby," Max called over his shoulder. He got a last glimpse of Bella as they shoved him out of the room.

One of them stayed behind. That threw Max off a little. He didn't want some vampire alone with Bella, where he couldn't protect her.

"What are you doing?" he heard her ask.

He didn't like the reply. "You've got to get ready. The Oracle wants you presentable for the entertainment."

Great. Max had planned on busting free right there in the hallway, backtracking and grabbing Bella on his way out. This was going to make things more difficult. He scrapped the plan. No way was he leaving without Bella, and he certainly wasn't going to set off a chain reaction of increased security when he had no clue where she was or how to get to her.

They marched him down a series of hallways and up a

couple sets of stairs. They'd been in a cellar—a huge old one, with arches and support columns you didn't find in your everyday suburban home. When they reached the surface the air was prickly with daylight. No direct contact, but that morning smell was in the air, and the feeling of wearing too-tight skin.

They took him to a large room in the center of the second floor, if he'd guessed his location right. The marble floor was cold under his bare feet. They must have taken his shoes when they'd chained him up. The dark wood of the walls stretched to a vast, domed ceiling swimming in ugly, fat angels. He had a feeling the cherubs and seraphim eternally paused in their harp playing to smile down on him weren't the decor choice of the current owner.

If they were, he'd enjoy killing her even more.

The windows were covered over with matching wooden shutters. They were huge, so there was no chance they'd be throwing those open soon, not if they weren't fond of barbecue. The covered oculus in the center of the ceiling troubled him, however. Especially with the rope that dangled from the shutter.

Another rope hung from the ceiling, this one passing through a pulley and ending in leather gauntlets. Cocky and Twitchy tied Max's wrists into the leather cuffs and jerked the rope, hauling him up to his tiptoes.

"I didn't peg you guys for the type who'd be into this sort of thing," he quipped through clenched teeth as his shoulders dislocated. They had him at a real disadvantage now.

"What did you say to me?" Cocky demanded, grabbing the front of Max's T-shirt. His feet slipped from beneath him and he spun on the rope, squeezing his eyes tight against the disorienting twirling of the room. Cocky laughed. "Not so tough now, are you?"

Twitchy laughed with him, but nervously. He had a right to be. Before Max left this place he was going to fuck them up.

"Get out of here."

The quiet command caught the attention of all three vampires, and Max craned his neck on his next turn to see who had issued it.

Anne ambled slowly through the arched double doors. She'd gotten rid of the feathery coat, but her hair looked the same, a thick fall of springy coils scraped back so tight her skin looked like it might pop off. Max stretched his legs, toes grasping at the slick marble. He managed to stop his spinning, but the effort was hell on his calves.

"Don't you look comfy?" Anne observed as she circled him, the buckles on her knee-high combat boots rattling with each step. She regarded him for a moment with an unreadable look, then smiled the same girlish smile she'd always given him when he'd visited Movement headquarters. "Max."

"Care Bear." He tried to nod, but the effect was ruined by his arms stretching above his head. "So, what's the plan here? Truss me up and let these morons spin me until I vomit to death?"

She laughed, the unrestrained, mindless laughter of an eternal teenager. "You always were funny."

"Apparently not enough to save my ass." He pulled himself up, the muscles in his arms screaming. "Any chance of letting me down a little? I'm tall enough."

"You're going to be as tall as a pile of ashes when I'm done. The Oracle's gonna let me kill you." Her tone implied he should be greatly impressed, or happy for her.

"Well, why don't you pull that rope and get it over with?" It was a risk, but he was ninety-nine percent sure she wouldn't do it. Not yet. "I'm not one for pointless small talk."

"Cha, right. Like that's going to work on me." She gave a long-suffering sigh. "Not that I'm not used to people underestimating me."

Cry me a river, bitch. "Well, that's kind of why you were such a good assassin. No one saw it coming. Shit, I didn't think you'd lie to my face and stab me in the back."

"I know, right?" Her face lit up in appreciation of his recognition. "People never got it! They think just because I *look* young, I don't have the experience or the smarts to pull stuff like this off. Not that sucking up to me is going to get you off the hook or anything, but thanks for, like, getting it."

"It appears I live to get things. Like shafted by my supposed friends." He tugged on the rope. Synthetic. It stretched a little. He could get the balls of his feet down now. And she was so wrapped up in her own drama, she didn't notice.

"The Oracle gets it, too." Anne turned away and walked to a long table at the side of the room. "She says it's one of my strengths."

With a flourish, Anne pulled back the canvas draping the table to reveal an assortment of weapons, branding irons, power tools and surgical implements.

Keep her talking, Harrison. Keep her talking or your

worst trip to the dentist is about to be grossly outdone. He twisted his wrists in the cuffs, but they held. Damn bondage weirdos and their escape-proof fetish gear. "So, what's her game, anyway? I mean, is she working with the Soul Eater or what?"

"Oh, please!" Anne snorted when she laughed. "Do you think I've never seen a James Bond movie before? Right, I'm going to spill all my secrets to you."

"The only reason Bond villains were stupid to spill their secrets was because Bond always got away." Max tugged the rope for effect. "Not like I'm going anywhere."

She cocked her head, considering. "Yeah, okay."

Suppressing a sigh of relief when she dropped a cordless drill, Max gave the rope another discreet pull. All he needed was a little more slack…

But he also needed to hear what she'd tell him.

"What do you already know?" She eyed him warily.

This was where playing it cool would come in handy. He had to act as if he was casually interested in the stuff he really wanted to know, but not so casual that she'd decide to quit wasting her time and get on with the torture. "Not much. Why don't you give me the rundown. It'll kill some time."

"Right, like you don't just want to keep me from carving into you." She rolled her eyes. "Fine. Did you know that the Soul Eater was, like, trying to become a god?"

"Yeah, that was the message your boss gave us. Right before she broke your back? Remember that?" He gave her a sarcastic look.

Anne clearly didn't appreciate it. "Yeah, I remember. Now, do you want to hear the rest of the story or what?"

He inclined his head. "Continue."

"Okay." After a dramatic pause, she did. "Well, you know how she, like, blew up the Movement? She was talking to me for the whole month that I was healing from when she broke my back. I could hear her voice in my head. So she freed me, I helped her pick off a few Movement staffers, and now I get to be, like, her right hand."

"That's great, but I wasn't really curious about your life story here. I figured most of that out myself."

She rolled her eyes again. "I'm getting there. Anyway, this whole time I'm in a coma, I hear about how the Soul Eater is trying to become a god, and she's gonna string him along and make him think she's helping him when she's, like, furthering her own agenda."

Surprise, surprise. "And that agenda includes?"

"Chaos." Anne laughed. "Oh my God, did I ever tell you what I thought about the Movement?"

"Apparently, you didn't think too highly of them." He wriggled his hands again. When her sharp gaze snapped toward his wrists, he shook his head. "I'm just trying to get comfortable. So, the Movement pissed you off enough you'd want the Oracle to have free reign on planet Earth?"

"Okay, I went from being the highest paid assassin on their roster to being a receptionist. A receptionist? I could have stayed human and done something dumb like that." She paused. "You know, if I'd been born, like, ten centuries later. But the point is, I was told they had a contingency for when assassins couldn't work anymore. I didn't know it meant getting busted down to secretary."

"So, you're going to help her destroy the world because

you're unhappy with your retirement benefits?" Max laughed. "Yeah, no, you're way more mature than you look."

"Oh, shut up. You're so righteous and everything because *you're* not filing papers all day for room and blood." She crossed her arms and pouted. "Like it matters, anyway. I'm not stupid. I know that once she gets some power, a lot of us will be stupid enough to stick by her. The smart ones, like me, are going to lay low."

"And you don't think she'll find you?" Here it was. The desperate bid for freedom. He hoped she didn't peg it as such. "Listen, you can stop all this now. There are Movement people working against you guys, and you're gonna lose. But if you get me out of here, if you get Bella out of here—"

"Oh, that's sweet." Anne snorted. "You want to save your doggy girlfriend from certain death and you think you can scare me into doing it. Yeah. That's not going to work. I have a vaultful of money waiting for me, and part of that payment is contingent upon my new boss getting her hands on your illegitimate baby."

Max swallowed his anger. It wouldn't help him burst out of the cuffs, and she would probably end their little dialogue and start cutting him up like a jack-o-lantern. "Yeah, that's the part of all this I can't figure out. Was she just waiting for someone to achieve the impossible? I mean, I don't like to brag, but vampires don't get chicks knocked up every day."

"Don't give yourself too much credit there." Anne made a disgusted face. "For one thing, it was supposed to be your little blond friend, the lady with the ugly shoes you brought in to see the Oracle a couple of months ago. And when that didn't work, that witch thought she'd try it out with you. And then it was back to the drawing board, because we didn't think it would ever happen. 'We' being the Oracle and the Soul Eater. They've been working together for a while now, and the Movement never knew! Anyway, she only needed a natural-born vampire to fulfill her prophecy. But a natural-born lupin? I mean, wow! Could you ask for a happier accident than that?"

Max closed his eyes. Of course. The night with Dahlia. He could almost taste that potion again, all sugary and hot in his mouth. "Yeah. Lucky you."

"Well, once the Oracle gets the baby, she's gonna try and lure the Soul Eater up here to drain it and eat its soul. When he gets here, boom. No more Soul Eater." Anne dusted her palms together as if the old vampire's ashes already dirtied them.

"And the baby?" Max didn't bother covering his intent as he pulled on the rope. A hard jerk, and the cuffs miraculously slipped a fraction of an inch. "What are you going to do with the baby?"

Anne noted his struggle with a wry smile. "Oh, don't worry. She's not going to hurt her. She's going to raise her, like a daughter. And stop wriggling, you'll never get free."

She turned, apparently tired of the game. "I was going to wait until they brought your girlfriend in to watch, but I'm not that mean. You used to be on my side. I'll just rough you up a little so it leaves marks."

"Gee, thanks." He pulled again on his restraints, more motivated than before when he saw her pick up a pair of wire cutters from the table.

Anne returned, eyeing his twisting hands. She held up the implement. "Shall we?"

The Soul Eater's mansion—I'd stopped thinking of it as Cyrus's—was as frightening as I remembered it. Of course, it was frightening for more sensible reasons now. Before, when I'd come to steal Dahlia's blood, I'd been afraid of my past. My current fear was deeply rooted in the present and near future.

We crouched beside the back wall. I'd never seen the grounds and mansion from this angle. I doubted many people had, including those who owned the huge lot we'd encroached upon to get to our location. We'd sneaked past a night watchman, across a dark lawn, past tennis courts and a swimming pool, and found the crumbling brick wall that separated a normal looking garden shed from the Soul Eater's guardhouse.

I understood now how the mansion had been so isolated. Though the house was visible, distinct figures were not. We spotted shapes moving in the windows, but couldn't tell what they were doing. Sounds didn't carry this far, either. Dense hedges surrounding the place absorbed the noise before it could reach us—high hedges forming a maze.

"We'll all go through the maze," Cyrus said at my elbow. "I know the way to the other side, and Nolen and I can easily hide there until you come back."

"But how will she find us?" Nathan hissed through the darkness. "We need a rendezvous point."

I held up my hand. This wasn't the time for them to start arguing. "I'll remember the way. We'll meet at the end. If there's trouble, if someone discovers us, it's every man for himself, okay?"

"No!" they both whispered in unison.

I shushed them. "Do you want someone to hear you? Listen, I can take care of myself. I'll be invisible. It's you I'm worried about."

"I'm not going to leave here if you're in trouble. That's asking too much!" Nathan shook his head vehemently. "I won't do it."

"Listen to me!" I grabbed his hand and squeezed it. "I have blood ties to both of you. You can keep track of me that way. If something happens that you lose me, or I can't communicate, you'll know it's too late. Promise me that if you can't hear me, you'll leave."

The pain that flashed through Nathan's eyes was visible despite the darkness that surrounded us. He nodded once in agreement.

"Then let's go," Cyrus said softly, motioning toward the wall. "Carrie, I'll boost you up."

We'd found a spot where the barricade had broken near the top, so the climb wouldn't be too difficult. The drop on the other side might be another thing entirely, so I braced myself mentally as I placed one foot into Cyrus's cupped hands.

Carrie!

I looked at his upturned face, his features sharp with desperation in the faint moonlight. I touched his cheek. "Hey, we're not going to the firing squad. Boost me up."

It wasn't the death drop I'd anticipated on the other side. In fact, the wall seemed to be taller on the side we climbed. After landing, I stayed low, crawling to hide behind a nearby tree. It wouldn't provide great cover, but it was nice to have something tangible between me and the guardhouse.

Cyrus followed, then Nathan. I beckoned to them, but Cyrus shook his head, motioning toward the maze. Apparently, we'd done all the planning he thought we needed.

In the time I'd stayed with Cyrus at the mansion, I'd never ventured into the hedge maze. I'd see the Fangs go into it. I'd seen Dahlia run to it to escape pursuing vampires at the New Year's party. But I'd never braved it myself. Mazes have always given me the creeps. I don't like the uncertainty of not knowing where to go or how to get back. It wasn't any better tonight, when possible death was thrown into the mix.

I followed Cyrus, Nathan close behind me. A rule I'd learned about mazes as a child was "always go left." I saw now it wasn't a fail-proof rule. We twisted right and left, following angles, then curves, through narrow corridors and wide, circular spaces.

"How do you remember this?" I asked, feeling secure enough in the cloistered darkness that I raised my voice.

"Shh!" Cyrus whispered urgently. "There could be guards. This path intersects theirs several times."

"There won't be. Dahlia ate them all." I wished I hadn't said that. Thinking of people being eaten destroyed the modicum of confidence I'd built up since coming over the wall. "But how do you remember your way?"

"Practice. Also, concentration and patience. All things that I am out of," he said, distractedly. "She ate them? All of them? I rather liked a few."

It seemed too short a time before I had to leave the

cover of the maze. I'd dreaded the close, confusing space, but I dreaded the house at the top of the hill more.

"Okay, got the stone?"

I held out my palm. Nathan pulled a leather pouch from his pocket. Leather, for some reason, was unaffected by the charm, something we'd discovered when he, but not his watch, had disappeared when he'd handled the stone. He opened the pouch now, spilling the amulet into my hand.

"You're good to go," he said quietly. "Be careful, Carrie."

"I will." I could already feel myself vanishing. "I'm going in now."

They watched me all the way up the hill, even though they couldn't see me. I know, because I stopped halfway and looked back. There was something voyeuristic about it, watching them watching me and knowing they didn't know. They stood side by side, too visible at the opening of the maze. They should have known better, but I wasn't going to blow our cover by shouting at them. Nathan's features, sharpened by stress and the eerie shadows of the maze, showed his pain and fear more acutely than I'd ever seen them. Because he'd admitted to me, and to himself, that he loved me, he thought I was doomed.

It was the same for Cyrus. How alike they were. They both thought their love would be the thing that killed me. How alike, and how self-centered.

Keep moving, sweetheart, Nathan prompted through the blood tie.

A little guilty that he'd heard my thoughts, and surprised that he knew I'd stopped, I turned and continued the long walk to the house, and to the Soul Eater.

Twenty-Two: To Worse

"So, you didn't tell them anything? In the whole time you were there, you didn't tell them why you were coming here or who you were looking for?"

Max lifted his head. Sweat mingled with blood dripped into his eyes. "What did I tell you?"

Anne regarded him coldly for a moment. "Why do you have to make this so difficult? I really liked you. I was even going easy on you. But you just keep pushing and pushing."

There was a sickening crunch, one he'd come to identify as bone being crushed between the blades of a wire cutter. He concentrated on the sound in an effort to ignore the pain as she snipped another finger to the first joint. If this was taking it easy, he silently thanked himself for being so nice to her all those years.

"I don't like doing this," she said with a sigh. "Well, I do like it. Reminds me of the old days. Torture was kind of my thing."

Another section. He'd been keeping track. So far, she'd done away with his pinkie and half his ring finger on his left hand. He'd looked down once, saw the split flesh and splintered bone littering the floor, and puked. Now he kept his eyes up, focusing on the oculus that would eventually open and let in frying sunlight.

Don't pass out before Bella gets in here. Pull yourself together, 'cause she is going to freak.

The huge doors scraped open. Anne spun him to face them. "Oh, look who's here!"

A vampire pushed Bella's wheelchair. They'd dressed her in a black velvet gown with laces on the front, and her hair was down, like some princess in a low budget fantasy movie. Only this princess looked worried and tired. He tried a lame attempt at a wave and realized he'd only managed to wiggle his injured hand, flinging droplets of blood across the marble floor. She gasped and paled.

"You look like Morticia Adams," he quipped, but his voice was hoarse from screaming.

She moved as if to lunge from her chair, and the vampire behind her gripped her shoulders. "Don't move again."

"Do not hurt him again and I will not be tempted to," she said, as threateningly as she could manage.

Max hoped the tremor in her voice was from fatigue and not worry over him. *I'm not dead yet,* he thought, willing the words to materialize in her brain. But he didn't have telepathy, and he knew it was pointless.

"I was just trying to get your baby daddy here to tell me what you two were up to." Anne knelt beside him and lifted his bare foot, fitting the wire shears over his little toe. "You wouldn't want me to maim him any more than I already have, would you? Why don't you spill it?"

Bella lifted her chin and looked away in casual defiance. "Why should I? You will kill him anyway."

Good girl, Max thought, digging his fingers—the whole ones—into the leather cuffs as Anne snipped the toe away. He didn't want to scream in front of Bella. Hell, he hadn't wanted to scream when it was just him here. But it was a losing battle. He didn't scream now, but a low, shuddering whimper escaped him, possibly more pathetic than crying out.

"Stop it!" Bella shouted, again trying to rise. The vampire behind her pushed her down, striking her across the face.

"What the hell do you think you're doing?" Anne threw her implement of torture down and stalked toward Bella.

"Stay away from her," Max shouted, but he wasn't entirely sure how he'd back up that command, with his hands tied and blood leaking out of him all over the place. Still, if she was going to do something to Bella… He pulled on the restraints, wincing at the pressure on his mangled digits. His hand slipped down a fraction. The brutal, agonizing pain put a damper on the tiny victory.

Ignoring him, Anne confronted the vampire behind Bella. "If you touch her again, you'll fry right along with him."

At least Anne didn't seem interested in hurting Bella. That took a load off Max's mind. Anne was very, very good at hurting. The thought of Bella learning that firsthand… Jesus, he had to get her out of there.

"Speaking of frying, when does that happen, exactly?" He jerked at the gauntlets again, half praying he'd get free and half afraid of how he'd fight two vampires when he wasn't exactly in fighting shape. "I mean, this is getting kind of boring."

"Oh, this is boring you?" Anne returned to him, spinning him to face away from Bella. Anne went to the table and rubbed her hands together like a kid looking at a dessert cart. "We can move on to something else. Like…this?"

She came forward with the cordless drill, giving the trigger a few experimental squeezes. "How about it?"

"I'm not telling you anything. Obviously, *she's* not." He jerked his head to indicate Bella. "So, I guess if you really want to torture me, go ahead, but you're wasting time."

Anne grabbed the rope securing him and gave it a tug, pulling him up so his feet had no chance of touching the floor. "I'll decide whether or not I'm wasting my time."

"There has to be something left to burn, when the boss gets here," the other vampire warned. "Or I won't be here when she does."

"You won't be here anyway, because you're not invited." Ever the teenager, Anne delivered the blow with practiced snottiness that would have been devastating to someone in the eleventh grade.

Max couldn't see what effect it had on the vampire. "So, when does she get here?"

"What, are you afraid?" She took a step closer, still holding the rope. A second tug set him swaying, just a bit.

He thrashed his legs. He hoped it looked like an attempt to keep her away.

"Is little Max afraid of the big, bad girl?" She squeezed the trigger again.

Almost close enough. She was almost close enough, and his hands were nearly out of the cuffs. He'd have to time it exactly….

She took another step forward, raising the drill. "How about…the eyes?"

"How about, no?" Max swung forward with the momentum he'd built up, knocking the drill from her hand as he locked his legs around her rib cage. She'd made a mistake starting with his fingers, one that had worked to his advantage. Wet with his blood, the leather had become slippery. The missing digits made his hands small enough to slip from the cuffs, and the weight of his body did the rest.

He took her down with him. They landed with a thud, skidding across the bloodied marble. He didn't want to think about the sticky pieces of his former fingers getting crushed beneath them. He had her pinned now, so it would be a damn lousy time to get distracted. Before she could collect her wits to scream, he grabbed her head and twisted, snapping her neck. It wouldn't kill her, but it would sure incapacitate her.

The vampire who'd been guarding Bella raced forward with a roar. Max grabbed the drill, depressed the trigger and caught him in throat as he charged. "Sorry, couldn't have you calling for help."

The vampire writhed on the floor, directly under the oculus. Max grabbed Anne's limp, unconscious body by the legs and pulled her beside her cohort. "Sorry, kid. You were a good egg, for a while."

Shielding his eyes, he pulled the rope, flooding the room with light.

"Max, no!" Bella screamed. In the blinding pain of the moment he saw her stand, and fall.

"Damn it, Bella!" If she'd have stayed put, his chances

would have been much better. He skirted the direct beam of light, his skin sizzling from the limited exposure. He managed to scoop her up and deposit her into the chair again before he burst into flame.

"Will you be quiet? Do you want the whole freaking house to come in here?" He stopped, dropped and rolled into a shadowed corner. "Wheel yourself over here and let's go."

The horror on her face as she approached broke his heart. He knew how he must look. Blood on his arms, dried and fresh. Mangled hand, missing toe. He couldn't have looked too hot *before* he'd inadvertently set himself on fire.

The sickening stench of burned vampire reached them. Bella gagged and covered her nose. Lifting his head, Max saw the piles of ash where the bodies had landed. The blue ball of flame of Anne's soon-to-be-ex heart extinguished with a fizz.

"Hang on," Max instructed Bella. Then the wind came, making a maelstrom of the cavernous room, destroying the wooden shutters over the windows. Bella dived from the chair to shield him from the light.

"I have killed many vampires and that has never happened," she said, almost accusing.

"She was old," Max explained. "Despite what she looked like, she was really, really old."

During the night, when he'd lain awake relishing what might have been his last few moments with Bella, he'd realized he would probably have to kill Anne. He'd imagined himself being somewhat more…sorry about it. Funny how having his fingers cut off a little bit at a time had changed his attitude.

Bella touched his shoulder, then recoiled. "You are badly burned. How will we escape here? You cannot fight. I will applaud you if you can walk."

"Well, prepare to give me a standing ovation, 'cause we're getting out of here." He climbed to his feet and flattened himself against the wall. "Forgive me if I don't help you up, but I think I've had enough barbecue for today."

Jumping down in her chair, Bella groaned. "If it comes to pass that I will never walk again, please do me the favor of killing me."

"At least you've still *got* all your body parts, working or not." He waggled his ruined hand at her. "Follow me."

He inched along the wall, avoiding the sunlight that now flooded across the floor. Getting to the door would be the hardest part. Once they were outside it, the chances of finding another open window were slim. Unless the Oracle didn't mind looking for new employees every dawn.

Another few steps and he would be there. If he didn't lose his balance and fall into a shaft of sunlight first.

As if in answer to a prayer he hadn't uttered, the light dimmed.

"Max, what is happening?" Bella asked, her last word nearly drowned out by the clang of steel shutters. The windows and oculus were covered, leaving them in darkness.

Not a good sign. "Go!" he shouted, racing to grab her. But it was too late. The doors slammed shut before them.

"We are trapped," Bella whispered, eyes wide.

A mechanical whirring drew their attention to the other side of the room. A section of the tall paneling began to shift. Improbably, the whole section swung around, reversing itself. On the other side was an attached dais with a large, ornate throne.

And on that throne sat the Oracle.

Invisibility wasn't a subject I'd given much thought to. Still, I think my logical expectation would have been that being invisible would make you lose your inhibitions and become a little reckless. In reality, it made me feel exposed and overcautious.

Maybe the situation would have been a little different if I were using my invisibility to spy on the men's locker room at the gym instead of sneaking into a house I'd tried desperately to escape from before.

When Cyrus ran the place, it had been crawling with guards. But he'd been paranoid. As I eased open one of the French doors leading from the terrace to the foyer, I noted that the Soul Eater seemed pretty confident no one would try and oppose him.

Then the alarm went off.

For a split second I panicked. Since when had there been an alarm system? And I'd thought Dahlia had killed all the guards? Then I remembered that, though I might not have anyplace to hide, I was wearing the best camouflage possible. Still, being invisible didn't make me noncorporeal. Which became a real concern as the room flooded with guards.

Oddly enough, some of them I recognized. They were the Soul Eater's personal retinue, trained to obey their master's whims, most likely on pain of death. They'd been there the night of the Vampire New Year, accompanying their master to his feeding. I'd probably get an extra helping of torture before they killed me.

I slipped into the corner under the stairs and watched as they assembled, praying none of them copied my get-out-of-the-way idea and discovered me. Fourteen of them milled about, weapons drawn—shiny, black stakes with gleaming metal tips—scanning the room in a state of determined readiness.

"Nothing here," one of them barked, both to the guards in the room and into his headset. "I want two men at the top of those stairs, and stay there. Another team searches the servants' wing. I want two more casing the kitchen, dining room and ballroom. Go in threes to search the grounds. The rest of you get back to your posts, and keep your eyes open. They might have tripped the alarm to distract us. Go, go, go!"

The guards scattered as quickly as they'd assembled. Somewhere, someone turned off the alarm, and an unnerving silence descended.

Creeping from my hiding place, I willed myself to stay calm. Someone hypervigilant—or a vampire—might be able to hear me.

The door to the study was open. I noticed no one had been posted there, so it seemed a good place to start. I was halfway across the foyer when I heard steps coming down the stairs.

Dahlia swept into the room, clad in a diaphanous black gown. Her sleeves fluttered behind her as she stalked toward the study. I froze, holding absolutely still to keep from making a sound. My palms grew damp. It became a little more difficult to keep my grip on the slick stone, my only camouflage.

She paused, turned her head slightly. Then, without warning, she spun and held out both hands. "Illuminate!"

The room flared with bright, white light. It penetrated the space where I stood and destroyed any shadow on the floor. Her eyes narrowed. She knew someone was in the room with her, she just couldn't see me.

"Let the guards handle it, my darling," a deep, cultured voice called from the study. It sounded almost like…

A visible tremor racked Dahlia at the sound of his voice. An almost identical reaction to what Nathan had experienced in the presence of his sire.

Oh, God. Dahlia was the Soul Eater's fledgling.

It made sense, now. Why Dahlia had been feeding Cyrus information. She knew that eventually, she would find herself on the Soul Eater's dinner table. If she played both sides, someone might rescue her.

She'd lied to me. I was outraged, but not surprised. Dahlia was clever in ways that continued to mystify me. If I'd thought I'd had her—or her motives—completely figured out, I'd been a fool. No one would ever really know what she was up to. My mistake had been believing that she'd been sired by one of the Fangs, as she'd told me. She'd been in relentless pursuit of Cyrus's blood. Why would she have settled for a lesser prize? She could have had my blood the night I'd fed from her and she'd stabbed me. But she'd wanted power.

I followed her to the door of the study, timing my steps

to echo hers. She tried to trip me up, once. I'd been count-
ing on it. She'd have noticed by now that her spell book was
missing. I'm sure she had a clue as to why the guards
hadn't—and hopefully wouldn't—find the intruder.

In the study, a fire burned in the fireplace. All of the
lamps, delicate art nouveau creations, lit the room cheerfully. Seated at the desk, his long, white hair bound in a single braid that coiled on the floor, was the Soul Eater.

He turned at the sound of Dahlia's entrance, and smiled.
He looked so much like Cyrus, but with the added mystery and elegance of age. My heart lurched in my chest.

But he's not me, Cyrus reminded me through the blood
tie. *He's so much worse than I ever was.*

"You look lovely tonight," Jacob Seymour said, inclin-
ing his head in Dahlia's direction. "Is there some occasion?"

"None, really." She sank into a large, leather armchair
with a winged back, looking like a queen on a throne.
There was no way that was an accident. "I thought we
could try the potion again, if you wanted to."

He made a noise of disgust. "We have been over this
time and again. Julia has captured the werewolf and her
vampire companion. We'll have the child soon enough."

"There's no reason not to continue as planned,
though!" Dahlia sat up straighter, pounding the arms of
the chair with her fists. Her knuckles were white with tension. "We have no idea if the child will be born vampire
or werewolf. Or lupin."

"The baby will be a lupin," the Soul Eater retorted
calmly. "A natural-born vampire and werewolf combined.
What use would I have for a mere vampire child?"

"A right hand?" Now Dahlia was reaching. She'd out-lived her usefulness and she knew it. "A son. With the power of a natural-born vampire. Maybe if Cyrus had been—"

"My son is not the issue!" The Soul Eater stood so fast he knocked over his chair and the delicate writing desk. Papers fluttered to the ground, all scribbled on in handwriting that I was sure belonged to him. I moved cautiously toward the desk as he continued to rage.

"I have warned you never to speak of him in my presence!" He advanced on Dahlia, throwing aside his overturned chair. It bounced off my legs and I muffled a shout of pain and surprise. Luckily, neither of them noticed, wrapped up in their rage and fear, respectively.

Dahlia crawled backward like a crab on her hands and feet, too tangled in her voluminous dress to create much room between her and the Soul Eater.

"I should destroy you now!" As his voice raised in volume, it grew in intensity, the voices of his past victims joining in the hellish chorus. I'd heard that voice once before, and I shuddered to hear it again.

"No!" Dahlia screamed, holding up her hands. "You need me!"

"Need you?" He continued to advance.

Carrie! Go, find what you have to and move on! It was Nathan's voice in my head, involuntarily replaying images of the night we'd both barely escaped this room with our lives. The night Nathan's son, Ziggy, had died at the hands of his sire.

I dropped to my knees and scrambled toward the mess of papers. Letters, a sequence of them, made out to Julia.

The second I touched one, it disappeared. I had to read them silently where they lay, transmitting their contents through the blood tie.

Julia,

I hope this letter finds you well. I have arranged a transport for you and the werewolf for the week of the seventh. This will ensure it is well past the time of the full moon.

I noticed, along with the fact his notorious charisma did not translate to paper, that beside the scattered letters were a handful of envelopes. All were addressed, simply, to "Oracle." There were no addresses.

Father uses personal couriers. Cyrus's contempt echoed through my head. *You won't find the address there. But he will have it. Look in my bedroom.*

His bedroom, I snapped back. *I'll go when I can move.*

The Soul Eater grabbed Dahlia by the hair and hauled her to her feet. At least, sort of to her feet. She tripped and her legs tangled, leaving her to twist by the handful of red curls he grasped. "Do you know how many there are like you? Who will do as I say and not make ridiculous demands? Witches are not hard to find. It's an obedient one I've yet to come across!"

He released her hair and grabbed her throat with his clawed hand. "You will not speak to me of this again! Do we have an understanding?"

A tear escaped the corner of her eye, forced out by the pressure of suffocation. She gasped and scratched at his hand, squeaking out a pained "yes" before he threw her backward. She knocked over a table as she fell.

I sprinted for the door, thinking to escape when I wouldn't be heard over the ruckus Dahlia's weeping and falling caused.

"And you! Don't move another inch!"

I froze.

Twenty-Three:
Back from the Dead

"**Y**es, I know you're there." The Soul Eater moved closer to me, as though he could see me despite my invisibility. He sniffed the air, a smile twitching the corners of his mouth. "Do you think I can't smell my fledgling's blood in you?"

I clutched the stone tighter. *Run! Just get the hell out of there!* Nathan screamed in my head. I tensed, ready to follow his advice.

The Soul Eater laughed. "Oh, Nolen. He was always so dramatic. You have nothing to fear from me."

Carrie, don't listen to him! Cyrus's thoughts set up a panicked buzz in my mind. I clapped my hands to my head, trying desperately to keep my wits under the onslaught of my sire's and my fledgling's frantic urging.

"Be calm," the Soul Eater advised. His tone was patient and reasonable, cutting through the pandemonium in my head. "You know how to quiet them."

Block the blood tie? In my confusion and pain I dimly

remembered telling Cyrus and Nathan that I wouldn't, that they could stay in contact with me and know everything was all right. It was so tempting to follow the Soul Eater's directive. So I did.

"There," Jacob said, stepping toward me. "Now, show yourself. I won't hurt you."

For some horrible reason I couldn't fathom, I believed him. I let the stone tumble to the floor.

His eyes lit up with cold fire in recognition. A smile bent his lips, lips that were so like Cyrus's. "Oh, this is a pleasant surprise."

"You remember me?" Why did that make me feel special, somehow?

Dahlia staggered to her feet, her face cut and bleeding. "You!"

"You may leave now, Dahlia. I am quite finished with you." He didn't look at her, until she opened her mouth to protest. Then he fixed her with a piercing glare. "Unless there is something else you wish to offer me?"

She backed to the door, her eyes wide with fear, and left us alone in the study.

As if he hadn't just threatened to steal a person's soul right there in front of me, he beckoned me closer. "Come here, let me get a look at you."

I went to him, drawn by some invisible cord that seemed to bind us. Nothing like the blood tie. It was pure charisma.

"Of course I remember you. You were my son's…well, plaything seems so crude."

"Because it is." But I don't know why it didn't offend me.

"Pity, what had to occur between you. But you weren't

suited for each other." He reached out, gripped my wrist. "You're much too strong for him."

"Is that a compliment?" It was hard to tell. It was hard to think at all. His hand burned where it touched my skin.

"It's an…observation." He lifted my wrist to his lips. I didn't resist him, even though it seemed certain he would bite. Instead, he pressed a kiss there, and I shuddered. "When you killed him, that created much trouble for me."

"Did it?" I pulled my hand back slowly, actually reluctant to break contact. "I won't apologize."

The Soul Eater chuckled. "I wouldn't expect you to."

"Because you know me so well?" I heard the sarcasm in my voice, but I didn't feel the conviction that bolstered my words.

He laughed again. "I can see why my son enjoyed your company. Please, sit. Talk with me. After five centuries, the days grow tedious, especially with such…pointless companions."

"And you two seemed to get along so well." I sat on the couch, where he instructed.

He righted the chair and turned it to face me before sitting. "She has her uses. I must admit, I found her enjoyable for a time. But I grow tired of people so quickly. It's a character flaw on my part, and I accept it. So, tell me. What have you come for?"

"I want to know where the Oracle is." There was no point in hiding it from him. I doubted I would survive to make it out of the place. If I could get the information, maybe I could relay it to Cyrus or Nathan. "The Oracle has my friends. Tell me where they are."

He laughed. "Now you underestimate me, Carrie."

"You won't let me live to get out of here. Might as well tell me. Satiating my curiosity could be…fulfilling my last wish." Even as I said it, I knew he wasn't stupid enough to fall for it. He didn't have a pathological need to gloat over his impending victory.

He stood and paced leisurely behind his chair, then to the fire. There was a cut-crystal decanter of amber liquid on the mantel. He poured a glass and offered it to me.

I declined with a motion of my head. "I need to stay dry. I hear you can be dangerous."

"In more ways than you know." He moved toward me and pressed the glass into my palm. "Drink it."

I took the glass. "Is it poisoned? Spiked with holy water?"

"I wouldn't do such a nasty thing to you." He poured himself a drink, as a show of good faith, probably, and sank into his chair. "I do remember you. I remember when you knelt beside my coffin and put your devious hands on it. And I remember how wounded you were when I did not fall into the same trap that my son did. How naive you were, how refreshingly stupid."

"I can't say Cyrus was much better." I couldn't help glancing at the floor. We sat in the very room where I'd first encountered the Soul Eater. The room in which I'd killed his son.

"No, Simon was always too headstrong. From the time he killed his brother, I knew it. He could never accept that he wasn't my first choice as fledgling. He would never see the larger scope of my actions, only how they affected him." The Soul Eater shook his head ruefully.

"Talk about not seeing the broader scope! You killed his wives, you didn't care when the only maternal figure in his life burned to death, your goons killed the girl in the desert—"

"What girl in the desert?" Jacob leaned forward, clearly intrigued and…amused? "I hadn't heard about any girl."

"I won't be the one to tell you." The fact I'd even mentioned it disgusted me. "But you can't blame him for becoming blinded to betrayal. After living with you for so long, it probably felt natural."

"Very good, my dear." The Soul Eater laughed, a deep, seductive sound that didn't have the callow edge of his son's. "Well, I did kill a few of his companions. But his first two wives, they killed themselves. And his stepmother, what a useless woman. I suppose he told you his suspicions of me."

I glared at him. "Never. When I knew him, he was blinded by his loyalty to you. He acted like the sun shines out of your ass."

"Do you have to be so crude?" Jacob clucked his tongue. "I must say, I'm proud he never spoke ill of me to you. It showed he had at least some sense."

"It shows less sense that he stayed under your thumb for so long." I let the comment hang in the air for a moment. "Tell me what you did to his mother."

"*Step*mother," the Soul Eater corrected. He propped his steepled fingers in front of his mouth, cold blue eyes glinting in the firelight. "She was useless. Perpetually pregnant and useless. I had two daughters by her. Neither of them lived past infancy, thank the Lord for small mercies. But the experience of bearing a child and watching it die…well, it ruined her. Chores were neglected, my children ran wild. All except Cyrus, foolish brat that he was. He doted on her, as if anything he could do would break her from her self-pitying spell.

"The day she burned, I'd had enough. I came in from the field—I was a simple farmer then, with no land of my own, toiling day after interminable day for another man's gain. I came into my house, and the fire had died. It wasn't a cold day, mind, but with no fire came no supper, and my bones fairly ached with hunger. I thought of my sons, scattered to the winds, doing God alone knew what while their stepmother wallowed in her sniveling sorrow, and I'd had enough. I went for kindling, built up the fire and when it was large enough, I pushed her into it."

Cyrus's tortured memories flashed through my mind. The loving mother figure, enrobed in flames. His only friend and ally in the cruel world of his childhood, burning to death before his eyes. And Mouse, left to burn away in the desert as he watched.

The Soul Eater made a disgusted noise. "Well, in any case, he's dead now."

So, he didn't know the truth then. How could he? Dahlia had obviously meant to kill Cyrus, and probably reported the deed finished when she'd told the Soul Eater.

"You're a monster," I rasped, still trying to swallow my shock.

"And you're a simpering fool!" His hand shot out to grab me by the throat. Rage lit his eyes and hard lines bracketed his mouth. Still, he wasn't the Soul Eater I'd feared meeting tonight. I hoped that creature didn't show his face while I was around.

He took a deep breath and released me, smiling tightly. "I'm sorry. Forgive me. I have no wish to harm you."

I find that hard to believe, I thought, but said nothing.

"You intrigue me, Carrie." He regarded me with an intensity that burned. "You may have been too strong for my son, and certainly too strong for my fledgling, but you're no match for me. A challenge, certainly. It would take us a long time, I think, to tire of each other."

"Well, I'm already getting tired of you," I retorted. But it wasn't true. When Cyrus had been my sire, I'd been drawn to the danger in him. In him I'd seen reflected all my basest desires. He'd offered me a life of indulgence and hedonism, and I'd been able to turn away in disgust. But the Soul Eater… Everything about Jacob Seymour seemed *right.* As if he could do no wrong simply because he believed nothing was wrong. It made him powerful, and power remained my weakness.

I begged myself to remember what had happened before, how unhappy I knew I would have been if I'd stayed unquestioningly at Cyrus's side. The Soul Eater didn't *need* me. I'd wanted that so much, someone to need me. Now, it seemed the furthest thing from my mind. I wanted to need someone else, and the best possible person to need would be one who could provide.

I was falling under his hypnotic spell again.

"Think of it, my dear. I have but a few full-time companions, none that I share my *interests* with." He gave me a pointed glance, leaving me no illusions as to what those interests were. "And you'd benefit from our alliance in other ways."

"What? When you get tired of me my soul gets a gala installation in your lower intestine?" I shook my head. "No way."

"Oh, I wouldn't have to consume you, Carrie." He waved his hand as if shooing away my foolishness. "Use your head. My fledgling knows what I'm up to, and he's likely told you as well. Why would I need or want your pathetic little soul? I didn't sire you. I have no use for you."

"A minute ago you were practically down on one knee, and now *I'm* pathetic? You sure know how to win a girl's heart." I stood as if to leave. "So, if that's all—"

He threw out his hand and an invisible force knocked me back to the sofa. "Impressive, yes? The power…it's all you've ever dreamed of, and more."

I glared at him. "And you'll use it against me every day of my life, making me your mindless puppet. I've already been through that with your son. What is the price you ask, oh great one, for this dubious honor?"

With an evil smile, he came toward me. I couldn't move as he leaned down, his teeth bared. He had fangs, even though he wasn't in feeding mode. At least I hoped he wasn't. His nose almost touched mine, and his breath was cold against my face as he spoke. "This is why my son couldn't tame you. I will not have the same problem." He slapped me hard across the face. It caught me off guard and I tasted blood.

"The price for letting you live," he hissed, gripping my

hair to punctuate his last word, "is that you will bring my fledgling to me!"

"Nathan?" I gasped through the pain. "No way. Kill me now."

He lifted me by the throat and flung me across the room, literally. I bounced off the wall and landed in a broken heap on the floor. In my head, breaking down the wall I'd created to block him out, Nathan's anger—with me, with his sire—and his pain assailed me, skewering my mind in a thousand agonizing places. "Nathan, no!" But I'd meant to call out to him with my mind.

The Soul Eater laughed, and the sound twisted into the tortured screams of the souls trapped inside him. His eyes glowed red and his face contorted. "Let him come. Let my wayward child come home to me, as he's longed to do so many times."

"No!" I scrambled to my feet and broke for the door, but the Soul Eater was on me in a second, holding me back.

"Struggle! He'll feel your fear and it will quicken his pace." Jacob's hands turned to claws around my arms, and the stench of decay overwhelmed me. "You will be rewarded for your compliance."

Bile rose in my throat. I choked it back. "He'll kill you! And I'll help, I swear it!"

"And you'll die like all the others who've tried." His words died into an anguished cry, the chorus of voices in him raising to protest their eternal torment.

The door of the study ricocheted off the wall as it burst open. "The hell she will!"

"Nathan, no! Get out of here!" I tried to escape from the

Soul Eater's grasp, and to my surprise, he let me go easily. I hadn't anticipated it, and wound up on my face on the hard marble.

When I looked up, I saw what had taken Jacob Seymour so off guard.

His son Cyrus, presumed dead, standing in the doorway.

Cyrus showed no hint of bravado as he entered the room where he'd once died. He met the Soul Eater's astonished gaze head-on. "Hello, Father. There are a few things we need to discuss."

In all the time he'd worked for the Movement, Max had never seen the Oracle conscious. She actually seemed less frightening, and that was dangerous.

She sat on a carved wooden throne with a back that pointed up like a church steeple. Her head, normally bald, was covered in an Egyptian-style wig, her thin body robed in a loose red dress. She held her head regally, but appeared fragile, like a mental patient in the starring role of the asylum's *Cleopatra*. Her frailty actually caused a stab of pity in him.

He knew better, but Bella…she might have been through assassin training, but she was still a woman, and women had sympathy. Sympathy that would get her killed.

"Come." The Oracle pointed at Bella and crooked her finger. The wheelchair shot forward with such speed that when it stopped, Bella fell out, spilling to the floor.

When Max tried to run to her, he couldn't. He added telekinesis to the list of shit he hated about the Oracle.

"Hey, bitch!" he shouted, hoping he'd catch her attention with his boldness and she wouldn't just twist his head off his shoulders. "You know, for wanting that baby, you're not being too gentle with the mother."

"What happens to the wolf does not concern me, only what happens to the child she carries, and it is in no danger." The Oracle turned back to Bella. "My daughter is strong in you."

"She is not your daughter," Bella shrieked, pushing herself up with her arms. "She will never be yours!"

"You presume to correct me?" The Oracle laughed. "I, who know all?"

"For knowing all, you sure don't have much common sense," Max shouted, desperate to get the Oracle's attention off of Bella. "Why would you hook up with the Soul Eater? He'll double-cross you faster than you can come up with one of your stupid prophecies."

The Oracle crooked her finger and pulled him forward, his feet tangling together as he resisted her. She brought him to within inches of Bella, smiling cruelly. "You doubt the legitimacy of my prophecies?"

Trying for bravado, he laughed. "I do. Hell, half the time we can only figure out what they're about after the thing happens. That's not a real handy skill, making general observations and then pinning them on an event after the fact."

"I have never done such a thing. It was your Order of the Brethren that decided I spoke of a future that would include them." She closed her eyes, hands clutching the carved arms of the throne. When she looked at them again, her eyes were obscured with a haze of blood. "Their time is over."

"Yeah, kinda got that when you toasted the place." Max

tried to move his arms, and when he managed, there was nothing to do with them. It wasn't like he could *fight* the Oracle. It was a losing battle before it even started. "But you're still asking for a world of hurt teaming up with the Soul Eater. He's not a real trustworthy guy."

The Oracle laughed. "He is a pawn. He has no power over me. He has my heart. He could have killed me at any time. But he doesn't, because he is weak, and he does not know how to proceed without my help."

"But you sent him your heart," Bella said, wiping a trickle of blood from her split lip. "He has your heart."

"He does." She gave another eerily knowing laugh. "He does."

Max shook his head. "He's totally going to kill you."

The Oracle leaned back, her eyes fading slowly back to normal. "He desires power above all else. He will not kill the source of it."

"But he won't coexist with someone who has more than him. He's trying to become a god. God means all-powerful." The Oracle's hold on Max had slipped a bit, and he bent to help Bella.

The Oracle made a fist and drew his spine painfully straight. "He will never reach that level. I will use him up and discard him."

"For what? To get yourself killed for free? Hell, I could have done that for you." Max grimaced as her invisible hand tightened around his spine. "If you're going to kill me, kill me!"

The Oracle relinquished her hold. "My vision is not clouded by lust for power. I will not fall as easily as him."

Max stretched his neck, hoping his back wouldn't collapse into dust. "Then what's your vision? Lay it on me, babe. I got time."

"You have less time than you believe." The Oracle pointed at him, but didn't use her destructive powers. "I am establishing a new order. With the Soul Eater's help, I will destroy all those who would oppose me. When he has exceeded his usefulness, I will dispose of him. Those loyal to chaos will reign."

"Chaos?" Max raised an eyebrow.

Seemingly pleased at his interest, the Oracle nodded. "The world will become a vampire's paradise. Mortals will weep in fear at our feet and tremble before us. The earth will become saturated with the blood we cannot drink for the abundance of it."

"Sounds…nice." He cleared his throat. "But that doesn't sound like chaos. I mean, you're using the term 'order,' you're talking about people worshipping you. Sounds kind of like what the Soul Eater is doing."

"Let me finish!" She held up her hand and snapped it closed, and his jaw tightened, teeth shifting against each other under the pressure. "Lowly ones will rejoice, powerful ones will seek more power. It will be as it is now, but only for a time. They will soon realize they are not bound by laws or sides in a never-ending war. They will begin to turn on each other.

"Vampires will hunt vampires, new Soul Eaters will rise. Others will kill them. No leader will emerge who can sustain his rule. All the earth will be lost in darkness and blood."

"Why would you want that?" Bella whimpered.

Tenderly, the Oracle reached down to touch her face. "I would not expect a lowly werewolf to understand."

"What does the kid have to do with it? I mean, if you're superpowerful, why do you need a baby to help you?" *Why do you need my baby?* He fought to keep the unspoken question from surfacing. The bitch might get him, might get Bella and their daughter and everything important to him, but she wouldn't know it. He didn't know how, but if she didn't know what they meant to him, he got to keep a part of them. Just for himself.

"The prophecy." It was Bella who spoke, her sorrow cutting straight to his heart. "I didn't want to tell you. I wasn't ready to let you know."

"What prophecy?" He looked from the Oracle to Bella. "What prophecy?"

"There is a prophecy among my people, made by the Oracle long ago." Bella's head dipped. She wouldn't look at him.

When the Oracle spoke, her voice was low and mechanical. "The sword forged of blood. A natural-born vampire."

"But she's not a vampire. Bella's a werewolf. The baby will be a lupin," Max protested, though he was pretty sure it wouldn't matter.

The Oracle spread her hands, an expression of bewilderment on her porcelain face. "So, I may control the wolves, as well. It is not a setback. Be proud. The child you gave me will rule after my one hundred years of chaos."

"You're doing this all for just a hundred years?" Max sputtered in disbelief. "That's like a blink of an eye to you!"

"If I have the child, the natural-born vampire, the course of events in those hundred years can be altered considerably." She leaned forward with a predatory smile. "Through her, chaos could rule without end."

So that was the plan. She would make his child a monster. Even though it was a kid he'd never seen or held, the thought made him ill. "Fuck you."

"I do not appreciate your vulgarity." The Oracle turned to one of her sentries. "I want him dead."

The vampire approached, pulling a stake from her belt. *This is it. I'm going to die.* Max swallowed, but the lump in his throat wouldn't go down. He'd always wondered if he'd be afraid. And he was. *I'm going to die, and it's going to be some third-rate vampire crony who does the honors.*

"No, not you." The Oracle held up her hand as the vampire paused midstrike. "Bring the one who just arrived. The present from dear Jacob."

There was an interminable wait as the vampire crony, looking more than a little pissed off at not being allowed to kill him, left the room. While she was gone, the Oracle didn't speak. She sat, looking bored, on her throne, occasionally tapping her fingernails on the carved wooden arms.

"Max," Bella whispered, as if the Oracle wouldn't hear them only a few feet away. "I do not think we will survive this."

"No. I do not think you will." The Oracle's laugh filled the room, pounding Max's brain like a sledgehammer.

It was echoed by the slamming of the big doors behind them. The Oracle's face lit up. "Ah, there you are. Come here. Kill this vampire."

"Why?"

The voice sent a shock of recognition through Max. But he couldn't place where he'd heard it.

The Oracle's eyes narrowed. She obviously didn't like being questioned. "Because I asked it of you. Call it a test of loyalty."

"I call it a poor excuse to drag my ass out of bed before sunset." The voice moved closer with a jingling of chains. "But yeah, no problem."

The body that went with the voice passed Max, insinuating himself between the Oracle and his intended victim. He was stocky, his brown hair shaved from the sides of his head in what would have been a Mohawk if it weren't so long. "So, give me a stake."

The vampire guard threw him one, and he caught it before it could pierce his chest. "Nice one, lady. Thanks."

Then he turned.

It was the kid. Nathan's dead son.

It was Ziggy.

Twenty-Four: Ashes to Ashes

Everyone always says, "You should see the look on your face," or, "I wish I'd had a camera." Both of those statements went through my mind as the Soul Eater laid eyes on his formerly dead son.

Cyrus strolled into the room like he still owned the place, head held high. "Surprised to see me?"

Nathan followed close behind him. His steely expression softened with relief when he saw me, but the emotionless mask snapped quickly back into place. "It's a dysfunctional family reunion."

"She told me you were dead." Jacob's right arm flailed, reaching for something to brace himself on. He seemed a tad more flappable than you'd expect someone to if he walked around calling himself the Soul Eater.

And Cyrus fed off his father's shock like a fire sucking up oxygen. I knew Cyrus well enough to know this was the first time he'd been in this position. "She tried. She failed. But what I want to know is, why did you send her to do it?"

"I didn't!" The Soul Eater backed up as Cyrus advanced on him.

Before Jacob could call for the guards, Nathan grabbed the overturned couch and flung it at the doors. They slammed closed under the weight, and the sofa fell neatly to the floor, effectively barring anyone from entering. The guards would be strong, but they were still just humans. The Soul Eater's taste in furniture ran to heavy, expensive pieces. If anyone came sniffing around, the sofa would at least buy us time.

"We don't need any extra company," Nathan said coldly, advancing on his sire.

"Get back, Nolen!" Cyrus commanded, stopping him in his tracks. "This is my fight and mine alone."

I felt the conflict in Nathan. He wanted to honor Cyrus's wishes—it was *his* father about to be killed, after all—but he was driven by his desire to avenge his wife. To avenge himself.

It's okay. I waited until he looked at me, and put out my hand. He came to stand at my side.

There were tears in his eyes. *It's really going to be over.*

Nathan had never been this stupidly optimistic before. The Soul Eater wasn't dead yet, and I'd learned never to believe in the logical course of the future. Logical didn't really apply in the vampire world.

The Soul Eater drew himself up straight, regaining some of his regal manner. "Dahlia is a troublesome and disobedient girl. I warned her repeatedly to stay away from you, but she didn't listen. If she turned you, it was her own initiative."

"Oh, she didn't turn me." Cyrus took a few steps toward the fire. "She bled me and left me for dead."

"Then she didn't do a good enough job of it!" The Soul Eater stalked off on his own path. It was almost comical, the way father and son paced identically, alike in their rage. "You are weak. Even a human could have fended off that cow of a witch!"

Then, as if he was struck by lightning, the Soul Eater's eyes narrowed. He turned to Cyrus. "But you did. She told me as much. She didn't turn you. How do you stand here if she did not turn you?"

And in another flash of inspiration, he rounded on me. "You!"

I backed up as he came forward, and Nathan got between us. The Soul Eater knocked him aside as though he were made of straw.

"Nathan!" Torn between wanting to dive for him, to protect him and see if he was hurt, and my instinct to flee the Soul Eater, I found the latter winning out. But I wasn't fast enough. Jacob had centuries of reflex training over me. The instant I thought about running, he had me.

"Perhaps you were the weak one." He spun me, my back pulled up tight against his chest as his clawed hands gripped my arms. Nathan and Cyrus stood, their helplessness written in the dire expressions on their faces, unable to save me. Unable to do anything, really, until the Soul Eater made his next move, and that might leave me dead.

"Now your resistance toward me seems all the more peculiar. Nolen at least had some fire in him, some passion. Simon…oh, my dear Simon." His hold relaxed, and he brought one hand up to stroke my neck. "What ever are we going to do with you?"

I couldn't tell if he was talking to Cyrus or me, so I didn't answer him. Through clenched teeth, I whispered, "Let me go."

For a moment, he seemed to consider it. Then he gripped my chin and pulled my head up. "Isn't it funny, that my son is your fledgling, and my fledgling is your sire? We're blood related, in a way."

"Then what you were proposing before would be incest," I wheezed, barely able to catch my breath.

"Why are you doing this, Jacob?" Nathan attempted to draw the Soul Eater's attention away from me. It worked, but only a little. I could breathe again, but my head was still pulled up at an uncomfortable angle. My spine popped and my muscles screamed in protest.

Still, I sent Nathan a mental *Thank you.*

Hang on, sweetheart. His gaze met mine for just a second before he addressed the Soul Eater again. "Why are you on this demented quest? Do you really think there isn't going to be another vampire just as ambitious as you are, gunning for you once you become a god? Imagine the kind of trophy you would make!"

"More ambitious?" The Soul Eater cackled at that. "Have you met an ambitious vampire in your life? Look at yourself. You could have stayed with me, never wanting for anything, if only you would have done what I'd asked of you. Instead, you chose to live out your pathetic existence serving those who would see us subjugated and exterminated. Living in a filthy apartment and running your pathetic shop full of superstitions you've never believed.

"And you, Simon! All I ever asked is for you to carry

out my wishes, to be my eyes when I could not rouse from my slumber. But you were more concerned with finding a woman to adore you, as if that would make you more of a man. You embarrass me!" He gave a grunt of disgust. "If you intend to serve me, I suggest you rid yourself of your insipid humanity.

"A new age is dawning, my children. Vampires will rule this earth, as we're meant to. No more of this 'the meek will inherit' preaching from the Movement. Let the meek have the kingdom of heaven. The strong shall rule on earth." As he spoke, his hand tightened around my neck. His body trembled with rage. "The Oracle has fulfilled her role. She has secured the child I need. She sees a vision of chaos, thinking to impress me with horror. But the true horror will come when I rule, when I kill the Oracle and reign in her stead."

His hand at my throat relaxed once again, stroking down the column of my windpipe. He took me by the hand, the strength of his grip a warning, and turned me to face him. "Despite your failings and your naive alliance to those who would destroy me, your death is not essential, Carrie. You're of my line. You could serve me. Or can die here tonight."

"If they die, I die." I said it with as much steel as I could inject into my voice, but I was terrified.

The Soul Eater smiled. "So brave. I should kill you for that alone. But I am feeling kind tonight."

"Thank you?" I looked over Nathan and Cyrus, saw their grim faces. They knew better than I how the Soul Eater displayed his kindness.

He hooked his index finger beneath my chin, lifted my

face and gazed into my eyes. "You may pick which one of them lives."

"Excuse me?" I blinked rapidly, as if that would help me clear my head. I couldn't have heard what he'd said.

"You can pick which one lives." He shrugged elegantly. "Oh, they'll both die eventually. I need Nathan's soul to complete my ritual, and I'm sure my son will do something to rouse my anger before long. But at your word, one of them can leave this house tonight."

I looked to Nathan. *What do I do?*

I trust you. The reply didn't help me, but it was the only communication we could manage. The Soul Eater made a move….

I'm not sure what he intended to do. But in that second, Cyrus rushed forward, a stake drawn. He swung the weapon at his father, and before my eyes could track the Soul Eater's movements, he had Cyrus's arm bent at an unnatural angle behind his back.

"Why do you fight me?" Jacob sounded pained as he twisted Cyrus's arm. I heard the bones crack and saw the stake fall from his fingers as he screamed. The Soul Eater grimaced. "Why would you make an attempt on my life?"

"Because I know you're a coward! You'll kill her, just like you kill anyone else who threatens your power!" Cyrus shouted. The tears rolling down his face were from the pain in his arm and the grief he felt. Both sensations overwhelmed me, and I clutched my chest, crushed under the weight of his sadness and frustration. "You won't steal her from me!"

The Soul Eater looked taken aback. "She is worthless. You value her life above mine?"

"Yes, I do!" Cyrus cradled his ruined arm to his chest, mouth frozen open in a silent cry of anguish as he dropped to his knees in defeat. "I don't know. I'm tired of this pain."

I wanted to go to his side and wrap my arms around him. But it was his father who comforted him, placing a hand on his head. "And I can take it from you. My son. I can take it all from you."

Don't listen to him, I begged him silently, but my thought bounced back to me with a desolate echo. Cyrus wasn't listening to me. He'd made up his mind.

"Let me help you, son." The Soul Eater knelt at his side. "Come home to me."

He's going to drain him! I screamed silently at Nathan. *He's going to drain him and re-sire him.*

Calm down, Carrie. Don't say a word.

If I'd been in the right frame of mind, maybe I would have recognized the sense in Nathan's words. But all I felt was unimaginable pain that my fledgling would be stolen from me, that my life would be meaningless.

That's why I didn't see the stake Cyrus had pulled. My gaze was focused on the Soul Eater's face as it changed, his fangs as they pierced Cyrus's skin.

So I screamed, "He killed your stepmother!"

The Soul Eater paused. I couldn't stop talking. "He pushed her into the fire. He was the one who killed her."

The Soul Eater actually withdrew, as if to apologize. He saw the stake in Cyrus's hand and raised his arm to strike him.

Cyrus was faster. He kicked his father's feet from beneath him. Jacob landed hard on his back and couldn't recover before Cyrus pinned him with a foot to the chest.

"You killed her?" His face contorted in rage. "You killed *her?*"

"She was a worthless cow," the Soul Eater wheezed. The sound of his ribs slowly crunching under Cyrus's foot was followed by a gurgle of blood from his mouth. "And now, I'll send you to join her!"

He planted his feet on the floor and sprang up, grabbing Cyrus's arm. But he grabbed the wrong one. It took only a second for Cyrus to implant the stake firmly in his father's chest.

I braced myself for the whoosh of wind and the violent storm of ashes that was sure to follow. But nothing happened. The Soul Eater's shout of pain died into sinister laughter.

I thought of Cyrus's heart, how he'd kept it in a box.

I thought of my own heart in its casket in Nathan's bedside table.

The Soul Eater's hand closed around Cyrus's neck. He lifted him off the ground with one arm and wrenched the stake from his chest, releasing a spurt of blood.

Then, without another word, he stabbed Cyrus in the heart. There was no rush of wind, no spectacular flame. Cyrus's second vampire life ended in an inconsequential burst of ash.

Crippling pain gripped me, almost exactly what I'd felt when I'd sired him. But that pain had been a sort of stitching together. This was an agonizing rending of the fabric that had bound us. And the last thing I heard through the blood tie was his scream of terror.

I collapsed to the floor at the same moment the Soul Eater did. He clutched his chest as though his hand could stop the blood that poured from him. A ball of blue flame shot upward from the wound, but still he didn't burn.

"It's not his heart," Nathan whispered, staring in horror.

The doors flew open. Dahlia rushed in, screaming.

Kill me. Let her kill me. When it seemed I couldn't stand another second of the pain, it doubled, tripled, multiplied into oblivion. I stared at the spot where my fledgling had stood, rocking with my knees drawn up to my chest.

"No!" I'd never heard Dahlia sound so crazed, and for her, that's saying something. But it didn't register with me immediately. Not until Nathan was pulling on my elbow—how long had he been doing that?—urging me to my feet. When I didn't stand, he swept me up in his arms, cradling me to his chest, and charged through the window. A flash of light illuminated the study—probably a spell of Dahlia's intended for us—and then we were slipping down the lawn the way we had the night Nathan had lost Ziggy in the very room I'd just lost Cyrus.

The irony would have been more poignant if I hadn't been losing my mind to grief at an accelerated pace.

Once we were off the grounds and hidden for a moment, he slowed. I noted from a faraway place the blood streaming down his face from cuts left by the shattered window glass.

"Carrie, are you all right?" He shook me. "Carrie, say something. Say something!"

I turned my eyes to the sky. "I can't see the stars."

And then I couldn't say another word.

Twenty-Five: Bite

❧⟶◦⟵❧

It only took a second for the kid to make up his mind. Max saw the decision-making process in slow motion: recognition, realization that the plan must be changed, new plan taking shape.

Ziggy lifted his arm as if he was going to drive the stake into Max's chest. Bella screamed. The kid spun and let the stake loose. It punctured the Oracle's chest, fast and clean, but she didn't burn.

She laughed. The laughter grew louder as the guards approached them, stakes drawn. Without hesitation, the kid slipped two from his sleeves straight into his hands, and let them fly in quick succession. This time, the strikes hit home. The vampires exploded into dust.

Ziggy turned to the Oracle. "Hold still, bitch, unless you want another abnormally large splinter."

"You think you can kill me?" The Oracle laughed again, twisting the stake free from her chest. "You think you can cause me pain? You have no idea of pain. No concept!"

"Oh, lady. You have it so fucking wrong." He reached

into the back of his shirt and pulled out another stake, twirling it in his hand as he raised his arm.

Max had worked with a lot of assassins in the past. The Movement had the most specialized hand-to-hand training program outside of the Israeli military. But Max had never seen reflexes like this, let alone spatial accuracy in the blink of an eye.

But the kid didn't get a chance to use his mad skills. Without warning, the Oracle burst into flames, from the feet up. Fire shot from her eyes and mouth, her fingers melted and flames licked up her arms from the stumps.

"Looks like the Soul Eater had the balls to do it, after all! This one is gonna be bad," Max called to Ziggy, dropping to cover Bella. "Grab something and hang on."

The Oracle screamed—no, roared was more like it—as the flames burned her body. The skin dissolved slowly, leaving her a creature of raw muscle and tendons for a split second before they flaked away to ash, leaving nothing but a skeleton suspended around a ball of blue flame. When the flame extinguished and dropped to the ashes on the ground, the wind came.

The shutters tore from the windows. The sun had set— at least that was in their favor—but being sliced in half with a piece of metal would be just as bad.

"Keep your head down," Max shouted over the howl of the wind. The last word had just left his mouth when a chunk of debris whacked him in the back of the head. His arms gave out and he fell onto Bella. A sharp pain in his shoulder a second later indicated another piece of flying something had taken a chunk out of him. "Son of a bitch!"

The Oracle's bones, still suspended, were surrounded by a cyclone of her own ashes. They eroded away as if being scourged by a superaccelerated desert sandstorm. And when they were gone, so were the ashes, and the wind.

"You guys okay?" Ziggy helped Max to his feet. "Dude, are you okay?"

Max brushed him aside. "Bella, are you all right?"

"Yes. A little…dizzy." She trembled as he helped her into the chair. "I will be fine."

Max turned to Ziggy. "Yeah, we're fine."

"*She's* fine." Ziggy gestured to Max's shoulder. "You're bleeding."

Max touched his shoulder and winced. "Yeah, something hit me. And then something else hit me."

"Something *bit* you," Bella said quietly. When Max looked at her, questioning, she dipped her head. "It was the only opportunity I thought I would have."

Ziggy's eyes went wide. "Wait a minute, you're a—"

"Werewolf," Bella finished for him.

"And you bit him. That would make him—"

"A lupin."

Max froze. "My God. Bella. Why—"

"We will need a place to hide. To hide our baby. The clan will not accept you if you are not one of us." She stated it like he just had to accept it, like there was no other way. "They will know you are a lupin, of course. But the elder will understand the circumstances. She will let you stay. And if not, we will seek out Titus's sanctuary."

"What the fuck, Bella?" Max spun away, kicking a twisted chunk of what used to be a shutter. "What the hell happens now? When the full moon comes or the daylight gets me? What the hell happens now?"

He felt her approach, felt her at his side before she got there. It was so like the blood tie he'd shared with Marcus…but not violent or fearful. This was like….

Coming home.

She laced her fingers with his. "Whatever comes, we will figure it out together. The three of us."

He squeezed her hand. "This isn't how I expected to end up, you know?"

"Guys, I hate to break up your moment, but we have to get the hell out of here. Those weren't the only guards in the place, and I can guarantee others are headed up those stairs right now." Ziggy ran toward the section of wall that had rotated to reveal the Oracle. "They'll be behind here, too. Are you ready for a fight?"

"It's all we've been doing for the past week. I think we'll manage." Max looked at Bella. "What about you?"

"Have you ever known me to back down from a fight?" She smiled encouragingly at him. "Even half-crippled?"

"Listen, guys, if we make it through this, you gotta do something for me, okay?" Ziggy held Max's gaze so long it became a little uncomfortable.

Still, Max nodded. "Sure, kid. I think I've got a pretty good idea what you want."

"Good." Ziggy put his hand on one of the wooden panels. "Ready?"

Max took Bella's hand and squeezed it. "I love you."

"I have always told you that." She smiled up at him. "We will be fine. It is not our destiny to die today."

"Good. Then let's kick some ass."

Ziggy pushed on the panel, and they started to move.

Twenty-Six: Grave

~~~~~

At the end, we went underground. Literally.

We stopped at the apartment briefly, where Nathan loaded up on blood and weapons, then he took me down to the bookshop. He put a Closed for Remodeling sign on the door and locked us in, then began pushing aside the counter. I wondered what he was doing, but it was from a faraway place, and not enough to motivate me to speak. The counter, which I'd always assumed was fixed to the floor, moved aside after a lot of work on Nathan's part. Beneath it, a trapdoor slid aside to reveal a narrow wooden staircase leading into a subbasement.

It was what I'd heard people in the area refer to as a Michigan basement, with a dirt floor and stones packed into concrete to form the rough walls. There was a sleeping bag and a cooler, a camping lantern and a utility sink connected to a single hose that disappeared into the floorboards above. Nathan unrolled the sleeping bag and helped me into it, and I could feel the dampness from the floor seeping into my bones already. He went back up the stairs and

I heard him pulling the counter in place to cover the hole, before he slid the trapdoor closed.

"We'll be fine for now," he said, taking the stairs faster than he would have if they'd been a bit less steep. "Max will be on his way, and we have enough blood for a couple days. And anyone who comes into the shop probably won't…" He stopped when he looked at me, and cursed.

I know what he probably saw. My eyes, glassy and blank as I stared at nothing, seemingly checked out of my head. But I was there. I saw everything, took in everything that was happening. I knew when the Soul Eater recovered, he'd come looking for us. I just couldn't make myself not long for death. And my despair was so complete, I couldn't speak to tell Nathan not to bother, to save himself.

I heard his thoughts, though, and his anger. Anger at me for mourning Cyrus, anger at himself for being angry with me, and fear that we would be found. *If I sleep, I won't think, and he won't be able to find us.*

So he climbed into the sleeping bag beside me and held me close, despite the fact that I'd probably assumed the temperature of the floor beneath us. We lay like that, probably for days, in the dark, because Nathan was afraid the light from the lantern would show through the cracks in the floorboards and give us away. He barely spoke to me, except to offer me blood, which I refused. Twice we woke to voices and footsteps upstairs. Nathan went completely still with fear beside me as we heard the intruders overturn bookshelves and tables in their destructive search.

The seclusion was good for me, though. With nothing else to concentrate on and nothing to distract me from my grief, I moved through it quickly. I didn't talk to Nathan—I wouldn't ask him to understand—but I did talk to myself, inside my mind. I began to understand why I couldn't speak. It wasn't a prison, but a retreat. I wouldn't have been able to put my pain into words, anyway. I taught myself to forget the pain of losing Cyrus, and remember the joy of loving him. The hatred I'd felt for him when he'd been my sire was important to remember, as well. It kept my sorrow in perspective. I had loved him, but I couldn't divorce him from the monster who'd made me, or it would hurt all the worse.

And when I woke one night—or day; it was hard to tell with no windows—I could talk again.

I rolled to my side and touched Nathan's face. He snapped awake as if waiting for me to come back to my senses, his eyes full of concern. "Carrie, are you all right?"

No, I'm not. "Why didn't you ever tell me about this place?"

A quick intake of breath warned me of the explanation ahead. "In case I ever had to use it. In case you…went to the other side again."

"Oh." I picked at the zipper on the sleeping bag. "I was never on the other side."

"You were always on the other side, Carrie." He touched my cheek. "Or on your own side. You've never truly been on my side."

"I have to be on my side. If I'm not, who is?" I thought of Cyrus. No, he was never on my side. No one was.

"I would have been." Nathan said it so earnestly, I think he believed it.

"No. You wouldn't have." And it was something I had to learn. No one was ever truly devoted to anyone else.

There was a long silence. Then Nathan put his hand over mine. "I do love you. I didn't say it because we were going to die."

"It has nothing to do with love." I didn't say that to wound him. "I love you. But you hurt me. And I hurt you. Whether we love each other or not, we can't ignore that, or we're just…building our foundation on sand."

"I know."

We didn't say anything else. I think we reached some sort of understanding. Our timetables were off once again. One of us was ready to open up and love, the other was retreating into solitude. But I needed time to grieve and think and let what had happened change me. At the end of that change, maybe I could build a relationship with Nathan out of the ruined components of our previous attempts. Or maybe I'd be strong enough to start from scratch. Maybe it would be easier, both of us coming from a place of loss. Perhaps that unequal footing had been our problem all along. But right now, I needed to be me, not "us." And it wouldn't be fair to give him anything less.

It was the damnedest thing, life. Once you decide exactly how things are going to go, something—or someone—comes along and messes it all up.

Max looked at Bella, really looked at her for the first time in days. She sat ramrod straight on the bench at the T station in Salem, working hard to keep her balance on the seat without the aid of her legs to steady her. They'd ditched the wheelchair—the Oracle's people would be looking for a werewolf in a wheelchair—and had used all manner of tricks to get themselves this far.

Her eyes drifted shut a moment, then snapped open, a new, more firm resolve visibly gripping her. Max smiled. Now that they weren't in mortal peril, weren't walking blindly into danger, he realized how stupid he'd been. Of course he loved her. And yeah, there was a chance something might happen to them. It wasn't fair, it wasn't the life he would have picked for himself, but there it was. And he would be an idiot to throw away what he had because someday, something might hurt him again the way Marcus's death had.

God, he could be dense sometimes.

"When the train arrives, we will take it to North Station," she repeated for the fifth time since they'd sat down. More to keep him awake than to actually reiterate the facts in her mind, he was sure. Bella's mind was like a steel trap. "There will be a car there for us, to take us to the airport. The helicopter will be there."

"Now, is this the helicopter that takes us to your clan, or the helicopter that takes us to the sanctuary?" He hadn't listened in on Bella's whispered phone conversation in Ziggy's car. Max didn't want to jinx things somehow.

"To New York City. My father's jet will be waiting at JFK, to take us to Rome." She closed her eyes, intentionally this time, and breathed deeply. "Back home."

He didn't know what to think about the prospect of meeting Bella's family. Her obviously rich family. "Listen, if they don't like me—"

"It does not matter if they like you. What matters is keeping this child safe. They will understand that." She placed a hand on his knee and gave a comforting squeeze. "Now, don't you have a call to make?"

Reluctantly, he pulled the phone Ziggy had given him from his back pocket and flipped it open. "How do you do this?"

"Dial the number and talk." She pointed out, arching her eyebrow as if to imply he had lost his mind.

"That's not what I mean." He glanced at the sky, starless thanks to the bright lights of the nearby condo development. "How do you tell someone goodbye? How do you say, 'Nice knowing you, I'll never see you again?'"

Bella's eyes took on a faraway look for a moment, then turned with pity to him. "You do it knowing that it is for the best."

He opened the phone and dialed.

Later, I finally ate. Nathan had to prop me up on his arm and hold the bag for me to drink, but the blood restored me somewhat. By the end of the second bag, I could sit up and remain conscious. But I tired quickly, and I'd nearly nodded off again when the sound of Nathan's cell phone, muffled in the sleeping bag, woke me. Groggy, I sat up, fumbling for it. "I think you have voice mail. I can't believe you didn't put that on silent."

Nathan reached for the phone, glancing up at the ceiling of our little tomb. After a long moment, when he'd decided no one was lurking upstairs, he opened the phone and punched in some numbers.

I watched his face scrunch up with tension, then melt in relief at whatever he heard. "Oh, thank God. Max and Bella are all right."

He listened to the rest of the message, then handed the phone to me. It was already replaying, Max's voice sounding better than it ever had as he assured us of the Oracle's death and informed us of his plan to go into hiding with Bella.

"I can't go into details. You guys just have to trust me that this is for the best. And I really hope you're okay. If you need someplace to hide, use the penthouse. It has great security, and Carrie is still cleared with the doorman.

"Something else went down up here. I have no idea how to tell you this, but here's the deal—" A loud burst of static cut off his words, and the message ended.

"I wonder what that was about?" I looked up at Nathan for some kind of enlightenment.

He shrugged. "I have no clue."

We fell silent for a minute. My voice shook a little as I said, "So, I guess that's the last of him."

"Sounds like." Nathan moved to the bottom of the stairs and reached up to open the trapdoor. "We're all clear. No one has been back for days."

I followed him up the stairs. It felt good to get out of the hole. To stretch and get my feet under me.

It was less good to see what they'd done to the shop. The door was torn from the hinges. Tables were overturned, merchandise crushed underfoot.

"Jesus," Nathan whispered beside me, and his horror at the scene pierced my heart.

"Most of this stuff… I mean, it's not like we could have

been hiding in a box of tarot cards. Most of this they did just for the hell of it." I covered my face.

"Well, it's a good thing we're going to Chicago, then," Nathan said in that manful, stiff-upper-lip way only guys have perfected.

I bent and scooped up a few tumbled stones—amethyst, if I remembered the inventory right—and juggled them from one hand to another. "Are you going to be okay?"

"It hurts my customer base to close down without warning. There are special orders waiting to be called, things like that. But since I'm obviously not coming back, I don't think it will be an issue." Nathan paused. "I'd rather lose my money than my life. Or your life, especially. But it's the memories that really hurt when I think about leaving. Ziggy was a child here. Some days I wake up and swear I can hear him running down the hall."

"We don't have to leave forever," I said hopefully. I certainly couldn't foresee spending the rest of my unlife camped out in Marcus's condo.

"I know." Nathan drummed his fingers on the thin strip of metal that used to surround the glass of the counter. "But who knows what they'll do to this place while I'm gone."

The thought of leaving Nathan's home—my home— twisted my heart. Like so many times before, I wondered if it was worth it. Had it been worth it to go into that morgue after John Doe? Had it been worth it to lose my mortal life, if this was where it all led?

Yes. A resounding yes. Despite the horrible things I'd endured, being a vampire wasn't the worst thing that could have happened to me. I'd experienced paralyzing sadness, but I'd also had incredible joy. I had a new perspective on where my place was in the world.

I had a new perspective on myself, too. I didn't have to be a wannabe human, hating myself every moment for being what I am. I didn't have to be a monster, either. I could be a sort of…ethical vampire. Or not. I had the rest of my life to figure it out, if I wanted to take that long.

And I had Nathan. He'd waited out my unhealthy relationship with Cyrus. Twice. He'd proved he would wait again, until I figured more out. Because it had taken him so long to tell me he loved me, I knew he really meant it.

Of course, as always, I have no clue what lies ahead. We stand on a fearful precipice and the currents of events beyond our control push us closer to the edge, with no way of turning back.

But at least now, I'm not alone.

Read on for a quick bite of

BLOOD TIES BOOK FOUR:
ALL SOULS' NIGHT

Available now from all good booksellers!

Prologue: Daymare

Some days, I dream of the time that I spent in Marianne's soul. Or is that the time that she spent in me? In reality, it was horrible, but in the dreams, it feels wonderful. Powerful. Another soul gliding over mine like silk, whispering in my head.

I stand over Nathan. He's still restrained, babbling, senseless with fear and the spell his sire had cast over him, bleeding from the wounds scored deep into his flesh by his own hand. Marianne leans tenderly over her husband, kisses his mouth, calms him. And then the power swells up inside me, and she screams for mercy in my head. All I know is blood and tearing flesh. Darkness and warmth with the copper-tinged smell of slowly ebbing life urging on my bloodlust.

I don't even consciously drink. I don't feel or taste the blood, and though I know, somehow, that I am dreaming, I find it unsettling, as if some understanding is just out of my reach. If only I could see the greater picture.

I consume without drinking, reach my fill without satisfaction. And when I raise my eyes to the evaporating darkness, I see the ballroom where Marianne met her fate. All around me are the bodies of people I know: Nathan, Max, Bella, even old friends long since dead, like Cyrus and Ziggy. Their blood is on my hands. Their life in my veins. Their tortured screams rolling through my head like the sweetest symphony I've ever heard.

And then Jacob Seymour is there, seated at the head of the massive dining table. He wears a crown of thorns and the blood that drips from his wounds is black tar, staining his white hair and shining golden robes. A huge, silver-domed platter covers the table, and I remember—in that dream memory that doesn't quite see reality the way it happened, but still manages to catalog every horror you've ever known—what will come next. Clarence appears, as if from nowhere, his dark, regal face a mask disguising the hate he feels for the task, and removes the cover. On the platter, arranged in a way that is familiar, yet shocking, is Dahlia, her skin pale and mottled blue with death, a carpet of rose petals beneath her halo of red curls.

And then, with the voices still screaming in my brain, I laugh. Blood flows from my mouth, splashing to the tabletop, my hands, my lap that is suddenly and inexplicably dressed in a voluminous gown to match Jacob's attire, and I laugh.

But when I wake, I'm screaming.

FIGHT EVIL.
BECOME EVIL.
SACRIFICE EVERYTHING.

With the Soul Eater on the verge of god status, it's time to take a final stand, even if it means losing everything I love.

They say that good always triumphs over evil. I hope that's true. Because the odds aren't in our favour and the fate of the world is in our hands.

www.mirabooks.co.uk

MIRA